SCYTHIA

MONGOLS

Turfan

Aksu

Osh Kashgar

Tarim Lop Nor Dunhuang

Terek Davan Pass

Ho Tien Taklamakan Desert

Great Wall

Khotan

Kunlun Mountains

Lan Chou

Chang An Yeh Ch

CHINA

INDIA

Taprobane

THE SILK TREE

By Julian Stockwin

The Silk Tree

THE SILK TREE

JULIAN STOCKWIN

Allison & Busby Limited
12 Fitzroy Mews
London W1T 6DW
www.allisonandbusby.com

First published in Great Britain by Allison & Busby in 2014.

A CIP catalogue record for this book is available from
the British Library.

First Edition

ISBN 978-0-7490-1795-8

Typeset in 11/16 pt Adobe Garamond Pro by
Allison & Busby Ltd.

The paper used for this Allison & Busby publication
has been produced from trees that have been legally sourced
from well-managed and credibly certified forests.

Printed and bound by
CPI Group (UK) Ltd, Croydon, CR0 4YY

AUTHOR'S NOTE

The genesis for *The Silk Tree* came when my wife, Kathy, and I were in Istanbul doing location research. She discovered a rather lovely silk scarf in the Kapali Çarşi, the ancient Grand Bazaar. While she was chatting with the merchant I idly wondered how silk had been brought from China to the West. Intrigued, I did some research on the subject and the creative juices started flowing – I knew I had a story I had to tell! Part of the task of a writer of historical fiction is to recreate city landscapes of the past in his mind's eye and for *The Silk Tree* this meant sixth-century Constantinople (as Istanbul was called then).

So, what is known about the secret of silk? China kept the secret for over 1000 years and legend there tells of a princess who smuggled eggs out in her headdress when married to a prince of Khotan. In the West, accounts generally agree that it was two monks that returned from China in 551 AD with the secret of silk, and although documents vary in their details – each providing tantalising references and with no one version standing out as definitive – I have based my novel on these. Many of the characters in the book did exist and it was fascinating researching their lives.

Top of a novelist's desire when writing is that his readers enjoy the book, but I also hope *The Silk Tree* has opened a window to a world that we in the twenty-first century can only wonder at.

At about the same time there came certain monks. They promised Emperor Justinian Augustus that they would provide the means for making silk from Sinae where they had learnt the art. After they had announced these tidings, they returned thither and brought back eggs of a worm that feeds on leaves of the mulberry. Thus began the art of making silk in the Roman Empire.

Procopius, Byzantine scholar and historian
– Ὑπέρ τῶν πολέμων λόγοι

DRAMATIS PERSONAE

* indicates fictional character

*Aldar	caravan escort soldier
Antonina, Lady	wife of Belisarius
*Arif	young cameleer
Barsymes, Peter	Count of the Sacred Largesse under Justinian
Belisarius	Roman general under Justinian
Chang Le, Princess	wife of Gokturk Lord Bumin
*Dao Pa	mystic
*Grotius	Nabatean merchant
Hao	chancellor at court of usurper Wen Hsuan of Northern Ch'i
Hsiao Ching	Emperor of the Eastern Wei, overthrown by warlord Kao
John the Cappadocian	disgraced former tax collector for Justinian
Justinian	Justinian I, Emperor of the Eastern Roman Empire, ruled 527–565 AD
Kao Yang	warlord who usurps emperor, becomes Emperor Wen Hsuan
Kao Yeh	Crown Prince of Ch'i
*Khosrau	torturer in employ of Marcellus
*Korkut	Rouran silk merchant

*Kuo	Ying Mei's uncle in Chang An
*Kuo Ming Lai	chancellor and grand chamberlain to Emperor Hsiao Ching
*Kuo Ying Mei, Lady	daughter of Kuo Ming Lai, aka Lady P'eng, aka the Ice Queen
*Lai Tai Yi	Gold Lily lady-in-waiting to Ying Mei, Ah Lai familiar name
*Liu	court eunuch
Lord Bumin	the Khagan of the Gokturks
*Mansur	caravan master and trader with the barbarians
Marcellus	Count of Excubitors at court of Justinian
*Marius	Quintus Carus Marius, Roman legionary, aka Brother Matthew, aka Ma Lai Ssu
*Master Feng	torturer
*Messalia	merchant in Constantinople
Narses	grand chamberlain to Justinian
*Nemasus	compulsor (tax extraction agent) of Justinian
*Nepos	chariot driver for Blues faction
*Nicander	Nicodorus of Leptis Magna, Greek incense merchant aka Brother Paul, Ni K'an Ta
Peter the Patrician	Master of the Offices, the court of Justinian
*Priscus	chariot driver for Greens faction
Procopius	Byzantine scholar and court historian at the time
*Su Li	Sogdian caravan master based in Chang An
*Sueva	Spanish cargo agent in Brundisium
*Taw Vandak	Tibetan lama of the oasis kingdoms

Totila	leader of Ostrogoths
Ts'ao Fu	court poet
*Velch	compulsor (tax extraction agent) of Justinian
*Wang	chief scribe to Kuo
Wen Hsuan	new Emperor of Northern Ch'i; overthrew Hsiao Ching of Eastern Wei
Wu Kuo Chin	general of Imperial Bannermen
*Wulfstan	northern barbarian guard, John the Cappodician residence
*Ya	Uighur commander of caravan escort
*Yi	beastmaster at court of Emperor Wen Hsuan
*Yuan	court eunuch
*Yulduz	caravan master
*Zarina	Korkut's wife

CHAPTER ONE

The dilapidated building on the outskirts of Rome stank of farm slurry – and rank fear hung heavily on the air. Nicander's stomach contorted painfully with hunger. He rubbed his legs, cursing the sparse, angular timbers of the hayloft where he had been hiding since the day before.

He glanced below. In the fitful moonlight coming through the holed roof he could see the three farmhands still cowering in a corner. Next to them a mother rocked her infant. An older child stood close, her eyes flashing fearfully at every sound.

Now the old man was dead. His two slaves squatted next to the body, sunk in a stupor of misery. At least there would be no more of his tortured whimpering. He wore a toga, making him out to be a patrician of sorts, but it hadn't saved him from a brutal, casual hacking by the invaders before he had managed to flee.

Outside in the darkness a distant wolf howled. A mourning for the travails of a proud city falling to the forces of darkness. Nicander shivered at the flesh-crawling sound. In the Year of Our Lord 549 a great empire was now meeting its end.

He hadn't heard any drunken laughter or sounds of rampaging destruction from the farmhouse for some time but the nearby villa was a different matter. The Ostrogoths were again busy at their plunder there, but if they heard noise they would come looking . . .

He eased more into the shadows. If they broke in, would they be content with butchering the half a dozen below and not glance up? He caught himself – the little group were fellow human beings. But what could he do? He was just one man without so much as a knife. They were strangers; did he owe them anything? Coldly, he concluded that they were in no different position to himself, helpless before the flooding tide of barbarians. Therefore, like him, they must take their chances with whatever scraps of fortune the gods threw their way.

It had all happened so fast. The capital had long moved to Constantinople while the ancient city of Rome had declined and decayed. However, the Emperor in the East, Justinian, had been increasingly successful in his bid to restore the old glories of Rome. He had unleashed the gifted general Belisarius on the Huns, Goths and Ostrogoths and other enemies until the populace felt they could breathe easily. But then he had unaccountably recalled his general, in a fit of jealousy, some said. The beaten hordes had seized their chance and struck back, the wild and cunning Totila of the Ostrogoths thrusting aside the leaderless army to take Rome itself.

Nicander would never forget that night. The rumour had spread that traitors had opened the gates to the Ostrogoths. Panic-stricken crowds scattered before crazed horsemen wielding axes and swords, screaming in bloodlust. An unstoppable flood came on and on, fanning out among the ancient magnificence to plunder and destroy. The wise had hidden. Those witless with fear who had not were mercilessly run down and killed. Females were raped in full view on the street.

Hoarse yells, screaming, flames; the reek of destruction drifting in a choking haze. The chaos and carnage had never abated.

Nicander had watched from his hiding place as his warehouse was set alight by the rampaging barbarians, two hundred thousand solidi worth of incense going up in thickly scented smoke. He was a merchant with a business in the old quarter of the city but now that was over – he was finished and he'd lost no time in fleeing for his life to the countryside while the Ostrogoths were greedily occupied in their looting.

14

He'd deliberately fled alone, fearing that groups of people would be more likely to attract attention. It had been a terrifying and exhausting struggle over the hills with his little bundle of possessions, avoiding scattered bands of marauders until daylight had threatened. He had looked for the nearest hiding place and found this ramshackle farm outhouse, but was taken aback to find it already occupied by others in the same dire need. They had spent the day in a trembling funk, waiting for who knew what. Towards evening a throng of Ostrogoths had cantered past to plunder the villa close by.

All night they had cringed at the harsh shrieks of the family there as they provided bloody entertainment for the conquerors. Bursts of noise and coarse laughter came on the air, along with periodic splintering crashes. The cries had fallen away in the daylight hours but who knew when they would emerge to come after fresh victims. Now the drunken revelry had begun again.

Italia was being overrun. Nicander knew he had to get out, quickly. The northern ports would all be taken but if he pressed on hard to the south he could probably make Brundisium, and there take ship, away from this madness.

He tried to shut out the unsteady maundering of the mother as she attempted to comfort her infant, the older child still standing by her side, mute and rigid.

He was not a warrior but a peace-craving merchant, certainly no hero. Should he go now, or hope the marauders would tire of their revelries at the villa and move on? Either way there was the prospect of stumbling on one of the murderous bands roaming the countryside.

There would be no mercy seen when—

A blow on the door sounded like a thunderclap, then came harsh, smashing hits. Cold fear gripped Nicander – it had happened and they were hopelessly trapped!

The door gave way, sagged and fell flat. With his heart in his throat he stared down and saw limned against the moonlight a single large figure, sword in one hand, a shapeless pack in the other.

There was a terrifying moment as the man looked in suspiciously then, in the same second that Nicander registered that his weapon was a regulation Roman gladius, the infant gave a loud shriek. The legionary dropped the pack and hurled himself forward. 'Shut it!' he hissed savagely to the mother, the sword threatening. She gripped the baby tightly, pleading with her eyes.

It was too much for the child, who began screaming hysterically. The soldier tore the infant from her, and in a practised sweep slashed its throat, the screech instantly turning to a bubbling sob. He dropped the limp body quickly. The sword flashed out again, stopping an inch from the mother's breast.

There was a petrified silence, then the woman fell on the dead child, her sobs muffled by its stained clothing. The soldier stood back, tightly alert, his sword still drawn while his hard eyes passed over them all. He let it fall to his side and went to the doorway and looked out, listening intently. Then he sheathed the weapon and returned.

'Who's to speak for you?' he demanded to the space in general. His Latin was crude and direct.

Nicander couldn't move. The ruthless execution had paralysed him with its lethal effectiveness.

But then a shameful thought crept in: if there was going to be any chance of survival, this man of inhuman decisiveness might be the means of achieving it.

'I will,' he found himself saying.

The soldier's eyes flicked up to the hayloft in surprise. 'Then get down and speak!'

Nicander dropped from his hiding place and tried to keep his voice steady. 'Nicodorus of Leptis Magna. Nicander.'

'Greek!' grunted the legionary in contempt. His plumed helmet was missing but he wore body armour which was stained with blood over the right side.

'And running from the Ostrogoths – like you!' Nicander retorted.

16

A strong hand shot out and grabbed the front of his tunic. The man's hard face thrust into his, the expression merciless. But then he nodded. 'It's the truth of it, Greek. We're beaten, the fucking square-heads did it again and this time Rome itself pays.'

He made play of smoothing Nicander's tunic and added contemptuously, 'Who are your mates, then?'

'They're not my friends. They were hiding here when I took shelter.' He held the big man's eyes. 'You didn't say who you are, soldier.'

'Does it matter, Greek?'

'Just being polite, Roman.'

Unexpectedly, the big man smiled. 'Don't get your dignity in a twist, then, Greek.' He grunted. 'It's Marius, legionary of the Decius twenty-fourth Pannonian as no longer exists. Quintus Carus Marius,' he added, smacking a fist to his left breast in mocking salute.

Nicander inclined his head. Around them was the stillness of horror, only the muffled distress of the woman audible. 'We have to get away from here. What's it like out there?'

Marius ignored him and pointed at one of the huddled farmhands. 'You! What did you hear outside?'

The lad stared back in mute despair.

Marius's hand dropped to his sword and he took a pace forward. 'Answer me, you fucking cowards!' he snarled.

'In the last few hours, sounds only from the villa,' Nicander said carefully.

Marius swung around to face him. 'Right. That's to the north.' He smiled mirthlessly and scooped up his pack. 'So I'm away to the south. Best of fortune, Mr Greek, you're going to need it!'

'Wait!' Nicander thought furiously. It would be daylight in a few hours and then his fate would be sealed. There was no way he was going to leave his bones in this godforsaken corner of a crumbling empire. He had moments only before the soldier left them to their doom.

It was a long shot, but the only card he had. 'Aren't you forgetting something, legionary?'

'What?' snapped Marius.

'Your duty as a Roman soldier!'

Marius stiffened. 'You dare to speak to me of such, you Greek swine!'

But Nicander sensed he had touched a nerve. 'Yes, you've surely not forgotten your sworn oath before the legate – to defend to the death Rome and its citizens!'

'Have a care, Greek! I'm not throwing my life away for this worthless rabble!'

Nicander's face hardened. 'You've lost a battle but this doesn't end your duty to your country.'

'What do you know of soldiering! I've a bigger charge – to preserve myself as a trained legionary for when we strike back.'

Nicander stepped between Marius and the doorway. 'These are Roman citizens. They've a claim to your protection. Are you going to turn your back on them all, each and every one, to save yourself?'

'Yes!'

Taking a deep breath, Nicander drew himself up. 'Then the glories of old Rome mean nothing to you. The wars against Hannibal and his cohorts when all was said to be lost, then brave legionaries turned the tide? Teutoburg Forest and three legions exterminated – but avenged? And you're going to—'

Marius's eyes had a dangerous gleam. He bit off savagely, 'Those times have gone, Greek! There's nothing now.'

But Nicander had seen something that might give him one last chance. He glanced at the single iron ring on Marius's hand. 'I doubt Mithras agrees,' he said, almost in a whisper. The cult of the bull had gone underground since Christianity had triumphed but still had adherents in the military.

'Is it not true the god smiles on those who hold honour more precious than life itself?' he went on.

He could see it hit home.

Marius recoiled. 'So what do you expect me to do? Take 'em all on myself?'

Nicander felt the tide turning in his favour, but he knew he needed to play it very carefully from now on; the Roman had taken the infant's life without a second thought. Would he kill him for his insolence?

Folding his arms he said, 'You're waiting for a centurion to tell you what to do? These people are looking to you, Mr Quintus Carus Marius, to think of something.'

The legionary strode to the doorway and looked out, seeming to be struggling for a decision. After a moment he turned back with a grim expression. 'You're a sad bunch o' losers – but for the honour of the twenty-fourth – there might be a way. When the square-heads find more loot than they can carry, they let out a wolf's cry to bring up their mates.'

'Yes, and—?'

'I'll go outside and draw 'em away like that. You and the others can then get clear.'

Nicander smothered a sigh of relief. With the attention of any wanderers out there elsewhere, he would lose no time in making off into the night and blessed safety. 'Yes, Mr Legionary. A fine plan, worthy of your calling.'

'You're just looking to save your own skin.'

'Not at all,' Nicander came back. 'These people will need a leader in the days to come.'

'And that's you?'

'Can you think of anyone else?'

Marius glanced around the forlorn group. 'No,' he agreed, with a sour smile. 'Get 'em on their feet.'

Nicander motioned to his sorry charges then said, 'I wish you well, Marius.'

The Roman did not reply, but gave an ironic army salute. He turned and loped noiselessly out into the night.

Some minutes later the call of a wolf sounded in the darkness.

'Get ready!' hissed Nicander.

Another howl rose further out, long and insistent. Nicander listened intently. Excited shouts came from the villa, no doubt men streaming out toward the call.

'Go!' he said urgently. The slaves would not leave their master and in a fury he kicked at them until they obeyed, followed by the listless farm workers, pushing them out bodily into the cold night air.

'Where's the woman?' His voice was taut with nervous tension.

She was still inside, crouched over the body of her infant. He tugged roughly at the older child. 'Get her out of here – if she's not with us, you're both dead! Understand?'

He didn't wait for a reply and returned to the doorway, listening. The cries were now off to the right and distant. They had to make their move – fast!

Pulled by the older child the mother emerged slowly, holding the dead body to her breast, her ragged sobs distracting. Nicander cursed under his breath but wheeled about and led off to the south, a line of dark woods beckoning in the dull moonlight from beyond the fields.

He moved quickly, through a patch of clinging undergrowth and then on to the bare earth of a ploughed field, stumbling forward, propelled by the sick fear of what might happen to them, discovered in the open.

Panting, he made the edge of the woods and crashed on through into the gaunt shadows and the cold stink of forest litter. He turned and looked back, the others were in a slow, straggling line and this pointed like an arrow to where he was. Distraught, he beckoned them on. One by one, they lumbered in, the mother last of all, still clutching the dead child to her breast.

'Quickly!' he urged, then lunged deeper into the forest gloom.

At a small clearing he stopped to catch his breath. How could they carry on like this?

He spared a thought for the legionary. He would be dead by now, overwhelmed by vengeful Ostrogoths, but it would have been a quick end. That such a brave man had to be sacrificed was a pity, but now he had bigger problems.

He knew vaguely where south was, but this would lead them into the densest part of the woods. His thoughts raced – did he let on about his plan to make for Brundisium? There were only so many ships and the more that tried to crowd into them, the less his chance of getting away.

And surely it was insane to think this sorry crew could keep up for the many days' slog there, anyway. What were—

'I'm h-hungry,' the small voice of the older child broke in.

'Shut up!' he snarled.

He tried to bring to mind the teachings of the ancient Greeks that he was made to learn in his youth. Did the Stoics or the Cynics have anything to say about any moral necessity for the fittest to sacrifice their chances for the sake of the weak?

'I want s-something to eat!' moaned the child. Her mother was no longer in touch with reality; her eyes empty and, slowly rocking, she dangled the dead baby's body listlessly.

He needed more time to think, to decide what to do.

'Now!' the child wailed. 'Someone give me a little piece of bread, anything.' She started to cry.

'Hold your noise!' Nicander spat. 'I'll go find something, just shut up!'

He struck out into the woods, eager to be away. Quickly he was deep into it, pushing through the thickening undergrowth between the trees until a broad track crossed his path at an angle. At last he could move freely – but to where? And how could he find food in a ruined countryside seething with barbarians? Perhaps this track led somewhere or – a chilling thought came. If it did, then it was more than likely . . .

Suddenly he felt hoof-beats through the ground and in a paroxysm of terror threw himself into a thicket, scrabbling at the leaf litter and thorns, desperate for concealment. The first riders came around the bend and he froze, praying they were not looking down. The horses thudded nearer in a gallop, then, just inches away, thundered past, the displaced air of their passage buffeting him. He was left with the stomach-churning reek of Ostrogoths on their way to plunder.

When they had passed he got up, trembling. The track in fact curved further and in sickening realisation he saw that it must pass close to where he had just left. However there was no slackening in the hoof-beats as he heard them die away on leaving the confines of the wood.

He straightened and tried to gather his wits. But before he could focus, in the distance, from the direction of his little group, he heard shouts, hectoring and triumphant. Instantly he realised what had happened. The Ostrogoths had seen footprints in the moonlight on the bare field and these had led unerringly to their victims.

As the first unhinged shrieks came, Nicander could do nothing but stand dully, listening as it grew into a hellish chorus as the slaughter began.

CHAPTER TWO

His muscles were a raw torment and his feet burnt, but Nicander tramped on. He'd joined a flood of others desperate to get away from the scenes of ruin and carnage, fear driving him mercilessly. While the Ostrogoths were busy looting Rome he had to make best speed to Brundisium. It was the biggest port in the south: a capacious harbour, hundreds of vessels. He knew it well from the distant days when he'd been part of the family business, trading out of Leptis Magna.

Now, finally, he was close to his destination. And with it was the prospect of safety and release from suffering.

The journey had not been easy: frenzied stumbling across the Pontine Marshes to get out of reach of the marauders, then buying a place in an overcrowded cart at a ruinous price, only for the horse to go lame. Days of soreness had turned to agony as he'd flogged his body to the limits of endurance.

He'd tried to keep clear of the obvious route, the legendary Appian Way, but there was little avoiding the arrow-straight efficiency of the ancient engineers. And now he found himself toiling over well-rounded stone paving, ever alert for the wild thunder of hoofs behind that would tell him it had all been in vain.

Around the bend the wind caught a thick and cloying stench. Bodies.

No one was taking time to bury them and as the human flood converged on Brundisium he saw many more corpses, roughly pulled aside from the road.

God help it, he'd be glad to be quit of this place of death and desolation.

He patted his groin furtively. There was still a reassuring weight in the pouch that nestled snugly there. In his makeshift knapsack he'd planted a handful of siliqua, the coins debased and near useless, together with a scatter of obsolete sesterces, big and impressive, but also valueless. However those in the pouch were solidi, coins of gold, his entire fortune.

Nicander reached the crest of the last rise before Brundisium and gazed down into the wide plain and the town. His eyes searched feverishly – the harbour was virtually empty! There were two small ships out of reach at anchor offshore. Apart from that, nothing of the hundreds from the old days.

Picking up his pace down the road he tried to grapple with the consequences: if he couldn't get away the only other port of size was Tarentum, days of pain over to the west.

But he couldn't face any more. Must he take his chances here when the Ostrogoths came? Where could he hide? He hobbled on bleakly, fending off wretches begging for a crust, others on their knees in supplication for release from their misery.

There were roaming gangs out to get their hands on the pitiful scraps of wealth travellers kept to bribe their way to survival. When nightfall came it would bring scenes from hell – if the Ostrogoths didn't arrive first.

Nicander forced his mind to try to find a way out and remembered that on the gently curving south side, out of sight past the old burying ground, ships were hauled up for repair to be fitted out for their voyages. It could be . . .

He took a short cut through the marshes and rickety tenements; there were far fewer people and he allowed his hopes to rise. Then, above the rooftops – the lofty broad spars of a ship! A *corbita*, a large vessel of at least 4000 amphorae gross tonnage.

Eagerly he slipped through an alley leading to the docks but, as soon as he got out in the open, he realised it was hopeless. The ship was alongside but almost hidden by a crowd of hundreds; beseeching, shouting, weeping. He pushed through and saw that there were men with weapons in a ring of steel, guarding the crew who were at work ejecting its grain cargo into the sea – they now had a far more valuable freight.

There was one last chance: the cargo agent's office was on the second floor of the building behind. Would he still be there and perhaps be able to sell him a place for gold in hand? His little hoard was not impressive but he knew the man and . . .

'Sueva! How go you, old friend!' The big Spaniard glanced up, gave a quick grimace and went back to his counting, each kind of coin in a different money bag. A sour-faced Moor looked on impassively.

'I'd hoped to catch you here,' Nicander went on, in as friendly a tone as he could muster.

'Won't be for much longer,' Sueva said darkly. 'Someone just saw the square-heads firing a farmhouse. They'll be here before nightfall.'

'Yes. Unfortunate. Sueva. I've need of a passage out of here. I don't suppose that for a premium fee—'

'Can't be done.'

'Oh?'

'There's sixty-seven head going in that *corbita*. We're not taking any more and that's final.'

'I can perhaps find gold . . . ?'

'No.'

'Is there another ship leaving soon—'

'That's the last. If I were you, my little Greek, I'd scamper off as fast as you can before this town starts getting exciting.'

On the wharf the crowd was growing but was still held at bay by the armed men. Moving closer, Nicander heard cries and curses as the throng was forced aside by some kind of disturbance at the far end.

It was a group being escorted toward the ship – the lucky few who were getting out with their lives. His heart pounded. Unless he could think of something he was going to be left here, probably to die this very night, butchered by the barbarians.

He tried to pull himself together, he was a merchant, a businessman, and surely should be able to come up with some sort of deal. The pay-off would be saving his own life.

But weariness and pain had dulled his wits. He could think of nothing as he watched the fortunates being shepherded to the gangway and over the bulwarks.

And then a tall, well-built man in a shapeless cloak strode up the gangway – there was something familiar about him!

At the top he turned briefly and their eyes met. It was Marius.

For a long second the legionary held the gaze, then made to step onto the deck. He hesitated – and turned to face Nicander again.

'There he is!' he suddenly bellowed. 'Been looking everywhere for the sorry bastard! My Greek slave! Get aboard this instant, you runt. Now!'

A guard reached out to collar Nicander. He allowed himself to be propelled up the gangway – but the captain swaggered up and barred the way. 'And who's paying, then? Full price it is, even slaves.'

He glared pointedly at Marius, who folded his arms and looked meaningfully at Nicander.

Near panic, Nicander faced away and scrabbled for a solidus.

'Ha!' guffawed the captain. 'Your skin's worth only a pawky single? I'll have another four o' them or you gets thrown back, my little cockerel!'

Five gold solidi for a couple of weeks' voyage! His face burning, Nicander handed the coins over.

'Right, get along, then,' the man rumbled and stalked off.

Nicander hurried over to Marius, near incoherent with relief. 'I . . . I—'

'Well? Pick up the bag then, slave!'

'What? You don't mean—'

'You need a taste o' the whip to get you going, Greek?'

'Marius, we've—'

'It's Master to you, runt!'

'I . . . I – y-yes, Master,' Nicander said, ready to do whatever it took to keep in favour.

'Stuff that! Can't you Greeks take a joke?' Marius snorted and stalked off.

Nicander followed him forward to a chalked area of deck, presumably where they were to spend the voyage.

Already the ship was being prepared for sea, sailors elbowing the milling passengers out of the way as they bent on sail.

The ship poled out, and the big square sail was heaved round to the wind. It filled with a loud slam and banging before it took up, and a cheerful rippling began as they pulled away.

Closer to the open sea the vessel gently heeled under a keen breeze.

Near weeping with relief, Nicander stammered, 'I can only thank you from my heart for your—'

'Don't waste your words, Greek. I don't know why I did it – reckon it was your spunk when you took that hopeless bunch out into the night.' A suspicious look came over his face. 'So where are they now? Did you—'

Nicander pulled himself together, 'Oh, right now I'm not sure. There was a band of Goths came up and I remembered your cry of the wolf. It worked, as well, but I couldn't find them afterwards,' he concluded, avoiding the big man's eyes.

'Oh? How did *you* get away, then?'

'Ah, I climbed a tree. Easy, really – they were only looking on the ground.'

'Good thinking, Greek. So how did you leave your tree with 'em all around you?'

'Ah. That. Not so difficult. I waited for a square-head to ride under the branch then fell on him. A right tussle it was but he dropped his axe and I let him have it straight between the eyes and rode off on his horse, that's all.'

'Well, quite the little warrior!'

'It was nothing,' he said hastily. 'How did you . . . ?'

'Not so smart as yours. Four of them came at me, put 'em down, then took another couple on my way out. Hard hacking all the way,' he added laconically.

The entrance of the harbour came up and then they were through – into the blessed expanse of open sea.

'Marius, just where are we off to? What's our port of call?'

The legionary said nothing and fumbled in his pack. He brought out a small cloth bag and threw it at Nicander. 'Beans, Greek.'

'It's actually Nicander, Marius.'

'Right, Nico.'

'Nicander.'

'Get a move on, or you won't make the head of the line for cooking. *Nico*.' Without a word Nicander went off.

Some time later he came back with a steaming bowl and they used their fingers to sup the frugal meal together.

'So it's Constantinople, then, Marius. I heard the crew talking.'

'Yes.'

'Never been there. Have you?'

'No.'

'Then it's a new place for us both. Have you given thought as to what you'll do there?'

Marius grunted and patted his pack. 'Seeing as how the square-heads won't need this loot where I sent 'em, I'll put it to good use for myself. You?'

'I'll see what kind of fist I can make of it in Constantinople.' Nicander tried to sound convincing, as much to himself as to Marius. 'Bound to be opportunities for an experienced businessman!'

The Eastern Roman Empire was a great melting pot; races from Greece, the Levant and the unknowable civilisations that lay in the interior to the east. Surely with his skills he could make something of it there! Returning to Leptis Magna was not an option. That would mean admitting defeat: he had left home against his father's wishes to set up on his own in Rome.

'Right. Well, I suppose we should get some sleep,' he murmured. Outside their chalk square, the deck was carpeted by bodies. He pulled out his travel-stained chlamys. Marius quickly had his greasy wool campaign

28

cloak tightly around him and with a practised endurance sat with his back to the bulwark and head on his knees.

Nicander lay down. Even in his fatigue the decking was hard and unforgiving. Right aft there was a cabin with lights within and no doubt soft beds and wine . . .

He turned restlessly, looking up at the stars gently wheeling above, regularly obscured by the triangular top-sails.

Would fortune smile on him again? On a merchant with little capital, one of so many nameless souls fleeing the barbarians?

Sleep refused to come.

Setting foot on dry land could not come too soon for Nicander. At least the sailing had been uneventful. Their ship had followed the well-worn track eastward, navigating by known headland and seamark as vessels had for a thousand years. And now, after the slow, week-long journey through the winding length of the Hellespont into the Propontis, they were at last coming within sight of their destination.

Nicander watched as the light-blue misty coastline ahead firmed into darker blue.

It was a changed world now, one where Rome was diminished to a carcass for the plucking, finished as a country, let alone a world power. He had no real feelings for it any more; he'd lost his business and nearly his life because of their pathetic living in the past. They still maintained the pretence of glory with a senate and consul and all the flummery of an imperial history while letting their institutions decline and rot.

It was different for Marius. Brought up as a true Roman he was staunch in his loyalty and protected against reality by the traditions and ceremony of the legion. And secure among his comrades, he'd been blind to the inevitable. It must have been a cruel awakening to have been broken in battle and see all he held dear and honourable crushed under a barbarian horde.

How would he take to the other, more oriental Roman Empire? Nicander had dealt with quite a few merchants from these parts; clever, metropolitan and sly. They had done well under Emperor Justinian, who had transformed the climate for trading with his laws and firm rule, preserving a bastion of civilisation in the face of the human torrent that was flooding in from the vastness of Asia.

And would he himself prosper or fade? With so little capital and no friends . . .

The land ahead took on colour and detail. Constantinople was beginning to emerge to the left, occupying the end of the peninsula across his vision. On the right was Chalcedon, which lay in Asia. Between the two cities was the Bosphorus Strait, leading through the mountains all the way to the Euxine Sea.

Nearer, a massive sea wall ran right along the foreshore, vanishing into the mists to the left. Above it were houses and larger edifices, glittering white in the morning sunshine. The wafting air brought the scent of land.

The ship's twin rudders were put over as their course was laid to round the peninsula, and as they closed with the shore new sights came into view. A tower, a lighthouse – domes, tall buildings – and a great palace. And there next to it, unmistakeable, was the marvel of the Church of Sancta Sapientia – or Hagia Sophia as he knew it, a breathtaking vision in marble.

Close by it were the stern porticoes of some kind of senate building, looking as if it had been magically transported from Rome, and further round the end of the peninsula, gardens and olive groves, meadows and valleys.

They did not continue on up the Bosphorus but followed the headland around. A noble acropolis stood high on the wooded promontory.

On the left, a long and narrow waterway opened up, bustling with small craft – the Golden Horn, the legendary end point and focus for so much exotic trading.

Sail was shortened, lines thrown ashore and the ship worked alongside the stone wharf. The high-class passengers were escorted off first, then Nicander and Marius joined the flood of others down the gangway and found themselves on the blessed solidity of the land.

'So. Where do we . . . ?' Nicander began but tailed off when he saw the outstretched hand.

'It's farewell, then, Greek. I wish you well.'

'Where are you going?'

'Join up, o' course! Legionary like me, good to be under the eagle banner again.'

CHAPTER THREE

The sound of the fretful infant's crying set Nicander's teeth on edge. The Sarmatian woman had no time to care for a child – she had her hands full running the *tabernaria*, the street eatery beneath his room. He'd rented the little place from her crude Thracian husband and daren't risk losing it by complaining, not with the way things were at present.

The whining continued on and on and Nicander saw red. He jumped up and decided to go to his small lock-up and check if the shipment had arrived. Anything to get away from this racket.

Snatching his chlamys he swirled it on, hoping the dash of colour at its hem and polished bronze brooch at the shoulder would conceal the shabby tunic underneath. He clattered down the wooden stairs, flashing a glassy smile at the woman pouring something from an amphora into a giant pithos set in the floor. A stomach-churning reek of rancid oil and stale fish billowed out from the array of hobs at the back of the *tabernaria*.

Outside there was little relief from the fetid closeness. He stepped off briskly.

In this capital city of Empire, despair marched side by side with monument and splendour. From his tenement in the fringe area it was only a couple of streets and he was at the Artopoleia with its bustling commerce, and then the four columns of the tetrapylon marking the end of urban Constantinople.

A diseased beggar on his knees clutched at Nicander. Irritably, he kicked him aside; most were frauds and made a tidy living out of their condition. There were church sisterhoods and others who found their salvation by ministering to the poor – why should he be singled out?

It had been a serious blow finding that his line of business was closed to him. There was a guild of incense traders licensed by the state and they were not interested in making things easy for an outsider. And without serious capital there was no prospect of setting up in competition with them. He'd had to look for some other entry-level venture, for no one was going to extend credit to yet another exile.

He was approaching the edge of town, broken up with vegetable plots and artisan workshops. He hurried; all he'd been able to secure was an agreement to provide pomegranates to a monastery and if his Syrian supplier let him down again he stood to lose it.

At the converted stable he eased open the door of his lock-up and saw it was quite empty. The old watchman he had hired to act as storekeeper was lying on sacking in a corner, snoring heavily.

'Get up, pig!' Nicander shouted.

The man rolled over but didn't awake.

'Stir yourself,' he bellowed, landing a kick.

'Wharr?'

Nicander caught the stench of cheap wine, he'd get nothing out of him. There'd been no delivery and he left with only the satisfaction of slamming the door with an almighty crash.

He started back, trudging on in a black mood.

Ahead was a building site – yet another villa or church in construction – and he winced at the noise, hurrying past the busy scene. At the roadway groups of men lay sprawled on the ground, waiting to be taken on as labourers by the hour.

He noticed one in a dusty tunic, unusually with a cowl concealing his face. Suddenly he got up and made for him.

Alarmed, Nicander braced himself.

The man flicked back the cowl. 'Ah, Mr Nicander, good to see you!'

'Marius?'

The proud legionary was kneading his hands, not catching his eye. 'Do I see you in good health, sir?'

'Quite well, thank you,' Nicander replied cautiously. 'And yourself? How's the army treating you?'

'I'm not with 'em any more,' Marius said stiffly, then added, 'You – you're now in the way of business as a merchant, as you said you would?'

'Fruit from Syria and so on. I've just come from my warehouse, checking on deliveries. I've a contract with the ecclesiasticals which sets fair to lead to big things if fortune allows.'

'So you're doing well, Mr Nicander.'

'So-so. I'm rather busy, what with all this business to attend to, so I'll have to bid you good day, old chap, and be on my way.'

A hand shot out and clamped on his arm.

Nicander glared until it fell away.

'Look, I'm no good at begging. Don't make me do it, friend.' Marius's eyes hardened, then he looked down. 'It's like this. I fell out with that mongrel army, took a run. Thought to set up as a bootmaker but the toad who rented me a shop found my silver loot and thiefed it, threatened to turn me in.'

He came closer, his voice a whisper as though fearing someone might overhear. 'So, well, I thought as how you might have a place for me in your company. Anything – anything at all! I don't fear to get my hands dirty, and if you'd give me charge o' your slaves I'd sweat 'em!'

'Well . . .'

'Or even lumping. I'm good and strong still . . .'

'*Anything?*'

'Look, I'm desperate, Mr Nicander. Huck out your drains, swab down your warehouse, polish your pots . . .'

Recalling how the legionary had toyed with him when he'd come aboard the ship in Brundisium he couldn't help replying, '*Why* is Marius desperate, I'm thinking? Is it because no one will take him on? Then, should I?'

'You're making me beg. You gave your word not to.'

'I made no such promise!'

'Then . . . then you want me to beg, damn it.'

'Well, I—'

'On my knees? Kiss your sandals?' Marius continued in a savage growl.

He scruffed Nicander's chlamys, lifting him off his feet. 'I've never begged to any man in my life and I'm not starting with you!'

Nicander tried to say something but the big legionary drew him close to his face. 'You lot just don't know what it is to be right out o' luck, not a coin, not a future, no pride and all no fault of your own, *do you?*'

He let go. 'I'd have thought you a better sort, but then I'm no hand at judging men. Sorry.'

'It was of no account,' Nicander said, shaken.

Marius gave a mock bow. 'Well, *sir* will be wanting to get about his business. I won't detain *sir* any longer.'

'Wait – when I said that the business was doing fine, I didn't really mean that well. In fact, not so prosperous that . . . and to tell the truth, not so brisk at all that I can think to hire any man.'

'Oh?'

'But . . .'

'Yes?'

'Tell me, Marius, have you somewhere to stay at all?'

'None of your business, Greek.'

'It's just that . . . I've a small place near the Artopoleia. If you're embarrassed for accommodation at the moment perhaps . . .' He'd come to know the man on the voyage out and had developed an odd regard for his character. And even though they were so different, they were facing the same fate . . . to have someone to talk with, share the wretchedness . . .

'I couldn't pay my way in a fine mansion like yours,' Marius responded. But there was a knowing look in his eyes.

'On a temporary basis, of course, I can see my way to suspending any fee incurred.'

'We could share meals, it'll be less for both.'

'As it happens, there's a *tabernaria* close by which I know well.'

'Hah! So there's something in it for you then, Greek?'

He sighed. 'Call me Nico, then, if you must.'

Nicander could swear that the child had not left off whining the whole time he'd been away, only pausing to watch the big man in a cowl go up the stairs with him.

As they entered the room, Marius said, 'It's decent of you, Nico. Letting me stay and that.' He looked around at the humble furniture. 'I'll doss down there,' he said, pointing to the ragged carpet against the opposite wall to the bed. There was no hint of sarcasm Nicander could detect.

The child's fitful crying broke out again.

In a voice that had been heard above the din of a battlefield, Marius bellowed down, 'Shut it, or I'll come and tear off your poxy head!'

The sound stopped as if cut off with a knife.

Nicander fought down a rising warmth. 'You've had a tough time of it, then.'

'Been kipping on the steps of St Demetrius. Hard as a whore's heart and noisy with it, they at their business all night. Look, if you've a bit o' bread, I'd take it kindly . . .'

Nothing less than a fish soup and a jug of rough watered African wine could meet Nicander's feeling that he was no longer alone.

Marius lifted his cup. 'Here's to rare times,' he grunted and drank heavily.

When he finished he fixed Nicander with a shrewd look. 'Business not so good, then.'

'Oh, fair, a slow start I'd have to say.'

'So it's bad.'

The elated spirits fled under a tide of depression. His head hung in despair.

'Not your fault, mate,' the legionary rumbled. 'The world being so fucked up.'

The evening was drawing in, shadows deepening in the dingy room. Nicander found the oil lamp and brought flame to it.

They both stared pensively into space until Marius broke the silence. 'Seems to me a right shame.'

'What's that?'

'Well, you and me. Now we understand each other, a pity we can't work something out. Team up, come together on some venture.'

'Such as?'

'I don't know! Get in the ferry business? I can pull an oar better than the pathetic weasels I've seen.'

'Capital.'

'What's that you said?'

'We've no coin. That's the rub,' Nicander said bitterly. 'No capital, no investment; no business, no profit.'

Marius glowered.

'I'd willingly join you if I could think of a venture not requiring capital, I really would.'

'Well, what are you doing with yourself now? You said something about fruit.'

Nicander sighed and explained what faced him in the fruit supply business. 'Without the pomegranate shipment I'm finished anyway,' he concluded.

Marius gave a tight smile. 'Ah, now that's something that can be left to me. Tell me about this Syrian.'

Next day, as if by magic, the pomegranates had arrived. Disbelieving, Nicander set about arranging delivery.

'He's sorry for the inconvenience and will do better next time,' Marius said with a wicked smirk. 'What now?'

Then it was the oranges. A private arrangement with a ship's master to regularise. Again there was no trouble, once the legionary had seen to it.

CHAPTER FOUR

'How's our capital, now, Nico?' Marius asked as the coins were carefully counted.

'Improving.'

'Can we—'

'No. Capital is blood – we don't shed it unless we have to. It's our way out of this stinking hole, but we need to build up more.'

'Damn it all, when will that be?'

'At this rate . . . perhaps a year or so, then—'

'I don't *want* to wait that fucking long!'

'This is what we have to do, Marius.'

'Take a chance on it, man! Where's your courage?'

'No!'

'I say, yes!'

Nicander's face tightened. 'You're entitled to half the assets, Marius. Do you want them now? Shall I put them in a bag?'

'A plague on your money-grubbing ways, Greek.'

'Patience is the hardest lesson in business.'

'A pox on that, too.'

Rage suddenly clamped in. 'You stupid bastard, Marius! Can't you see? Do you think I want it to be like this? Let me tell you, not so long back you'd see me running my own incense business, seventy men taking my wages, a turnover of a hundred thousand solidi, a reputation in the city. Can you just try to think how it feels for me to be grubbing about in oranges and pomegranates at the beck and call of any pig with an obol or two? Can you?'

Marius's face went dull red. Then with a crash, his fist slammed down.

'Now you listen to me, you . . . you poor pissed-upon bastard! How do you think I'm taking it? A first-class Roman legionary, service in Syria and Dalmatia, there's enemy bones out there because I'm good with a blade – now all I'm told to do is put the frights on some witless idiot on a barrow stall!'

He heaved a deep breath.

Both men slumped back in their chairs.

After a space Nicander said, 'Look, I do appreciate what you're doing. It's hard on both of us . . .'

He picked up his accounts and opened the ledger. 'This Nabatean Grotius,' he said wearily, 'I advanced him an amount to cover his lemon shipment and now he's crying poverty and won't return it. If you could go and persuade him to his obligation . . . or it'll leave me embarrassed in the matter of the currants deal.'

Marius flung open the door. 'M'friend, m' friend!'

He rubbed his hands in delight as he sank into a chair with a wide grin.

'You have the coin, then?' Nicander asked, surprised as the legionary had only been away an hour or so.

'Better'n that, Greek!'

'Oh?'

'Grotius. He begs to be released of his arrears.'

'*And* . . . ?'

'I said we'd agree to it.'

Lost for words, Nicander blinked in confusion.

Marius continued enthusiastically, 'In view o' what he had to say.'

'Which was, might I ask?'

'Ha! What you didn't know is that the fat toad is in with the Blues faction in a big way.'

'And what's that got to do with us?'

The brutal Roman circus of gladiators and Christian sacrifice had long since been overtaken in Byzantine popular entertainment by other offerings; now it was wild animal baiting and, above all, chariot racing between the Blues and Greens factions.

Marius retorted triumphantly, 'In two days there's a fix, and Grotius is on the inside!'

'So?'

'He says it's certain, as only he's in the know and he trusts we'll look kindly on his position while we collect our winnings.'

'Do I hear you – you're saying we should risk our precious capital – on a bet?'

'Right enough. I can tell you on the quiet, he's staking his wife and two daughters to slavery on it.'

'No reason for us to be demented as well! Now look, Marius, betting is the business of fools. Can't you see he's throwing out an excuse so you leave him alone?'

'This is our chance to make a hill o' cash! Greens have had a good run with Priscus, their crack driver, they're calling odds of sevens at least on a Blues win. We put—'

'No!'

'I say we go for it!' Marius growled. 'Anything which sees us on top o' this world instead of—'

'You fool!' Nicander said. 'We've not one shred of proof that there's such a fix being planned. You'd throw our money at a bunch of losers and—'

'Look, he'll take us to see Nepos, the Blues driver. Introduce us. You can ask him yourself!'

Grotius met them outside the Blues faction clubhouse. 'So pleased you could come, gentlemen,' he said with an oily charm. 'It might be better to sport these favours?' He handed a blue cloth spray to each of them to pin on their tunics. His own had an ostentatious silver clasp, Nicander noted, already regretting his agreement to humour Marius.

'My party,' Grotius told the heavyweight pair at the door and they proceeded into the noisy interior.

Seeing the marble panelling, ornate classical statues and the occasional flash of a senatorial toga, Nicander suspected that Grotius was a man living to the limits of his means.

He also knew the factions were more than simple supporters. Enormous sums were granted to them by the Prefect to manage the public shows. In Rome there had been four factions but now the Blues and Greens had it all between them. They played to the masses and ran an operation that included top charioteers and circus spectaculars.

They could effortlessly whip up the mob with professional cheerleaders and gangs and were therefore a formidable political force, even having the power to address the emperor directly in their own interest.

Nicander trod carefully around the carousing groups as they followed the corpulent merchant. Female cries that left no doubt as to the activity within came from behind closed doors. A stream of slaves bearing exotic sweetmeats and jugs of wine jostled past. Occasionally, well-dressed patrons nodded familiarly at Grotius then looked curiously at his guests.

At the end of the long passage Grotius knocked firmly at a door.

'Who the fuck's that?' came a deep voice from inside. 'I'm tired. Go away.'

'Ah, Nepos, old friend. It's Grotius and I've a pair of your greatest fans who beg to meet you.'

'Oh? Well send 'em in if you have to, then.'

Rush dips guttered as they entered and a rich stink of horses lay on the air. The charioteer reclined on a leather bench. Two women were at work on his oiled back.

'This is Nepos, gentlemen, the supreme chariot driver of the age!'

He rolled over to face them. Impressively big, with muscular thews and a deep chest, he had the dark of the Thracians. His hair was a riot of black curls in the old Roman style and he sported a pugnacious beard.

Nicander felt his presence overbearing. 'Good sir, we're here to express our best wishes for your contest with the Greens.'

Cruel eyes took him in. 'You've got money on me, then?'

'O' course, Mr Nepos,' Marius came in quickly. 'Knowing you'll win, like.'

'What do you mean?' The charioteer snapped, sitting up suddenly.

'That your loyal Blues have taken precautions to—'

'Get out!' Nepos snarled at the two masseurs.

'Now, what—'

'These are some of my closest friends,' Grotius said, grovelling. 'It behoves us to share our good fortune.'

'They know . . . ?' He sprang lithely over and seized him by his tunic, drawing his face close. 'How many others have you blabbed to, you Tyrian bird-brain?'

'None but these, Master Driver, truly! And I can say they're in great admiration that it's your own cunning that came up with this winning stroke against those arrogant Greens.'

Nepos let his hands drop. 'So they should be, runt.'

'I would be so gratified if you'd show them something of our little surprise.'

The big chariot driver hesitated, then gave a wicked grin. 'Follow me.'

Below the clubhouse were the workshops and Nepos stopped at the one with two lounging guards. 'Just remember,' he muttered darkly, 'the Greens have got it coming!'

Inside were workbenches and timber racks, but in the centre was the sleek and oddly large bulk of a racing chariot. Not much more than a platform on wheels with a raised breast-rail and side panels, it was clearly designed for victory. In weight it was pared down to the very limits of prudence: wheel spokes nothing but spindles, iron fittings like filigree and a single supporting beam fore and aft. On the side was emblazoned a large blue escutcheon. The whole gave an impression of arrogance and speed.

Nepos swaggered over to it and lightly stepped aboard, cutting a magnificent figure as he looked down on them. He dropped to a racing crouch, one hand stretched to the 'reins', the other furiously cracking an imaginary whip, his lips curled in a contemptuous sneer. 'It's the last lap, the Greens are coming up on the outside. I sees 'em, gets ready. They're coming . . . we make at each other. Priscus doesn't give way, the prick. But next time he gets it – like this!'

There was no giveaway motion that Nicander could see but with a shocking clatter a small wooden pole suddenly shot out from the side of the chariot, ending yards away.

'See?' It didn't take much imagination to conceive of its effect on an adjacent chariot, thrust into flimsy wheel spokes at speed.

Nepos leapt to the ground and bent under the platform to replace the device. 'That's all it is!'

The concealed pole was held by a simple leather spring which was restrained by a small peg protruding up through the platform. The driver had only to tread on the peg to set it off. And with both of his hands in sight working reins and whip there could be no accusations of interference.

'Ingenious!' Grotius chuckled. 'And will see us rich as Croesus!'

Nicander and Marius returned to their tenement.

'I told you it was a certainty, didn't I!' Marius crowed. 'Worth staking all of, say, ten golden solidi, don't you think, Nico?'

Nicander didn't reply but went straight to his accounts.

'Did you hear me, Greek? At least ten – why not fifteen?'

Nicander flipped the ledger firmly shut and looked away.

'So just five, then.'

There was no response. 'Come on, that's not so much – is it? This is our big chance! Have we ever seen anything like it since we came to this pox-ridden place? We can't let it go without—'

'You know nothing of finance, do you? Five solidi – how much do you think this can yield on just a single voyage in olive oil? No? I'll tell you. It returns as eight. A profit of three on five.'

43

Marius stared back obstinately.

'But this is a four month turnaround voyage. And danger of pirates and tempest.' His eyes held Marius's with a sudden intensity. 'Three solidi! Enough, perhaps, to keep us in meat for six months. And then back to that woman's stinking fish. But let's say we take our five solidi to the races at a solid sevens. Thirty-five solidi! Think of it – put on a Cyrenaican grain venture we'd be talking near fifty! Reinvested in another, and one on the side in marble and we'd be looking to moving out of this . . . this situation in a year.'

'Well, let's do it! The five on Blues to win!'

Nicander didn't answer, his gaze unseeing.

'Why not?' Marius blazed.

Nicander reached for his slate, his hand flying as he made calculations.

'This is why not,' he said, holding it up.

'What's that to me?'

'If instead we settle all we can rake together on a certain sevens, we stand to make six . . . hundred . . . and . . . seventy . . . gold ones! We clear out of here, set up on The Mese and get our start! The world ours for the taking, Marius! With that kind of cash we get respect, investment capital and decent living all in one hit! We'd be on our way!'

Marius blinked, startled at what seemed so out of character in his friend. 'Yes, but don't you think—'

'Who's holding back now! Courage, brother!'

'That's all our savings, and most of our purse too. What if something goes wrong?'

'We saw with our own eyes what's in plan, and the Blues' greatest man to do it. How can it fail?'

'I . . .' rumbled the big legionary awkwardly.

'Look, remember what Grotius said at the end. We don't place the bet until they're at the starting line. Gives us the chance to wait for the secret signal from Nepos that'll tell us the Greens haven't rumbled what's going on. Nothing to risk now, is there?'

'What if—'

'You've objection to the high life? Slaves, fine wine, Palmyran dancing girls at dinner?'

'But—'

Nicander slapped his hands down on the table. 'An end to it! All or nothing – what's it to be . . . ?'

CHAPTER FIVE

'We walk in beggars, we leave rich men!' Nicander cuffed Marius affectionately on the back as they approached the bulking mass of the hippodrome, a full quarter-mile long and capable of seating a hundred thousand – a fifth of the city population. Located at the end of Constantinople's peninsula, together with the palaces and churches, the Senate, Patriarchate and Praetorium, it stretched from where the main street ended at the Hagia Sophia all the way to the Bosphorus.

The colossal structure was simple in layout: an elongated circuit with a tight turn at each end and along the centre, the *spina*, a central barrier adorned with noble statues from Rome's glorious past. A twisted bronze column rose thirty feet above the *spina*, topped with three serpent heads. Stands reared sharply up around the entire length, save the northern end, where the starting boxes and entertainment rooms were located, surmounted by copper prancing horses.

It seemed all the world was converging there. Patricians and beggars, souvenir touts and contortionists, great ladies and courtesans, thieves and urchins. All streaming in for the race of the season. The raucous hectoring of officials mingled with the strident brass of the Excubitors' military horns, the jeers and catcalls of rival supporters and the ceaseless hubbub of excited spectators.

On the side closest to the Bosphorus, the structure formed a wall for the Great Palace compound, giving the Emperor private entry to his box, the kathisma. The opposite side, facing inland, was where the people flooded in through the black gate. The Greens supporters began massing to the left of the Emperor's box, the Blues to the right, and the two found seats there.

Nicander couldn't suppress a growing thrill; he'd never seen an emperor and Justinian was the most powerful ruler in the world. He'd rescued the pride of the Romans, built the breathtaking Hagia Sophia, and had kept the faith and his peoples secure against the barbarian hordes.

There was movement at the kathisma. The ivory gates were flung open and six flamboyantly dressed soldiers strode out. Their officer looked about importantly, then returned inside. Moments later, hidden trumpets flourished a fanfare.

The crowd quietened to a hush.

Nicander held his breath: he and Marius were no more than a hundred yards from the royal box. A vast roar went up as Emperor Justinian appeared, an image of white and gold, the glitter of precious stones, a sumptuous purple cloak. On his head, a tall pearl diadem, and at the shoulder of his Greek-style chlamys a massive clasp worked in gold and rubies.

The great man moved with the deliberation of age but was not stooped. He was alone, no empress shared the moment with him for the fabled Theodora was dead.

Justinian, one hand on his breast, gazed down inscrutably on the seething thousands. Suddenly he held up both hands. The roar fell away and a herald appeared to the sound of the trumpets.

'In the name of Our Lord Jesus Christ! The Emperor Caesar Flavius Justinian, Vice-regent of God, conqueror of the Vandals, the Africans, the Goths and Allemani. Pious and renowned, victorious and triumphant, ever august. Hear him, his people!'

For most of the crowd the stentorian voice was barely audible and when Justinian began speaking it was impossible to make out his words. But it was enough that their emperor was addressing them. He sat down to a surge of excited anticipation – the games had begun.

From the far end of the hippodrome burst dozens of gaily dressed performers, spreading rapidly down the track, their acrobatics, contortions and clowning a preliminary to the animals.

The bears were brought out for baiting, but the crowd were not in the mood for any delay before the coming race. They were hastily removed.

Then there were movements in the starting boxes. A spreading roar went up at the appearance of four chariots, two Green and two Blue, each with four horses. Their drivers were dressed head to toe in their colours, which also decorated the horses and chariots. One by one, the teams saluted the Emperor then raised their hands to receive the acclamation of the crowd.

Eventually the chariots were eased forward to the white cord, the horses snorting and jibbing in nervous expectation.

The noise died. Justinian solemnly raised an outstretched hand which held a crimson silk cloth. It fluttered for a moment – then fell.

A colossal wave of sound erupted. The horses leapt forward, whips lashing without mercy as the charioteers strove for advantage. The four teams swept down the straight towards Nicander and Marius, swerving at maniacal speed in a breakneck contest for an inside place at the turn. They fought their way around the end of the *spina* in a tight bunch, wheels skidding, the drivers leaning at extreme angles.

A Green took the lead.

The chariots flew down the straight, dust swirling, the frenzied roar of the spectators never slackening. Then around the far end and back up the other straight.

A gilt ball dropped on a pole of the *spina* signified a lap completed.

The Green was still out in front by a couple of lengths, a Blue in hot pursuit, the other two jockeying for position close behind as they came up to the turn below the Emperor.

Nicander was shouting and screaming with the rest, barely aware of Marius next to him bellowing and flailing his arms like a madman.

The chariots crowded into another turn. The lead Green was going all out, setting a cruel pace for the Blue that was close behind.

Then Nicander saw that those following were the two star charioteers: first Nepos for the Blues then Priscus for the Greens – and they were separated from the leaders by a significant three lengths.

Was this a ploy to reserve everything for a ferocious last lap?

When would the fix go in? To be certain of the outcome Nepos had either to be in the lead or second coming up – but there were still two ahead vying for position! If either of these second-rank drivers won, their fame was assured and as they made for the turn they were neck and neck, slashing their foam-streaked horses into madness.

Then, in a split second, everything changed. As they went into the turn, the lead horse of the Green chariot out in front seemed to stumble and hop and his other horses, confused, slackened their pace. The driver skilfully slewed his chariot clear of the onrushing avalanche of horses and riders but he was out of the race.

This left the two Blues in the lead. The Greens supporters screeched their dismay.

Now the final turn lay ahead. Nepos, flashing a glance behind at Priscus saw his chance and lashed his horses to their limits, gradually pulling up level with the leading Blue. They stayed together, denying Priscus the Green any chance at the inside in this last, critical turn.

The crowd went wild. But yet again the situation changed – the first Blue was visibly tiring, spent in reckless efforts to stay in front and was dropping back. Priscus saw his chance and began a move to overtake. All three closed the turn – if Priscus could manage the manoeuvre the race would be his!

But then the first Blue deliberately went wide. It blocked Priscus but gave Nepos the inside at the cost of his own position in the race. Priscus, however, tugged savagely at his reins and fell in behind Nepos on the inside. They came out of the turn skidding wildly and into the final straight.

From somewhere Priscus found the last vestiges of strength in his horses and began pulling up with Nepos, whose glances behind betrayed that his own foam-streaked animals were at the limit of their endurance.

There was an overlap! Nepos swerved to discomfit Priscus who sheered away but came back quickly still overhauling the Blue. There was blood streaking the back of Nepos's horses – he swerved again but there was no deterring the Green and they swayed dangerously close together.

The fix! Do it now! Nicander's heart hammered but he knew Nepos would only act when Priscus was in exactly the right place for the deadly blow.

Transfixed, he watched as the Green drew level, Nepos's head flicking over again and again as he made his judgement. Nicander remembered the position of the trap – Priscus would have to be precisely two feet ahead before—

In a heart-stopping moment the chariot seemed to explode, pieces cartwheeling and bouncing. The maddened horses plunged on with the wreck furrowing the dust behind, the helpless charioteer dragged along behind, entangled in the traces.

But this was not Priscus – it was the Blue! Nicander felt numb: the opposition must somehow have got wind of the fix and put in their own.

Nepos desperately went for the knife down his back to cut himself free but he couldn't reach it and his frantic horses thundered on. He was sandpapered to death in front of the screeching crowd, while Priscus cantered on to an easy victory.

In a haze of unreality Nicander and Marius watched the garlanded winner receive his prize and laurel crown from the hand of the Emperor then turn to receive a deafening acclamation from the masses.

Fighting their way clear of the riotous supporters streaming from the hippodrome the pair, headed for home – the stinking stew they had so hoped to be rid of.

Neither spoke, the crushing enormity of what had happened too great for words. In the gathering dusk gangs of the Green faction gleefully set upon any Blue they could find, but at the sight of the big legionary they left the pair alone.

They passed a wine shop overflowing with raucous customers. Marius snarled a curse. 'Wait!' he mouthed and loped off down a side alley.

Nicander became uneasy when he didn't reappear after some minutes.

Then Marius, cradling a heavy amphora, burst from out of the alley, pursued by a livid innkeeper. Nicander thrust out his foot and the man chasing him was sent sprawling headlong on the ground.

'Where are you going with that?' he panted after catching up with Marius.

'What do you think!'

Nicander glanced back into the darkness. 'Better you play it smart – put it over your shoulder and follow your master, slave!'

Marius growled but fell in behind him for the trudge home.

In their shabby quarters Nicander got a rush dip going and found a knife to pierce the hard wax around the stopper. It came free and the heady pungency of wine filled the room. He sniffed appreciatively.

The amphora yielded up its contents, a dark, rich red wine.

'No water?' Roman wines were strong and always diluted to taste.

'No water.'

Nicander didn't argue and poured for them both. 'To damnation in hell for this stinking city!' he said and downed his wine in one. It coursed to his belly in a flooding tide of guilty release. He wiped his mouth on his hand and pronounced, 'A Falernian niger – and a good one.'

Marius held out his empty cup. 'Will do me whatever it's called, by the gods.'

They drank deeply again, then Nicander threw at Marius, 'Would never have happened if you hadn't made me bet.'

'Or you hadn't staked the lot!'

They lapsed into silence; given what was ahead there seemed little point in debating blame.

They were facing the unthinkable.

Marius tossed back more wine. 'Be quit o' the place! Get out, go somewhere a man can breathe clean air again!'

'Oh? Where? I can't think of anywhere not crawling with Goths or Huns, can *you*?' He snorted. 'Of course, there is one way that will keep us safe and warm, never short of a bite – security and all that.'

'All right, Greek. What?' Marius said morosely.

'Sell ourselves into slavery. That way we get silver in our pocket and not much work – can't be bad!'

'Be buggered to that! I'm a free Roman and—'

'Calm down, I'm only joking.' Nicander said wearily. 'If Leptis Magna is still standing, I *suppose* I could go back there,' he muttered. He'd not told Marius about the feud with his father and in truth he doubted a return would be welcome. 'But without a single sesterce – *and* assuming I could raise the passage money. How about you? Could—'

'I've got no folks,' Marius said tightly.

'Then . . .' Nicander felt a curious pang at the thought of parting with the strong-minded and plain-speaking man he had come to know and respect. 'I suppose for now we could throw ourselves on the state, register for the bread handout.'

'I've never begged before and I'll not start now!'

'Then it leaves us with only one thing.'

'What?'

'Pull off a crime so big we're right back in the picture.'

'Now you really are joking, Greek.'

'You've got a better idea, then? Well, if we're not to thieve our way out of trouble, there's only one way to turn an honest coin and that's in business.' The wine was doing nothing for his concentration but Nicander pressed on, 'We've got to find something that has solid returns and quick yields.'

'Business? I know the biggest there is!'

'Oh?'

'Yes! With my own eyes, I saw it. In charge of the fore-escort to Ankara.' His brow furrowed in concentration as he recalled the details. 'Four carts, eighty men, all on the quiet. I asked my centurion, he said it was gold – payment to the Persians. Over a ton! Told me it was to pay the bastards for silk as can only be got from them. Each year, six loads o' gold go to Nisibis and gets handed over. Just think about it, Nico – tons of gold because the poxy priests and royal court can't do without their silk!'

'And you want us to lift a shipment!'

'Listen, Greek! You asked about a big business, I'm telling you one! You're the mighty money man – let's see you make something out of this silk thing!'

Nicander tried to throw off the wine's fuddle. Maybe there was some little corner which they could ease into. 'Ah, I grant you, if we get into it, why, we've chance for a good earner . . . but there's always going to be need of capital.'

'But what about those damn Persians?'

'What do you mean?'

'Got a stranglehold on the whole stinking silk trade. Can't get past 'em to buy directly, demands we pay in gold, nothing else will do.'

'Ah. So if we can get around them, we can set up a business deal?'

'Not a hope. I tell you, they have the lot in their hands. I heard about it! The ships, the border, those caravans o' camels, they control it all. How? Because they has an arrangement with the seller, takes their entire lot for cash in hand. Are they going to listen to a piddley three-obol dealer? Forget it, Greek!'

Nicander glowered at Marius as though it was all his fault, but it was obvious that while the Persians were sitting astride all the trading routes there was no chance of importing on his own account.

Then an idea floated into his mind. A beautiful, magnificent idea. Yes, it truly was!

He smiled. 'I've had a thought!'

'May we be blessed to hear it, O Master?'

'Marius – it's simple. We grow our own! Silk, that is. Start in a small way, sell smart, build it up. Only need to get a peasant to lend us his farm until . . .' He tailed off in wonder at the scope of his great plan.

'How?'

'What do you mean, how?' Nicander slurred, resentful at anything said against his precious idea.

'Well, where do we—'

'Simple! I read somewhere silk grows on trees. What can be easier than we go and help ourselves to a load of seeds? Buy 'em, steal some if we have to – and if we can't sling a bag of seeds over the shoulder and tramp across the mountains with it, we're . . . we're . . .'

'Hump back and plant in the farm? Yes!' enthused Marius.

'I think we've got something!' Nicander crowed. 'Let's drink to it!'

CHAPTER SIX

The next day they left the bedlam and distractions of Constantinople behind and sat together on rocks warm with the sun high above the shore of the Bosphorus.

'We need to think,' Nicander managed to croak. 'Think and plan!' He was feeling a little better after Marius had come up with an old legionary restorative but, in future, he swore, the wine would be well watered.

Marius turned to him. 'Answer me this. If your idea's so fucking good, why hasn't anyone else come up with it?'

'You have to understand the business mind, Marius. Men of finance want as little risk as they can arrange, no daring plans for them. You see, what they're always after is to squeeze better deals on import, sharpen up percentages, margins, build on things as they are. What we're going to do is to get around the whole damned thing, cutting out everybody in the middle. But now, we've bigger problems. Like . . . for instance, how do we get a handle on the costings?'

'You tell me,' grunted Marius.

'Well, there's nothing simpler than to walk away with a bag of seeds. It's getting there in the first place. Why, Sinae where the Seres live, it must be thousands of stadia off – across Persia, over the mountains somewhere. How do we—'

'A march across Persia will take you a month at least, Greek. I heard there's Huns beyond – with surprise we'd get through them in, say, another month, if we leave off attacking the bastards. Mountains? Always tough going. And then the other side – the Seres might not take kindly to so many boots on their soil.'

'Boots? What the hell are you talking about!'

'Come on, Mr Businessman, where's your thinking now? An expedition into hostile territory; I'd not feel secure without we have at least a cohort of pedes and cavalry to match. I'm no officer but even I can see we'd need camp support to the same numbers. Say a thousand or so?'

'Do you know what you've just said?'

'I suppose if we have to go around the Persians then it'll add at least another month – or so. A tight expedition, and I'll agree the numbers might be a bit thin for what we're thinking.'

'Marius – you've just put paid to the whole thing!'

'Wha—?'

'Where are we finding the money for that? We can't afford a couple of serving slaves, let alone half an army!'

Marius replied huffily, 'Those Huns are mad bastards – I should know – where we're going we'll surely need a hell of a stout force to keep 'em off our backs.'

'Can we find our way around them?'

'No. Maybe we can dodge the Persians for a while but then we have to go east – this means right through the buggers.'

'So what this is now saying is we'll need to be funded, get some sort of investment capital into our venture.'

'Right, so we do that.'

'Heaven give me patience. Marius – if an investor puts more money into this than we can, he gets control. And profits in proportion. We take all the hard stuff, he sits back and piles it up.' He shook his head. 'Come to think of it, what's to stop the bastard liking the plan and then ditching us entirely for his own operation?'

'So no money man can be trusted!' Marius paused. 'But there may be a better way.'

'Tell me.'

'Who's to get the biggest kick out of what we're doing? Remember what I said about all that gold – it's the Emperor! Six tons of it a year going out of the country – if we can stop that, he'll be so happy he'll put up statues to us both!'

'State funding. I can see how it'll work. In return for the subvention we undertake a perpetual contract to supply. On exclusive terms, naturally.'

Marius rubbed his hands. 'Yes, that. Get him to pay!' He stood up impatiently. 'Hey, now – what are we waiting for? Let's move!'

Nicander's mind raced. It was too easy . . .

'Marius. Sit down. Spare a minute to consider what we're thinking of. We two, not quite in the front rank of the citizens of the greatest city in the world, do knock on that great bronze gate of the Grand Palace and demand to see His Top Highness, the Emperor of Byzantium, Justinian, because we've a good idea we want to share with him, and him alone.'

A fleeting memory of the vision at the hippodrome came. He shivered – their impertinence verged on the sacrilegious and the palace was a byword for intrigue and betrayal. To enter without a friend or guide, into that labyrinth . . . 'On second thoughts don't think that's such a good move. Perhaps we . . .'

'We get someone to speak for us!'

'And lose our idea? I don't think so.'

'All right, then we've got to go in ourselves, for fuck's sake!'

'Who do we see first? Come on, just who do you know in the Grand Palace has the ear of the Emperor? Will not let on to others, will—'

'So we find a bastard who knows!'

'Who?' But even as he spoke, it came to him. 'I supply Sarmatian grapes to that villain Messalia. And he's got one very picky customer out in the country.'

'So?'

'John the Cappadocian!'

'Who?'

'Count of the Sacred Largesse – or was.'

'What's the point of this, Greek?'

'Well, I got it all from Messalia, the gossip. John the Cappadocian's a legend – the most grasping and cruel tax collector of all time. Spared none, high or low, however hard they squealed. Justinian relied on him to pay for his wars and he didn't fail him. It's said he handed over fourteen times his own weight in gold every year, rain or shine.

'For years he had the top job at the treasury – and power and riches – until he fell foul of Empress Theodora, who plotted to bring him down. To please her, Justinian stripped him of his wealth and banished him. After she died he let him back, but to live out of town, poor and in disgrace.'

'And he's . . .'

'He knows every secret in that palace, everyone's – and he can tell us how to get to the Emperor.'

Not far from the massive red-striped Thedosian Walls, nearly hidden among an olive grove on a small estate, was their quarry. It had been several hours' walk under the hot sun and Nicander, in his best tunic, with Marius as presentable as could be contrived, stopped to rest.

'Remember, let me do the talking. This is the most famous money man of the age and won't be accustomed to plain speaking.'

'If it please y' highness,' Marius replied in mock grovel, hoping it hid his nervousness at the prospect of addressing a minister of state, however fallen.

Nicander too felt apprehension. This was their only chance and he would need all his merchant's cunning and guile to bring off their objective.

This was the man who'd, in his day, wielded his power directly under the Emperor and who was even said to have run a private prison within the Praetorium for the torture and execution of offenders in the matter of their tax affairs.

How would he take a visit from the likes of themselves?

There was a high fence around the modest villa with a gate that led through to a garden arbour then into a courtyard. Nicander took a deep breath and strode forward as if he had every right to, Marius at his side.

In one silent, deadly move the apparition of a northern barbarian sprang in front of them, lank-haired, clad in wolfskin and leather and with wild eyes. A hatchet leapt magically into his hands.

'To see His Excellency,' stammered Nicander. A sharp call came from inside the courtyard and the guard stepped aside reluctantly.

There was a table under the dappled shade of a latticed fig tree spread with a simple meal: a jug of wine, olives, bread and honey cakes. A man sat there, a sheaf of notes beside him. A dog cringed beneath his feet, its eyes only on him.

Nicander approached with as much confidence as he could muster. 'Two gentlemen desiring to consult with His Eminence John the Cappadocian.'

There was no doubting that this was he – a near-feral presence radiated from the man, terrifying, unnerving. He was repellently corpulent and dressed in a short chlamys that left his fat legs, hairy and gross, thrust out naked before him. But his eyes gleamed with a fierce intelligence.

'You're a colonial Greek – a merchant, I suspect. And your friend is an exile Latin. I wonder why you came?' he pondered. 'If it's to gloat over my fall then please be aware I shall ask Wulfstan to first break your heads and then throw you out, but I fancy it's for some other reason. Am I right?

'And if you're thinking to sell me some oriental nostrum then I'm gracious enough to allow you a ten-second start before Wulfstan comes after you,' he added with a cruel smile.

Nicander gulped. 'Sire. We come for quite another purpose.'

'Oh? Go on.'

'On a concern that if it came to a true conclusion would be of profit to us both.'

'You're not being very clear, but continue.'

'I – we seek advice in the matter of a business venture of some degree of delicacy that Your Excellency is well placed indeed to advise.'

'I see. Would this be connected with my knowledge of the Byzantine court by any chance?'

'Sir, I will be plain with you.'

'That would be a splendid start.'

'We have a scheme that promises to be of great benefit to the Emperor but requires first we approach him for funding.'

'Ah, me. And I'd hoped the day would bring me diversion of a more worthy nature.'

The dog whined softly. He kicked it.

'Sire, it's to be—'

'If you had any notion of how often I've heard those words you'd pity me with all your heart, you really would.'

'But sir, this is truly a great opportunity,' Nicander pressed. 'A once in a lifetime chance!'

John the Cappadocian yawned, patting his mouth in mock politeness.

Marius bristled and before Nicander could stop him he leant forward. 'Six tons o' gold!' he snarled. 'Year by year! Enough to interest Your Greatness?'

'Your friend has a . . . direct manner. Yet he knows how to pique my interest. You must tell me more about it. We shall leave names aside for now.'

They were motioned to sit and cups were summoned for wine.

'So. As I understand it, you have an idea, a scheme, which you are sanguine will engage the Emperor's attention. It has, however, the fatal flaw that, by its nature, a degree of pelf is required to be laid out before it may be set in train. Is this correct?'

'It is, sire.'

'Do dispense with the court flummery, there's a good fellow. I've been a common citizen these years past and have no hankering over its return.'

He downed his wine, then sat back with a cynical smile and poured more. 'I rather fancy that unless you're frank with me in all particulars we shall not make much progress.'

Nicander hesitated. If he gave away their precious secret, their only asset, and it was taken from them, it would be all over. On the other hand if they did not go forward they would have nothing.

'I should tell you . . . all my idea?'

This was met with a pitying half-smile.

'Ah. Then this is what we propose. Should we succeed in our scheme as a result of your offices, then a due proportion of our increase we shall return to your good self.'

'Yes, a fair and proper course, undoubtedly. Now, why are you not concerned that your scheme, once divulged, will be taken by myself for my profit alone?'

He stuffed a honey cake into his mouth. 'Then I'll tell you. Since I cannot fund you myself I must yield to another. I have thereby surrendered any chance of return. If on the other hand I guide you to a successful conclusion there is a remote possibility I shall be remembered. This is not certain but assuredly better than nothing at all and my rational course therefore is to aid your venture. There is no risk attached to me, it being your necks that are at hazard, neither is there any question of my venturing any coin of mine upon it as I haven't any, and thus I remain perfectly safe.'

Raising his cup he finished the wine in one. 'Gentlemen, for the sake of the entertainment it brings to my lonely existence, I shall assist you. Shall we begin with your names, you being so evidently in possession of my own?'

'Ah, Nicodorus of Leptis Magna, merchant. This is Quintus Carus Marius, legionary, late of Rome.' Nicander went on, 'The silk trade in the Empire, sir. We're aware at the first hand how this is cruelly hurting our sovereign lord in the outgoing of his treasure and revenues.'

'Your six tons of gold a year, yes. I would have put it nearer eight.'

'Our plan, sir, is to bring silk itself to Constantinople.'

There was an irritated wave of a be-ringed hand. 'That's a nonsense, Mr Nicodorus. You'll know the Persians would not countenance any interference in their comfortable relations with the producers!'

'No, sir. We mean to mount an expedition to bring back the seeds of the silk tree and grow it in our own land! We will then be independent of imports and thumb our nose at the Persians, and who's to say – may we not look to export to the world?'

John the Cappadocian slowly sat back and looked at them, each in turn, his glance first speculative then covetous. 'Might I be told how advanced you are in this . . . adventure?'

'It were better we left details to after our consultation with you, sir.'

'That's not quite what I meant . . .'

Nicander picked up on it immediately. 'That is to say, we have no other interested party, none we have discussed the matter with.'

'I see. Mmm . . . a novel and, I'm obliged to say, intriguing idea. Yet there are difficulties. Do you wish to hear them?'

'Sir?'

'The first is that if your intent is to farm silk and sell it on the open market, pray be disabused of that notion. Justinian will never allow an industry of such wealth to remain free. He will of a surety seize it for himself and create a state monopoly.'

'Ah. Then—'

'You will be compensated, no doubt. But the greater difficulty is in the getting of the seeds. As I understand it, silk comes from Sinae or Serica as some would call it, the land of the Seres people. This is at an unknowable distance beyond even the Persian frontier. Cloud-piercing mountains have been mentioned, I believe. To reach it, therefore, your expedition cannot but enter upon the lands and territory of King Khosroe of the Sassanid Persians with whom, let me remind you, we are currently bound with a fifty-year treaty of perpetual amity.

'He will naturally resist any Roman attempt to break his hold over the silk trade and if your party is armed, as it must assuredly be, then it will mean war. The Emperor is sorely distracted by the loss of Rome and would never contemplate another Persian war, no matter what the advantages. I cannot readily see how you will overcome this, gentlemen.'

'We'll go around them.'

'March a small expedition into the very lair of the Goths? I rather think not.'

Nicander replied hastily, 'Then we go in disguise! Just we two, honest merchants about our business.'

'And be instantly taken up as Roman spies? Your Persian is an epicure in the arts of torture – the very least you might expect is to be impaled through the anus and raised on high as a caution to us all.'

John the Cappadocian smiled serenely. 'However, I like the conceit of disguise, on reflection it merely needs refinement. I can well see how it might be handled.' He steepled his hands.

'Please go on, sir,' Nicander said.

'Then it is this. A brace of devout and intrepid gentlemen of god, of whatever species they may be, might without excessive hindrance pass through the lands of Zoroaster about their holy mission.'

'Be buggered to that! I'll not prat about like a poxy monk for any man!' Marius burst out.

'Did I say you must? You asked me for advice, I'm laying out the alternatives, wherever they might lead . . .'

'Yes, yes, please continue, sir!' Nicander spluttered, glaring at Marius.

'So, you do not propose to go in the nature of a military expedition. This will greatly reduce expenses and will be looked upon favourably.'

Nicander brightened.

'Yet the sum needed will remain substantial.'

'For our travel needs?'

'Not so. You will be begging your way in the usual fashion and, of course, living frugally. No, I was more thinking about far kingdoms and strange peoples. I would find it singular, indeed, should your way be not greatly eased by the judicious laying out of inducements.'

'Bribe our way out of situations.'

'That is not the customary term, but it will serve. And naturally when in the fabled land of the Seres, will not your persuasion to loosen their grip on a trifle of seeds be in the nature of things golden?'

For the first time it was all looking possible. 'It does appear we have a basis for moving ahead on the project,' Nicander replied. 'What do you think are our chances – with Emperor Justinian, that is?'

John the Cappadocian eased into an oily smile. 'Why, I would have thought quite positive. The idea will, without a doubt, attract his interest and a few hundred thousands to him is neither here nor there. With my considerable help you will gain his attention in this.

'You will, of course, be presenting a costed estimate based on a comprehensive plan with distances, timing and good evidence of your knowledge of the impediments to be encountered. Whether he will consider you yourselves as suitable for the expedition will depend on your credibility, otherwise you will be thanked with a pittance for your suggestion and others will be appointed.'

'I understand, sir. We'll begin work on it immediately! There is the question of gaining audience with His Imperial Majesty. How . . . ?'

'The usual sanction is to petition for a hearing, but this requires you state your business first with the referendary regulating such access. I do not recommend this course if you desire discretion in the matter of your idea.'

His flabby brow furrowed. 'The Master of the Offices is the untouchable Peter the Patrician, who would never countenance private access, still less the wooden-headed Marcellus, Count of Excubitors and not a man to cross.'

He reflected for a moment. 'I fear our greatest obstacle, however, will be the cunning and entirely corrupt Peter Barsymes, whose reptilian hide is as slimy as his manner. You will know him as the Count of the Sacred Largesse – Emperor Justinian's privy treasurer.'

The 'our' triggered a sudden thrill in Nicander.

'No! Leave this to me. The matter is too delicate for precipitate action. Do prepare your plan, return with it and we shall discuss it together. I will ensure it reaches the ear of the Emperor, do not doubt it.'

Heaving himself upright he leant across, holding their eyes. 'Meanwhile – trust no one! Speak not to a soul, distrust the very walls. The palace is an evil place, where behind a genial manner every man's hand is set against his brother, where a father sells his daughter for power and gain, and worse that I cannot speak of it. Go now, we'll meet again when your plans are ready . . .'

CHAPTER SEVEN

Nicander fought down his exhilaration. From utter despair to the situation now – when anything seemed possible!

'I really do believe we're on to something. I reckon at the very least Justinian will reward us handsomely.'

Marius merely grunted in reply.

Nicander allowed his thoughts to roam. Their spoils would probably be vast: this was no less than the saving of a king's ransom in gold at a time when the Byzantines needed all the wealth they could find to preserve the country's borders against the tidal surge of barbarians.

It seemed so unreal: this wretched squalor and the talk of gold and empires in which he was a central player.

He glanced at Marius, who now had a brooding expression.

'I do think that notion of going as monks makes a lot of sense, don't you? On the way back we can even hide the seeds in a holy relic or some such.'

There was another ill-natured grunt.

Nicander sighed; he was not going to let Marius's mood spoil the moment.

'So. A plan. It's got to be a good one, credible and appealing to an emperor. How do we start?'

Marius sat unblinking, a scowl now darkening his face.

'We've first got to work out a route that takes us past the Goths and other foul heathens. And to make us sound credible we have to know in detail what we're talking about. This will, as well, tell us what's ahead so we can plan for it, put it in the costings. Where do we get such information? It has to be from impeccable sources and as comprehensive as we can manage. Of course! The library, right here in the city! All the knowledge of Serica and the East . . . it must have everything.'

There was still no response from Marius and Nicander was beginning to be irritated by his sullen attitude. Did he not see the scale of the task?

'Be in classical Greek or legal Latin, naturally,' he went on, 'Shouldn't be too much of a problem. Only thing is, so much to get through.'

Suddenly Marius got to his feet with a venomous glare and stormed out.

The next morning Nicander was vexed to see Marius's mood was still there but he decided to let whatever was riding the man pass in its own time.

He took up his satchel. 'I've had a few thoughts about topics to investigate. I don't have to tell you that I have to be disciplined in this or I'll not cover the ground in time. So I'll be off, then. Don't know how long I'll be.'

But just before he reached the door Marius thrust himself across it, barring his way. 'You don't fucking need me now, do you!'

Nicander stopped in his tracks, taken aback by the outburst.

'Admit it!' Marius snarled. 'All your grand plans, prancing off to a library – you don't want an old caligatus getting in the way, spoiling your pitch! I'm no fucking use to you any more, right?'

'Why—'

'So what do I bloody well do? Hey?'

'Well—'

'See! I saw you with that scumbag John the Cappadocian. He only spoke to you, didn't he? Didn't say shite to me. You're going off to speak to Emperor Justinian yourself – can you see him giving me the time o' day? No way!'

'It's not like that—'

'I'm a shame to you! To drag about and act dumb all the time – you don't have to fling it in my face, I know.'

'Marius—'

'You're going to dump me. But have the guts to tell me first!'

Nicander sat down slowly. So that was what was goading him.

'I've no intention of getting rid of you, Marius. In this venture you've equal shares with me.'

The legionary breathed deeply. 'Listen to me, Greek. Don't you dare patronise me. You go out of that fucking door without you swearing on all that's holy that you'll not betray me . . . you won't find me here when you get back!'

In a rush of feeling Nicander realised that he was about to challenge fortune for the greatest stakes of his life yet he had not a single one to trust, any to whom he could safely open his heart, lay out troubles and frustrations, share the burdens – except this bear of a man with his strong, uncomplicated views.

He stood and clasped Marius's hand. 'We've gone through so much together . . .' He paused, aware that a lump was forming in his throat. 'And in what lies ahead I want you with me. I'll swear, if you insist, but I allow before all that you're my true friend and . . . I could never let you down.'

At first there was no reaction. Then the other big hand came out and a smile surfaced. 'Friends. Yes. You and me, Nico – that is, Nicander,' Marius added with a self-conscious chuckle.

'No, m' friend, it's Nico.' He grinned. 'But only from you!'

CHAPTER EIGHT

In a haze of excitement Nicander stepped out along The Mese. His destination was the public library of the Emperor Julian of two centuries before – since the destruction of the Library of Alexandria, the acknowledged centre of learning of the civilised world.

Their great venture was now under way!

At the Forum of Theodosius he turned right towards the arched aqueduct of Valens. Where it met the rise of a hill there was a modest basilica, opposite the grander buildings of the university and overlooked by the Praetorium.

A number of stalls outside sold knick-knacks: stylus and wax tablet sets, finger guards and offcuts of parchment. One of the industries in the library was the copying of decaying papyrus documents to vellum, prepared from more long-lasting animal skins. With a few of his precious remaining coins, Nicander purchased several small pieces on which to make notes.

The library had the reek of ages past. He made his way inside through an old-fashioned columned doorway passing rhetors, grey-and-black robed learned scholars. An open space filled with desks stretched ahead to an apse and a dais with a pulpit-style desk where the stern literary steward sat.

There were three open floors with an endless warren of scroll nooks in the lower, broader shelves for the codices in the upper.

Nicander found an empty desk and looked about at the scores of students perched on stools working silently. They took no notice of a newcomer but an assistant steward quietly appeared at his side. In low tones he explained the structure of the library and Nicander was soon at a well-thumbed index.

The first thing he wanted to equip himself with was all there was to be known about silk. The ancients would have what he sought!

He asked for a well-remembered tome of his youth – the *Naturalis Historia* of the elder Pliny, who had lost his life on the seashore of Pompeii as the volcano rained destruction.

Several volumes of the work arrived. Sections on geography, nature, more.

In a dissertation about silk at origin, Pliny's view was that it was nothing more than an insect's lidle weaving of a cocoon. A commentary below by another declared that it was in fact the hair of the sea-sheep.

Nicander asked for a further volume. It got worse: this one mentioned that in far Sinae gigantic spiders were held prisoner in cages and spun silk while being fed on condemned criminals. Yet another reference stated that silk was scraped from the underside of the common mulberry.

It was deeply unsettling. How could the ancient scholars disagree so?

He found his eyes focusing on the literary steward. Taking his courage in hand, he threaded his way between the rows of desks.

'Learned gentleman, I have a question.'

The august figure frowned.

'Sir, I'm engaged in the writing of a paean to beauty, in particular to that of man-wrought silk, and I rather thought it would lend a pleasing turn to the conceit if I were to make reference to its origin.'

The man's face cleared, apparently satisfied that he was to be troubled for no less a reason than the sublimity of a poem's creation. 'Why, surely you're aware it grows upon the silk tree?' he replied in ponderous tones. 'The authorities are clear on this.'

'As I thought, sir. But Pliny and some others would have it otherwise.'

'Your minor scribblers are never reliable. As to the good Pliny, there have been instances where regrettably he has been found to be in error and his observations in this case are not to be relied upon. The more substantive of the classical authors are the authorities you will wish to consult. The Virgil *Georgics* spring to mind – as does the *Phaedra* of Seneca the Younger.'

In a wash of relief Nicander found among the heavy-going homilies of Virgil that silk did indeed originate from trees, and in fact there was a mention of a fine-tooth comb of special design used by the Seres to harvest the precious substance from the leaves.

He then turned to the *Phaedra*, a gruesome play of taboo love, suicide and a cruel man's relentless will, persevering until he came across a reference to silken garments won from the silk tree in far away Serica.

He could now move on to the next objective: where was Sinae and how to get there.

Accounts by travellers would no doubt reveal what he needed and he busied himself at the index. The first he decided to consult were the reports of the envoys of Marcus Aurelius Antoninus to the mysterious Seres. They would be a logical beginning to his reading, even though they had been written a good three centuries earlier, in the period before the Roman Emperor Valens had been slain by the Persians and their entire access to the East cut off.

The assistant steward brought the work. While filled with exotic details of impossible beasts it was written neither by merchants with an eye to the practicalities nor a geographer, or even a military man concerned with where they were. And it was plain that this was not an official mission, only a half-hearted attempt to open communications, which was admitted to have failed.

Nicander pored over more accounts. The revered historian Ammianus Marcellinus was the most detailed. He had compiled a picture of Scythia – and Serica beyond – but it was a wild tale of Syziges and Chardes, Alitrophages and Annibes, in wearisome succession, together with dogmatic assertions on climate and terrain that made no sense. But Marcellinus did confirm the production of silk originated from a soft fine down spun into thread, gathered from the trees while the leaves were continuously moistened.

The rest just spoke of dragons and gryphons. Nothing on the location of the land of Serica.

Once again Nicander made his way up to the pulpit. This time he was awarded a look of benevolent indulgence.

'Sir, you were entirely correct in the particulars concerning the source of silk. Yet my enquiring mind thirsts to know more – where in the world is this Sinae, that gifts man with such beauty?'

'Quite so. It is to your credit, young man, that you so ardently seek after such knowledge in this crass commercial world. And in furtherance of a work of literary art I believe I will help you.'

He wrote something on a slate and handed it over. 'Go to the Chamber of Apollo and present this.'

Nicander anxiously waited in the small room. Shortly the attendant returned with a single sheet.

It was a map by Pomponius Mela in the reign of Claudius Caesar, from a time of empire and conquest. Nicander examined it carefully; he knew maps of the mercantile kind which detailed market areas but this was different. It was of the entire known world, the *oikoumene*. The centre was dominated by the Mediterranean, with the continents radiating out from it, the whole surrounded by a boundless ocean.

He quickly found familiar territory: Africa to the right with his birth town of Leptis Magna in tiny script, Europa to the left, Constantinople among the densely packed legends in the middle. He eagerly scanned the map, searching for Serica. It was right at the top.

Nowhere on the map, however, was there a marking to show north or south, nor any indication of distance. At the edge of the land mass, there was on one side, the burning Ethiopian Sea, on the other the frigid Hyperborean regions. Hispania was at the bottom limit.

Having found Serica was as maddening as it was enticing, for the entire region existed without a single notation, neither town nor river. The only information he could draw from the map was that by comparing relative sizes,

71

the distance to reach the Seres was nearly as far as the entire length of the Mediterranean!

The next item that was brought was a fat roll of vellum, a foot broad, twenty feet long, infinitely detailed. An *itinerarium*, used within the Roman world when travelling between one town and another along public roads, it listed distances and inn stops. This particular one claimed to record *every* road and town that existed.

There was no pretence at scale or topography; it was simply a lengthy skein of routes originating from Rome to the furthest reaches of Empire. At one end was the outermost extremity of the west, the now-lost province of Britannia, and at the other were the last outposts of civilisation to the east, tailing off with a tantalising reference to the legendary island of Taprobane and a bewildering confusion of barbaric names beyond Scythia that had no meaning to him.

Nicander rubbed his eyes, determined to persevere.

A third item arrived, a map of the world by the famed geographer Ptolemy of Alexandria, his *Geographia*.

Along the base of the map and its sides was a series of numbered lines. The accompanying gloss explained that these were real-world degrees of latitude derived from observations of the sun's altitude, the longitude degrees arbitrarily assigned to make a regular square with the latitude. The entire land mass therefore was distributed under a grid of these lines which had been said to have been taken from actual measurement and should thus at last give a true picture of distances and directions.

Finally here was both a scientific and practical map! It looked much different to the others: Rome and indeed Italia seemed impossibly small against the vast expanses of Asia and Africa and Constantinople was almost lost over to the left.

Nicander concentrated, trying to take in how it all related. The frigid regions in the north were at the top and the burning deserts at the bottom. He'd heard that the limits to the world were impassable snow and ice in the north, warming by degrees until in the far south the heat reached the point where the sea itself boiled. He could see how the mass of Africa curved down and around to connect with south-east Asia on the other side, enclosing a vast inland sea with Taprobane in the centre.

The Seres. They were over to the right, past mountain ranges, deserts and vast empty spaces. Over one hundred and twenty of Ptolemy's longitude degrees, which when brought to real terms was a distance to be measured in thousands of miles!

The steward pointed out that in addition to this world map there were separate regional descriptions on other sheets.

Fighting weariness, Nicander took in the one of the extreme Orient. There indeed was Serica, the land of the Seres, the other side of an impassable desert. Before it was Scythia, the inner home of shadowy tribes so savage and bloodthirsty that it was said the Huns and Goths were fleeing before them to fall on softer civilised peoples.

This map divided the Scythians into the Western *hippophagi*, the horse-eaters and the Eastern *anthropophagi*, the man-eaters. The rest of the sheet was vacant space – was it because travellers never returned from there to tell the tale?

Nicander was about to give up when the literary steward entered the room holding a large, brightly coloured map. 'I came to bring you this,' he said with pride. 'It is lately produced and contains all we know of our place in creation.'

It was the work of the cartographer Cosmas Indicopleustes. His map was apparently constructed on an entirely new theoretical principle. Nicander tried to show enthusiasm as the steward explained that this was based on a sensible flat earth and was in the form of a rectangle with raised corners supporting a curved heaven. And modelled after the design of the tabernacle of Moses and being divinely inspired, it could obviously be relied upon.

But it completely contradicted all other sources.

Night was drawing in as Nicander headed back, bitterly disheartened. His meagre notes offered virtually nothing on which to begin laying down detailed plans for an expedition and he'd seen little to suggest there was anything of value left to discover.

As he passed by the Nymphaeum, several prostitutes waved gaily at him but he had no taste for playful banter and trudged on, ignoring the insults that followed him.

In effect he had established three things only: that silk was indeed harvested from the silk tree, that the land of the Seres was all but unknown and that it was at a staggering distance, in an uncertain direction through barbarian hordes of unimaginable ferocity.

Now he would have to face a trusting Marius waiting for answers.

CHAPTER NINE

The seediness of their living quarters drove in on Nicander.

Marius looked up from the table. He was fashioning something in leather, his hard, capable hands sure and swift.

'A bloody long time!' he growled and got up to check a pot. 'I've had a mess of lentils going since sundown.'

Nicander did not enjoy such crude Roman peasant fare but knew his friend had a fondness for it. He took his bowl and ate with as much relish as he could muster.

'So how did you get along, then? Read a hill o' books and things, I suppose.' Marius was literate in Latin but only painfully so.

Nicander sighed. 'Quite a few.'

'Well?'

'I found the subject very complicated,' he mumbled. 'A lot of things to take in.'

'So hard going, then.'

'It was, yes.'

'I thought of a way to find out about Seres.'

Nicander bristled. 'What?'

'Calm down, I couldn't spoil your fun with the books, could I?'

'Then please tell,' he said sarcastically, 'just what is it that's better than research in the greatest library on earth?'

'Fellow down the street I know. Back with his family after a long trip. I met up with him today.'

'This better be good!'

'Interesting job he's got – camel wrangler with the silk caravans as trade across Asia with the Seres. Just asked him how far, like, what direction you go in.'

Nicander sat back. So simple – so obvious!

'Well – what did he say?'

'Not a lot, he couldn't. Like 'em all he only picks up on the caravan this side of the border, that's Nibilis for him. See, the Persians don't allow crews to go through their territory, they might learn something, so they has their own.'

'Oh.'

'That's not all. He says that they've foreigners – Sogdians or something – taking charge of their caravans up to there, come from way into Asia and he often talks with 'em while they hand over. What they told him is that no one at all goes the whole way.'

'They must – how do we get the silk, then?'

Marius chuckled grimly. 'Hey now, and you're a merchant and haven't picked up on it!'

'What, damn it?'

'Why, just that it's all organised between 'emselves. Freight gets loaded, taken on to another town, sold in the market where there's a profit. Then the new owner sends it to wherever he's heard there's a good price, and so on. Who knows how many changes. That's why it's so bloody expensive to us, everyone adding their profit on top, and why nobody knows where the stuff ends up or comes from. So, Nico, there's no one sending silk from Sinae to Constantinople – no one at all!'

'And nobody who can say where the caravan's been or going.'

'No. Crews change at different places – he said his friend goes on another stage with the caravan across the plains in camels and when they come to the mountains hands over to others with oxen and donkeys. He thinks there's a mighty desert beyond but he's not sure.'

Nicander put down the unfinished lentils.

Marius gave an awkward smile and picked up what he'd been working on. 'For you,' he said, almost apologetically, 'Try 'em on. Need to impress His Nibs, won't we.'

It was a pair of sandals of the *carlatina* pattern, a single piece of leather used to create a soft-soled sandal with a pleasing openwork cross lacing. 'Why, these are wonderful, Marius. And – and just the thing to go before an emperor,' he finished lamely.

'Right. Well, can't sit about, what next?'

Nicander knew he couldn't put off telling him the truth.

When he had finished, the big man said nothing, his face set.

'So it's come down to stupid fairy tales and maps which don't agree and now with what you learnt from your friend . . .'

They sat wordless for a long time.

'A hit o' wine?'

'No, Marius. I'm not in the mood.'

'And as for our greasy friend John the Cappadocian,' Marius rasped, 'I think the bastard knows more than he's telling us.'

Nicander grunted agreement. He wasn't looking forward to facing him but could there be something they'd missed?

CHAPTER TEN

John the Cappadocian greeted them with irritation. His eyes were bloodshot and his robe stained.

'You're finished so soon? I expected something of a proper plan, decently put together.'

'There are difficulties that have arisen. Sir, we need your advice.'

Swearing, John cleared the table with a sweep of his arm. 'Sit down.'

The sound of the smashing pottery brought a slave running.

'What is it, then? Am I to be disturbed for every little problem you meet?'

'Silk does grow upon trees, sir, I now have sufficient confirmation of that.'

'I'm glad to hear it.'

Gathering his courage, Nicander went on, 'What is proving harder is to find a suitable route to Serica. No two authorities agree and the ancients are not helpful. Sir, might I ask that in your time as an officer of state did you ever hear of the Seres in any way?'

'As I told you before, I've heard of them, but then so has everybody. Are you telling me you've no reliable indication of where you're headed?'

'Not at the moment.'

John the Cappadocian slumped back with a bitter smile. 'Then you've got a problem. All I know is that it's a damn long way off, in some godforsaken place somewhere at the end of the world.'

He held Nicander's eyes. 'I take it you've asked to see the records of that . . . what was it . . . the Antoninus delegation. Didn't I hear they'd actually reached there and came back?'

'I have, sir, and others. They didn't – or couldn't – say where they were, and the fools didn't bother to write down anything of value in terms of direction or distance.'

'That doesn't augur well for your plan, sir. What will you do now?'

'The secret's out there somewhere,' Nicander said doggedly. 'We'll keep looking until we find it. Then let you know, of course.'

He got up to leave.

'Why the hurry? Stay, take a little refreshment.' It was an order: two more cups were signalled.

Marius shot a warning glance at Nicander, but he took no notice. While there was any chance . . .

'All is not lost.'

'Why do you say that, sir?'

'Just a thought, that's all.' There was a self-satisfied smile touched with a hint of spite. It brought Nicander to full alert.

'May we know it?'

'Perhaps. Tell me, what is your objective in this?'

Wary, he answered that it was the securing of the seeds of the silk tree.

'No, Mr Greek. The real object.'

'I – I don't understand you, sir.'

'Surely it's the acquisition of wealth by whatever means? Those baubles of comfort that so ease the pangs of old age . . . ?'

'As a man of business I do accept that the increase resulting—'

'Then I believe there is a path to that same objective – requiring only a little courage, far less effort and with the gratifying consequence that it goes a little way into . . . squaring accounts between myself and the Emperor Justinian.'

This was edging into dangerous waters. Were they going to be pawns in some palace power struggle?

Nicander was aware of Marius's disquiet but John the Cappadocian was probably the most successful money man of the age, brought low only by the spite of a woman. And he had just this one chance to talk at the exalted level of emperors and gold, statecraft and business.

'Your advice to us is always to be welcomed,' Nicander said as neutrally as he could.

'Very well. We go inside – in this evil city there are ears everywhere.' He heaved himself up and led them into a sparsely furnished room. The window looked out on olive trees where a slave hoed the soil in desultory fashion.

'Aha – the boot is on the other foot! Before I reveal my idea, how do I know it will not be taken from me by a pair of out-of-town adventurers? Hey?'

'Sir, I don't—'

'Be easy, Greek. I'm only in jest. The situation remains as before. I cannot perform it, and I'm bound to your own good selves for any fortune that might result.'

'Then what is your idea, sir?'

'The same as your own . . . taken a little further.'

He went on briskly, 'The seeds of the silk tree. Brought back to be planted in a sacred grove for the enrichment of the whole Roman Empire. This cannot fail!'

A dreamy expression appeared on his face. 'I can see it all: two holy men from the edge of Empire, thinking it their sacred duty to inform their ruler that having particular knowledge far beyond that of mere libraries, they are prepared to venture to far Sinae to acquire the seeds for the glory of the Byzantine Empire and its illustrious ruler. They lack only the means to do so.'

'Special information?'

'I rather think something more in the way of a token, a visible sign that not only do they possess the knowledge but are themselves the only ones able to take advantage of it. A species of immunity, if you like, preserving the idea for their own furtherance . . . and profit.'

'Sir, I don't follow you,' Nicander said. 'We have no special knowledge and no prospect of any.'

'Yet you'll agree, should these two men appear with some, their way to being funded is assured? Our ever-avaricious Justinian would think nothing of settling five hundred thousand gold solidi on them for a return of eight tons of gold a year!' His eyes gleamed wolfishly.

'But how—'

'These monks come with a tale. They were on pilgrimage from somewhere outlandish like Sheba, when the winds seize their ship and after a harrowing experience which would wring pity from the hardest heart they are cast up in shipwreck. They are rescued by a passing trader who is from Serica and takes them there. Where they meet the King of the Seres who offers them hospitality and his prayers for their safe return. When they are ready to leave, he gives them a letter decreeing those named therein as honoured guests of the kingdom. This they offer to Justinian as proof that they will be welcomed back should they return.'

'And only them.'

'Just so. And while in Serica they see the silk trees, how they are cared for, how to use the peculiar combs and so forth as no one else has. Who else might Justinian send, but these two worthy monks?'

With the assistance of one slightly less than genuine document they would get their funding! It was a lifeline but . . . 'Sir. There is an impossibility. We do not know where Serica is!'

'What a charming innocence you possess, sir! I asked clarification of your major objective which you were kind enough to disclose. You know not where the Seres are. At the point of sailing these two are not in conflict.'

'You mean . . . ?'

'Our monks are again unlucky in their voyaging. This time, soon after departing, they are swallowed up by the sea and they and their treasure are never seen again. How sad, is it not?'

It started to sink in slowly and Nicander felt his face pale. Was John the Cappadocian inciting them to a deception, a fraud against Emperor Justinian himself?

He glanced at Marius. His expression gave nothing away.

Nicander asked for a moment with his friend and they went out to the olive grove.

'I owe nothing to this shite of a city after what I've been through,' Marius spat. 'Why not make something out of its greedy sods who'd see us go out to be gutted by the Huns if there's a profit in it somewhere for them?'

Nicander hesitated, troubled about the morality of such a deception. But *just supposing* they went along with it. They'd have the entire money chest for the expedition in their hands, which, after paying off the captain and crew, would amount to a colossal haul. Guiltily, his mind toyed with the prospect: unable to come back to Constantinople, he would be returning home with a fortune beyond their wildest dreams. His father would have to eat humble pie while *he* dictated how the capital would be invested . . .

John the Cappadocian was waiting for them, a faint smile in place.

'We can see the merit of your suggestion, sir, and we—'

'I thought you might. And now you'll do exactly as you're instructed in the matter – no more, no less – or it's finished here and now!' There was no mistaking the rap of authority, of accustomed power, as the terms of the relationship were ruthlessly laid down.

'We understand.'

'Then to work. From this point on, you're in the character of monks, holy men. You'll practise this until you think yourselves born to it.'

'How do we—'

'To start with – you speak Latin, always. You have the mother tongue?' he asked, looking at Nicander.

'I do,' he replied. As most of his incense business had been concluded in metropolitan Rome, he knew it well enough.

'And you?'

'Learnt on my mother's knee.'

The rough-tongued *sermo vulgi* brought a wintry smile. 'You'll need a trifle more polish than that, Holy Father. Perhaps ask your Greek friend to . . . ?'

He turned back to Nicander. 'So – to raiment. Lose that bronze clasp, if you please. And those sandals are much too fine for a poor cleric.'

'Ah, I've been shipwrecked and the good people of Constantinople have not been backward in seeing me restored in the matter of attire.'

This brought only a raised eyebrow. John the Cappadocian looked at Marius in dismay. 'Do droop a little, fellow. You're strutting around for all the world like a Roman legionary in disguise. It will never do for a begging cleric.'

He called for more wine. 'So, to your origins. You come from the distant reaches of Empire, perhaps in the deserts to the far south of the Holy Land? You've been cut off from civilisation for some reason, that's why no one has heard of you or your king.'

Nicander came in, 'That's because our river dried up – took another course, and the desert has driven us away from the coast and kept us isolated from the world of man.'

'Good. Your new king, however, being of an enlightened nature, wishes to know more of the world—'

'We were colonised in the time of Constantine, our conceiving of the Christian faith is primitive and our king seeks to know the truth.'

'Yes. You two have been sent to discover this truth. You embark in a ship and—'

'We set out for India! A place of mystery and holiness. We sail for days and nights without end but then—'

John the Cappodician nodded in satisfaction.'Now, to your names.'

'I am Brother Paul and this is Brother Matthew of the fellowship of Saint Agnes, the kingdom of Artaxium Felix.'

'They will suffice.' He paused. 'Now, Brother Paul, just why is it that you are offering to repeat your voyage at great hazard to yourselves? What is your purpose? I will tell you, as I know what will touch the Emperor most. It is that you desire that on the proceeds a great church be built in your kingdom, and that Justinian sends multitudes of his unemployed clerics on a mission to direct you back on the path of righteousness. That is all you desire. Riches of this world are to be rendered to Caesar, as it were.'

'I understand,' Nicander said gravely.

'Then I believe we may proceed.'

There was no look of triumph, avarice, even of satisfaction – only one of calculated resolve.

'Your part now is to be who you seem. If you fail, this is to your misfortune, not mine. I am not implicated, I shall deny all. In return, however, I undertake to place you before Justinian in the best possible light to make your case – the details of which you will leave to me. Now, in what form shall your precious letter be?'

CHAPTER ELEVEN

It was a long walk back but, in a whirl of elation and trepidation, Nicander barely noticed it.

As long as they kept their heads all would be well: they would be confirming what was generally believed about silk and its growing. Their claim could not be disputed – there would be no one from 'Artaxium Felix' to cause them trouble, for it didn't exist, and there were none who had travelled to Serica or knew enough about it to confound their story. Above all, the stakes were so staggering that any hearing of it would want to believe.

Aware of tramping feet behind, he turned. It was soldiers – praetorian guards under the command of the Prefect of the city and responsible for good order, a not unusual sight on The Mese.

Marching stolidly, they were in two columns led by a centurion. Nicander and Marius stepped aside to let them by.

But the columns divided, surrounding them. The centurion bawled, 'Take 'em!'

Brawny arms seized Nicander. He did not resist, noting in shame that it took four to subdue Marius.

It soon became apparent that they were being taken to the Praetorium, the headquarters of the Prefect himself. The place of secrets and terror.

What had they done? It couldn't be his library visit, they had neither his name nor where he lived. And he'd done nothing wrong – yet – and as far as he knew was unknown to the authorities. This was probably a case of mistaken identity.

At the reception desk his protesting was ignored and the pair found themselves thrown into a prison cell. Ragged moaning punctuated with screams sounded down the passage as the hours passed.

Then suddenly there was the clash of doors and four guards appeared. 'Out! March!'

They wound up a worn staircase to a richly appointed office.

A thin, ascetic-looking man with an expression of disdain rose from a desk. He was in flowing white, edged with scarlet, the rich embroidery of a silk tablion proclaiming high rank.

'I am Peter Barsymes, Count of the Sacred Largesse. Be aware my time is limited and I will not be trifled with.'

Nicander gave a start. This was the one he had been warned about.

'You were seen at the villa of the disgraced John the Cappadocian. Twice. Do not attempt to deny it, I have competent enough informers. Once might be accounted coincidence, but two times . . . this suggests an assignation. What were you doing there – answer!'

'Sir, we are castaways. We were rescued and returned to our land but we have information of such importance that it is only for the ear of Emperor Justinian himself. We were given the name of this gentleman as being one who could arrange a meeting.'

'Convince me. If not, I swear your end will not be pleasant!'

It all now sounded so unbelievable but Nicander persevered with the story of a remote desert kingdom, their honest seeking after truth.

'And this *information* for the ears of the Emperor only,' Barsymes snapped. 'You will tell me, that I may be judge of its value.'

'Oh, this is impossible, sir! We have sworn—'

'Do you realise that I am at the right hand of Justinian always? There are no secrets between us, you may safely disclose your information to me.'

'Sir, we cannot! It is—'

'Before you go before the Emperor I must be sure his time is not wasted on idle talk. Tell me!'

'Very well, sir. But I crave that the room be empty of all but yourself, what I have to say being of such gravity and . . . and of interest to those of a sinful cupidity.'

Barsymes's eyes gleamed. 'Get out! All of you! Guards, wait outside. Now, speak!'

One thing was certain: John the Cappadocian was out of the game, their pathway to Justinian stopped.

But just possibly this power behind the throne might restore it!

Nicander's voice fell to a whisper as he outlined their story and the plan that the seeds of the tree be acquired for the Empire.

'Do you . . . have you any idea what you're saying? This is incredible!'

'But only what is due to our illustrious emperor,' Nicander murmured. 'We ask merely that we might seek assistance from him for an expedition to Serica.'

Barsymes gave an oily smile. 'A fine and worthy object! However, I doubt the Emperor need be troubled. I have it in mind to finance an expedition myself.'

'Sir, you'll dispatch your own men?'

'You've suffered much, and are not to be imposed upon again. If you'll leave me the details I'll ensure you're both handsomely rewarded.'

Yes, in a sack at the bottom of the Bosphorus!

Nicander thought furiously. 'I'm devastated to be the one to bring objections, but if it's others who venture forth, there will be a difficulty.'

'Oh?'

'The king of Serica decrees that none but we two named in the document we have shall be made welcome in his country.'

'I see.'

'It is a long and dangerous road to Sinae, sir. On the outward journey there will be need for much expense, many bribes, unforeseen costs.'

'You'll not want for outlay – be assured I have resources I may count upon.'

87

'The return journey will be much easier,' Nicander stammered. 'A few dozen seeds is a paltry cargo. Sir, as yours is the investment, the seeds are your property. Have you given thought to their cultivation? They require particular soil and much labour in the harvesting, and will—'

'Thank you, Brother. We'll attend to that, I promise you. Now, you see to finalising your plans, I'll take care of the funding, and we'll meet again soon.'

He went to the door and barked for the guards. 'These two good men are my friends and not to be vexed with petty attentions when next they visit.'

'We've done it, Marius! In just a few weeks—'

'We've done it, right enough. The bastard took the bait, but when he starts asking questions among his poncey friends he's going to wake up and we'll be nailed to the wall!'

'What questions? Nobody knows us! That's the great thing about it all. John the Cappadocian is going to deny he's anything to do with us, and who's to say we're not who we claim to be?'

'You're so bloody confident – I'm not! This is way over our heads, out of our league as much as a worm to an eagle. I've never had a word from a nob in all my life, now in a couple of days I've been pawed over by two! I don't like it, and I want to get out before it's too late, Nico!'

'Take it easy, Marius. Think about it – Barsymes stumbles on two innocent holy men with the secret to wealth beyond his wildest dreams. All they ask for is to be funded to get it. No big risk to him, that's our worry, he just sits back and waits for the gold to shower down. All we have to do is come up with some sort of believable plan and sail off with the chest of riches and vanish. Can't be much simpler than that!'

'If he smells a rat—'

'How can he? I keep telling you, nobody knows either about us or Serica! And the thing I particularly like . . .'

'What?'

'Barsymes insists we're on a private venture – the palace is not involved

88

any more and it's in his selfish interest to keep very quiet about it. So for us it means no need to get worked up about seeing the Emperor, or even to go into the Grand Palace which, I tell you now, gives me the shakes just to look at it! We've the chance to be not just comfortable, but rich – wealthy! And we're only talking a few weeks away! Just play your part – and we're there!'

A grin eventually surfaced. 'What the fuck! Let's go for it.'

Nicander went over to the corner and found their pot. He emptied it on the table, a solidus here and there but mostly the worn dark bronze of a follis. With a practised eye he assessed their pile and divided it into two. 'There's enough here to see us over the next few weeks – and some for tonight! I say we go out and celebrate. Soon we'll have more than ever we could jump over!'

CHAPTER TWELVE

The early evening streets seemed noisier and more foetid than usual, but Nicander was not going to let that affect his mood.

'Fish or meat?' he asked happily, a vision of a slab of roast shimmering enticingly before him.

'A brace of ox ribs from Thessaly,' Marius replied immediately. 'With all the trimmings.'

Their stroll changed to a purposeful stride at the thought but a cry from a slave loping towards them brought the pair to a halt.

'Good gentlemen – I've been searching everywhere for you. Magister Barsymes asks that you spare him an hour. There's someone he'd like you to meet.'

This was probably to make acquaintance of some lower ranking functionary they would be working with instead of the great man himself.

They turned to retrace their steps back toward the Praetorium, but the slave stopped them. 'Oh no, sirs, not there. At his home! This way, if you please.'

They were shortly outside one of the exclusive residential buildings near the Grand Palace, like the others showing only a small portico entrance in an otherwise blank façade. It led into a vast interior courtyard with a fountain flowing.

The slave beckoned them up marble steps to a top floor room, passing a careless display of wealth on all sides. 'Be used to it, Marius,' Nicander whispered. 'It'll be us soon!'

A richly dressed woman rose from a couch, her lustrous rust silk dalmatica set off by gold and pearls.

'My Lady Barsymes,' Nicander bowed, remembering just in time to speak in Latin.

Her strong features registered distaste. 'Be careful with your words, sir. I'm no creature of that toad. You are addressing the Lady Antonina, wife of Justinian's foremost general, Belisarius.'

'But why . . . ?'

'I used the name of that reptile to bring you here to my house.'

Unease seized Nicander. What on earth could she want with two such humble persons?

'I am at a loss, Lady, to understand . . .'

Antonina purposefully straightened an ornate emerald ring on her right hand, then looked directly at him. 'To be strictly correct, I have no great wish to, to . . . but by your actions you have interested me.'

'We—'

'I'm a woman and cannot bear a mystery. And this one is particularly deep. I want the answer, and all Constantinople knows I'm not to be denied. Do you understand me, or must I . . . ?'

'My Lady, anything I can—'

'Then tell me this. Why is it that in the last few days you have been seen with both that loathsome John the Cappadocian and the slimy pig Peter Barsymes? Not only are they the two most powerful money men of the age but they hate and detest each other to a degree.'

'It's nothing really,' Nicander mumbled, desperately trying to think. 'We—'

'Don't waste my time, or you'll rue it! I make it my business to know everything of consequence, everybody's petty plots, secrets and crimes – that way I'm not to be surprised when things happen.'

A look of cruel calculation came on her face. 'Or shall I make a guess and you'll tell me if I'm right? Very well – I say that the Cappadocian is plotting to restore his place before Justinian by a clever false betrayal of Barsymes, for which he needs information from the inside, and you're the one to feed it to him?'

'N-no, My Lady, that's not—'

'So. It's the other, and more serious for all that. These two are colluding in a master plot, some wicked design that requires them to join their forces together. They loathe each other so you are the go-between, and therefore know everything. Right?'

Nicander flashed a helpless glance at Marius.

'Great lady. May I explain everything?'

'Do so.'

'We're holy men from a far desert kingdom and . . .'

He stumbled through his story.

'A fine tale. And all lies.'

'No, no, My Lady. This is the truth!'

'Don't insult me!' she spat. 'I know the world more than most, and holy men you're not! Where's your doleful look, snivelling whine, begging manner? And for one born and bred in the desert you're as milk-white as a babe!'

'I-I . . .'

'And all that dog vomit about silk seeds. Even I know silk comes from spiders, and you're not going to keep those in a bag all the way from Sinae!'

'But—'

Her voice dropped. 'I don't think you quite understand your situation,' she said slowly. 'I've only to lift that bell and the general's men will rush to my rescue, you having talked your way into my room. When he hears of this, you'll be begging for a crucifixion as the more merciful. Yes?'

Nicander nodded helplessly.

'So let's begin again. Just what are you doing with those two vultures?'

They were cornered like rats with no alternative but to confess the full extent of what they planned, and hope for mercy.

Stony-faced, she heard him out, down to the final twist.

'Now, let me get this right. You two plotted to defraud the Emperor with a wild scheme, then let Peter Barsymes take it over? In some colossal sum as would see either in some difficulty?'

'Yes, Lady,' Nicander admitted miserably.

Antonina stood transfixed for a moment, then shook her head in wonder.

Suddenly her body convulsed, and she screamed with laughter. 'Oh, merciful God, but I've not heard such a merry tale in all my life!' She bent double, choking back tears of mirth. 'It's priceless! That I could see their faces when—'

'My Lady, you're not—'

'Good God, no! I wish you well of your . . . enterprise.'

Her face suddenly tightened. 'Screw those rat-faced fuckers for every obol you can get and you'll have my great thanks for it. You know it was that prig Justinian who recalled my husband away – in case he should win a popular victory over Totila the Ostrogoth?' She smiled. 'May I offer you some advice?

'Barsymes is entirely corrupt and there's nothing he will not stoop to. Trust him no further than you can spit. Avoid the palace like the plague – it's a cesspit of betrayal and intrigue. There are some like Peter the Patrician who are straight enough, but he's an emperor's man to his gizzard. And Marcellus – thick as a short plank, always gets the wrong end of the stick. But dangerous. He's Count of Excubitors, which means he's in charge of protection for the Emperor, which gives him a lot of power.'

She paused, then added, 'But Justinian is the one to fear. Been on the throne for years and years and knows all the tricks. Since poor Theodora passed on, he's turned sullen and unpredictable and the whole empire is heaving with spies. But then of course you don't have to worry about him now, do you?'

There were sounds of movement below. 'Oh, that sounds like Belisarius. You must dine with us!'

Struck dumb by the giddy speed of events, Nicander could only nod an agreement.

'Antonina?' came a voice on the stairs.

'Here, my love.'

She turned to them both and urgently whispered, 'I wouldn't mention the last detail of your venture, it would confuse him.'

'No, Lady,' Nicander promised fervently.

Belisarius was grey-haired but clear-eyed and still in glittering parade armour. 'Ah, you have guests?'

'Two gentlemen on a holy mission, my dear.'

'Then the least we can do is offer them the hospitality of our table.'

They descended the stone stairs and emerged into the courtyard, Antonina on her husband's arm as they crossed toward the triclinium, the dining room. Slaves were already carrying silver pitchers of conditum and ornate platters of exotic food there.

But before they could begin the meal a dozen soldiers crashed into view, weapons drawn.

Belisarius's sword leapt into his hand and he thrust Antonina behind him.

An officer in a crimson cloak called imperiously from the doorway. 'General Belisarius, you are taken, sir.'

Seeing him, Antonina came out from behind her husband. 'Marcellus! You gave us such a fright. What is going on?'

'Stand aside, Lady Antonina. I mean to put the general to the question!'

'What in Hades are you talking about, Marcellus?' Belisarius roared. 'You break into my house and—'

'You've been fairly caught, sir! Consorting with known plotters! You'll come peacefully or—'

Antonina stormed up to Marcellus. 'You fool!' she threw in his face. 'You never stop to think, do you! The greatest and most loyal commander in Justinian's army and you'd risk your own standing with His Majesty by arresting him? Where do you keep your brains – in your boots?'

'I must have answers to my questions, My Lady,' he replied, his cheeks turning red.

'Then you'll not get them from Belisarius the Goth-slayer! Get out of here, you oaf.'

Hesitating for a moment, Marcellus lowered his sword. 'Well, I'll take these two and wring the truth from 'em – then I'll be back!'

CHAPTER THIRTEEN

Frogmarched to the bowels of the Grand Palace, they were fettered to dank, slimy walls. The icy grip of the chains broke through Nicander's paralysis of unreality. The guttering light of an oil lamp illuminated instruments of pain and the merciless face of the torturer.

Excubitor Marcellus waited impatiently for the soldiers to leave then crossed to them. 'Now, I've not much time to waste on filth like you. Make it easy for me and you can have it quick and clean – tell me lies and I'll let Khosrau loose. Understood?'

He leant forward until he was inches from them. 'You've been skulking about, first in John the Cappadocian's villa, then Magister Peter Barsymes is seen being very amiable towards you – this is not his way towards low-life. Then I'm brought word that the same day, if I chose, I could find you being heartily welcomed into his home by none other than the great general Belisarius. So what am I to conclude? I think it speaks for itself, but I'll let you tell me in your own words.'

He whirled on Marius. 'You! What's the meaning of it all?'

The legionary stared back in contemptuous silence.

'Very well.'

In sick realisation, Nicander knew what was next.

Turning to him, Marcellus eased into a smile. 'Why, what a shame to tear about such soft skin – or will it be the hot iron? I haven't really decided yet.' His tone became mournful. 'Why don't you tell me? It would save so much hurt and pain, when you know I'll find out in the end . . .'

Nicander threw Marius a look of apology. He knew he did not have his friend's powers of endurance but could he bluff their way free?

He blurted hoarsely, 'All right, I'll tell you what you want to know.'

In jerking, terrified sentences Nicander explained about the silk tree expedition and its need for funding, but was cut off impatiently.

'Utter pig's turds. If all this silk seed nonsense really needed was support, any right-minded citizen would go straight to His Resplendency and fall at his feet.'

'It's true, *I swear it!*'

'Don't try my patience, dog. There's only one reason you've been to see all those grand names . . .' He drew a savage breath. 'It's all a monstrous plot against the life of our most Divine Caesar, Emperor Justinian!'

'*No!*'

'Yes! You're part of a wider conspiracy touching every corner of the realm, and I'll screw it out of you, this I swear!'

There was nothing else for it now. 'No – it's . . . I'll confess.'

In broken sentences Nicander admitted that the whole thing was a fraud, calculated to lift riches from those investing in the expedition.

'Enough! You think I'm simple?' barked Marcellus. 'You're determined to make it hard for yourself; I can accommodate you. Khosrau! Start the fire – I'll be back in an hour.'

'Marius!' Nicander gasped. 'He's not believing any of it!'

There was no response.

'What can we do?'

Marius snarled, 'Die like a Roman, Greek!'

Time passed infinitely slowly, then the door crashed open.

'Right. Shall we start the fun?' Marcellus went to the brazier and lifted an iron. It was a flat arrow-shape and glowed white-hot. He sauntered over and flourished it before Nicander.

He flinched in terror, his mind near unhinged.

Marcellus lowered the iron. 'I think not.'

He selected a more elaborate one, a distorted corkscrew. Speculatively he held it up, watching Nicander's eyes following its every move.

The Excubitor tested its heat. 'Ah yes, this will do. I should tell you we normally have a little ceremony before proceedings really begin, more of an entertainment for you.'

A young pig was brought into the cell on a long rope. The animal snuffled about, investigating busily, its farmyard snorts out of character in such a place of torment. It made its way over to the chained men, looking up in puzzlement with innocent eyes.

It was a mistake.

Marcellus stabbed down with the white-hot iron, directly into its pink body. It shrieked in pain, convulsing and thrashing while the Excubitor twisted the iron expertly. The reek of burnt fat rose up as the crazed animal screamed its life away.

Trembling, the handler lifted up the carcass and hurried out.

'There, now. We know what it's going to be like, don't we?' Marcellus said. 'Then shall we begin? Who's to be first?'

Almost fainting with horror, Nicander tried to flog his mind to reason. There were only minutes of sanity left to him – then, as if in a dream, he heard the dry, age-withered voice of an old man standing in the doorway. 'Marcellus, I thought it was you! Good God, are you at it again?'

He was frail but in a crimson-edged robe that told of a rank of eminence.

Marcellus looked taken aback. 'What! Can't you see I'm busy?'

The old man approached and whispered something.

Marcellus snorted. 'If you must! Damn it, why can't I be left to get on with it?' Then he roared peevishly, 'Guards! Go with 'em.'

Released from their chains, Nicander and Marius followed the old man out along a passageway into another building.

He stopped at a heavy wooden door. 'That will do.'

The guards took up position outside and they entered what appeared to be a monk's cell.

Nicander fell into a chair and stared up at their grey-haired saviour. 'Sir, who . . . ?'

'My name is Narses. I am grand chamberlain to His Clemency the Emperor.'

'And . . . and you . . . ?'

'The Lady Antonina got word to me of your misfortune. Marcellus does have a tendency to get the wrong end of the stick but he means well. I told him I would be continuing the questions for now.'

'But—'

'I can say he won't be seeing you any more, if that is your concern.'

Narses's eyes took in the spartan simplicity of the room. 'No doubt you are at this time living in a mean and humble abode. Now this you may consider *your* cell, holy brothers, guest of His Sacred Majesty. Is it to your satisfaction?'

Nicander mouthed, 'Th-thank you, sir.'

'We'll send for your possessions but for now I think it advisable you stay here and not venture out. You are perfectly safe with me. Meanwhile, you'll want to bathe – I'll have fresh raiment sent here for you.'

Reeling at what might have been their fate, Nicander managed to ask, 'This is kindness beyond the usual. May I know . . . why are you treating us with such . . . benevolence?'

'Why, is not this self-evident?'

'Sir?'

He gave a benign smile. 'The Lady Antonina mentioned your expedition plans. To me this is a splendid enterprise, worthy of the best adventurers in the land and deserves well of us. And because it bears so as it does on the revenue situation of the state, I am taking immediate action.'

'Wha—?' Nicander scrabbled to make sense of what he was hearing.

'I'm overriding the usual protocols – when you are ready I shall take you before His Benevolence, Emperor Justinian himself, to present your case in person.

'Given the nature of your mission we must see to it that you have every facility at hand and no interruption while you polish your case before you see His Refulgence. Involving as it does questions of wealth beyond the commonplace, we must also regard it as a privy secret of state. This means that I must ask you to remain in this cell while you work and refrain from discussing this with anyone – no one whosoever.'

He went on, 'I'll ask the Patriarch to relieve you of any clerical or ceremonial duties and make arrangements for your food to be brought. I do beg you will forgive our discourtesy to a guest but the matter presses exceedingly. I know the Emperor would look ill upon any delay once he learns of the expedition.'

After Narses had left, Nicander sat on the edge of the bed, his head in his hands.

Marius paced up and down. 'What's to do, Nico?'

'Let me think.'

In a short time they would be expected to present themselves and their 'project' before Emperor Justinian. To bring out a reasoned, credible plan to recover the seeds of the silk tree from the other end of the earth – when they had no idea at all where or how to get to them.

Nicander groaned, 'We're going to cross the Emperor!'

'Where's your backbone, Greek? That was our plan before, if you recall! We've a chance for the big money and now you're turning cold?'

CHAPTER FOURTEEN

Nicander gathered his wits, trying not to let the imminent prospect of confronting an emperor affect him. The fact that it was so past belief that a penniless outsider like himself would be in this position insulated him from the actuality.

He worked hard. Going over all parts he ensured there were answers to every possible objection, provisions for failure, background detail to add plausibility.

This was what he was good at, for wasn't he the one, in better times, who'd planned and put in place the successful cross-country myrrh route to Cyrene? And not forgetting that it was his own delicate talking with the desert Garamantes that had secured the Carthage frankincense concession.

When it was all there, he made Marius 'emperor' and delivered his presentation over and over again until he was sure of it, then he sent word to Narses that he was ready.

The old man's eyes glowed. 'Excellent! This day I promise, you will be before His Resplendency.'

Before the morning was out, he was back. 'It shall be so. Directly after the Reception of the Western Kings you are granted a privy audience in the Daphne Palace! This is all but unprecedented, you are honoured above all.'

Nicander was giddy with excitement and nervousness. 'What do we do – that is to say, the formalities . . .'

'For a privy audience there is nothing laid down in the Scroll of Ceremonies, do rest your concern. It is a simple matter: when bidden, you approach, kiss the slipper and remain on one knee until released.'

'Yes, and . . . ?'

'I took it upon myself to acquaint the Emperor in a small way of the petition, your expectations and likely success should you meet with his approval. He was most interested.'

'Thank you, sir.'

'Do let me give you some frank advice, Holy Brother. His Sacred Clemency is not one for form and custom. Efficiency and clarity are his watchwords, therefore I advise that your presentation be brief and to the point, sparing in honorifics and platitudes. As well, do remember that his mind is sharp and watchful and unforgiving of loose thinking. And whatever else, never utter an untruth – this he cannot abide in any man.'

It brought Nicander up with a sudden chill as the scale of what they were going to do returned.

Narses added, 'Then I will call for you in two hours and together we will attend at the Magnaura Great Hall for the grand reception, after which we will have our audience.'

After he had gone, Marius turned to Nicander. 'Be buggered to it, Nico, but I don't mind telling you I'm . . . I'm bloody troubled . . .'

Narses was wearing his full ceremonials: a richly embroidered dalmatica with the tablion of high rank, an infinity of precious stones sewn to his robes, shoes and headgear.

The Imperial Palace was not a single building but a bewildering series of massive marble edifices. The three made their way through a great courtyard faced by other grand structures. They joined others progressing past the great bronze gate to the white colonnades which led to a domed red-stone hall.

Entering by the smaller of three doorways they found themselves in a hushed throng in a great vaulted space. At the far end in the raised apse was a grand throne, illuminated by light from lofty windows.

Leaving the holy men in a corner with strict instructions to remain there and speak with no one, Narses moved off to greet the dignitaries.

Nicander and Marius took in the spectacle of hundreds of nobles, ministers, generals and grand officials of state, waited upon by white-robed servitors and flanked on all sides by soldiers in gleaming plate armour.

Toward the centre of the assembly were the barbarian kings from the shadowy wilds north of the frontier – Gepids, Avars, Uighurs, others. Here to be wooed and impressed by the sights and sensations of civilisation.

The hum of conversation died at a new sound: from far away the ethereal purity of a choir floated on the air. It strengthened: after each stanza the melodious clash of cymbal, then the voices again – both deep and rich, pure and high in a delivery that lifted the soul.

The head of a procession entered the hall. A great golden ornamented cross was borne in front, behind it thuribles swung, the rich odour of incense wreathing the air. Then two holy icons carried high and crowned with myrtle, and another cross.

The choir, dressed in simple vestments and carrying lighted tapers followed, eyes raised to heaven in sonorous chant. It processed into the centre of the gathering and then moved towards the throne, dividing each side and ascending the stalls in the apse behind it. Then all was silent.

With a blast of sound at the doorway from the braying of bronze trumpets the Emperor stepped into view in a blaze of splendour – a heavily jewelled purple pallium cloak over gold breastplate fastened with a brooch of four immense pendant pearls, a red and gold diadem of heart-stopping magnificence. The ruler of the world!

Justinian moved with stately deliberation, followed by a host of nobles. Nicander was transfixed as the glittering image passed across his vision.

A murmur spread, growing in strength: 'Divine Caesar! Ever august!

Victorious and triumphant! Emperor of the Romans! All hail to thee!'

The progress moved on, followed by every eye.

The great ornamented cross was set down and Justinian knelt before it in prayer. He rose and kissed it then ascended the throne.

A richly dressed officer of state strode forward, the feared Master of Offices, Peter the Patrician. From a parchment scroll he declaimed in ringing tones. Nicander could not make out the words but in a heady breathlessness he watched the proceedings unfold.

One by one the barbarian kings were brought before Justinian where they rendered obeisance and in return were blessed and awarded gifts. At certain points the choir made intercession. It was a masterful display – the sounds of angels ringing out, the wafting incense, splendour and brilliance.

Then it was over.

The procession formed up; this time at the head, following the cross, Justinian. With all the pomp and glory of the throne of Byzantium, it proceeded out of the Magnaura Great Hall, passing close to Nicander.

A wave of stark terror overcame him – how could he continue with his plan, stand before that vision and present a business proposition that was entirely false?

As the procession receded, he reached for control: in minutes he was going face to face with the Emperor. He had to go through with it or . . .

As if in answer, a strange feeling of calmness stole over him; one of ringing destiny.

Narses came for them. 'His Sacred Majesty disrobes. We will await him at the Daphne Palace.'

Nicander stepped forward but Marius hung back.

'I can't do it!' he muttered hoarsely. 'What if he speaks to me? Wha-what do I say?'

'Come on, Marius. I'll be doing the talking.'

'He'll have a go at me – and then I'll . . . I'll say a wrong thing!'

'Not if you've taken a vow of silence and cannot speak.'

They swept on; past the Delphax with its noble columns, the domed

Onopodion, the low colonnaded Consisterium, more. A concentration of grandeur and solemnity.

Finally they emerged opposite the Daphne Palace. The actual residence of the Emperor, it was faced with columns but there were no windows or doors to be seen except for the main entrance. There, wreathed smoky-white marble columns supported a façade of the utmost elegance, the approach steps a contrasting dusky red stone.

They rounded the end of the building to a lowly entrance and passed inside a single plain doorway which led into a room beyond.

Narses held up his hand.

They heard movement in the room; the scraping of a chair, the chink of a goblet and a slight cough.

Narses gave them a warning glance, then knocked and disappeared inside. There was a murmur of voices and he emerged. 'His Divine Majesty wishes you to enter upon his presence.'

Keyed to the highest possible level, Nicander told himself this was really only a bigger league sales pitch, much like the time when, single-handed, he landed that Epirus deal in front of the Exarch of Achaea himself, or that masterly performance when . . .

With a single backward glance at the stricken Marius he stepped forward. To stand before Justinian, Emperor and Caesar of the Roman Empire, its people and dominions.

Sitting at a desk that was not much more than a bench he looked up.

Nicander saw before him a man of years, an abstemious and heavy face, brooding and unsmiling. Bare-headed, he wore a plain rust-coloured chlamys secured with a simple gold clasp which, with a single massive ring, was the only ornamentation.

'Approach!'

Heart in his mouth Nicander went to him, knelt and kissed a worn slipper, remembering at the last minute to stay on one knee.

'Rise!'

Pulse racing, he raised his eyes to meet those of the ruler of civilisation.

'From where do you hail, good Brother?' The tone was benign, encouraging.

'Sire, I am Brother Paul and this, Brother Matthew. Our home is the kingdom of Artaxium Felix, which is in the desert, past the mountains of Hawazin and beyond the land of the Carnaites.'

'You're a Lakhmid?'

'No, Majesty,' Nicander replied, not sure what that meant. 'We are an ancient race, much decayed in fortune since our river changed its course. We've been cut off by the advancing desert and have lived alone, away from the outer world for centuries.'

'Are you then a pagan? Your Latin does you credit, I ask this only to establish your standing before God.'

'Why no, sir! Our little kingdom was established in the time of your illustrious predecessor, Alexander Severus, at the time of the first Persian wars. We were loyal to Rome but the last we have of the true way was the Christianity of the blessed Constantine. From that time we have been alone.'

'So you're then untainted by the ungodly heresies of Arianism, the Monophysites or even, our good Lord forbid, the Nestorians?'

'Majesty, we have stayed by the teachings of our blessed Saint Agnes to this day.' He crossed himself devoutly.

'I see. Your fellow brother – has he anything to say for himself?'

'Oh, no, sire! He remains under a vow of silence made on our miraculous return. Seventy-eight days, one for each of the years granted unto our Lady Agnes.'

'Most proper in you, Brother. Then I must hear your tale from yourself only. Do go on.'

It came out easily; modest in delivery, compelling in what it implied and it held Justinian's rapt attention.

'I wonder why I have not heard of these wanderings – most travellers are only too eager to prate on about their exploits.'

'Sire, we're only humble holy men, unversed in the literary arts; we are newly returned, anxious to impart our secret most urgently to Your Clemency before others steal it.'

'A worthy object. And it was in Serica you saw the silk trees?'

'We did, Resplendency. Such a picture in a warm dusk, when the ladies of the village gather with their combs and panniers waiting for the moon. They sing strange but beautiful songs and no man may join them, for only the agility of the female hand is sufficient to garner the harvest of silk from high up on the topmost leaves.'

'And . . . the seeds?'

'The silk tree requires particular care, the soil well watered and animals kept away until they be of a stature to stand alone. The seeds are small, many would fill a common purse but these are well guarded, for it is feared that the Scythians to the north might well plant their own and be seen abroad in all manner of rich silks, to the despising of their industry.'

'Hmm. I can quite see that – silk is not for the common people, still less barbarians.'

Nicander tensed as the Emperor's face hardened.

'Now you propose to return with these same seeds of the silk tree. How is it you can feel able to return the kindness of the King of the Seres by robbing him of his secret in this way?'

'In the eyes of God, all creation is gifted to all men – it is so written. Is it right therefore to withhold the fruits of creation from others so?'

A wintry smile came and vanished quickly. 'Very well, shall we now hear something of your plans?'

'Yes, Excellency. It is a long and arduous journey across desert and mountains to Serica, through uncountable Hunnish tribes and vile kingdoms – the worst of these are the Persians. Nevertheless, we who have experienced so much know that there is another way. We mean to embark in a ship and sail to the fabled isle of Taprobane, which lies at a distance into the Erythraean Sea far from any Persian or barbarian. There with our precious decree of protection we will induce a trader of Seres to take us on to his country.'

'A wise and well-thought plan. I had feared you would present a scheme requiring me to mount an expedition of size to cross Persia, which would undoubtedly mean war.'

'Thank you, Majesty. It was always our intent to keep costs and gross outlay to a minimum by setting aside ambassadors and an official delegation, leaving merely ourselves to support.'

'I see. Nevertheless, an enterprise as you propose will still require funding at a significant level. Travel at an unknown distance, subsistence, additional attire to meet a variety of conditions . . .'

'Still far less than a military-led expedition, sire.'

'True. Then for the sake of example, should we hazard, say, funding in the amount of five hundred gold solidi? Would this be too generous, do you believe?'

'It is in our thinking, that to cross lands beyond the protection of the King of the Seres will require a different course. It is the usual practice to hire unemployed soldiery for guards, which we feel a reasonable expense. And there are always unenlightened rulers who will levy exactions on travellers under penalty of refusing to allow them passage. In fact, there are many such traps for the unwary and it were folly to hazard the success of the venture for want of proper funding. Excellent Majesty, the Persians are exacting fifteen solidi a pound for raw silk.'

'It's more than that, but I'll let it go.'

'At seventy grains weight for each solidus, seventy-two in a pound, then each pound of silk is two, three ounces of pure gold. Thus, to import a single ton of silk the Persians must receive no less than four hundred pounds weight of gold. To satisfy an empire will therefore take in the measure of some tons' weight of gold every year – all pouring into the treasury of the King of the Persians and no revenues you may call upon to offset this outflow.'

Justinian's eyes narrowed. 'For a holy man it seems to me you're worldly beyond your station, Brother Paul.'

'Clemency, I knew you would require detail and considered thought, so I made it my business to have the facts at hand.'

'Go on.'

'Sire, I merely wished to point out that when in possession of the seeds this drain will cease. No more tons of gold to your bitter enemy – perhaps even a net inflow when you begin exporting your crop to others. Surely this is worth an investment of, say, four thousand . . . ?'

'You present a compelling argument. Just for my curiosity, pray, what reward do you seek for your services? A fee against—'

'Sire!' Nicander blurted, shocked. 'This is not the way of one in the fellowship of the holy Saint Agnes!'

He allowed a beatific smile to settle. 'If it pleases, Your Effulgence, it would gratify my king were you to establish a church to Saint Agnes and provide us with such monks as are necessary to teach our people the true way of the Lord in these parlous modern times.'

'A church? I would think that possible. And clerics – you shall have them both. Provided you are successful in bringing back to me the seeds of the silk tree.'

'Then . . . ?'

'It does seem you have a case, Brother Paul. I'm minded to assist. If you're going forth to cross the earth at great personal hazard, why should we not risk our own paltry three thousands?'

'Sire, four.'

'Hmm, four. Now let me help you, Brother. The tribute convoy to Persia leaves shortly. You will have escort and rations all the way to the shores of the Erythraean.'

'Thank you, Majesty,' Nicander managed.

'Further, I would not have it on my conscience if I allowed men of God to go into the world without they have attendants. You shall have two of my finest compulsors to look after you. To carry your bags, as it were, and assist in bringing safely back my seeds.'

'This won't be necessary, Your Resplendency, we—'

'You will be provided with a holy relic to present to your king. Perhaps the finger bone of Saint Anthony?'

'You are most generous, Divine Majesty.'

'And holy scriptures, of course. You have no objection to the writings of the sainted Athanasius?

'So now there is little more for you to concern yourselves with. Return to your cell with our blessing, to fast and prepare yourselves spiritually for the journey. Rest easy, holy brothers – you will be guarded day and night, have no fear. Your attendants will take care of the chest of funds when they have been assembled. You are to be relieved of responsibility and anxiety for all profane existence.'

CHAPTER FIFTEEN

They spoke in whispers – the guards posted were only paces away outside their cell.

'You think . . . he knows?' Nicander said, his voice unsteady.

Marius grunted, lying on his back on the simple wicker bed and staring up at the dark ceiling. 'So why let us go?'

'We're trapped in this cell. Peter Barsymes won't go near us now, John the Cappadocian is no use – he'll deny us anyway – Lady Antonina dare not show herself at this level. We're on our own, Marius – do you hear what I'm saying?'

'That's good – we don't need anybody now.'

'Are you mad? We're caught up in a crazy scheme that'll see us on a boat to nowhere or the edge of the world, and you say we don't need anybody?'

'I'm saying it's all down to us, and that's how I like it.'

'So what do you suggest we do now?'

'We wait for the right moment and get out fast with the doings, why not?'

'The attendants, *remember*?'

'Two little servants? Nothing to worry of, Greek.'

'These are compulsors!'

Marius levered himself up. 'So?'

'Known in the business world as "tax extraction agents", and hard men, believe me, friend!'

'Oh?'

'They know all the tricks, have been everywhere, eat a Sarmatian muscleman for breakfast – each – and are blind loyal to Justinian. Only sent in where other persuasions fail.'

'Why . . . ?'

'Can't you see it? There's two ways to look at it. Either he believes that we're two innocent holy men needing protection from a wicked world, can't be let out alone – or he wants us to get the silk seeds, then these two seize 'em, and after disposing of us in a permanent way, present them to their master, secret safe.'

'Ah . . .'

'So we're in trouble either way, my good friend.'

CHAPTER SIXTEEN

'What's that bloody noise?' Marius groaned, awakening in the pre-dawn light.

The insistent knocking made Nicander stir, too. 'See what the matter is,' he muttered, pulling his blanket over his head.

Cursing under his breath, Marius opened their cell door. Two men stood patiently. 'What do you want?' he growled.

'Are you gentlemen not yet risen? Sorry to disturb. We're your attendants come for you,' said the taller of the two.

'Can we enter? Get acquainted, like.'

'Well, make yourselves at home!' Marius said sarcastically as they pushed past. Both, he noted, wore a knee-length chlamys, plenty of room to conceal weapons.

Nicander emerged from under his blanket. 'Why are you here at this hour? We're—'

'Ship sails soon. We're to see you on it.'

'I don't think I caught your names.'

'I'm Velch the Tuscan and he's Nemasus of Massilia.'

'We're here just to keep you gentlemen safe, looking after details, like. Wouldn't want a nasty barbarian taking advantage of you holy gentlemen, now would we?'

'So, you're guarding us. And our chest, too?'

'Ah, now you've no need to worry yourselves about that there,' he chuckled. 'It'll all be taken care of – just you get us to this Seres place and we'll be doing all the rest.'

Nicander didn't miss the quick flash between the two.

'We're holy men and used to our privacy. I trust this will be respected?'

'Of *couuurrrse!*' purred Velch. 'We'll be no bother at all.'

Nemasus produced two small bags from the hallway, which he tossed on one of the beds. 'You can take as much as you like on the boat – as long as it fits in those. We'll be back in an hour.'

Velch stood in the doorway, Nemasus to one side.

'We are ready to proceed,' Nicander said, looking pointedly at their bags.

The two compulsors did not move.

'Our luggage?'

'We don't carry bags. Gets in the way of a sword arm, like. Now, if you holy gentlemen would go on ahead where we can keep an eye on you.'

In the quiet of the early morning the little group moved through the palace compound and out to the small harbour by the lighthouse.

Alongside the breakwater was a dromond, the sleek sail galley that was the navy's chief battle weapon. It was being loaded by a chain of labourers and the yards already had sail bent to them.

The entire area was secured. A double line of armoured soldiers cordoned off the approaches to the vessel and a burly ship's corporal made much of looking up their names on a slate before they were let through. At the gangway an officer also checked a list.

Hundreds of feet long, the dromond was equipped with fifty oars and two lofty masts with diagonal lateens across them. A full deck ran fore and aft, both for sheltering the oarsmen beneath and to serve as a fighting platform for archers.

As they boarded, Nicander spied a series of squat cases lashed down in a row on the centreline under cloths. Their chest would be amongst them.

They were escorted aft to the clear area before the cabin and left with their bags until they could be attended to by the busy crew while the compulsors disappeared below. With a hundred men-at-oars pouring aboard, sailors hauling on ropes and the last stores being struck down it was no time to be in the way.

There was a long, piercing whistle followed by three short ones. Sailors sprang into position, lines were thrown ashore and they were poled clear. Then a sharp order rang out, along with a rumble of wooden thunder as oars were shipped and brought to a ready position.

The captain looked about, sniffing for a wind. Satisfied, he raised his hand.

A bull roar erupted from forward. The oars lifted and fell in a chorus of creaks, bit into the sea then lifted once more – and with a slither and thud dipped again together.

Nicander looked up to see the dry land retreating feet at a time. The ship gathered way and began slipping further off until, imperceptibly, their world changed to a watery one.

Soon all the familiar sights of Constantinople took on a different perspective, the great Hagia Sophia becoming model-like, a vision in white. The low bulk of the vast hippodrome was nothing more than an apologetic hump beyond the sea wall stretching down the coast.

His thoughts were interrupted by another barked order. The oars ceased their rhythm and the ship glided to a stop. They were now well out into the Propontis. Two other galleys took position ahead, on either side.

More orders cracked out and running feet thumped on the deck as sailors raced to their stations. Lines were thrown off, yards hauled around and sail was shown to the wind. As if bowing to Oceanus, the ship leant at an angle and with a final rumble below, oars were brought in and housed.

'So, our last view of Constantinople,' murmured Nicander.

Marius remained silent.

'You do realise, if – *when* – we've got it in the bag we can't return. If something else happens, we'll be cooked like a goose. Either way, this is the last we'll be seeing of the old place.'

'You sound sorry.'

'Sorry! When every face I see could be in the pay of someone out for our blood – when you can't trust a common serving maid, public races are corrupt and you're dragged off the street to a torture chamber on the orders of some thick-brained idiot!'

Marius muttered something that Nicander did not quite catch.

The morning breeze strengthened and the ships stretched out together, their wake astern slowly dissolving into the distance.

A ship's boy approached. 'You the holy buggers?'

'Brother Paul and Brother Matthew,' Nicander said reprovingly.

'You lot go there, then.' The lad pointed to a small cloth hutch, one of five, set up on deck from lines carried back from the mainmast.

They humped their bags and found that their accommodation consisted only of two straw mattresses and a tiny locker with eating utensils.

'Better'n some I've been in. They'll bring blankets at night, I'll guess.' Marius grunted and snugged his bag as a pillow at the head of a mattress.

Outside there was nothing to be seen but a vast, endless grey-blue sea.

Marius stretched out. 'So. We're on our way, then.'

'We must be heading for Alexandria. Ever been there?'

'Bugger that!'

'We'll be putting in at a whole lot of ports beforehand.'

'You know your way about, then.'

'Well, I've been in the incense import–export business since I was a nipper. I know ships and shipping and there's going to be at least a dozen stops down the coast before this one ever gets to North Africa.'

'Well, we'd better get to planning,' Marius came back.

'What'll we do about those two bruisers?'

'Stands to reason – we get rid of 'em.'

Nicander frowned uneasily. 'You can't just—'

Marius rolled over and fixed him with a grim stare. 'Nico. We make a break for it, whether it's with the loot or no, those bastards – under Justinian's direct orders – are going to kick up such a fuss as will have the whole country crawling with troopers. We'd have no chance. So . . .'

'Still . . .'

'Them or us.'

This was not how Nicander had seen things work out. 'Putting that aside for now, I thought we'd first ask for our chest because we need to check it, then we know where it's stowed. So we'll be ready for any chance. After all, no one suspects us or what we're going to do so, in a quiet port somewhere, we slip off to visit a monastery with our heavy holy scriptures in our bag . . .'

Marius grunted, closing his eyes in dismissal at the current conversation.

Restless, Nicander went out on deck.

There was a brisk breeze coming in over the quarter and the ships made a fine picture slashing through the easy swell. He looked up at the soaring curve of the big lateen sails, taut and fluttering at the edge. They seemed so much more workmanlike than the usual broad square sails of a merchantman.

He strolled forward. The rowers were visible each side under this main deck, taking it easy while they could.

Right in the bow was a slightly elevated forecastle. He peered over into it and saw their attendants, lounging with a cup of wine in the quarters of the weaponeer.

Velch raised his drink in mock salute. 'Anything you need, Holy One?'

Nicander gave a wry smile: they obviously knew all the tricks, including how to find a comfortable berth. Here on the open sea they had no need to constantly watch over their charges.

As the afternoon came to a close the ships downed sail and headed purposefully under oars in to the darkening coast. This was the long Hellespont that separated Europa from Asia, and led to the outside world.

Nicander knew that at the narrowest part of the seaway was the port of Dardanellia, a trading harbour where the customs imposts for the Empire were exacted. That's where they must be headed first.

He racked his brain, trying to remember what he'd heard about the port. Yes. On the Asian side opposite to Constantinople – berths alongside, an amiable population. A river, hills and wooded valleys not so far off. Beyond that still was the anonymity of the ancient lands of Troad and Lydia.

He and Marius had managed to see exactly where their chest was. Stowed under a pack of glassware right at the front of the second case, number XIV, it was only three feet long. It contained, however, over forty leather sacks neatly laced at the tops, packed tightly together under a layer of parchment scrolls and an intricately worked reliquary containing a finger bone of Saint Antony, together with other religious oddments.

Fearing the attendants' interest, they had tut-tutted that the scriptures were so scanty but allowed it was all there, making much of seeing it safely restowed.

For now they must just be alert. Once it became clear how the ship was to be secured they could finalise their plans.

Ahead, slightly to the left, Nicander saw the first outer settlements of Dardanellia. The narrows shortened and the town grew in size but, one by one, the ships pulled past without slackening pace.

In bewilderment he watched as they left the confines of the strait and moved out into the eye of the sunset and the vastness of the Mediterranean Sea. A few miles further they raised an island, rounded it and dropped anchor.

Nicander returned to Marius, disheartened. Even if they got away with the chest by boat or whatever, on an island there was nowhere to go.

They spooned up the greasy slop that passed for supper in sullen silence.

'There'll be a proper port before long, never fear,' Nicander muttered.

But it was the same all the way down the coast of Asia Minor. Even a naval ship did not navigate across the seas out of sight of land, it followed well-known headlands and seamarks to its destination and moored safely in a bay by night. Potable water for the rowers was brought aboard from the shore and the next morning they were on their way again.

After a week they reached Cyprus and the port of Paphos, ancient and with a thriving town where they loaded provisions and water for the next and final leg – across to Alexandria.

'This is how we'll do it,' Nicander told Marius. 'I know Alex well. The docks are along the waterfront below the Timonium. Cargo is landed next to the ship under local guard until customs have assessed it and duties are paid. Then it's freed to be moved into the warehouses while the inland shippers bring up their wagons. That's when our men go to work.'

'Our men?'

'Who will have been paid to relieve the shipment of the goods we've told them to.'

'Then?'

'Meanwhile the four camels I'll hire arrive and during the night we vanish.'

'While the sailors and rowers are on shore, getting on the juice. Yes!'

CHAPTER SEVENTEEN

They made landfall in two days and turned in along the sandy shore of North Africa until they came up with the capital city of Egypt.

'You've not been to Alex,' Nicander said as they approached the double harbour. It was hot, the dry smell of dunes and the wafting pungency of camels sharp on the air.

'No, never.'

'Well, you're in for treat. Look, there.' He pointed to an immensely tall, stepped square structure at the edge of the sea. 'The Pharos! You can see its flame from an unbelievable distance at night.'

The ships curved around to enter the harbour.

Nicander could see their captain measuring distances and speeds by eye. The entrance right by the Pharos was not wide and he was prudently coming in with more control. The oars began their steady pull until at about half a mile off they were suspended to allow the other *dromonds* to enter first.

'See, when we get inside we go across to the docks, and there we'll be right before the Library of Alexandria. And of course Cleopatra's Caesareum which she put up for Julius Caesar but ended up dedicating to Marc Antony—'

'Damn your history, why aren't *we* going in?' Marius snapped.

Their *dromond* made no move to enter, heaving gently to the waves, oars motionless. Nicander frowned. 'That's odd.'

They were at the wrong angle to see much inside the harbour but there was no reason to wait indefinitely after the others had gone in.

But then they were moving again. The huge, rearing Pharos passed on the right.

'The docks are over there,' Nicander said, pointing past the noble Caesareum to the untidy clutter of wharves and ships across the harbour.

'And our mates are over there!' Marius gestured to the left where their escorts were tucked into a small cove with a single pier.

They were not headed for the common docks – the landing was to be away from public gaze.

'Now I see why we didn't go in. They've taken the time to set up a full perimeter – see all the men over there?' Marius pointed to the continuous line of soldiers surrounding the private dock.

'Stops other buggers coming in, stops us going out,' he added bitterly.

Their *dromond* curved around smartly and ended alongside. Ropes were secured and the vessel stood down from sea.

'All ashore – everybody off!'

Snatching up their belongings, the passengers found themselves ushered to a spot well clear as an immediate start was made to land the precious tribute cargo.

'Come along, you gentlemen,' an anxious official encouraged.

Nicander and Marius were hurried past the Palatinate barracks to where a long line of horses, mules and carts stood patiently with their handlers. Names checked yet again, passengers were assigned to their carts or mounts. In minutes it was complete and the first cargo cases began arriving under escort.

Nicander shook his head in rueful admiration at the faultless organisation.

'No chance here,' Marius said in a low voice. 'We'll have to come up with something else.'

The tribute convoy prepared to get under way. Their conveyance was one of the laden carts, where they sat each side of the mule-driver while the compulsors were well behind them in another.

Marius watched the escort form up. A substantial detachment of cavalry in the lead, a sizeable formation of foot soldiers behind. At any threat there was speed at the front and force at the rear.

'Where are we headed to?' Nicander asked their driver.

The unsmiling Nubian raised his eyebrows. 'East. Myos Hormos, o' course.'

It seemed this was a simple journey across the delta of the Nile to end at the head of the Mare Rubrum, the Red Sea – and at the hazy boundary of the Byzantine Empire.

There were shouts from the head of the convoy – then they were off, grinding and creaking along the last streets of Alexandria and into the open country beyond.

Nicander and Marius looked out over the Egyptian landscape: stately date palms, neat reed houses on stilts, waterways and fields where peasants bent to their labours.

It was hot and close after the breezes of the sea and their monks' robes itched and rubbed. Clouds of flies came up from the droppings as each cart went over them and far overhead buzzards wheeled. The jingling of the cavalry and the tramp of marching soldiers added to the general noise.

'Be damned to it, but I'm not having the bones shaken out of my body!' Nicander grumbled, and dropped to the ground to walk beside the cart.

'Well, what now?' Marius grunted, joining him. 'Can't see how we can do anything with this lot about us.'

'I think I have a way.'

'It had better work or we'll end up in some godforsaken hole out on the borders.'

'Listen – all this good land is here because it's watered by the Nile. Once we get to the other side it's a different story. Probably two or three days across the desert before we reach Myos Hormos.'

'So?'

'This time of the year I've never known it not to be plagued by sandstorms from the south. What we do is wait for one to strike! It's easy to see them, a great wall coming at you across the desert.

'Now, what everyone does is get down out of the way until it's past. Not us! I saw where our chest went – number XIV, in not the next but the following cart. They'll all be stopped, no one looking, so we feel our way down to it, give the driver a bump on the head and lead the cart out into the desert. That's anywhere to the right, and keep on going. These storms last for hours – by the time it's all over we've vanished. Can't delay the convoy to go looking for us – we're away!'

'What about water, food?'

'This cart's got provisions for three, that one will be the same. Only a couple of days to reach somewhere like Memphis, won't be a problem.'

The country slipped by, soon looking all the same. Occasionally, the tedium was relieved by a river or waterway crossing, the horses splashing and kicking in relief, and then it was back to the endless grind and bump.

At nightfall a stop was made at a hamlet. Under a full military guard there was nothing to be done and wearily they stretched out in sleep.

Time passed: four days after leaving Alexandria they met the Nile, a placid blue sliding mass of water. The ferries took many hours to ship horses and men across and then they were headed to the south-east and the desert.

Abruptly the carefully tended small fields and clusters of palms gave way to sand. Ahead stretched a nondescript stony desert with nothing but a few fraying bushes and the white sticks of dead wood protruding from the side of small dunes.

They stayed the night, resting horses and men and taking on water, then the next day they headed out into the desert.

The ancient road petered out. With no substantial stone to work with, the engineers had resorted to laying impacted gravel that wound between the low dunes. But the route was now seldom used and it had become a rutted dreariness.

The convoy moved on in the heat and dryness, the heads of horses drooping and the steady pace of the men slackening as they faced the deeper reaches of the desert. Night was spent under the stars and the next day was the same again.

'When's your sandstorm coming, then?' Marius demanded.

Nicander didn't reply.

They plodded on, the discomfort of their garb a growing penance in the heat.

The convoy reached the shores of the Mare Rubrum, a harsh glitter that spread across the vision.

They followed a coast road through reedy shallows, threading past hillocks and outcrops to the outskirts of a decaying town, Myos Hormos.

A halt was called while the cavalry rode ahead. In an hour riders returned to announce that they could proceed.

They moved on, past bleak scoured ruins of houses and overgrown gardens to the quay, which was deserted. There were precious few signs of life.

The convoy stopped; Nicander could see a knot of officers arguing, one throwing down his pace stick in anger. Eventually the order was given to make camp.

This was done in orderly fashion, sentries posted and the men released into the perimeter limits as military routine took over.

Nicander sat morosely in the shade of their cart. He glanced sideways at Marius. The old campaigner was asleep.

The tinny sound of a small bell intruded from a low building away to the left. Nicander squinted in its direction: a church of sorts, summoning what must be a tiny congregation in this hellhole of burning heat.

Then a thought struck. 'Marius! Get up, you lazy sod!'

It took hard persuading before Marius would abandon his shade to trudge over to the little church. But when they returned each had on, in place of their monk's robe, a blessedly cool linen tunic – they had left two holy men at the chancel fingering in wonder their new-won woollen robes, given in exchange.

But the relief was only temporary. The day became ever more oppressive and even talking was fitful and exhausting.

'Bugger this, Nico. We're going to be on a boat out of this stinking place – but leaving the Roman Empire! Away off into . . . who knows where. We've got to—'

'Didn't you hear what the mule-driver said? We're to go the whole length of this Mare Rubrum to the end, where you'll find the kingdom of Axum. The independent kingdom of Axum. Owes nothing to Justinian, or the Persians, just makes a pile of coin being in the middle.'

'So . . . ?'

'So Roman law doesn't work there. The compulsors can go and rot themselves, we're not under their control any more. Just have to find some way to relieve them of their weapons and they're powerless to call for help. And another thing – this is where we part company with the tribute convoy. They take ship for Eudaemon and the Persian Sea, while we . . . well, as we sold to the Emperor, we're supposed to find a ship going to Taprobane.'

'You're saying if we move, it has to be at Axum, or we're done.'

'Exactly. The chest will be guarded only by those two, and we can surely turn up a riot that sees us end with the box and vanishing into the crowd. Not only that, there's no way they can start a commotion, no one will take notice of them.'

Marius scratched his bare knee. 'You seem to know a lot about this Axum?'

'Of course! Never been there myself, but this is a famous place for incense. You get frankincense and myrrh from across in Saphar and at the same time, nard and the rest from the south. They double their money by adding in spices coming up from the Cushites and even ivory and slaves from the barbarian marsh people.'

The hired ships did not arrive for another day but they were no fine *dromonds*. Flat, broad and ugly transport craft, they were designed for livestock. The two holy men were given places on deck under an awning, unlike the hapless souls of the escort who were accommodated below.

It was long days of endurance in the baking heat and reflected glare of the sea before they finally raised the kingdom of Axum.

There, the jovial king had welcomed his Roman visitors warmly as representatives of the state that was piling so much trade wealth into his coffers. He had gone out of his way to meet their requirement, a ship on passage to the fabled Taprobane for a pair of holy men and their attendants.

Nicander and Marius had no chance to make their move: it had been a smooth exchange out of one ship into another, their hard-joking escort of soldiers entertaining them with lurid tales of what they might expect on their venture into the Erythraean Sea.

The trading dhow's long curved bow met the swell with ease in a long upward swoop, triumphantly descending the other side in a swash of white, under the urging of its soaring lateen sail. On the after deck Marius sat wedged into the low bulwarks, holding on for dear life in the liveliness of their ship's movement and staring hopelessly back at where they'd come from, a fearless soldier – but no sailor.

The last of the smudge of blue-grey that was Arabia had lessened by the hour until it had disappeared, and now all that was left was a blazing sun high in the sky and sea – an alien, watery expanse that stretched as far as the eye could see in every direction.

'Where are we?' he croaked, every legionary sense of place and purpose now irrelevant.

'The captain knows what he's doing,' Nicander replied, feeling none too brave himself.

But they were heading straight out into open waters instead of hugging the coast as any prudent Roman would have done. The Arab captain, in broken trading Greek, had said only that they were following the season's winds that blew always from one direction in summer and in the opposite in winter, and this was what provided their direct route to Taprobane.

Nicander had never heard of such a regularity of nature and immediately distrusted him. In the Mediterranean everything from calms to storms could be expected from any direction at any time at the whim of the gods.

The captain also talked darkly of the perils of the deep: the monsters surging out of the depths with no warning, the giant rocs that plummeted

126

down from invisible heights to snatch unfortunate sailors from the decks to take back to feed their chicks. And an immense white octopus that rose up at night and ate ships whole.

Nicander had additional anxieties. The Erythraean sea was in the centre of the world; in the north was the land mass of Asia and the further you went the more frigid it got, until past Thule the human body froze in its last posture like a statue for all eternity. In the south there was no land, therefore it stood to reason that in that direction, in which it got progressively hotter, it would reach the point where the sea itself started to boil. No one had ever returned from the burning region to tell the tale.

What if there was a storm and the mast broke? Without sail they would be carried before the wind. And no one had ever worked out where the winds blew to in the end – it was quite possible that they would be driven ever further south, to end in a dreadful fate as they reached the boiling sea.

He decided to keep his concerns to himself. 'We've a stout enough ship,' he added in half-hearted encouragement.

'You think so?' Marius hissed. 'Look! Look at this – did you ever come across such shite workmanship!'

To his horror Nicander saw that there was not a nail anywhere. Even the hull planks were held together with nothing more than twisted fibres and thongs. They were trusting their lives to a seagoing vessel that was just sewn together.

Nicander glanced back at the Arab captain at the steering oar, his unfocused eyes on a distant horizon as he chewed some kind of dried leaves. 'But that's the least of our problems. This voyage is only going to end in one of two ways: we're going to be shipwrecked or worse – or we're going to safely arrive at Taprobane. If we get there, those bastards forward will be watching very carefully while we carry out the plan we set before Justinian, which, if you remember, calls for us to wave our magic letter and demand the nearest trader of Sinae to take us there.'

'But . . .'

'Damn it, Marius. There'll be nobody from Serica there and the people of

Taprobane will soon tell them so. We'll be exposed, unmasked – they'll take us prisoner back to Justinian as frauds and no doubt we'll be entertained by Marcellus again.'

'We've got to get away, then,' Marius said.

'Tell me,' Nicander said, glancing pointedly out over the vast, empty sea. 'Just how you propose to do this?'

The big man looked down.

'Let me sum up for you. We're no longer looking to flee with a chest of gold, we're looking to save our very skins! Just that – anything that sees us disappear. Not a sesterce to our name, but still alive.'

CHAPTER EIGHTEEN

Yeh Ch'eng's early morning light was delicate and pure, befitting an imperial city of China.

It touched the myriad rooftops, their upswept eaves and finials slowly taking colour. Soon it streamed into the apartment of the Lady Kuo Ying Mei. She sat by the window while her elaborate hairstyle was completed, braided up into an elegant double knot and secured with pearl pins by Lai Tai Yi, her Gold Lily Lady-in-Waiting.

A red-crested bulbul broke into song among the pink and yellow flowers of a nearby tree. Ying Mei sighed with contentment. 'How enchanting, and from so tiny a creature!'

'Your father would say that it is a sign of heaven's blessing, my child, that daintiness is sent to bring beauty to strength,' Tai Yi offered. The blossom of the plum was revered as a symbol of fortitude.

'Just so, Ah Lai.' She could use the familiar form of name, for Tai Yi had cared for her since birth and personally instructed her in the intricate ceremonial and etiquette expected of one attending on the Emperor himself.

The mention of her father, however, brought a frown. An only child, Ying Mei had become his confidante. As grand chamberlain to the elderly Emperor Hsiao Ching, he was becoming more and more enmeshed in the intrigues and betrayals that were sapping the dynasty of the Eastern Wei. A Confucian scholar and accomplished calligrapher – and a deeply honourable man – Kuo Ming Lai took his duties seriously and was pained by the incessant rivalry and treachery, much of it centred around the ruthless and tyrannical independent warlord Kao Yang. His bellicose manoeuvring out in the eastern counties was unsettling the peasantry and tales of his bestiality and callous indifference were widespread.

Why the Emperor had taken a course of appeasement and benevolence toward him was a mystery but he had, tolerating the military posturing for reasons which were hidden from mere mortals. She had heard that, in response, the warlord had sworn loyalty and promised to disperse his army at an early date.

Ying Mei stood, quite unconscious of the swan-like grace of her figure as she extended her arms to receive the broad-sleeved cream silk robe of the Presence. It was sumptuously embroidered with flowers and motifs from nature, with contrasting panels of rich brocade. Tai Yi fussed at the garment then fastened a wide girdle in the golden yellow of the imperial court under her breast.

With her fragrance pouch settled discreetly beneath her gown, Ying Mei went to a rosewood chest and carefully drew out a small case.

Leaving by the lion-carved gate that led into a shady courtyard, she approached an ornamental pond with multicoloured carp swimming languidly among the lilies. She paused to offer them a tidbit. Then into the stillness came the summoning of the stone chimes; she hurried on toward the Inner Court.

It had been a long time since her father had first presented her but she still felt a thrill of anticipation as she waited by the door of the Throne Room. A blank-faced eunuch in a cream and chocolate-brown robe with an elaborately embroidered breastplate and peacock feather cap motioned her in.

With quick, dainty steps she took her place before the Celestial Throne and knelt deeply, head bowed, arms extended to each side. A yellow gauze hanging from the gold ornamented canopy hid the Emperor from mortal gaze; she knew, however, that he was there, able to discreetly observe all that went on.

An incense brazier sent gentle spirals of smoke up into the lofty expanse above. On either side, Imperial Guards in rich surcoats with burnished halberds stood at attention and to the right was Grand Chamberlain Kuo Ming Lai, in full court gown and scholarly cap, his hands clasped within his sleeves, his countenance impassive.

She waited, her head touching the ground until, at a word from him, she rose and extracted a richly ornamented loose-stitched book from the case.

It was Emperor Hsiao Ching's practice before the business of the day to listen to five verses from the *Analects of Confucius*. Ying Mei's task was to read these passages, carefully chosen by the Grand Chamberlain.

Lifting the book with dignity and reverence she found the first selection and paused. As usual, her father had chosen a generality to begin.

To one side the soft reverberation of a gong sounded. In a courtly high-pitched chant she began: 'The Master says: he who governs by his moral excellence may be compared to the Pole-star, which abides in its place, while all the stars bow toward it.'

She inclined her head and waited.

The gong reverberated again.

'The Master says: "I will not grieve that men do not know me; I grieve that I know not men."' Ying Mei's gaze remained resolutely on the parchment: this was a scholarly admonishment at the Emperor's recent leniency toward the warlord Kao Yang. It could only bring trouble, for the man was an unprincipled viper and—

Another soft boom.

'The Master says: "Observe what he does; look into his motives . . . can a man hide himself?"' She remained bowed; it was a call to take heed of the reckless vainglory of the man, his barely concealed ambitions and dark streak of cruelty.

The melodious note from the gong never came. Instead there was a strident triple strike as a dusty messenger ran in, throwing himself prostrate before the throne.

No one except an imperial herald with tidings of the utmost urgency came into the Presence without obtaining leave at the highest level. First Eunuch Yuan shot a glance at Kuo.

'What is this news, that you disturb His Imperial Majesty so?' the Grand Chamberlain demanded, ignoring Yuan, who stood tight-faced.

'Great mandarin, General Wu desires you should be aware that Lord Kao Yang is under arms and advancing on the city.'

Ying Mei caught her breath. Not only had Kao Yang betrayed the Emperor's trust in refusing to disband but he was now insolently approaching the capital.

'Sire, what I have feared has come to pass,' Kuo said to the hanging gauze. 'It is time to—'

'Wu has six banners of Yeh spearmen. We are not concerned.' The voice from within, however, was weak and elderly.

The Grand Chamberlain persisted. 'Do not underestimate Kao Yang, Sacred Ruler. His spies and agents are everywhere and they cry disloyalty and insults to your august name upon the common people. If we—'

'Minister Kuo! The Wei Lord of Ten Thousand Years is not to be dismayed by mere posturing. Instruct General Wu to offer Kao Yang mercy. If he submits to me this day, then his life will be spared, and that of his family. If not, then the wrath of heaven will surely be called upon his head. That is all.'

'Sire, it is essential that—'

'Enough! Let the readings continue!'

Ying Mei returned to her chamber shaken. The times were strange and disturbing. She recalled the portent of a golden eagle taking a fox within the imperial compound that had terrified many by its thinly veiled meaning; there were mutters that the previous month's partial eclipse was the sun turning his gaze from horrors to come. Now, the warlord Kao Yang was not so far from the capital. Had he come to pledge fresh allegiance to the Emperor or was there a real threat? She knew much of the imperial army was away, dealing with an uprising among the peasants.

She busied herself and tried not to worry: in China's long history there had been other disturbances and challenges to an emperor's rule, this would not be the last.

Within the high walls of the palace, the morning wore on in its usual measured calm and after a delicate midday repast the Emperor honoured his court by attending a recital of music on the pipa, a five-stringed lute, played by his ladies at the Hall of Tranquil Longevity. Despite a subdued atmosphere, Ying Mei brought smiles of delight with her gay, 'White Snow in Spring Sunlight', and then the more introspective 'Flute and Drum at Sunset'.

Another lady of the court stepped forward shyly to take her place, but in the stillness before she began, faint but insistent sounds of a disturbance came from somewhere out in the city. The Emperor frowned and Kuo immediately dispatched a uniformed eunuch to investigate. He returned minutes later, politely waiting while the pipa music drew to its close, then announced, 'Sire, it's nothing but the humble classes in a witless frenzy about the Lord Kao Yang.'

The Emperor held motionless for a space then said calmly, 'They are my loyal subjects and without understanding. It is within my power to ease their fears. Grand Chamberlain – this night I shall offer sacrifice before the people.'

Emperor Hsiao Ching then retired to the Hall of Bright Holiness to contemplate and purify.

The imperial palace meanwhile hastened to prepare. The Grand Master of Tao carefully cast his horoscope. It transpired that the hour before midnight was the most propitious. Heralds and runners fanned out to every office and department with orders from the Grand Chamberlain, others carried gongs and trumpets to announce to the populace what was about to take place.

At the appointed time, on either side of the Imperial Way, thousands silently came up to witness the ritual that would see the Emperor join earth to heaven in personal supplication. The great families of state took position about the altar at the steps of the Supreme Temple in strict order of seniority. From her place in the centre, Ying Mei had a privileged view of the processional way, lined by the Imperial Guard in their finest robes with the Emperor's insignia on their tabards. At the other end she caught sight of the ceremonial chariot being brought to the door, drawn by a pair of magnificent black horses.

The people pressed forward: peasants, beggars, shopkeepers, entertainers, thieves, brothel-keepers, all eager to catch sight of their near-mythical emperor.

Then, piercing the night, came the pure sound of trumpets, followed by shouts of command up and down the line of guards.

Flares blazed into life at the gateway to the palace as Emperor Hsiao Ching of the Eastern Wei dynasty appeared in all his glory. Resplendent in his dazzling yellow robes embellished with the five-clawed imperial dragon, he gazed out on his people. A giant drum began pounding and all along the line of guards, kindled torches were raised in a stunning spectacle.

The chariot ground off, the imperious figure of the Emperor looking neither one way nor the other. As he passed, his subjects fell prostrate and the air was wreathed with the fragrance of incense.

At the steps of the temple the Emperor dismounted. Officials and noble families quickly knelt in obeisance. He progressed up to take position at the altar, then turned and faced the multitude.

On one side of him Grand Chamberlain Kuo held the jade-bound *Book of Wei*, a compendium of proverbs and rules of the dynasty that came down from centuries past in the country's long history, written in antique characters revered for the excellence of their execution.

On the other, First Eunuch Yuan prepared the instruments of sacrifice.

Ying Mei could sense the guarded hostility in the two men. She knew her father resented the privileged access the eunuch had by reason of his personal attendance on the Emperor; he suspected that much of what he counselled was being overborne by Yuan to advance his own interests.

'My loyal subjects – listen now to your Heavenly Lord's words!' A spreading sigh came from the people who flung themselves down again in kowtow.

'We are gathered to offer sacrifice in order to gain the smile of benevolence from heaven in our need and . . .'

He finished and motioned for the people to rise, then beckoned to the Grand Chamberlain. Kuo stepped forward and opened the precious book. In a commanding voice he read the passages he had painstakingly selected, nodding in satisfaction at the humility and trust they were evoking.

A bronze libation vessel was brought forth; three-footed and of great antiquity, it was filled with precious wine and placed before His Imperial Majesty. With the utmost dignity, he raised it and drank, first to the heavens, then to the august earth, and finally, to the ancestors – and it was time.

At a discreet signal, a small pure-white goat was led out, bleating piteously in its anxiety. The creature was pinioned in front of the Emperor. A reverent hush descended on the crowd as the sacrificial knife – jade, with an obsidian blade – was presented to him. He raised it high, chanting sacred words known only to gods and emperors, and in the expectant quiet brought it down.

But the sacrifice was fumbled by the old emperor.

The kid screamed and kicked. In place of a clean slice across the throat the wound tailed off on one side. Spurting blood splattered those nearby as the animal, frantic with pain, went berserk. Unnerved, the Emperor stabbed and slashed until the creature finally gave up its life.

When it was over the Emperor stood before his people, bloodstained and hesitant. Trembling, he was unable to take the ancestral *Book of Wei* in his hands. The Grand Chamberlain held it for him, expressionless, while he feebly pronounced the sacred words.

The omens could not have been more dolorous. The Emperor mounted his chariot and moved off, a diminished figure. Down the torchlit way there was no doubt of what had passed: instead of the full-throated roar of acclamation due an emperor – *Wan siu! Wan siu! Wan wan siu!* Live ten thousand times ten thousand years! – there were only thin and fitful cries. The act of intercession and reassurance had failed.

CHAPTER NINETEEN

The captain announced that they would raise Taprobane in a day or so, save no monsters of the deep should appear in the meantime.

'We're never going to get away, not with those two around our necks,' Nicander said bitterly. 'And Taprobane – what in Hades is it like? Do they speak half-decent Greek? Or Latin? If we make a run for it, how do we survive without means – let alone get back to any kind of civilisation!'

'You want me to tell you?' Marius said.

'You're not saying we should give up, turn ourselves in?'

'No, sort it out now. They've got their orders. Get the seeds at all costs, then get rid of us.'

'You mean . . . ?'

'After they find out it's all a fast one, their only chance of clearing themselves before Justinian is to scruff us and make sure we front up to him to explain ourselves. Nothing else will save 'em. This is all to say that either way, in Taprobane we're finished.'

'But—'

'No. That's it – we're gone. Unless we solve everything in one hit – even to lay our hands on the gold.'

'I know what you're going to say, Marius, and—'

'We get in first. Knock 'em on the head and our problems fly away.'

Nicander's world shrank to a single focus. He was being asked to kill. When a human life flickered to its end under his hands, could he coldly just move on?

His rational self told him there were times when there was no other recourse – on the battlefield, defending oneself – but could he be like Marius, who he'd seen with his own eyes arrive at the decision to kill a child and then act on it? It had undoubtedly saved them all from the Ostrogoths but he feared he could never bring himself to do it.

'Marius, I'm not sure I could do it. Kill someone, I mean.'

'Barehanded? Yes, it can be tough for anyone not used to it.'

He edged toward the bulwark and furtively used his chlamys to shield a crude seaman's knife, its haft bound in worn rope but with a stout blade and wickedly sharp.

'Take it. Go for the throat and make it a good 'un.'

'Marius—'

'Don't worry about me, I've got a hatchet.'

'You . . . you don't understand,' Nicander said piteously. 'It's that . . . you have to believe me, I can't go up to someone and . . . and . . . just kill them!'

'Do it right, they won't feel a thing.'

'No! I can't . . .'

'What do you mean, you can't do it?'

'The knife, the . . . the blood . . . kill them, that is.'

'You might not like it, but there's times when you have to, Nico!'

'I – I know, Marius. But . . . but I really can't,' he ended miserably.

Marius breathed heavily. 'If you don't do your bit, where are we going to be? I can't take both of 'em at the same time.'

Nicander said nothing, his eyes pleading, but he took the knife.

'Look, we do it after the captain and watch turn in about midnight. Gives us time to heave the bodies in the sea after. And if you're worried about being caught, don't be. We're holy men, we'd never do a thing like that,' he added. 'Get some kip while you can. I say it has to be tonight, we haven't time else.'

Sleep would not come for Nicander. Brutal scenes of murder and death preyed on his imagination.

At last the captain did his final turn around the decks and disappeared. In the enveloping blackness of night the vessel settled into a creaking peacefulness.

A single lookout took his position right aft. He was staring away over the stern lost in thought – they had the ship virtually to themselves.

Marius whispered hoarsely, 'Now's the time! Are you ready?'

Nicander felt for the knife in rising panic.

'Good. Let's go, Nico.'

He started silently forward but Nicander was frozen to the deck.

'Come on,' Marius snarled, gesturing savagely. 'We've not got long!'

Nicander couldn't move.

'Right! You're leaving it all to me, you scumbag! Well, I know what has to be done and I'm going to do it. I'll take both of 'em on, be buggered to you, Greek!'

In a chaos of emotion Nicander's feet released themselves and he followed, his hand shaking so much he nearly dropped the knife.

The sharp bow came together at the prow and the compulsors had set up their 'home' there in the cool. The rest of the crew were under cover further in, taking advantage of the fatter turn of hull to sleep across-ways.

A sudden snort made Marius drop to his knee but it was only an unknown snorer.

He inched on to where the foredeck fell away to the open prow, looked back once at Nicander then eased forward the last few inches. He lifted his head up to peer over and down but quickly turned and gestured savagely that they should return to their sleeping place.

'Those fucking bastards! We haven't a chance – they've rumbled us!'

It took some time for the torrent of swearing and cursing to subside. Either suspecting them or from instinct born of their trade, the compulsors had given up their prime position in the bows and were now sleeping with the rest of the crew.

* * *

In the morning a drifting palm-tree was sighted.

'Ah. Tomorrow, maybe the next – we dock at Taprobane,' the Arab captain told them.

'Think of something!' Marius whispered savagely. 'Full on, we haven't a prayer against 'em with their weapons and soldier mates.'

'I . . . I can't.'

'Then . . .'

A coldness settled in the pit of his stomach. The fates had thwarted their every move, destroyed each cunning plan.

They had run out of ideas.

As the day progressed, the seas lost their energetic tumbling, and a long, slow swell came, a deep and languorous motion spreading ever on to the distant haze of the horizon.

The vessel slowed and the captain frowned in vexation. Two hours later vapour began rising from the sea and the distant haze grew more marked. The band of white swelled, reached out and the coolness of a tropic mist wreathed around them.

It thickened. Nicander watched as the ship's bow faded and their world contracted to barely a dozen feet about them, the passage of ship through the water now not much more than a muted chuckle.

It only delayed the inevitable, of course. The fog would burn off, the winds return and in hours they would meet their fate.

Nicander's spine stiffened. He couldn't do it! Not meekly resign to what was coming.

He began pacing the deck but when he reached the stern he stopped abruptly.

Surely it was not so simple!

'Sir, where exactly will Taprobane be?' he asked the captain innocently.

Surprised, the man hesitated and sniffed for the wind, a tiny zephyr coming in over the bow.

'There!' he pointed.

Nicander strolled over to where Marius stood glumly. 'Ready to leave? We have to move fast!'

Marius stared at him as if he was mad.

'Come with me – don't look around.'

He led the way aft. 'Marius, we've got just one chance to get away now before we land at Taprobane.'

He nodded almost imperceptibly to past the stern.

Marius followed the direction then went rigid and hissed, 'No! I'm not! I can't do it, you know I can't!'

Nicander gave a cynical smile. 'You might not like it, but there's times when you have to, Marius.'

'But . . . but . . .' he looked again in dismay at the two ship's boats which bobbed and snubbed at the end of the painter.

One had oars in, probably to act as the lifeboat, the other was bare.

'You can pull an oar, you told me.'

'Yes, but . . .' spluttered Marius.

'Sea's flat calm – we'd make Taprobane in a few hours. I know where it is. Then we lay low until the compulsors have quit the place.'

'They'd see us get our gear!'

'That's why we can't get it. We act now, this minute.'

'Leave our gear? Including the letter?'

Nicander looked at him with a twisted smile.

'Of course it's no bloody use, is it?' Marius said weakly.

'I want you to watch down the deck. Tell me the instant no one is looking. I'll pull the boat in and cut the rope ready. You jump in and take the oars, I'll push it off.'

'Yes, Nico, I'll do it.'

'Stout fellow,' Nicander said, recognising the courage behind it.

He turned to gaze out into the white mist astern as though in contemplation.

For long minutes he held his pose, then blurted nervously, 'Hurry up!'

'It's the captain,' Marius came back. 'He's talking to someone.'

'This fog won't stay for ever – we've got to get away before it lifts or they'll be after us!'

There was no answer – then a single word. 'Now!'

Nicander bent to the bollard where the lines were secured and pulled for his life. He strained and heaved but the boats were a dead weight.

'Help me!' he gasped.

Marius hesitated then, shouldering him out of the way, braced against the bollard and hauled mightily. There was movement, then more until it was hand over hand and they came up fast.

Nicander swivelled to glance forward. No one was looking their way.

Marius fended the boats off with his foot.

'Get in!' Nicander croaked.

Marius lowered himself in, clambering to the further one, with the oars.

Nicander snatched a look back – the captain was staring aft in astonishment. 'Quick! Get going!' he yelped, tumbling in the boat.

There was a commanding shout, then the sound of running feet.

Nicander fumbled for his knife and began a frantic sawing at the rough, hairy rope but it was strong and thick.

Marius had the oars in their pins ready to pull. 'Cut the fucking thing now!'

Finally the rope parted and fell away.

'Go!' shrieked Nicander.

With several quick digs on one oar Marius pivoted the boat about and then with deep, powerful strokes he had the little craft surging away.

As they disappeared into the embrace of the blank, cool whiteness of the fog, angry hails came across the water.

Nicander remembered the captain's direction: fine to the left of the bow. In the last seconds before the long shape was swallowed up, he had oriented. 'Cut around, Marius. Head that way.'

There were no sounds, only the rippling of water as they sped on into nothingness.

Nicander sank back. 'Do you know, I think we've made it?'

Marius continued to pull viciously.

'You can ease off now,' Nicander said. 'That is, we don't know how far you're going to have to row.'

'No!' Marius gasped between pants. 'If they see us when the fog goes, they'll sail after us. Those fucking compulsors will force 'em to.'

He lasted a full hour before he lifted the oars. 'I'm beat. Your turn.'

The last time Nicander had been at the oars had been on the lake along from Leptis Magna, entertaining a lady before he had left for Rome. She had an infuriating giggle, he remembered. He took the oars and settled to the task, leaning far forward and back to get the longest stroke as his brother had taught him. It was tiring but, pacing himself, he endured.

'When will we know we've reached Taprobane?' Marius grunted, trying to peer into the unbroken white wall.

'Look down into the water. When you see the bottom shallowing, give a shout.'

Marius stared into the translucent green depths.

After some time they allowed themselves a break. Lying as best they could across the unforgiving wood of the thwarts they sank into blessed rest.

Nicander groaned that they must continue, and he took the hateful oars to start the painful business again.

At least the fog remained. Thick and concealing, it was enabling their escape.

Their world had now shrunk to just them, their boat and a watery void.

'I think it's coming on for evening,' Nicander said nervously, noting the subtle change in the light.

'What if we don't make it to Taprobane soon?' Marius grunted.

'Only two choices: keep on or stop for the night.'

In the dark they could find themselves in trouble, perhaps careering onto a reef. It was decided that when it became too dim to see down into the depths they would drift until morning. Probably the fog would be gone by then anyway.

Evening drew in. After their exertion at the oars they felt the fog's clammy embrace keenly, condensation soaking their thin clothes until they shivered with cold. Pangs of hunger increased their misery. It became a trial of endurance.

During the night Nicander realised that by drifting they had lost their sense of direction. When they resumed the oars in the morning would they be on course, or heroically making for the boiling sea? Other horrors reared up in his imagination – sea monsters, a terrible storm, making landfall on a cannibal shore, a giant whirlpool from which none ever returned.

Dawn came at last: the fog was still all about them and as the light increased, their world seemed exactly as it was the previous day. The depths were innocent of sea bottom and there was a deathly silence.

With nothing to give a clue to direction they were helpless. Even if the fog lifted, would it disclose the same never-ending seascape?

He felt the prick of desperation. Without a scrap of food or anything to drink they would be unlikely to last long in this watery wilderness.

The sun rose – and the fog began thinning. The warmth was restoring but what would they see?

The mist began burning off in the tranquil calm.

'A ship!' he screamed, standing up.

By the gods, they were saved!

'Wave, wave!' Nicander urged in a delirium of relief.

'That, Greek, is our own fucking ship,' Marius said dully.

Nicander stared. They must have gone in a complete circle during the night. 'If we don't . . . we won't survive in this pawky boat,' he mumbled, his eyes fixed on the distant vision.

Without waiting for comment Marius took to the oars and began pulling to the ship.

By the time they reached it the side was lined with excited figures.

'Where've you been to, you madmen?' the captain blustered as they were helped aboard.

'Oh, Marius here was touched by the sun, wished by all means to be off the ship,' Nicander told him. 'He got in the boat and tried to get away. Just in time I leapt in and have persuaded him to return.' He looked around apprehensively for the compulsors.

The captain glared at them. 'You've caused a lot of trouble for us.'

'But we did return, didn't we?' Nicander said innocently.

'Yes, but the other boat, it still searches for you.'

'Oh, I'm sorry for that, sir, believe me.' If there were souls out there at peril of their lives looking for them he did indeed regret it.

'It is not safe to be in this place, not moving. The fog, it soon goes.' He paused. 'They are yours, those in the boat.'

'I don't understand.'

'Your servants. They insist to go in the other boat to look for you, would not let our sailors to take it.'

'You mean . . .'

'I cannot wait! It is dangerous to linger. I must sail on. You understand?'

Nicander and Marius caught each other's eyes.

Head hung, Nicander replied, 'If by this it is the means of saving the many we must concur. Do your duty, Captain.'

The sail rose on its yard and catching the slight wind there was a growing ripple at the bow as it gathered speed.

For long minutes the two looked back with grief-stricken faces.

Nicander broke the silence. 'Captain, you say it was only our two attendants in the boat, and they were insistent on this? I must beg of you, do allow us to check the contents of our chest. It is an unworthy thought, but not impossible, that they took advantage of our absence to seize the precious scriptures and baubles therein and make their escape. To settle our minds on the matter, might we . . . ?'

It was brought to the privacy of the captain's cuddy and they were left alone.

'I – I can't believe it!' breathed Nicander, as they spilt out the contents of several of the leather bags to the table, the gold glittering in heart-catching splendour. 'We have it! It's ours!'

There was row after row of the bags and a papyrus cylinder that yielded a hoard of diamonds. 'In case this Byzantine gold is not accepted,' Nicander said with a huge grin, as he lifted the coins in his hands and let them cascade down.

Marius stood speechless, hypnotised by the wealth on display.

'It worked!' he breathed finally, fingering the treasure with a childish glee. He looked at Nicander in wonder. 'It bloody worked!'

'It's ours to do with it whatever we want,' Nicander whispered. 'There's enough here to capitalise, why, an entire chain of incense importers. We get to Taprobane, get on the first boat back to Arabia . . . and let life start again!'

CHAPTER TWENTY

By the time a tinkling bell had marked the Hour of the Snake in Yeh Ch'eng, rumours were abroad and tension and fear in the air. From behind the filmy screen of the Throne Room, a strict decree was issued. Any who showed by word or deed that they doubted imperial powers to safeguard the land, or made reference to the motions of the warlord Kao Yang, was to be severely punished.

The palace conducted its business as usual but just before midday the sharp triple-strike of the gong brought a summons to the Throne Room for urgent news.

'Report!' Chancellor Kuo demanded to a prostrate imperial messenger.

'Honoured sir, I have an advice from General Wu.'

'Well? Speak!'

The man crouched closer to the floor and looked up fearfully. 'General Wu – he tells that the usurper Kao Yang has split his forces and it is now clear that this must be a move to surround Yeh Ch'eng.'

'And?'

'Sir,' came the trembling voice clear into the silence. 'He begs that the Son of Heaven is beseeched to leave the city this day as he cannot be certain of victory when he confronts Kao Yang tomorrow on the plains before Yeh Ch'eng.'

There was a chill of horror in the room. No one dared move. The Grand Chamberlain turned to the gauze and bowed silently, waiting.

Finally, the Emperor spoke. 'The herald has done his duty and we are appreciative of his efforts. We award him one sycee of silver, of value not greater than ten *wu chu*.'

Kuo nodded to the Chamberlain for palace revenue.

First Eunuch Yuan stepped forward and kowtowed. 'Great Majesty, this man stands in breach of the imperial decree forbidding talk of that traitor.' He paused significantly. 'There can be no exceptions. He must be punished.'

Smothered gasps and sighs left no doubt about the sympathy of the court.

'Beat him,' the Emperor said in a subdued tone.

Yuan's face distorted with a snarl as he took a rod and crossed to the cowering figure. He thrashed the messenger in strong, aimed blows. The man whimpered and writhed, still crouched in obeisance. Blood seeped through the back of his robe.

'Enough!' the Grand Chamberlain snapped.

The herald scrambled to crawl away and the hall quickly began to empty as the courtiers backed out with profuse bowing and ceremony.

The Grand Chamberlain was left alone with his Emperor. 'Great Lord, the news is painful.' Kuo had uneasily noted that the promotion of Kao Yang from warlord to usurper had not in any way been challenged.

'That Kao Yang has seen fit to ignore my mercy is his own failing that he will live to regret.'

'Nonetheless, sire, General Wu counsels a prudent withdrawal of the Emperor to a place of greater safety.'

'Do you?'

'You will know, Heavenly Lord, that I ever hold the Celestial Dragon's self as the most precious in this mortal world.' He paused. 'Yet an even higher purpose drives my words: the duty of a ruler to his subjects – the paramount requirement to preserve his sacred body to continue to stand between the divine and the worldly on behalf of his people.'

There was no response from behind the hanging.

'Therefore I have no alternative than to join General Wu in exhorting the Emperor of Eastern Wei to temporarily quit the city for a more tranquil place, there to—'

'Lord Kuo! You are forgetting one thing.'

'Sire?'

'We reign here over the people of Wei by right, and for one high reason – and one only.'

'Your Majesty.' Kuo bowed low.

'The Mandate of Heaven was conferred upon us. We hold the sacred trust to rule and none may deny it. While we thus retain the mandate the gods will extend their grace and protection to us and our kingdom. We therefore have nothing to fear from the Lord Kao Yang.'

'Then might I put forward another course. It has been overlong since the Emperor last made a progress among his peoples? Might not an appearing of the Son of Heaven among them—'

'Grand Chamberlain – Yeh Ch'eng has been the ancestral capital of the Wei from ancient times. Do you expect us to abandon it at the slightest alarm? No, it shall not be seen that the Emperor of Wei of this day scuttles away from his inheritance like a frightened rabbit! General Wu stands before the usurper invested with full imperial power and authority. He will not let them pass. And recollect that our soldiers are soon returning victorious from the southern rising and together they will sweep the rabble aside!'

'We pray that this be so, sire. Yet common prudence allows that—'

'Be still! The Emperor in full puissance continues to rule, and from the palace of his ancestors in Yeh Ch'eng. Your counsel is noted, and rejected. You may leave us.'

In his apartment Kuo sat at his elegantly carved desk with a heavy heart. It first bore a scholar's work some two centuries before, its red-stained wood now dark with the patina of ages. He gazed at the hanging frame of writing brushes, inkstone and jade seal and tried to let the tranquillity of far antiquity work on his soul.

His attendant and chief scribe Wang entered and waited patiently.

'The Son of Heaven stays,' Kuo said evenly.

'As we might have expected, Master,' said Wang carefully. 'He's an old man, and they have their memories.'

'Quite. Yet I will not deny it, the omens are adverse at this time. There is no sign that we are to be noticed by the gods and the Tao abbot refuses to cast any kind of prognostication, the villain.'

'Then . . .'

'Then we must look to our own situation, First-Born Wang.'

The younger man picked up on his tone, went to the door and closed it quietly. Then he sat respectfully opposite Kuo. 'Sir, Kao Yang is ambitious and impatient. He has shown his hand and must move soon. General Wu has little cavalry and cannot stand against Kao Yang's Mongols. I have in my bowels—'

'Yes. I'm rather referring to the inevitability of what must come, and hence what alternatives are left to us. Kao Yang is capricious and brutal. What he will do when he has supreme power does not bear thinking of.'

'I . . . understand, Master. You are saying that we must consider the case in which the Emperor does not prevail and is . . .'

'As the will of Heaven dictates, of course.'

'Just so.' Wang hesitated then continued softly, 'There are those who have already made disposition. Lord Chu was summoned by the throne and has not answered. The Lady Ch'i could not be found when her women begged audience and when Master Sung was sent for—'

'Rats will always flee before a whirlwind, as dragons will stand.'

'Some claim that it is better to serve the Wei by preserving their wisdom and knowledge for a victorious return.'

'This is a correct and worthy conclusion.'

'Then you will . . . ?'

The Grand Chamberlain faced Wang directly, and in a calm, considered tone replied, 'I desire you should now assemble the secretariat to gather together the records of the Eastern Wei and this day transport them to Luoyang for safety.'

'And you, Master?'

With a bleak smile Kuo said, 'For my own unworthy self there is no other course of moral value before heaven than to stay by the Dragon Throne.'

'Sir, this is madness!' gasped Wang.

'For many years I have served His Majesty and in return he has seen fit to render to me confidences and trust beyond any man's deserving. It is not within my power to flee while he stands alone to face his destiny.'

'Then . . . this is your decision?'

'It is.'

'Master – you must not!'

'My unalterable will.'

For long moments Wang gazed at his lord and preceptor. Then he replied quietly, 'Very well, Master, I accept it and shall honour you always for the lesson you have taught me. That loyalty has two tails. I have served you likewise, and in the same manner you have illuminated me with your inner thoughts. And that is why, while you remain by the Celestial Throne, I shall stand by you.'

In the silence that followed, the mournful cry of a shrike sounded outside.

'I go now to prepare the secretariat, Master,' Wang said after a space.

'Do send my daughter to me, and . . . thank you, First-Born Wang.'

'My Lord?' Ying Mei rose from her bow and looked anxiously up at the Grand Chamberlain. 'You called for me?'

'My devoted *yuan kua*. Dearest child and warmth of my heart.'

'Father?' A chill began to settle. This endearment from her childhood – chubby melon – was always light-hearted and warm. Now there was nothing but seriousness and gravity about her father.

'I wish to speak to you, my daughter.'

Obediently she sat with lowered eyes.

'The times are grave and perilous . . . but then you know to what I refer.'

'Yes, Father. The usurper Kao Yang at our gates.'

'Just so.' A wintry smile appeared and went as quickly. '*Yuan kua*, you always were quick in your intellects.'

'If you say it, honourable Father.'

'Now listen to me. I conceive that the days to come in Yeh Ch'eng will not have a happy outcome. I wish you to go with your mother to Luoyang without delay. You will be safe with our household guardsmen. Do you understand me?'

Her face rose to his, pale and worried. 'Father, I want to know what it is you intend.'

'That does not concern you, my flower.'

She bit her lip. 'You'll remain with the Emperor, won't you!'

'My child, I have served the Son of Heaven faithfully until now and see no reason to abandon his presence for the sake of my own convenience.'

Tears sprang and she lowered her head to hide them.

'Do not weep for me, *yuan kua*,' he said tenderly, his hand going out to stroke her. 'To every man there comes a season – to endure or take pleasure in, it does not signify. The sages tell us that it is a measure of the man, how he means to respond.'

'Father, I disobey you!' she blurted.

She raised glittering eyes to his. 'Can't you see? With your noble example before us how is it possible for me to go – to leave you here, so steadfast and true! No, Father, we'll face what comes together, as our ancestors always did. I stay.'

Kuo turned away quickly. When he spoke at last his voice was husky. 'I have a daughter more precious than a thousand taels of gold – no, ten thousand. It will increase my worries a hundredfold but if you are set in your course I will not try to dissuade you.'

CHAPTER TWENTY-ONE

Nicander choked, 'So close! So help me, we were so close to . . . It's our own fault,' he went on miserably. 'We should have got away while we could.'

He and Marius sat cross-legged on the deck, prisoners, their hands bound behind their backs.

The captain's fears had not been misplaced: pirates had boarded under the cover of the last of the fog and overcome the crew before any defence could be mounted. They'd then systematically ransacked the ship, screaming in delight at the discovery of the treasure.

An island appeared on the horizon and they drew closer then anchored. White beaches overhung with palm trees quite different to those of Arabia, verdant growth and a lazy surf seething across offshore reefs.

The prisoners were manhandled into smaller boats for the trip through the breakers to the calm of a lagoon and then with a hiss of sand they came to a stop on the beach.

They were prodded into the undergrowth and made to take a path which led to a clearing and a stockade.

Inside it was a mire of squelching mud that stank of human waste.

Nicander's stomach churned.

'Put up a brave face, Greek,' Marius growled. 'Else they've won, haven't they?'

The legionary glanced contemptuously at the other prisoners. One wept, some stared into nothing, trembling and uncomprehending like whipped dogs.

'Whatever comes, take it like a man. Who quails knows defeat!'

'Yes, Marius,' Nicander said, drawing on the man's strength to rise above his fears and dread.

The gates were swung wide and a fat dark-skinned man dressed in a multicoloured cloak came into the stockade. He paused, grimacing at the smell.

A village headman encouraged him on, then six warriors forced the prisoners to line up.

The man inspected them, feeling a muscle here, rolling back an eyelid there. He chose three – then came to Nicander who looked past the impassive black face, trying not to catch his eye.

He moved on to the next. Marius. He paused . . . and jerked his thumb with a grunt of satisfaction.

The legionary was taken away, into slavery, head defiantly held high.

Nicander felt a lump in his throat threatening to choke him. He would never see his true companion and comrade again in this life.

The situation beat in on him; Marius was gone and with him the one rock of sanity in this rabid existence.

Then his friend's strength reached out to him one last time. Nicander clamped a ferocious hold on his emotions. Yes! He would face it like a man. For Marius's sake!

Wearisome days followed one on another. Nicander came to know every inch of the compound as he paced it out, round and round. He avoided the other prisoners, who had descended into feral bickering.

At one point he found his mind floating, ignoring bodily sensation, taking delight in a butterfly's erratic fluttering, the regularity of shadows.

In this out-of-world state at first he did not register that coming through the gate was a bruised, bloody but most definitely unbowed Marius.

His eyes focused on the unbelievable sight and then he hurried to him, stopping shame-faced before he gave away his true feelings. 'M-Marius!' he cried. 'You're here!'

'Ah, well. Seems I didn't make a good slave,' he growled through split lips. 'The bastard made sure he got his money back, though.'

He bent and stretched painfully. 'You look in good shape still. Anything happened?'

'N-no,' Nicander replied, unable to manage more.

'Well, don't get your hopes up, we being together again. I saw a big nob come in a ship. He could be after slaves – then we'd be off the same way.'

It was an unbearable thought and when they were lined up once more Nicander was frozen with dread.

This time the buyer was a mild-featured Oriental who went up to the line and sliced an arm down, then nodded at the right-hand division of five – which included them both.

The slave ship was a large dhow. They were chained to the side but at least being the last on they were close to the hatch and fresh air.

With no view outboard there was no clue as to where they were going. But the name of their destination would be meaningless. They were in a universe entirely unknown to civilisation: lands and peoples that existed in ignorance of the Roman world, every element and detail of their living different and disturbing.

Once there was a blow and as the ship heaved and rolled, rain mixed with salt spray soaked them through the hatch. They endured, Marius visibly fighting down his demons – if the ship sank, in chains, they would be dragged down to the depths.

Then came the calms. The sun beat down unendurably. One of the crew threw sacking over the hatch which provided some shade. The still heat stayed, their torment not even relieved at nightfall.

Were they headed into the fabled boiling sea?

Finally it seemed they had arrived at their destination and they were brought out on deck. Nicander peered ashore at a sizeable town set in a bowl of surrounding mountains. There was a staggering amount of green vegetation. Covering every inch of the steep countryside it came right down to the edge of the water in a wild explosion of growth.

Unloading began immediately. In some pain from cramped limbs they were taken to a wooden jetty, then the group was roped together and led off into the interior.

What was this land? To one side a monument like a highly decorated spike reared up, on the other an exotic temple with yellow-robed priests gave out a sepulchral boom of some giant bell. The houses were utterly different, on stilts clear of the earth. The people, whose strange oriental features seemed to Nicander to be each and every one the same, wore simple loincloths and a wound headdress. There were dark pigs of mysterious breed roaming, monkeys and numberless yellow dogs. Above all there was an odour of rotting vegetation and animal sludge.

They were brought to what seemed to be a slave market and forced to squat, still roped, while account was made of their existence. Then they were led off to an adjacent barracks where they were confined.

Mercifully they were unbound and Marius began to exercise in the army way. Nicander joined him but fell out panting when Marius pressed the limits. 'Just to feel I'm alive after that fucking sea,' he said with feeling.

'I'm guessing the slave dealer who bought us from the pirates is now going to cash in,' Nicander said in a level voice.

In the morning Nicander and Marius were taken into the forest, and made to wash under a waterfall. After they finished they were given a waistcloth – a simple front and back flap joined by a string – and a plain cap.

Their cast-off clothes disappeared, one more step had been taken on the path of losing their past, their identity, their being.

Nicander gave a half smile. They would be put up for sale before very long. 'Marius. Could I give you some advice?'

'Don't you always, Greek?'

'Well, it's like this. If you remember back home, there are two kinds of slave. Those who work their lives away in the fields and those taking it easy in domestic service. I know what I'd rather do. I beg of you, Marius, do try to be docile and biddable and you'll have a chance of being chosen for service instead.'

They were paraded around a small enclosure in a line. On one side were the buyers, eyeing them professionally. Occasionally one of them would indicate an individual to be brought for closer examination.

They circled again. Nicander lifted his chin, imitating the dignity of Marius in front of him.

A cane came out and tapped Marius smartly on the shoulder. He was taken out of the line and to the prospective buyer.

In a surge of desperation Nicander left the line and ran to the elderly oriental in a full-length silk gown, whose eyes widened with astonishment. Nicander flung himself on his knees and mimed a heartfelt plea to be kept with his friend.

There was a torrent of jabbering. For a long moment the man stared down at him then imperiously gestured at the slave-keeper.

They would go as a pair. They were now the property of the man in the silk gown to do with as he wished.

He spent some time inspecting them, peering into their faces, especially that of Marius, whose pale-blue eyes seemed to fascinate him. Delicately he reached with his cane and lifted the front of his waistcloth, revealing the white skin of his loins. Satisfied, he let it drop and asked a question in a strange, song-like language.

Marius shook his head and the man repeated it several more times in different ways. At the incomprehension he smiled sadly but seemed satisfied with his purchase.

While the rest of the human cargo lay in the pit of an open hold amidships they were granted a small compartment in the bows, sheltered from rain and sun. It reeked of dried fish but it was out of the merciless sun and even had two circular holes in the side for fresh air.

There were two other two ships in their argosy – an exceedingly strange sight with their high square poop decks, flat ornamented sterns with a central rudder and a hull curved fore and aft. Most peculiar were the sails, a single rectangular one on both masts but with many rigid horizontal battens across them. A red flag with curious black markings was at the masthead of each.

Nicander and Marius were regularly allowed on deck for exercise.

They were well fed, too. At mealtimes they were given a bowl of rice, topped with small pieces of meat and vegetables.

It was not until they had been at sea for several days that Nicander tumbled to why they had been given special treatment.

'It's because we're a rare breed, different to these we see around us. See how they're all black-haired and have those foreign eyes? Flat noses and dark eyes, every one. We stand out a bit – especially you, Marius.'

He fiddled with the new clothes they'd been issued, loose baggy trousers and a simple round-collared tunic that opened in the front and was held by a small sash. On their feet they had sandals with a sole of dried rushes.

'But that's good! If we're prize breeds we won't be worked to death on a farm, we'll be shown off at feasts and such!'

'Or we could be thrown in as gladiator meat. The crowds'll go crazy to see the end of a pair of ugly outlanders.'

CHAPTER TWENTY-TWO

The dawn came as it always did, a delicate rose touching every rooftop in Yeh Ch'eng in a show of splendour at the new day. But as the light strengthened, it brought another sight: spreading across the whole horizon to the north was an ochreous cloud, ugly and ominous. Lazily rising, it was driven up from the fine wind-blown soil around the Yellow River by the advance of a great army – of the warlord Kao Yang.

Rubbing her still-sleepy eyes, Ying Mei rose from her bed and went to the window. The yellow-brown line smudging the skyline was hateful and frightening. She could hear disturbances in the city as its significance spread.

She waited for Tai Yi to appear in attendance, but remembered that, of course, she had sent her away from the palace the previous night.

Then the bedroom door opened noiselessly and her Gold Lily Lady-in-Waiting entered.

'Ah Lai! Why are you here?' Ying Mei gasped.

'Is not this my place of duty?' she said, finding combs and ribbon.

'You must leave, Ah Lai. It's not safe any more!'

'My family have gone, they are out of harm's way, My Lady. But I would not rest if I thought my *yuan kua* was left unattended.'

She parted her mistress's hair and brushed it in long, practised sweeps, then

158

paused in mock irritation. 'Do keep still, my pet,' she said, positioning her head before continuing.

'But you'll—'

'Things will go hard for us all soon, and you will need someone to look after you, my dear. Don't worry, we'll make do.'

Ying Mei choked back her feelings.

Kao Yang struck early. In the Hour of the Rabbit, before the more auspicious Hour of the Dragon could come, it was clear that a clash at arms was taking place just beyond the walls of the city. Faintly, on the still morning air, brassy stridency, screams and the continuous din of weapons carried out from a whirling ocean of dust that was blotting out the bloody scenes.

Ying Mei ran into the courtyard, trying to escape the terrifying sounds. Past the ornamental pond, the lion-carved gates empty of guards, she fled instinctively into the sanctuary of the Inner Court – and the Throne Room.

The incense braziers were not lit and the close odour of ancient decay lay heavy on the air. There were few officials in attendance but five loyal guards stood to attention close to the hanging gauze.

'Is . . . ?' she gasped.

One nodded importantly.

She fell prostrate. 'Heavenly Lord, I beg forgiveness for my intrusion. I . . . I—'

'Be still, child. You come for reassurance from your emperor and that is a very natural thing.' The voice had a strength in it, a dignity that reached out to her.

'Sire – may I . . . c-could I s-stay here?'

'Granted – if you do read to us from the classics of Han while we . . . wait.'

She rummaged in a nearby chest: works sanctified by the centuries, the learning of scholars in remote dynasties of China separated by vast gulfs of time, yet joined to the present by a golden thread of enduring values.

It steadied her as she read; the written characters, strong and upright, scribed by long-dead sages who seemed to be talking to her directly. The *Book of Odes*, the *Great Learning*, the *Doctrine of the Mean*. Confucius, K'uo Tzu, Ch'uang Tzu. She felt their strength and certainty – and was comforted.

She was deep into the transcendent mysteries of the *I Ching*, the Book of Changes, when the Grand Chamberlain appeared.

He said nothing but proceeded to perform a ceremonial kowtow, the three times three of prostrating full-length before his emperor, his forehead gently touching the ground repeatedly in humble obeisance.

He rose at last, and head bowed, intoned, 'Great Ruler – the gravest of tidings. The Lord Kao Yang and General Wu met in battle and it is my solemn duty to inform the Dragon Throne that General Wu was overcome, his forces slaughtered. He was executed in the field.'

There was the briefest hesitation before he went on, 'This, therefore, is the last sanction. Yeh Ch'eng must fall.'

From behind the hanging a serene voice replied, 'We understand.'

'Does the Son of Heaven comprehend also that there is still a little time in which the way is clear for a retreat to—'

'The Empire of Wei will not be yielded up by flight. We will occupy the throne until heaven mandates otherwise.'

The Grand Chamberlain bowed silently and withdrew to the shadows where he stood motionless, waiting. Others joined him; quiet, expressionless, dignified.

A towering stillness descended.

Long minutes turned into an hour. Distant sounds of cries, the rumbling of massed horses and full-throated shouts came fitfully.

Another hour passed. The noise faded and there was now nothing but a death-like silence. It seemed to Ying Mei that the world was clamped into an infinite suspension of time, an unreal floating of the spirit in a state of—

The door crashed open and a dozen warriors burst in. Swarthy, and in field tunics stained from the battlefield, they bore Kao Yang's cruel falcon cipher.

Fanning out quickly, with swords up, they took commanding positions.

'Let no one move!' shouted an officer at the door.

Ying Mei's heart beat wildly but she remained by her father's side, her hands tightly clasped within her sleeves. There was no sound from behind the yellow gauze hanging.

The officer walked about warily among the stock-still figures until, apparently satisfied, he gestured to one of the soldiers.

Minutes later the stillness was interrupted by voices outside and then, with a shocking suddenness, the warlord Kao Yang was in the doorway, feet planted astride, thumbs hooked belligerently into a broad belt. Under a rich scarlet battle cloak he still wore his lapped plate armour. A tall, gold-tasselled hat looked out of place on his stout figure.

He glanced about arrogantly. 'Emperor of the Wei!' he bellowed. 'I've come!'

There was no indication from behind the yellow gauze that he had been heard.

The Grand Chamberlain came forward and bowed low. 'The ancient ways of piety and respect are not so easily to be set aside. The Son of Heaven is not accustomed—'

Contemptuously, Kao Yang knocked him sprawling. Ying Mei gasped but held still, trapped in thrall to events, as was the rest of the court.

Kao Yang strode up to the canopied dais and ripped away the fine gauze in savage tugs until the Emperor of the Wei was revealed. Sitting calmly, and dressed in full imperial regalia, he stared back unblinking at the intruder.

'Yield up the throne to me. Your reign has ended this day!'

'Make your obeisance, Lord Kao Yang,' the Emperor demanded quietly. 'The Mandate of Heaven has not passed from my hands.'

'Ha! Then how do you account for me being here, with you at my mercy like a common cur? The gods have withdrawn their favour, Yuan Shan Chien, and better you know it!'

A smothered gasp went up at the great disrespect shown by the deliberate use of the Emperor's common birth name.

'You would risk the wrath of heaven, Lord Kao Yang? To seek to depose the rightful emperor is—'

'I will have the throne! Take him,' he ordered the soldiers, gesturing savagely.

They hung back, clearly reluctant to lay hands on the person of their emperor.

'Remove him or I'll have you craven scum gutted and hung like sheep!'

In visible consternation, they still hesitated, some making ineffective attempts to move forward.

Kao Yang went red with fury but was forestalled as the Wei Emperor rose painfully and said, 'We do declare that we have been overborne by forces beyond our power to control and therefore this day must yield up our ancestral rights to another.' He moved to the front of the dais and with the utmost nobility descended the steps, ignoring Kao Yang. His five guards fell prone in a kowtow, remaining in the position even after their emperor had left the Throne Room.

Regaining his composure, Kao Yang snapped to the officer, 'Take them out and decapitate them.'

As the guards were dragged away, he challenged the room with a fierce glare, then turned and mounted the steps. At the top he wheeled about triumphantly. 'Take heed, you people of Wei! Know that you see before you your new emperor, the first in line of a new dynasty – the Northern Ch'i!'

It was done. It was now manifest that the gods had seen fit to withhold their protection, and thus whatever the fate of the old, allegiance and duty would transfer to the new.

In the appalled silence first one, then several quavering chants rose. '*Wan wan siu! Wan wan siu! Wan wan siu!*' Others joined in, then more, until the hall rang with fervent shouting.

Kao Yang held up a hand and the noise quickly died. 'Each of you will make his obeisance.'

As figures came forward to fall prostrate in the ceremonial kowtow, his eyes roved suspiciously over them.

'Send for scribes, secretaries,' he commanded. 'We wish set down from this hour the first records of the Northern Ch'i.'

The Emperor leant back in the throne, his hands casually stroking the lion knobs on its armrests. 'We shall now decide on our court,' he declared, a brief nod inviting a first candidate.

'Son of Heaven and Extreme Ruler, I am First Eunuch Yuan,' the man said in oily tones, falling to his knees before him, 'as has served the previous emperor to his entire satisfaction. Should you require a discreet and worthy—'

'Yes, we know. A eunuch who has had the ear of the Dragon Throne for far too long.' The Emperor looked down on him with contempt. 'We must make sure your secrets stay with you, dog. Strangle him.'

Three soldiers fell on the stupefied man, pinioning him as he knelt. A fourth wound a silken tie around his wrists and with a knee in the eunuch's back looped it about his throat and deftly twisted it tight, holding it in place while the body jerked and writhed. After it shuddered and gave a last spasm the soldiers dragged it swiftly away, feet first.

A few in the court turned to try to escape but were quickly held with a clash of weapons.

Sick with horror, Ying Mei watched the swelling nightmare.

'So. A new emperor reigns.' Kao Yang demanded loftily, 'Bring me wine, fruit from the ice pit. If we're an emperor we mean to live like one!'

There was a terrified hesitation, then a courtier was pushed forward. He fell to a grovelling kowtow. 'S-second Eunuch Liu, Great Ruler. Does the Emperor of Ch'i prefer—'

'Honest rice wine, toad!' The man scurried away as if all the demons of hell were after him.

With a suddenly benign expression the Emperor gazed about. 'Now which is the Grand Chamberlain? Step forward that minister and we'll take a look at you.'

He approached, then performed a measured kowtow in neat, formal motions. 'Kuo Ming Lai, if it please the Celestial Dragon.'

163

Heart in mouth, Ying Mei watched as her father waited for his fate.

'Kuo. And you stayed by your emperor. What does this mean, then? That you do not recognise the succession of the Northern Ch'i? That you'll refuse to disavow the dynasty of the Eastern Wei that is now past?'

The silky menace was chilling but Kuo replied in calm, even tones. 'If I had abandoned my emperor then I would not be worthy of respect as first minister to the throne. The next emperor would be wise to distrust any protests of devotion and thus cast me aside.

'However, the Son of Heaven knows that the sage Confucius confides that of all qualities in a gentleman, filial piety is the greatest. And if the Dragon Throne intercedes for us all, then it must be said that the greatest piety is due the Emperor. Sire – if the first emperor of Ch'i occupies the Celestial Throne, then all piety is due to his person. There is my loyalty and that is my duty.'

'Ha! They said you were good, Kuo, and they were not wrong. A wordy scholar, perhaps, but you mean well.'

The eunuch Liu returned with a platter of fruits, accompanied by a younger attendant who bore the imperial wine jug and white jade goblet. Shaking, Liu began to pour from the magnificent jug, aware that on it a sinuous carved dragon with five toes was entwined about a haughty crane, the insignia of the Eastern Wei.

'I t-tremble that the Lord of Ten Thousand Years does take offence at this poor article – about its decoration, I m-mean,' Liu stammered.

'Never mind that, you cretin – pour the wine!' roared the Ch'i emperor.

Liu hastened to obey and when the goblet had been snatched and drained, he carefully refilled it, then proffered the fruit.

The new emperor picked some grapes up suspiciously. They were fat and dewy from the ice pit and glimmered with a soft inner glow of red.

In an explosion of rage he threw them aside. 'They have seeds? These are not fit for an emperor, you vile cockroach! Get me mare's nipple grapes or by heaven I'll see you leave your bones at the Great Wall workings!'

It was a near impossible demand: they grew only in the desert oasis of

Turfan and would have to be shipped out packed in snow from the Tien Shan mountains.

Kao Yang glowered. 'Do we have to show you how to serve an emperor? We'll have some order in this court if we have to punish every last one of you. What do you say to that, Kuo?'

Calmly, he intoned, 'Confucius said, "The progress of the superior man is upwards; the progress of the mean man is downwards." Therefore it is to be understood—'

'Yes, yes, we know all that. And if you're going to be our grand chamberlain you're to learn that this court will be run just how the Emperor of Ch'i wants it.'

Kuo bowed wordlessly.

'Well? Do you want to be grand chamberlain? Swear to be our man, serve us only and so on?'

'As this poor person is able, sire.'

'Then you are so promoted. Let it be recorded.'

The small eyes grew calculating and cruel. 'And as you'll be serving me at all hours, we shall be merciful. Quarters will be provided for your family here in the palace.' There was a significant pause before he added, 'And from this hour they are not to quit the Inner Court for any reason at all – under pain of instant death! Does that please you, Grand Chamberlain?'

Ying Mei swayed with emotion. To be incarcerated within this insanity for ever – it was past imagining.

Kuo's voice was controlled, his manner faultless, 'As it is written: "A Prince should employ his ministers with courtesy. A minister should serve his Prince with loyalty."'

'Have a care, Grand Chamberlain. We don't take to those who are always throwing words in our face!' He drank deeply, then meaningfully held out the goblet to Kuo himself to fill. The Emperor's face was flushed, whether from the wine or the intoxication of power it was difficult for Ying Mei to tell.

'So. What is our first matter of state?' Kao Yang pondered aloud. 'Ah. It is – what should I do with the old emperor? Finish him now, or later? Public or private? Speak up then, Grand Chamberlain!'

'Sire, that is a difficult matter. I can do no more than echo the words of the great Confucius: "He upon whom a moral duty devolves should not give way even to his master."'

'The gods rot your tongue, Kuo! Have you nothing to say for yourself?'

'Our Heavenly Dragon will believe that the sages are our guide and safeguard, that we do not err in our—'

'Enough!' the Emperor roared, flinging the goblet at him. It missed, the priceless white jade shattering on the stone floor. 'You're besotted by words!'

His speech now slurred by drink, Kao Yang went on thickly, 'Reading too much, all those scrolls, hours an' hours – not natural!'

He slumped back, then eased into a cruel smile. 'I've a cure for that, Kuo! Just the thing – this'll stop your time-wasting!'

With a leer he hailed down the hall, 'Send Master Feng to me!'

A dwarf dressed in shapeless black clothing ran up and grovelled at the Emperor's feet.

'Are you ready for work?'

Dark eyes looked up, a gobbling and energetic nodding the only reply – the creature was mute.

'Very good.' The Emperor paused for effect then hissed, 'Put out his lights!'

'No!' shrieked Ying Mei, flinging herself prostrate.

'Do it!'

Two soldiers seized Kuo by the arms and rotated him to face about, then forced him to his knees. With an inhuman calmness, Kuo lifted his head to gaze down the hall to where Ying Mei had been taken, weeping brokenly.

'Now!'

Gibbering with delight, the dwarf fumbled inside his clothing and came out with a short, black instrument. He held it high for all to see. Attached to a simple handle was a small but very sharp curl of iron.

Gasps of fearful comprehension went up as it was brandished before Kuo, who refused to acknowledge it. The dwarf jabbed at his eyes but still he did not flinch.

In his last moments of sight, Kuo sought out his daughter and fixed on her with a terrible intensity – then the hook flashed out. It caught an eyeball and with a savage twist it was plucked out, simultaneously a knife slicing its nerves and muscles.

In a mist of horror and madness Ying Mei witnessed the other destroyed and then the dwarf stepped aside from his work and she saw her father's noble face, pale and streaked – with two empty, bloody sockets, where that morning his kind eyes had looked upon her.

CHAPTER TWENTY-THREE

'God only knows where we are on this earth,' Nicander murmured, a new despair setting in; the further into these fantastical realms they went the more impossible it would be to ever retrace their steps.

They finally shaped course for land, towards a vast, sprawling seaport set in a bay between bare mountains.

On deck for exercise, Nicander and Marius mimed to their new master to be allowed to watch. As they came nearer, a panorama of roofs with upturned corners, spiky monoliths and the occasional grand building with red and gold ornamentation came into view.

Nicander and Marius were held to one side as they came into the wharf. The wafting odour of humanity, cooking and other smells of the city was utterly alien.

The boat gently bumped alongside and with a rising babble men swarmed aboard.

The pair were quickly escorted over the gangway. People stopped and stared then broke into a chatter of excited comment after they passed.

Then it was into a crowded street, pushing through gaping crowds to a courtyard with three carts, each drawn by a huge beast that stood patiently. Their heads had wide, spreading horns that were held low in a crooked curved harness. On one of the carts was a large cage made of ridged wood.

'I'm not getting into that fucking thing!' Marius protested.

'I reckon it's not so much to stop us, more to keep the others off our backs,' Nicander muttered.

A crowd was building, some gawping and hesitantly approaching, others reaching to touch their faces.

Nicander hurriedly clambered in. Marius followed and they sat on the rush floor and peered out at the sea of faces.

With a crack of whips they jerked into motion.

Once over the surrounding hills the road settled to a slowly meandering route through fields of rice and grain, meticulously kept with narrow paths between and water channels in dead straight lines.

Workers with wide conical straw hats laboured on, not looking up.

The carts ground on through the flat and never-varying scene, hauled by the docile, plodding beasts.

What would become of them? In a land in which not even a word of the language made sense was there the possibility – as there was in the Roman world – that they could emerge from slavery and make a life? Both were unmarried – was there a woman for each out there who could take to them and their strange ways?

Or was it to be a path ending in miserable degradation, a spiralling down to the dregs of existence and a cur's death?

On the fourth day the terrain changed into a broad plain between distant mountains and on the following day a yellow haze on the horizon betrayed the existence of a great city.

As they rumbled into the fringes the cart stopped and a cloth was spread over the cage. When they eventually came to a halt the cloth was flung back and Nicander and Marius saw they were in the grounds of an opulent villa.

There were men waiting in silken gowns and exotically coloured vestments, some with halberds, all with blank faces.

They were hustled in through a tiled gate with stylised lions on each side and across an inner courtyard to a large room where they were left in the care of a strapping woman in black and white with three giggling maids.

Before they knew what was afoot they were stripped naked and taken to a large tub where they were scrubbed and pummelled. They were then allowed to recover in a thin gown.

When the women left them the merchant arrived with two others. There was much deliberation but when it was over two girls were summoned. They came with pots and unguents, brushes and sponges and got to work under the stern eye of the merchant.

The first item was their hair. By now it was long – shoulder-length and unkempt. This was combed and gathered into a fetching tail.

Marius's beard was a magnificent imitation of Neptune, fierce and curly, and greatly admired but Nicander's was a more modest growth which was neatly trimmed.

Next it was indicated that they should close their eyes and they felt something being smeared on their skin.

When they opened them again it was to see in a bronze mirror that black kohl had been applied making their eyes wild-looking and rounded to an exaggeration.

An attendant returned with folded clothes.

They held them up in puzzlement. A long, featureless length of white linen, edged in red and a loose tunic not too different to what they had been wearing. And finally they were handed a weighty brooch, cheap and worthless.

An exasperated woman shook the tunics at them until they put them on, then held up the length of linen. Confused, Nicander could not think what to do with it but Marius caught on.

'Makes a passable toga. We wear it like the old-timers did!' He flung the garment over his shoulder, settling it in front in folds.

The onlookers laughed and clapped, delighted.

'Well, if this is the uniform around here, I've had worse,' Marius muttered.

Then their headgear was brought in. Tall and ridiculous, it consisted of a low crown-like piece with peacock feathers fastened to flare in all directions.

It felt awkward but had a chinstrap to hold it in place. A pair of rigid clog-like shoes varnished in red completed their outfits.

The merchant indicated they stand before him while he inspected them closely. Satisfied, he called an attendant forward and seemed to tell him to carry on.

He proceeded with a mimed lesson in elementary manners. They should keep their silence and stand politely with their hands concealed in their sleeves, their heads lowered. When the merchant indicated, they were to go on their knees and bow, then to rise on command.

If this was all it was going to take to save them from work in the fields, Nicander was willing to go along with it. Marius's face was set, giving nothing away.

The merchant stood up suddenly, and imperiously rattled off orders. Men scurried away and they were beckoned outside to a carriage. They were motioned in, the merchant climbed in opposite and they set off.

Quite soon they arrived outside the majestic wall of a great complex, the structure gaunt and forbidding with towers at the corners, upturned eaves and shaded lookout parapets.

The gate was flanked by stone lions and well guarded. They dismounted, the merchant positioning them decorously before the carriage, while he went over to the guards. One disappeared inside.

'I've got my suspicions we're not done with adventuring,' Nicander said quietly. 'I believe this rogue is about to sell us up the chain to some patrician for a fat profit.'

At the gateway a tall, acid-faced man appeared. He was dressed in a florid vermilion gown, on his chest a gold-embroidered rectangle of office, on his head a black hat with odd wings each side of it.

The merchant indicated urgently; they obediently went to their knees and bowed to the ground. A barked command and they rose again, placing their hands in their sleeves as bid.

The man approached disdainfully, passing by them once. He returned, stared at Marius's blue eyes and reached out to stroke his beard. Then without

171

warning he brutally tugged down on it, nearly bringing Marius to his knees.

The legionary spat an oath but Nicander hastily calmed him. His words, though, aroused the interest of the man who asked something in his musical but utterly incomprehensible tongue. Marius smouldered but shook his head. The man tried again in a different, rougher dialect, with the same result.

The merchant anxiously intervened but the official waved him off, and signed to them in a lordly manner to converse together.

Marius turned to Nicander and grinned savagely.

'A right heap of horseshit, don't you think, Nico?'

'Why, not worth the avoiding of the meanest charioteer, I believe.'

The official beckoned the merchant back. They spoke together and he swept away without a second glance.

'It seems he's made a sale.'

Two men shortly appeared at the gate. One handed the merchant a folded parchment. He tucked it inside his robe and then impatiently gestured for Nicander and Marius to go with them.

CHAPTER TWENTY-FOUR

Inside the gate it was a different world. Ordered, a sense of ancient peace – but also menacing in its alien mystery.

Nicander and Marius were hurried along a confusing maze of alleyways into a wide courtyard. The reek of horses left no doubt where they were but as they entered a dark passage at the end they were startled by a sudden roar of some wild beast and the agitated chatter of monkeys.

Cages extended into the gloom, some with giant snakes slowly uncoiling, others with creatures they'd never seen before.

Their escorts stopped at a door set apart from the animals and entered, pushing Nicander and Marius ahead.

A small, remarkably ugly man sat at a table spread for a meal. He looked up in annoyance but after a heated exchange the escort left.

The man raged across the room to Nicander and Marius. Because of a crooked back he could not stand straight and craned his neck sideways to peer up at them.

He threw out a torrent of words then pointed to a side room.

When it was clear they didn't understand, he grabbed Marius, rotated him to face the room, then booted him hard in the rear.

With a snarl of rage Marius turned on him.

But in one catlike move the man leapt aside, his hand flinging over his shoulder and coming back with a small but vicious whip.

'Come on, Marius. The ringmaster here wants us in that room,' Nicander intervened.

It turned out to be a small sleeping area, and for want of chairs they sat on the bed.

The man took his time finishing the meal, burping with satisfaction.

Then they were summoned with a hectoring, animal-quelling roar.

Twisted back aside, the man was different to the others. His eyes were like their own, round and without the upper fold and he had a close-trimmed beard. Was he a tribesman from the outer lands?

Nicander and Marius stood uncertainly while he looked at them in puzzlement. At length he stepped back and barked something.

It was in no language Nicander had come across in his years of merchantry and he shook his head. The man tried again, this time in a rough patter that sounded for all the world like heavily accented Persian.

Then again – and unbelievably he was hearing Aramaic, the lingua franca of traders in Syria and Anatolia!

Stammering in his eagerness he managed, 'I'm Nicander of Leptis Magna. What is your name, sir?'

The man glowered in triumph. 'Hah! Knew you were foreign devils, soon as I clapped eyes on you.'

'What are you doing here, where are you—'

'Calm down, Nicandorus whatever. Bugger, but I'm rusty in this barbarian lingo! But thank the gods we can talk – we've one pile o' things to get done.'

Marius grabbed Nicander's arm. 'What's he say? Tell me, for God's sake!'

'You speak Aramaic! H-how is this possible?' blurted Nicander.

The man eyed him shrewdly. 'Let's be straight on one thing. Wherever you've come from I don't give a toss. Now, I'm the master, you bastards are my slaves and you do what I say. Understand that, Mr Nicandorus?'

'Yes, Mr . . . ?'

'You two can call me Beastmaster Yi.'

'Tell me!' implored Marius piteously.

174

Nicander ignored him. 'Mr Yi, sir. In all mercy, please, what country is this? Where under heaven are we? I beg!'

Yi eased into a smile and slowly shook his head. 'Then you really don't know, do you?'

'No! For pity's sake . . . !'

'I'm of Chalcis, in Syria. Know it?' He went on, 'That was a fine place to grow up. But then the Persians went through it on their way to sack Antioch and I was taken. The fucking bastards sold me on to a Bactrian as a stripling and I can't remember how come I ended here. Where are you from, then?'

Nicander hastily brought Marius up to date, then told their story to Yi.

'Byzantium? I'd keep a bit quiet about that, if I was you.'

'Why?'

'They knows nothing here about the other side of the world – only that someone out there is paying big for what they've got a lot of. Silk. They doesn't want 'em to find out, break their secret of how it's made or they'd do it themselves. So anyone from that side has got to be a spy, hasn't they?'

'I suppose so. Grows on trees, of course, doesn't it?'

'Silk? Don't be stupid. It's little insects weaving away like spiders.'

'But – how?'

'Don't ask me fool questions. Talk to the peasants, they're herding the worms.'

'No trees?'

'No, no *trees*. Now – you had it tough, but you've got it better than me – I had to start on my own, no one to speak the old lingo to me! Made it all on my own, I did.'

'Yes, Mr Yi. But – please tell, where the devil *are* we at all?'

'Well, you're in Chung Kuo. Means the middle kingdom, it being the centre of the world,' he added. 'The Romans call it Sinae, Serica or something. All these people, they're your Seres. Heard of it?'

Nicander gulped, speechless.

Yi went on, 'Here they sometimes call 'emselves Sons of Chin. I'd think

175

we'd have to call it Chayna, it being easier in Aramaic, and I suppose the locals are then Chinese.

'More'n that,' Yi went on impressively. 'This here is Yeh Ch'eng, and it's the imperial city, the capital of the Northern Ch'i dynasty.'

At the puzzled look he explained, 'You've come to the big one. This is where Emperor Wen Hsuan, the Son of Heaven himself, lives and rules – and this is his palace!'

'Then . . . why are we here?'

'Ha! Because that prick Hao is banking on you being the next big act at the Emperor's feasts.'

'Act?'

'Yes! Thinks you should prance about being fantastical foreign devils, frighten the ladies, you looking so queer, like.'

'But—'

'I know,' Yi said bitterly. 'Me! The top beastmaster in the kingdom! I'm proud o' my work, I've had leopards and lambs in a chase act, snakes as will play dead and alive, dogs walking backwards. And now they want me to put on a couple of *kuei lao* strutting about acting foreign. Won't work, I tell you.'

'This is why we're wearing this stuff?'

Yi nodded. 'The merchant who traded you to Hao wanted to dress you up to look like a *kuei lao*. See, years ago, the time of the Han dynasty – 'bout three hundred years ago, about the same time as, oh, Antoninus, was it? – seems that some Romans did come here, no idea how. Didn't do 'em any good, they had nothing to trade the Chinese wanted, and never came back. But they made a splash at the time, and ever since, they think all *kuei lao* wear a toga like in old Rome, and they'll expect you to look the part.'

Nicander tried to make some sense of all that he was hearing. 'So – we live here as your slaves, and our job's to be going on public show as . . .'

'As a *kuei lao* – foreign devil. I can't see it lasting,' Yi said acidly. 'And I'll be blamed. Wen Hsuan – he's barking mad and murderous with it, you know – he tires of things very quickly. I spend all the days the gods give me trying to

176

think of something new for the prick and, every time, I leave the room feeling for my head, that it's still there.'

'So it's important—'

'It's life and bloody death! If the bastard's not amused I wouldn't give a single lychee for your chances of seeing out the year. Savvy?'

Nicander murmured something appropriate and relayed it all on to Marius.

Then the germ of a notion took root.

'Say, Mr Yi. I've been thinking. By my reckoning we're all in this together. Why don't we come up with an act that gets in the crowd, wins them over to our side.'

'Oh?'

'Well, I've an idea, but we can talk about that later. What I'd like to be assured of is that we'll be looked after. Decent living quarters, regular routine, that sort of thing. Then we'd be keen in our work, wanting more – and giving all credit to you, of course.'

'You're still my slaves.'

'In a manner of speaking. I thought more along the lines of say, foreign devils together against the odds – friends, in fact.'

'Bloody cheek! I'll sleep on it.'

CHAPTER TWENTY-FIVE

Yi honoured his end of the bargain. They were given a room to themselves overlooking the upturned roofs of the city, unheard of for mere slaves.

Their beds were raised platforms with poles at each corner from which a red cloth curtain hung on three sides. The mattress was a woven rush matting and the pillow a polished woodblock, cut away where the head would rest. There was also a black lacquered low table; stools with cunningly crafted paw-shaped legs; a side table with drawers and some colourful hangings.

Nicander stretched out. 'So, we're here in Sinae – or I should say Chayna. But in the name of all that's holy, just what's waiting in store for us?'

'Pig swill and insults,' Marius came back. 'Expect that, and you won't be disappointed.'

'Don't come it the Cynic, Marius. If I've learnt anything from our adventuring it's that you can go from king of the world to boot-licker slave in the blink of an eye. More the Stoic is the thing – we don't know our destiny therefore we do what we can to make our present existence as tolerable as possible.'

'Where's your pride, Greek? We're from a great country and don't belong here. We're going back to where we can hold our heads up, sup on decent vittles and—'

'Marius. My friend,' Nicander said gently. 'Don't torture yourself with thinking we can return one day. You've seen the seas are swarming with pirates, we'd be taken again and be in worse straits. In any case, even if we did find the gold to hire a ship, where would we tell him to go? I've no idea which direction Constantinople is, have you?'

'I'm not a quitter! While I've got breath I'll go after any way that sees me back with my kind.'

A stable boy arrived with their supper, two bowls of rice topped with chicken wings. He put the food down on the table, trying not to stare at them.

'Rice, bloody rice! Don't they have anything else?' Marius grumbled but he tucked in hungrily.

Shortly after they had finished their meal Yi appeared at the door.

'Comfortable?'

Nicander looked up. 'Why, yes, Mr Yi.'

He gave an ill-natured grunt. 'Don't count on it, you bastards. I've got a lot riding on your performance and unless you come up with—'

'In a couple of days you shall have such an act as will have them marvelling. Leave it to us.'

'Nico, you'd better have this act worked out pretty good, or we'll be in big bother with Yi.'

'I have something in mind. Don't forget, I'm a Greek.'

'What's that got to do with it?'

'Saving your presence, Marius, we Greeks are the origin of civilisation, creating high culture even before you Romans hacked down your first barbarian. Then we were overmastered by you lot, who admired us so much you imported us in quantities to entertain you.'

'So?'

'Well, then we had us Greeks and our delicacies and refinement, being asked to lay it before those whose sensibilities are, should we say, yet to reach full flower.'

'What's your point?'

'It is to say that we found a way to do it. Every time we were told to declaim a noble piece of art to such . . . we put on an act! One calculated to please. It never failed.'

Heading off an angry retort Nicander went on quickly, 'So here we have a culture without philosophy, science and poetry. And we Greeks – and I count you as an honorary Greek, Marius – will go before them and give them what they want.'

'Ha! Not me! I'd rather die in a ditch than take on pansy Greek ways! No act – I'm a Roman, bugger it!'

'Marius, I don't think you have a choice . . .'

Their 'togas' were now trimmed with purple, a capital offence in Rome. They contrived a pair of sandals each. Yi grinned at these; the Chinese would regard it as a shameful display of the naked foot.

Their hair was dressed to fetching curls, and they wore 'laurels', woven from the leaves of the tao chu tree. Yi insisted they use women's white facial powder, which together with the kohl made them fearsome foreign devils indeed.

'Are you prepared yet?' Yi nervously blustered. 'Hao presses me, the villain, and I can't hold off for much longer.'

'We're ready, Beastmaster. Tomorrow night?'

'Right! If it doesn't . . .' He made a cutting-the-throat motion, glared at them both, and stalked off.

They were taken along myriad passageways, past ornamental gardens and ponds of golden fish and into a high antechamber. The hum of conversation came from a larger room nearby.

The guards in the doorway were dressed in flowing full-length russet gowns over which they wore long purple surcoats with enormous sleeves. Each had a sword held upright in a ceremonial scabbard nearly half their height.

Nicander marvelled at the workmanship, the sense of style that was so alien, yet so elegant.

Then his mind snapped alert. He would soon be going on before this emperor and his full court.

Yi was nervously tapping his side. Marius stood grim-faced in his Roman costume.

An ill-tempered bellow erupted above the chatter and noise.

'Get ready!' Yi hissed.

The conversations died, replaced by a scraping of furniture, then silence.

Nicander peeked into the room. It was in shadows, lamps glimmering warm and gold but enough to see the audience. In the centre of the far side was a raised dais, shrouded in yellow muslin. On either hand were opulent figures in luxurious silks and elaborate headgear. Their jewels picked up the light in a dazzling display.

Yi scuttled in with a well-practised welcome and the patter of an introduction, then called out loudly in Aramaic, 'Now, the foreign devils!'

At a signal from Yi, Marius marched in and halted, looking about him as though affronted. 'I'm a Roman and proud of it!' he roared, daring any to deny it.

To the side Yi translated with pop-eyed histrionics.

There was absolute silence and some of the ladies recoiled at the fearful sight.

'Tremble all who see me, you bastards!' bellowed Marius.

Whatever was translated brought a sudden snort of mirth from behind the curtain, which was instantly followed by a general tittering.

'Is there any witless bugger here wants to argue?'

Marius paced about, glaring first at one individual then another. They jerked back in fear.

Yi rolled his eyes and burst into animated commentary which brought an excited buzz and laughter.

This was Nicander's cue. 'Hey ho, old friend!' he said airily, as he strolled into the centre of the room.

Marius looked at him. 'Hello, you old bastard,' he boomed. They faced each other and began a complicated ritual of greeting, loosely based on the

Moorish touching of head, lips and heart repeated several times.

Yi gabbled away and it brought a sudden roar of laughter.

'Shall we eat at a tavern?' Nicander suggested. This was relayed on; there was an immediate silence of anticipation.

'Where?' said Marius, shading his eyes and looking about him. This was met by another roar and those at the back pressed forward eagerly to see.

Yi gestured impatiently; a table and two stools were brought in.

'Ah. We'll go there.'

Nicander and Marius sat with much ceremony.

'Serving boy!'

Yi scurried up with a slate, bowing and scraping.

'Do you have any beef?'

Yi 'translated', his horrified eyes wide, while the audience convulsed at this reference to actually eating a lowly beast of burden.

Yi turned back and shook his head sorrowfully.

'Then we'll have lamb.'

In his aside Yi could hardly contain himself and the room bayed with laughter.

He turned back in mock solemnity and shook his head again.

'What a useless tribe of shite-hawks. Then we'll have something else,' Marius said loudly, banging the table.

Yi's translation brought a mix of hesitant laughter and apprehension. He beamed and made a quick exit.

He reappeared grandly bearing their repast, miming avoiding the 'stench' of a giant, swollen rat. There was a hiss of indrawn breath and the room fell quiet.

Nicander and Marius looked at it gleefully, rubbing their hands in delight.

Yi then solemnly presented them with oversized chopsticks which they accepted with every expression of politeness, and set to. The rat was a cunningly crafted imitation but the audience was unaware of the deception. Nicander swiftly secured the rear end of the rodent and brought it to his nose to savour its aroma.

Annoyed, Marius snatched it back, his lack of command of chopsticks ensuring it fell to the ground. He then picked it up in his hands and began stuffing it in his mouth, ignoring the cries of disgust that came from all sides.

Nicander leapt to his feet crying 'foul friend!' and wrenched out a small wooden sword concealed under his toga.

Yi's commentary brought hoots from their audience.

Marius dropped the rat and reached for his wooden gladius and they joined battle, threading between the delightfully horrified onlookers until they could make their exit.

'Yes, well then. I agree – you did a fair job.'

Gruffly, he went on, 'And the Dragon Throne sees fit to command our presence again tomorrow night for a repeat performance.' He sniffed as though it happened for every act. 'More guests – probably wants to show off his new diversion.'

Downing his rice wine, he relented. 'Knew it'd go – there's been nothing like it in the whole country. *Kuei laos* don't grow on trees this side of creation. Well now, why don't you sup with me. I've a line to the Emperor's kitchen and get the leftovers. Mouth-smacking stuff, all you can eat – that is, if you can stand rich food!'

That night they dined on fish maw in broth, pork-stuffed eggshells, fragrant duck and a wondrous array of many other delicacies.

'That kind of vittles I can stomach,' Marius declared, flopping back contentedly.

Nicander had been giving some thought to their situation as they ate. It was all very well being treated like this but in the last resort they were slaves. And their situation could change as easily for the worse, and the key to it all was Beastmaster Yi.

It would be prudent to show an interest, perhaps an obligation to their master.

'I have to say, there's a lot to learn about this Chayna,' he said with effusive respect. 'Such an impressive country, so many wonderful things. But glory be, you couldn't wish for a better place to take it in!'

Yi gave an odd look. 'You think so? You're new to these parts. There's a lot you don't know.' He looked over his shoulder then leant forward. 'Top of which is . . . our beloved emperor is a right murdering bastard the like o' which puts your Nero in the shade. Let me tell you a bit about him . . .'.

Slurping his rice wine he concluded, 'All I can advise you is to keep out of it as much as you can, don't trust anyone, let alone an official. Stay away from the whole court thing. There's plenty of work here to keep you busy, animals need hucking out, feeding . . .'

Nicander nodded. 'Now, about our repeat appearance. How about this for an idea . . . ?'

The room was packed and lively with calls. Marius played up to it, advancing and threatening the hecklers with flaring eyes and foul oaths, while Nicander scurried right up to each, making much of not understanding a word they were saying.

It was his idea to close with the audience to make their presence personal and at every opportunity the two worked the gallery. It was a stunning success; each victim reacting in their own way to their confrontation experience, afterwards loudly telling their neighbour how brave they'd been.

At the same time it gave Nicander a chance to take in the Chinese themselves. He recognised the tall and acid-faced Hao but there were many he didn't, such as the jolly-looking man in golden silk who was laughing so much tears were running down his cheeks while his lady clutched his sleeve, overcome with mirth as well.

Next to the Emperor, concealed behind his yellow muslin, stood a dignified figure in dark silk and a tall hat with sequin pendants. He was politely joining in the amusement but Nicander stopped short when he saw that where the man's eyes had been, there were empty sockets.

Further into the recesses a chubby man in the finest robes in the room was lost in hiccups, his two friends almost helpless with mirth.

And standing at the back was the most beautiful woman Nicander had ever seen. In a sheer emerald silk gown edged in blue, her hair in an ornate style and her hands clasped within her sleeves, she held herself tall and patrician.

Her face was heavily made up and perfectly rigid; her gaze went through him without acknowledgement.

Nicander tried a comic turn but it failed – she showed no signs of emotion and a lady-in-waiting thrust in front of her, indicating in no uncertain terms for him to be off.

Rebuffed, Nicander returned to Marius for the final part of their act.

From somewhere behind the yellow gauze a bellow and chortle erupted to mix with the general heckling.

The happy noise fell away in awe and Nicander guessed that a critical point had been reached.

He fell to all fours and scuttled for his life to hide under a table. Marius picked up on it and showed every sign of terror as he too found a hiding place. They trembled, rattling drinking cups and utensils.

Yi fell in with the performance. He ran to the centre and in mixed Chinese and Aramaic implored them to come out. They refused, cowering in fright. Yi stumped over and pulled Marius out by his ear, followed by Nicander, which provoked helpless laughter. The two foreign devils then made grovelling obeisance, Byzantine fashion, contriving to fall over each other – and the evening was made!

Afterwards Yi came up to them with a nod of approval. 'Humph. Emperor sends you this,' he said, handing over a red silk packet, the traditional Chinese way of presenting a gift. Inside were four tiny boat-shaped ingots of silver. 'No use to you, o' course . . .'

'We'll treasure them as a keepsake from the Emperor,' Nicander said quickly.

'If you must,' Yi sniffed. 'Oh, and Grand Chamberlain Kuo desires a word. He's a big nob, so watch your manners.'

He led them to him. It was the man Nicander had noticed before with the empty eye sockets.

When he spoke his tone was gentle but commanding and Yi translated with respect. 'Asks from where you came.'

Nicander recounted their tale of two holy men untimely captured by pirates when on a mission of a search for knowledge. He hoped it would survive Yi's translation.

Kuo civilly inclined his head at its conclusion and quietly replied.

Yi nodded. 'He hopes you are not dismayed at your first exposing to the Chinese civilisation. Says that it's not all like that. Can't think what he means. Oh, and he says to keep from saying you come from over the mountains. Like I told you, they're tender here about letting in spies.'

Kuo bowed and left, his hand on the shoulder of a silent companion who led him tenderly away.

There were others who came to see and touch, and Yi was kept busy until Nicander called a halt, pleading fatigue. He made his way back leaving Marius in the centre of an admiring crowd, making fierce gestures and growling street Latin at them.

He lay on his bed and closed his eyes, letting the rush of events settle.

It seemed there would be no more selling on, being slave chattels, human animals. They had made their mark and were here to stay and it should not be beyond the wit of any good entrepreneur to make something of it.

But he didn't know a word of the language. He set his mind to finding a way . . .

'Where's Marius?' he asked Yi as he arrived with rice wine and cups.

'He's being entertained by the Lady Yiu. Hope he can stay the course! Fancy a supper?'

Yi summoned a slave with a selection of dishes and began tucking in.

Nicander held back; he had a larger goal.

'Beastmaster Yi. I'm concerned we can't keep going with this same act. It's only good for a few more shows, don't you agree?'

Yi frowned. 'What do you mean? It's a bloody good act, keeps 'em in a roar all night.'

'Yes, but they'll tire of it. We should get something new on the way, ready to throw in when it happens.'

'What are you thinking of?'

'Well, something that we can take further, change a bit each night.'

'What's that?'

'How about, "A foreign devil learns about Chayna"?'

He let it sink in then added, 'We can have him learn chopsticks, dress in the wrong toggery, take what the ladies say amiss.'

Then he added casually, 'And most hilarious, have to learn Chinese words, getting 'em all askew and wrong meanings, that kind of thing.'

'Ha!' Yi said. 'I think you've got something there. Chinese, why, it's like no other lingo you ever heard. Listen to this: *ma, ma, ma, ma*. Get it?'

'No, what does it mean?'

'The same word! You *sings* it four different ways, it's got four different meanings. What I just said was "horse, mother, curse, well?". See?'

'Not really.'

'You're a foreigner, that's not surprising. Listen again – I'm going to say a word. Twice. But in different tones. Ready? *Mai* . . . *Mai*. Hear the difference? *Mai, Mai*.'

He could – the first tone started low and rose up higher, the second descended down. 'Yes. What does the word mean?'

'Well, there you have it. You now have two words! The first means to buy, the other to sell. Get it?'

Nicander's brow creased. How odd – singing a language to get meaning. If ever he was going to get into business in this country he'd better be careful with his tones.

'It must be very tough to learn.'

'It is,' Yi agreed. 'But it's got a good side. You Greeks have got words big enough to choke a horse. Chinese only has one beat, one word. You just string 'em along in a line to make your sentence.'

'I think we're on to something, Beastmaster,' Nicander enthused. 'Sing the wrong note, get a crazy meaning! We can really have fun with this . . .'

CHAPTER TWENTY-SIX

Nicander, a trader who was comfortable among the many tongues of the Mediterranean, took to Chinese quickly. Hearing it spoken on every side from morning to night immersed him in the sound and feeling of the musical language – and he began developing an ear for it.

On show evenings his deliberate same-word-different-tone efforts brought the house down. Marius could only learn his lines by rote but his rough Latin manner got just as many laughs.

The act became more daring: some in the audience, like Kuo, were beyond teasing but a number of the more pompous officials were easy targets and one night Nicander even went so far as to take the Crown Prince himself as his mark.

Kao Yeh, Prince of Ch'i, was fat and witless. He had little to do, as the Emperor had no intention of dissipating power, and spent his hours in pleasuring, both public and private. He and his sycophantic followers were regulars at every evening performance, their presence marked by unrestrained chortling.

Nicander crafted a not too subtle routine involving him as a drunken reveller meeting another and completely mistaking the tone value of *ou*, the word meaning to vomit. The prince duly fell about in mirth.

Then the acid-faced Hao was the victim of an earnest enquiry about a taxation form – or was that a wireworm larva?

But he saved his most cunning confection for the beautiful woman who never missed a performance but always stayed in the shadows. He had never seen her smile – the Ice Queen, he'd privately named her. But there was something about her . . .

His sketch centred on a happy-go-lucky man about town coming upon such a paragon. In a series of loud asides he debated whether he should approach the lady in question and what he should say.

She must have known what was to follow but gave no sign of it, remaining cool and motionless.

He worked up to his climax – a play on *ping*, ice, but also ailment.

Turning to her, he prepared to deliver his line but saw in her features a starkness, a dark void of the soul – and the words came out weakly.

Then her attendant came forward and beat at him with her fan in a shrill invective that was too fast for him to follow. The audience was delighted but he'd been put off balance by the woman.

Afterwards Yi was unsympathetic. 'O' course! You know why? She's the highest o' the high, talking to the lowest o' the low. Can't expect anything else, can you? We call her "The Porcelain Doll" and wonder why she's not married off.'

He sniffed. 'Now just as you're getting laughs with this wordplay, I'm thinking you can land yourself – and the act – in a lot o' bother if you get rude with the customers without you know it. What I'm saying is, this court is a dangerous place and even if you don't mean it, if you hand out insults to the wrong man, well, who's to say what'll happen?

'So what I'm going to do is lend you Ah Lee, my brightest stable boy. He's getting the same orders as you – if you're not up to speed in Chinese in a very short while you're both for the chop! You can play the fool *kuei lao* as much as you like, but now you'll know what *not* to say.'

They scuttled off in a high storm of applause.

'By glory but I think some of 'em wet themselves with your last act!' cackled Yi. This was Nicander's deliberate mispronouncing of the number nine to become the male appendage, at a crucial point in an interchange between a man and a maid.

As Nicander and Marius helped each other out of their costumes, a gong sounded.

'Must be another act,' Yi said. 'Let's see if they can do better!'

The hum of conversations and occasional laughter died away. Peeking around a column Nicander saw an old man shuffling in, helped by a younger. He reached the centre and insisted on a full kowtow.

'Ah, that's Ts'ao Fu. A famous poet but too heavy going for me,' Yi whispered. 'Haven't seen him for a while. The Emperor's got no taste for it but if he's going to be mistaken for a scholar he has to put up with it.'

When the man rose he was handed a scroll which he held up proudly in a trembling hand and began reading. It was a thin, reedy voice – and barely audible.

There was an irritated shout from behind the gauze. 'That's better,' Yi murmured. 'He's called for the court cantor. That's their job.'

To Nicander's astonishment the crowd gave way for the Ice Queen.

'She used to read Confucius and stuff to the old emperor every morning. This one doesn't like to be reminded, like.'

'That's why she's here all the time?'

'Her duty, isn't it?'

She moved with a studied grace and after an impeccable kowtow took the scroll. With a respectful bow to the poet she stood to one side to read it.

Her voice was high and silvery, the correct delivery for an imperial court, but as she read her face blossomed into a transcendent radiance.

The poem was in quatrains; she gave it an artistic lilt and expression that brought it to life in a way that was truly enchanting. Nicander could only understand one word in five but he was held enthralled.

It went on until at a particular place she faltered, and glanced at the poet who drew himself up and nodded gravely.

She resumed but the words brought a sudden ripple of unease about the room.

'Be buggered, but the old man's treading on thin ice!' Yi muttered.

'What's he saying?'

'Why, not for your ears, really, but he's waking up the old ancestors and comparing them to this one.'

There was a sudden bellow and savage words from the yellow gauze. She stopped instantly and lowered her head.

The poet shuffled forward.

'That's torn it – inviting Ts'ao Fu to change his words. He'll never do it.'

Suddenly the gauze was ripped aside and for the first time Nicander laid eyes on a Chinese emperor.

He was magnificently dressed in the richest silks, pearls, jade, rubies and sapphires and wore headgear of an impossible elaboration but was grossly corpulent, his pig-like eyes nearly sunk into a fleshy red face.

He advanced to the front of the dais with an air of menace. 'We mislike your words, poet. Change them!'

'Sire, I write as the spirits call to me. I cannot desecrate their words.' The voice was old and quavering but there was a pathetic strength behind it.

'Do you question us?' the Emperor roared. 'No man defies the Dragon Throne.'

Ts'ao Fu stood his ground, remaining respectful but mute. It was moral courage on a scale that Nicander doubted he could ever find in himself.

In the icy stillness of the hall long moments passed.

Then the Emperor turned abruptly and ascended his throne once more. He addressed the poet, his voice silky with menace. 'You sit under the old pagoda tree in the Bronze Sparrow Park for inspiration, do you not?'

'I do, Great Emperor. I humbly listen to the seven worthies of the bamboo grove that—'

'Yes, yes. Well, we know what to do about that. Imperial Guard!'

An officer jerked to attention and knelt before him.

'Take our poet out to his pagoda tree where he got the inspiration for this dross. Then strike off his head as a warning to his seven worthies to do better next time!'

In a chill of horror Nicander watched the old man led away.

The Emperor settled back and beamed. 'Well, why all the long faces? Music! Dancing! Strike up there!'

It was now clear they were walking a tightrope. Sooner or later this rabid despot would turn on them. Nicander whispered to Marius. 'Just to say, m' friend, I'm with you now. I want to get out of this madhouse situation as fast as we can.'

But they had long discovered that the palace was impossible to escape from. And even if they made it to the open country, what then? Two foreign devils on the run would not last out the day.

There was movement outside their room. It was Yi, who gave way to another. 'Chief Scribe Wang, you bastards.'

A young man with the calm of a scholar bowed to them. 'The Grand Chamberlain wishes to see you, should you be free.'

'Go!' commanded Yi.

Kuo's modest lodgings spoke of higher and deeper reaches of the mind. In the first chamber were striking hangings of Chinese characters in many styles and exquisite watercolours of bamboo and flowers.

Beyond, was a neat room with solid, carved furniture; a single incense stick sent up a tiny spiral into the dark rafters of the ceiling.

Kuo met them with disarming courtesy. 'Do forgive the untidiness. I now live alone and cannot be trusted with the civilities.' Nicander tried to avoid staring at the Grand Chamberlain's face with its empty eye sockets.

There were no chairs; Wang noiselessly led them to a low raised platform, inset with carnelian stone.

'I shall not detain you long, gentlemen. I've asked you to me, more to indulge my own conscience than anything of consequence,' Kuo continued. 'The younger one. May I know your name?'

'Sir. It is Nicander of Leptis Magna.'

Kuo faced him and tried to say the syllables. 'Your grasp of our language is better than my foreign babbling, I fear. We'll have to find you a Chinese name.'

He hesitated. 'I believe you to be a man of intelligence, probably of some learning. That is why I asked you here, sir. I confess I feel it heavy on my spirit that you have, through no fault of your own, been deflected from your sacred purpose. To survive, you must suffer the indignity of actors, playing the simpleton for the common mirth.'

He paused, considering his words. 'I wish to say to you that such sacrifice in two learned gentlemen – without repine – has won my most sincere admiration.'

'That is most kind of you.'

'At the same time I would have you know that the Chinese character is not one that is readily perceptible in the confines of a court. Rather it may be found in the company of scholars, men of discernment and delicacy in the arts of the gentleman. As the Master Wang Hsueh Che here.'

Wang flushed with embarrassment, protesting his unworthiness, which Kuo politely ignored.

'I wish to say to you, that what you witnessed today was . . . in the way of a prince perhaps not yet fully enlightened in the *tao* of rulership under heaven. His youth as a warrior has made him impatient with the gentler and more demanding imperatives of an ethical ruler. I simply ask that you do not judge our civilisation by the hasty acts of one such.'

'We shall reflect on your words, Lord Kuo,' Nicander responded carefully.

'And . . . and I'm obliged to say it, that if heaven wills it, the future may well be more blessed than the present.'

'Sir?'

The Grand Chamberlain gave a slow smile. 'How I wish . . . but you are bound men and cannot choose your path. In the fullness of time, perhaps . . .'

'It makes no difference,' Nicander said later after relaying the conversation to Marius. 'There's nothing here for us except what we saw today. We have to get away!'

Yi was consumed with curiosity at this second meeting with the Grand Chamberlain and demanded to know what had taken his slaves to his residence.

Nicander saw no reason not to tell him and detailed the meeting.

'What did he mean by, "if heaven wills it, the future may well be more blessed"?'

'Oh, that's plain enough. The whole country hopes the bastard will drink himself to death, then Crown Prince Kao Yeh will succeed. He's a sot and an idiot but hasn't a grain o' spite in him. We'll then all breathe easy, believe me.'

They supped on delicacies from the royal kitchens but Nicander had little appetite.

Yi ate greedily then sat back. 'We really ought to tighten up the paying taxes act. How do you feel about moving to levels?'

'I don't understand.'

'Chinese levels. They love 'em. Let's find you an example. Ah – here at the palace, Historian Shih. Now he was originally a Uighur – that's a barbarian from the far borderlands. His name was some awful thing like Scythian. They had to give him a name they could get their tongue around so they gave him "Shih Toyun" which sounds like it to the Chinese. That's the first level of meaning.

'Now that makes him Mr Shih, but the whole three character thing means "One who holds up the clouds". This is clever, because he's taller than your ordinary Chinese. That's the second level.

'At the third level we have that anyone who tries to hold up the clouds is ambitious to succeed, reaches for the highest, one to admire. Then the final level is that *Shih* sounds the same as *Shih* meaning "scholar of history", which o' course is what he does. See?'

'You mean anything that's said can have all these levels at once?'

'Yes. Especially poems and stuff written down.'

Nicander frowned. His was a language of precision and logic, he was proud of its accuracy of meaning and definition. How could a language so loose compare to it?

'You'd have to be very careful how you addressed the ladies, I'd guess.'

'Ha! This is why I think we can do a lot with it. Hang a pause until they get it, let the brighter ones start the others off.'

They set to work but were interrupted by a gong somewhere beginning a regular boom.

Yi froze. 'I don't like it. That's the general signal to attend the Emperor. Never done except at sacrifice time or . . .'

He pulled himself together. 'Means all of us. At the Hall of Eternal Peace.'

It was the biggest of the palace halls, able to easily take the half thousand that were assembling. A vast, polished, black stone floor reflected the richness of the gowns and robes, the jewelled ceremonial headgear and peacock feathers.

Raised up on a dais at the far end was a colossal throne with extravagant carving glittering with gold leaf. It was set before an even more elaborately ornamented screen. On each side soaring dusky-red columns displayed tall yellow panels with giant characters in black.

The nobles and ladies assumed their places at the front, lesser mortals behind. From the back Nicander took in the sweep of majesty that was the Celestial Throne.

Then without warning there was a sudden crash as the main doors were closed. A detachment of guards took position in a single line around the assembly.

'This is bad,' Yi whispered. 'Never had this happen before. Wonder what's going on?'

There were frightened conversations, spreading confusion – would Emperor Wen Hsuan soon make an appearance?

A massive gong sounded. Then the personal bodyguard entered and formed up, halberds and swords gleaming. Finally the Emperor stalked in, glaring about him before ascending to his throne.

'The Great Lord, Ruler of all under Heaven, the mighty and ever-victorious, Emperor of Northern Ch'i.'

The stillness was so acute that Nicander could hear his own breathing.

195

'Summons his palace to hear vile and dreadful news.' The herald was so nervous his scroll trembled as he read. 'Signifying such foul omens that he deigns to speak to his liege subjects himself to allay their fears.'

The Emperor stalked to the front of the dais and looked out in terrible deliberation over the mass of his people, first to one side, then the other. Then he spoke in a heavy, intimidating growl.

'I would have you know that an odious and abominable plot against ourself, the Son of Heaven and intercessory with the gods – has been thwarted.'

There was a tremulous hush.

'Which was revealed in time by the selfless loyalty of one man – Chancellor Hao! Who brought to us proof of the plot, knowing it would cause us the utmost grief, but out of his duty to the Dragon Throne felt it necessary to acquaint us with its contents.'

Hao stood silent, head bowed, hands in his sleeves, the picture of rectitude.

'I have it here!' the Emperor roared, waving a grubby sheet. 'Treachery, betrayal and filial impiety enough to make heaven itself weep!'

He lowered it, letting the tension build.

'Kao Yeh! Crown Prince! Step forward and make your obeisance!'

At the front of the assembly there was a brief confusion and a chubby figure came forward and prostrated himself before the Emperor.

'Rise up! Come before me.'

The Emperor thrust the sheet violently at his son. 'Read! So all may hear!'

As he did so Nicander could tell what it was – a soulful attempt in verse at a bewailing of his situation, being the inheritor in due course of the greatest rank on earth but at the present time to be made to suffer under the tyranny of a despot.

'This is yours?'

It would be useless to deny – Chinese writing was as individual to the writer as a portrait of them.

'It is, Father – that is, Most Excellent and Wise Emperor of All Under Heaven.'

Without a doubt it was the result of a drinking bout which had young men competing in witty writings into the early hours. Nicander wondered if it contained clumsy attempts at levels of meaning which had been overlooked under the influence of the wine, but which now held a sinister significance.

It had to be Hao's doing. To secure the trifle would have taken planning and guile. The prize was obvious: complete trust by the Emperor and therefore power over the entire court.

'Then be it on your own head,' the Emperor snarled. 'To seek to usurp the prerogatives of the mandate of heaven – this is an act of treachery and filial ingratitude that may not be forgiven.'

He glowered at the hapless prince. 'You have one course of redemption and one only.'

'Sire?'

'Master Feng!'

From somewhere close by the mute dwarf scuttled out.

'Offer the chalice to Prince Kao Yeh!'

A dark-green jade cup was thrust under the prince's nose.

'No!' he stammered. 'I've done nothing wrong—'

Yi leant close to Nicander. 'It's poison!' he hissed.

'Take it!' roared the Emperor, shaking in fury.

'I-I can't, it's not fair, I didn't—'

'Seize him!'

There was a brief struggle as the prince was forced on his back on the front of the dais in full view.

His voice distorted into a shriek which turned to a bubbling squeal as the dwarf carefully emptied the cup into his mouth, deftly stepping back when his task was done.

The Emperor waited impassively until the last despairing spasms and contortions were over, then resumed his throne and declaimed, 'Thus dies a vile and treacherous usurper! By this let it be seen and known that there are none – not a one – who may seek to defy their emperor's majesty with impunity!'

197

Then he stood abruptly. 'We see among you those with base treason in their hearts! But it is in vain, for let it be known – such perfidy *will* be found out. I have given special powers to Chancellor Hao to go among you and root you out! Know and tremble, for no mercy will be seen for any who cry against their emperor!'

CHAPTER TWENTY-SEVEN

Back in the privacy of their quarters Yi didn't waste words. 'That's it! Not staying another fucking minute in this crazy place. I'm away!'

'But – you're Beastmaster. Where—' Nicander said lamely.

'I'll admit it was a good screw, but better out and away, than here with that mad bastard on the loose.'

'How about us?' Nicander spluttered. 'You can't just . . .'

'Watch me.'

'Could you first free us as slaves?' he ventured.

'No. You belong to Hao. Ask him.'

'Beastmaster, sir, *please*—'

'Out of m' way, I've got things to do,' Yi said irritably and hurried to his room. Soon they could hear sounds of furious activity.

'You have to take us with you,' Nicander called out in despair.

'No!'

'You can have the silver sycees the Emperor gave us.'

'Piss off, I'm busy.'

'Sir, please, we're—'

Yi stormed back to confront them. 'Wasn't I clear enough? I'm off, you lot are on your own. Do your act how you like, why should I care? Hao will find another beastmaster, it'll then be his worry, not mine.'

'We're marked, you know that?' Marius muttered darkly as Yi left. 'Any trouble in a city, it's always "get the foreign bastards" first.'

'It's the Emperor who's going to do us, believe me. One night he'll not like the act and have our heads sliced off just for the fun of it,' Nicander retorted.

'And without Yi we've got big bother. No one to stir the crowd, get 'em going, like.'

'Look, forget the act. If we can't find a way to get out of here . . .' But they had been over it all before and seen no solution. Why would now be any different?

In the early afternoon a messenger came. 'You are summoned before the Grand Chamberlain,' he announced loftily. 'He wants you to tell him what you're going to say at the next act, that it won't offend the Emperor.'

At the residence of the Grand Chamberlain they were ushered in to a little courtyard. Nicander sensed something was wrong – but couldn't put his finger on it.

Kuo arrived with the faithful Wang. 'I've asked you here to detail for me the substance of your next act before His Effulgence,' he said, rather more loudly than necessary. 'We should, I suppose, go somewhere quiet to discuss this – we don't want to give away the plot to others now, do we?'

They proceeded to a small building. 'This is my sanctuary, my place of meditation.'

Inside it was dark, lit by two lamps only on a high writing desk, but it was warm and enfolding.

Kuo went familiarly to the desk while Wang motioned them to a carved bench opposite, glancing outside before closing the door.

'Now. My apologies for bringing you here under false pretences,' Kuo said. 'The matter, however, is critical and pressing. I'm bound to say, to my infinite sorrow, that the Emperor has now transgressed the rules of conduct for a ruler far beyond those laid down for him by the ancient sages. I believe him now to be past redemption, remote from enlightening by any moral precept.'

He held as still as a statue for long moments and Nicander thought him lost to the world. Then he continued, 'Therefore my loyalty to his misrule is now withdrawn, for how can I lend my hand and heart to acts abhorrent to the meanest? It would make me complicit in them and that I cannot bear.'

'Master, why are you telling me this?'

'You are right. This is none of your concern. Only inasmuch as at this point I must place my life, and that of those I hold dear, in your hands.'

At first Nicander thought he had misheard. 'Your l-life?' he stuttered.

'I am about to make you both a proposition. One that if it came to the ears of Chancellor Hao or the Emperor would undoubtedly result in my summary execution. If you do not wish to hear it, you must go now.'

Every instinct screamed at him to leave instantly – not to get involved in a life and death palace intrigue as a lowly player in whatever plot was unfolding.

Before he could say anything, Kuo quietly added, 'I should perhaps tell you that the proposition will be to your undeniable advantage in your present situation.'

Nicander froze. If he left now it would be to abandon the only chance that had presented itself to them.

'Please go on, sir.'

'Should I provide you with a means of escape, gold, documents and so forth, would you undertake to be gone from here – with my daughter whom I would place in your protection as holy men I do trust?'

Nicander caught his breath. From anyone else but the all-powerful grand chamberlain the words would be incredible.

'Master, I – we're honoured in the trust you have placed in us. Do pardon while I explain the matter to my brother monk.'

He turned to Marius whose eyes lit up as he spoke. 'Take it! Go – what're you waiting for?'

Nicander held his gaze and whispered, 'I have deep worries. We'll be caught up in all this plotting up to our eyebrows, is one. The other is that do you want a woman, high-born at that – and they're the worst – around our necks while we're trying to get away? If we go with this, then whatever else we come up with has to be thrown aside, we'll only get one chance!'

'I say yes!' snarled Marius. 'Woman or not, I want out of here as I need air!'

'I don't like it! We'd be—'

'We're going! Tell him!'

Nicander realised if he didn't agree, Marius would go on his own and be damned to all else.

He turned to Kuo. 'Sir, we'll do it.'

The sudden easing of the man's body told its own story. 'You cannot believe how grateful I am that my daughter will be clear of this . . . this gathering whirlwind, and you have my eternal thanks for it.'

In a voice charged with emotion he continued, 'The details be pleased to leave to myself. It must be very soon, I fear. Do hold yourselves ready, for it will happen fast and without chance of return.'

'How will we know—?'

'We cannot be seen meeting again. The next time will be on the night of your departure. The signal will be a messenger requiring you to present costumes for my approval. Bring one, but I have to tell you that of your belongings you will only be taking what you have on your person.'

'I understand, Master.'

'Then I will bid you good night – and again, please know you have my most earnest expression of gratitude!'

Marius was beside himself in glee. 'We're on our way! No more poncing about, soon we'll be as free as birds!'

'You haven't thought about this much, have you, Marius?'

'What's to think? We're away out of it, thank the gods.'

'Has it ever occurred to you that this doesn't really add up? It's starting to smell – something isn't quite right. Answer me this: why is it that we, slaves –

and holy men too, let it be said – are being asked to conduct a high lady out of here? Why not a dedicated band of warriors, a tight crew of compulsors or whatever they call them here. Why us, who stick out as foreigners?

'And another thing. Why is Mr Kuo and his doggy assistant staying? You'd think he'd want to be gone, surely.'

Was it that they were to be sacrificed as cover to a larger plot?

CHAPTER TWENTY-EIGHT

The next afternoon an imperial herald arrived. 'Where's Beastmaster Yi?' he demanded.

'Oh, he's indisposed.'

'Message from His Celestial Majesty. Performance tonight – he wants it clear it had better be funny, he's got guests.'

'Yi *sheng* is not well. Can we not—?'

The herald gave a cynical smile.

'Without him . . .'

There was no response from the man.

'Message from the Grand Chamberlain,' a voice piped up behind him.

'Get away, young 'un,' the imperial herald grunted. 'Emperor before Grand Chamberlain, mate.'

'Oh, let him deliver his message,' Nicander said in desperate hope.

'Master Kuo wants you to present your costumes to him for approval,' the youth said. 'Right now, he means.'

'Ah, yes. Of course.'

His heart began pounding but Nicander managed to tell the imperial herald that the Emperor's wishes would be obeyed for the performance.

* * *

Their escape was on!

In the matter of belongings there was no difficulty. They had lost all they owned to the pirates and apart from their sycees had little to show for their time at court.

At the Grand Chamberlain's residence they were quickly brought inside and the gate firmly shut.

A servant hurried them to the meditation chamber. Kuo was leaning on his staff, serene and calm. Wang stood close by.

'This night you shall be made free. Are you prepared?'

'Master Kuo. There are things that are not clear to us. For instance—'

'All will be revealed to you in good time. I must first ask you – will you truly do this? As a father, the placing of my daughter in the protection of another is a matter I cannot take lightly. Do you both give me your word that you will stand by her until she reaches sanctuary?'

Satisfied with their response, Kuo continued, 'This is the plan. The Emperor will be exceedingly angry at her departure – we are both confined here under penalty of death, but more important, she would be seen as a focus for any popular rebellion, and would be hunted down mercilessly throughout the kingdom. It is my fervent desire that my dear daughter is safely quit of a land that is fast descending into a pit of chaos, therefore I ask that you conduct her to the only place where I can be certain she will be, heart and soul, safe from his reach.'

'Where is this, sir?'

'Out of China to the lands beyond the mountains – to your own country.'

'B-but . . .'

'In this way you will not only be able to depart from here, but also gain the means to return to your native soil. This is my assurance that you will have every reason to stay by her.'

Nicander fought a torrent of doubts. Just how realistic was Kuo being – did he know where the Byzantine Empire actually was, seeing that nobody here was aware it existed? Had he taken into account the pirates, outer barbarians, the incredible distances?

'Master, how do you plan we do this?'

'I desire you should journey to Chang An, where my brother is a merchant. From there caravan argosies of silks go west, into the setting sun to Ta Ch'in as of old. The precious cargoes are passed hand to hand, but where goes the silk, so may a traveller, I'm persuaded.'

'It will probably cost much, sir. A very great deal, I fear. And if—'

Kuo fumbled for a chest on a nearby table and laid his hand on it. 'In this coffer is enough to see you through to Chang An. There my brother will make arrangements for you to draw upon his account with his agents along the route. He is a well-established man and may be relied upon.'

A tidal wave of hope threatened to undo Nicander's cool while he rapidly brought Marius up to date.

He turned to Kuo, 'Sir, you may rely on us, too.'

There was one last detail. 'My country is not renowned for its charity, sir. If your daughter—'

'She will be given the means to subsist there independently as a lady of nobility. Your mission will be accomplished the day you set foot on your native soil, for you will understand it can never be permitted that my daughter finds herself reliant on the charity of holy men, however well disposed.'

Against all reason . . . a miracle was happening! In a very short time they would be free – and on their way . . .

Nicander felt a gush of warmth toward the older man. 'Master – what will happen to you? I mean, after—'

'Do not concern yourself. I am condemned the instant it is known that both you and my daughter have fled. I shall leave at the same time with you, but part to go elsewhere. My plans are well advanced. Master Wang and I together will fly at the utmost speed to a sanctuary I long for with all my soul, the Temple of Shaolin, where I ask nothing more than to end my life in the contemplation of the sublime.

'Timing is crucial. In a short while it will be dark. As the Hour of the Snake is sounded we leave, going by separate ways to meet again with my

206

daughter and her lady-in-waiting – at the imperial stables. There, we will be told what to do. Have you any questions?'

'What is the nature of our journey once we are outside these walls?'

'In the chest are all requisite passes and documents. In these you are holy men accompanying a lady on a perilous journey, for you will be hiring a conveyance to take her on an urgent visit on my behalf to her uncle in Chang An, who lies sick.'

'A lady on her own? Will not this—'

'You are holy men accompanying her, it is a well-understood custom. However, at this point I must remind you that under no circumstances should you admit to coming here from over the mountains. You will be suspected of being a spy and would never be allowed to leave China.'

'Then where do we say we're from?'

'Some kingdom or other, it doesn't signify. Only that you do not come from far parts of the west.'

'Yes, Master. Your daughter. She's a . . . lady and we are both men. Do you not think that—'

'You are men, but holy men. I understand your concern over her female needs but rest your fears; she will be accompanied throughout by her lady-in-waiting, Lai Tai Yi, who is a most loyal and determined individual.'

'Ah.'

'The chest will be in her charge, for you holy men should not be burdened with the cares of this world.'

'Only one more question, sir. Could you be clear as to who exactly you consider to be in command for the journey?'

'My daughter has been instructed to take wise direction from which of you shall be foremost in the making of decisions.'

He motioned to Wang. 'Now, might I suggest you prepare by putting on these monkish robes? They will allow those of my country to know you as holy men and will give you a certain protection. The divines in China shave their heads, but your beards identify you as foreign. These are not unknown, passing to and fro from Tibet and the outer world on their search for knowledge and you will have no trouble.'

He reflected a moment then added, 'And I've been giving some thought to your Chinese name. I rather fancy "Ni K'an Ta" for you, sir. It is by way of meaning "One who is able to distinguish great ventures". Is it to your liking?'

'Indeed, Master.'

'Then so shall it be, Ni *hsien sheng*. Now your friend. How does he like, "Ma Lai Ssu" do you think? It has the meaning "Earth god who tames wild horses". Will you explain to him?'

While Marius – Ma *hsien sheng* – gloried in his new name, Nicander said gravely, 'Master, we thank you with all our heart! If we could ever—'

'You have lifted a burden from me that has been monstrous these last months, and I go rewarded by being the instrument of restoring two brave and worthy seekers after truth to the land of their birth.'

A stone chime sounded softly.

It was time.

'Are we then ready? You gentlemen to the left, Master Wang and I go to the right. Then let us depart!'

In a thrill of hope they stepped out into the stillness of the night. Over in the palace there was the usual revelry and Nicander imagined the explosion there would be when the Emperor called for his performers.

He and Marius walked as quickly as they could to the stables, close by their own quarters.

They entered the dank and stifling building and stood in the darkness listening. There was a creak and the door at the end opened. Four figures; two men, two women. Nicander recognised Kuo and Wang, who motioned them into the courtyard.

There, the rising moon provided just enough light to make out features. Wang was holding the chest. One woman carried two bags. The other, standing tall and still, was the Ice Queen!

'I may have omitted to make introduction. This is my daughter, the Lady

Kuo Ying Mei. My dear, this is Ni K'an Ta and Ma Lai Ssu.'

Taken aback at the identity of his charge, Nicander nevertheless managed a bow, returned with a distant inclination of the head.

Kuo spoke urgently, 'We must not delay. Master Wang, is . . . ?'

'This way, everyone!'

They hurried over to the stalls where a large cart hitched to two horses waited. It was filled with animal dung.

'Aboard quickly, please!' the driver hissed, his eyes showing white.

Wang ducked under the cart and pulled a bolt. A trapdoor swung down. 'Get in!' There were gasps from the ladies.

Kuo was first, disappearing up into some recess. He was followed by the reluctant women and then it was Nicander's turn. He scrambled under the cart, then looked up – nothing but darkness. Guiding hands pulled him over to the side where he wedged himself in, gagging at the smell. Marius followed, then the chest.

Wang shot the bolt, gave a muffled farewell and they jerked into motion.

'Only a short distance and then he will let us out,' Kuo said in a shaky voice, adding that this was the usual run for the dung cart to the village, done at night to avoid offending smells while the palace was at work. The regular crew had been told that they were given leave to drink the Emperor's health that night and trusty men had prepared and loaded the vehicle.

It was well thought out: an internal box under the dung, invisible from the outside.

The cart slowed, then stopped. The tension was unbearable.

But soon it started swaying forward again. After a few minutes Nicander sensed a definite downward angle.

'We're through the gates!' Kuo's voice came weakly. 'Only a little while to the river.'

They heard a horse drawing near and the cart stopped. There was a knock, then the bolt slid across and the trapdoor swung free with a sudden intoxicating blast of clean night air.

Wang helped them out and they stood disoriented for a moment.

Behind was the black mass of the city walls, studded with lights. A little way in front of them glittered the river gliding past in the moonlight.

'This way, quickly!'

He led them to a meadow. In the dark it was difficult to make out shapes and he frantically looked about. 'There! A boat waits!'

They made their way through the thick turf, stumbling against grass clumps. Out of the dimness came animal noises as they pressed on in a fever of excitement.

Halfway across they heard sounds from the direction of the city walls: distant cries, a powerful war drum starting an urgent beating.

'We've been discovered! Go for your lives!'

They ran – the boat was not a hundred yards away up the river by the bank. A figure stood nearby.

A line of torches flickered to life along the city walls and a trumpet bayed out.

'No!' screamed Wang as their boatman, now just fifty yards away, panicked and shoved off without them.

'The slivey bastard!' Marius shouted and waded into the water, making for the fast-moving boat to intercept it.

It came on but he was up to his neck and the man had not seen him. As it passed by, a hand shot up and seized his ankle, pulling hard. The man gave a despairing cry and toppled into the water. Marius lost no time hauling himself in. He found the steering oar and brought the boat safely in to nudge into the shallows.

'Move!' he roared.

Falling over each other they scrambled aboard. The women disappeared into a shelter aft while Kuo and Wang squatted in the middle.

Marius seized one of the boat oars, gesturing to Nicander to take the other. Wang clambered up to the steering oar.

'Go!' Marius bellowed. They heaved mightily and the boat came off the mud.

Nicander stroked in time with Marius and the boat swung to face downstream.

They began to move out and away. Wang found the main channel and soon the banks were slipping past. Dare they hope?

Nicander did not have Marius's brute strength but with his best efforts he pushed and heaved, his lungs bursting, the ill-balanced oar a burning weight.

As they slid around a curve in the river, to their horror, they saw a squadron of cavalry on the bank. A challenge came to pull in.

Orders cracked out ashore. Half the soldiers reined in, extracted their crossbows and opened fire while the others kept pace. Bolts hissed past, some skittering in the water nearby. Two made a solid thunk into the hull.

'Keep down!' Marius gasped. Wang steered the boat away but another squadron came into view on the opposite bank. There was nothing for it but head midstream.

The river widened; they were out of range. But the cavalry squadrons either side cantered along effortlessly, waiting for their chance.

Nicander felt sickened. They would never lose their pursuers, and at some point the river would narrow or become shallow enough for horses, and then . . .

'The Four Pheasants Gorge – we cannot go around now!' Wang said grimly.

'What do you mean?' Nicander gasped.

'Ahead, around the bend the river narrows through a cliff chasm, goes over rocks. We cannot go on!'

They would be forced to land the boat.

On the banks the two squadrons slowed to a trot, the glitter of unsheathed steel appearing as they waited to see which side their prey would choose.

They heard the first dull roar of the gorge, a dark cleft through an escarpment of broken rocks that stretched across from either side. Flecks of white showed at its maw.

'We must go through – who's with me?' Marius roared.

Kuo spoke for them all. 'Better death in the cataract than at the hands of Wen Hsuan!'

211

Marius elbowed Wang aside and gripped the steering oar tightly. His eyes fixed on the approaching terror, calmly judging distances, angles.

Small whirlpools appeared and their onward velocity increased as they were gripped by the current. 'Get the oars in,' he rapped. 'Everyone, low as you can get – we're going through!'

Angry shouts came from the banks.

The thunder of water increased but even in the rising moon the narrows were in shadow – there could be anything waiting for them.

Nicander glanced at the shore. 'Look!'

On either bank the horses were being reined in, baulked by the craggy escarpment across their track, their riders brandishing weapons in frustration.

He peered into the darkness ahead in cold fear. They had escaped from one fate but were hurtling to another.

The sides of the gorge whipped past and a heavy roar battered their ears in the confined space. As his eyes got used to the gloom Nicander made out the figure of Marius, standing on the afterdeck, heroically straining to keep the boat from splintering against some lethal rock.

Their speed was now dizzying – vague black masses flicked by and the odour of churning water and pungent weed rose up.

Kuo and Wang crouched with Nicander in the middle of the boat. Ying Mei and Tai Yi huddled in the little shelter.

They plunged on. It was impossible to make out much ahead; the very next instant could see them smashed to their deaths.

The gorge seemed endless, the darkness near impenetrable. White lathering over deadly rocks showed as Marius slewed the fragile craft this way and that to avoid them. Nicander could only imagine the burning pain in his body.

The lip of the chasm was still relentlessly high. How much further?

Then a massive buttress jutted out from one side, obscuring what was ahead. It was also constricting the waters – and the little craft gathered speed into the roaring chaos.

Nicander knew it was beyond even Marius to take them through alone and hauled himself up beside him, grabbing at the oar.

'Tell me!' he yelled against the noise.

Marius nodded. 'Left!'

They thrust against the shuddering haft, the frightful strength of the shooting water transmitted directly to them.

'Right!'

It was working: they were slipping past the vicious hazards in the narrowing channel, but then the buttress loomed close. There was no sight of the river ahead which seemed to be curving around it.

'We take it in the middle!'

In a nightmare of speed and terror they shot past and into the void beyond – it opened up wide but just ahead, spreading right across their track was a continuous chain of white.

There was nothing they could do except scream a warning.

The boat hit and reared up before dropping with a rending crash on the other side: Nicander felt himself flung into the air and then plunging into the water. He was rolled and tossed, choking and helpless until it quietened and he managed to get his head above water. Thrashing about he saw that the boat had entered a broad patch of placid water and Marius was levering it towards a sandy outcrop.

He struggled towards it and was hauled in as the others scrambled, damp and trembling, on to the sand.

'Got to check the boat,' Marius croaked.

The craft was fast filling from a splintered plank. Without tools there was no possibility of repair.

'We can't wait here,' Kuo said through chattering teeth. 'The soldiers will find a way around before long – we must leave!'

'Then get in and bail – every last bastard!' Marius ordered.

They found whatever they could to use and when the boat was refloated even Kuo, feeling for the gunwale, bailed as hard as he could.

'Oars again,' growled Marius at the steering oar.

Nicander and Wang took up their labour once more. They were keeping pace with the leak – they had a chance!

The night wore on until, imperceptibly, delicate light stole in to lift the darkness.

Ahead, Wang spotted a familiar fork in the river. 'Heaven be praised!' he gasped. 'Ye Ching!'

At a rickety bamboo landing place their little craft came to its rest and they scrambled thankfully to the shore.

Wang made off quickly down the river path to the village while Kuo, clinging to his staff with weariness, called the rest together.

'It has been a cruel experience for us all, but as so often in our mortal existence, with a hidden gift. In the usual way we should have disembarked before the gorge, made our way across country to the tributary and in another boat followed it down the longer way to this conjunction. Instead we went by a more direct, and you will no doubt agree, a faster route.'

He straightened painfully. 'By this, we have broken through the search cordon and have arrived here at Ye Ching well on schedule. They have no proof that a single fleeing boat held their quarry and therefore they cannot afford to relax their pursuit in other directions. I'm certain that if we move without delay we will stay ahead of them.'

Wang met them at the inn. 'Sir, we are desired to wait in the private room while our transport is prepared.'

'We have little time to waste,' Kuo said briskly once they were inside. 'Thus I will tell you now what must be done.

'You will head as rapidly as possible for the north-west. You will be safe there after crossing the mountains at the Wu Tsen Pass; on the other side you will reach the Yellow River. From there it is a simple journey to Chang An and the rest of your adventure.'

'And you, sir?'

'Master Wang and I will be taking horse in the opposite direction, to Shaolin.'

'Then . . .'

'Yes,' Kuo said with infinite gentleness. 'It is therefore here that we must part.'

Ying Mei's features remained blank.

'First, I give over to you the chest. It contains sufficient means to get you to Chang An, together with required passes and documents.'

Tai Yi firmly took it in charge.

'Next, I ask my daughter to accept this staff of mine that has done me such service.'

'F-Father . . . ?'

'I do so for a reason. It is this.' From inside his robe he brought out an extraordinary object, a thick length of black hair, shiny with lacquer. He looped it over the tip of the staff.

'It is the tail of the yak, a beast not seen in China but much esteemed by the western barbarians. It is a sign to them that you are of noble birth and you will be respected. Receive it with my blessing.'

'And to you gentlemen – staffs also for your journey, but more than that, I now give my daughter into your protection.'

'My Lord, we . . .' Nicander struggled for words.

'I take that to be your accepting. Then . . . then if you will permit me, I would desire to take farewell of my daughter in private.'

Nicander motioned for the others to leave and they went outside into a bright early morning. There was a small carriage waiting, with gauze veils over the window spaces. Behind were four mules, two with saddles, two with packs.

A pair of birds began singing among the blossom of a nearby tree. The sweetness of their song brought a lump to his throat as he thought of the anguish that now must be in Ying Mei's heart.

Then she emerged. Pale but erect she stood and blinked, eyes overbright but her face a mask of control. Without a backward glance she went toward the carriage.

Impulsively Nicander pressed forward. 'Miss Ying Mei, do please understand how much I feel for you in this—'

She stopped . . . and looked into the distance, her chin lifting defiantly.

'How dare you!' Tai Yi thrust herself between them, her face pinched with anger. 'This is the Lady Kuo Ying Mei! Ni *sheng* – know that any communication from the likes of you goes through me, and me alone!'

Struck dumb, Nicander watched Ying Mei enter the carriage and draw the veil.

'In the future I'll thank you to remember your manners, foreign devil,' Tai Yi said icily.

CHAPTER TWENTY-NINE

The Yellow River was broad and slow-moving, its muddy waters sliding along as they had done for untold centuries through the featureless flat plain.

Settled under an awning on the timber cargo of the big lighter, Nicander watched the passing spectacle while Marius snoozed.

He looked aft. The amiable old man in a curious conical bamboo hat at the steering oar, who was owner and captain of the craft, gave a toothless smile. His whole family was on board in a tiny house-like structure perched right on the stern.

From above came the comfortable creaks of the single lofty rectangular sail, heavily slatted and needing little handling, driving them on at a steady pace.

Forward, Ying Mei and Tai Yi were keeping out of sight in the privacy of their own spacious temporary quarters atop the long timbers. He shifted in annoyance. There had been no thawing in the Ice Queen and in fact it felt as if she was going out of her way to antagonise them with her airs.

Damn her Chinese ways!

He had reluctantly accepted that there was a distance to be kept between a high-born and commoner but this was ridiculous – having to communicate only through her doughty and ever-vigilant lady-in-waiting, the averted eyes, the cold hauteur. The boatman and his wife were always fawning and bowing, overawed by her presence. Even Marius was uneasily polite and deferential in front of her.

Nicander had tried to get Ying Mei to utter words directly but never once succeeded. He'd come up with strategems, from saying there was a unicorn behind her, to pretending she was not there and passing sly comments to Marius on her appearance. None had broken the silence.

There was no future in a confrontation. No doubt he and Marius could seize the chest, but to what purpose? Her uncle was crucial to their deliverance and that needed her presence. The Ice Queen had the upper hand.

They left the broad expanse of the Yellow River for a tributary and with distant mountains always to the left, sailed on westward.

Nicander idly wandered back to the boatman, who grinned in pleasure at the break in the tedium.

'Ho!' he cackled, pointing to the horizon off to the right where a long, low dun-coloured smoke haze betrayed the presence of a great city. 'Chang An!'

Although it was hard going, as the accent in this part of China was flat and guttural, Nicander pressed the old man for information about their destination.

It was a very old city, perhaps the oldest. It had been the capital of the first emperor of China and counted on gnarled fingers by centuries, it was apparently two thousand years older than the Rome of Augustus – clearly impossible, of course.

Its size was equally fantastic – from excited sweeps of the arms it would need to be measured in handfuls of miles, but he'd not wanted to show sceptic and let the old man babble on about the sights and the pleasures in the venerable city.

Marius was not impressed. There was only one thing he was interested in and that was getting back to Roman civilisation and a decent feed.

The waterway was now busy; barges and lighters like their own, slim fishing craft and fat brick transports, pleasure skiffs and sampans – all the usual bustle at the approaches to a great metropolis.

Outer settlements began to appear along the bank, here and there pagodas on the skyline.

The Lady Kuo Ying Mei stepped out of her quarters. She had long restored her appearance, the slim silk gown with its elegant embroidery setting off her elaborate hairstyle, her ceruse-daubed face restored to its impassive rigidity. She looked about with cool detachment.

The captain hurried up, enquiring of her lady-in-waiting if there was anything she desired. It seemed not and the man was dismissed.

The sprawl of settlement became continuous. They dropped sail and were pulled down a long canal against the wind by hundreds of whipcord-thin men.

What they had seen before was the overflow of buildings outside the city. Inside a rectangle of great, towering walls twenty feet high and pierced only once each side with a single set of three gateways, Chang An proper was indeed immense in size.

Peoples of all kinds in every sort of dress were coming and going, quite ignoring the arrival of yet another boat from the outside world.

Tai Yi was soon engaged in spirited bargaining for the hire of their transport.

The merchants' quarter was well known and they set off, My Lady in a curtained sedan chair, Tai Yi sitting next to the driver of a cart, the foreign devils on the tailgate.

Passing through one of the city gateways they came on an impressive sight – arrow-straight, immensely broad treelined avenues that disappeared into the distance in a regular grid. Minor boulevards and streets led off them and there were canals with pretty arched bridges and every so often a noble pagoda or vermilion eaved mansion showed above the roofs.

They swung off the main avenue and proceeded along a street with high, blank walls on either side. They turned again, into a residential district. Then, past the hubbub and commotion of a bazaar, they came to street stalls selling fish, pastries and flowers.

Through more urban bustle they crossed another broad avenue and continued along by a residential ward, spacious and well guarded.

Abruptly, they stopped by a dignified entrance. Painted on each panel of the heavy wooden gate were demons. Above, a large red triangular flag trimmed in yellow with huge Chinese characters in black flapped lazily.

Nicander dropped to the ground. 'Looks like we're here.'

Tai Yi spoke with a guard who went away, returning quickly to open the gates.

Waiting inside was a group of people, in the centre a small figure in a flowing blue robe, his face so creased with pleasure his eyes almost disappeared.

Ying Mei went up to him and bowed.

Words passed between them; she turned and beckoned the others forward. 'Dear Uncle, you know my lady companion, Lai Tai Yi, who has served me steadfastly since I was a child. Those two are foreign holy men, Ni and Ma, who are accompanying me in my visit.'

Kuo looked at them in keen interest. 'From where do they hail, Ying Mei?'

'A long story, Uncle. It were best left to later.'

'But of course – I forget my manners! Do enter, my child, take some refreshment while you tell me why you are here. You are most welcome, most welcome!'

They were led along paths lined with peonies and trees, through several courtyards, and then past a series of modest buildings of a charming style to a formal hall.

It was delicately appointed in the same spare, elegant taste as his brother.

They sat by a low table, Ying Mei close to her uncle. A set of tiny porcelain dishes was brought and a larger container used to decant a fragrant steaming liquor.

Kuo told Nicander, 'You may not yet have tried jasmine *cha*.'

Nicander lifted the dish and caught a subtle aroma – there were tiny leaf fragments and a dried white blossom floating in the tea. It was delicious.

'Now, my dear, tell me. How is your father?'

Ying Mei replied without emotion, 'Uncle, this is why I've come. I beg that before you hear me, you desire all of your household to leave save yourself.'

In the same controlled tone she laid out what Kao Yang's usurping of the Dragon Throne had cost her family.

It was the first time Nicander had heard the full story, and despite himself, his heart went out to her.

To stand helpless while her father was mutilated, to hear that her mother had hanged herself in shame soon after, and that all the time she had been living with the constant fear of being taken up as a concubine by the tyrant was deeply shocking.

She had held her dignity for her father's sake and, like him, had done her duty as she saw it. With the Emperor's cruel putting to death of his own son they had felt released of the bonds of loyalty.

Kuo's face went pale and when she passed him a letter from her father his hand trembled.

He read, twice, then turned aside.

She waited quietly, her face an impenetrable mask.

Recovering himself, Kuo addressed her gently. 'Your father is a great philosopher, a worthy disciple of the sages and a loving and dutiful father. And I will not refuse him. But in this he is asking for more than he can possibly realise. The obstacles to be faced are very severe. On the other hand you have little choice: your fleeing the Emperor's court has earned his rage and vengeance – you will be hunted for the rest of your days. Or his.'

He went to the door and looked out, then resumed his place. 'So – you seek to leave China for exile in the Western Lands. Are you still resolved on this?'

'I am.'

'Not Japan or Korea, as others have done?'

'My father despises their debasing of our civilisation, and as well, fears that the Emperor's agents have influence even there.'

'So he wishes you to be entirely out of the reach of the Emperor.'

221

'Yes, Uncle.'

'Therefore beyond the influence of our civilised ways, into the land of the barbarians. This is hard indeed, my child.'

'Our history has many instances of a princess journeying beyond civilisation in obedience to her father. How am I to be so different?'

'Very well. I bow to your wishes, my dear. Now, you gentlemen . . . ?'

Nicander answered. 'We have sworn to your brother that we will stand by his daughter until she has reached her sanctuary.'

'That is most noble in you, sir. May I enquire where you come from?'

Wary, he knew the question would not have been asked if Kuo had mentioned it in the letter.

'Sir, from a small kingdom far away, it is of no consequence for we came by sea. We are seekers after truth and have travelled far in our wandering.'

'I honour you for it. Yet the obstacles remain a threat to you all. I shall be frank. I am a merchant in silk and it is in my interest to know of far places to learn of the market there, prices, demand. Yet my knowledge extends only to the oasis towns in the great desert before the mountains. Past these, no one knows what is there.

'We merchants consign our stock and sell to the highest price as advised to us by our agents in those places, the most distant of which is in a place called Aksu, still far from the mountains. That is to say, this is as far as my knowledge and influence extends. I cannot help you any further. After Aksu . . . you are on your own.'

'How will we go on from there?'

'You will join a caravan leaving here for those regions. They are large, some several hundred camels is the usual number. These go to an agreed destination, like Dunhuang, Khotan and such, so the merchant may plan to send his freight there. On arrival there may be an entirely different caravan going on – the silk is transferred and the original caravan returns. The furthest I personally have sent a freight is Kucha. The merchants in the various cities know the market prices and conditions further on the route, having their own agents out there. They can advise of caravans going on and make arrangements for you.'

'So we travel by camel caravan.'

'Yes. Do understand that the purpose of these caravans is the moving of freight – you are only a variety of goods requiring special handling.'

'Then people regularly travel?'

'On the nearer routes, often. Officers relieving outer garrisons, imperial messengers, merchants consulting agents, but the further parts very rarely. In fact, I can tell you that I know of not a one who has gone beyond the last oasis towns, as you must. There have been famous travellers who have gone into the mountains, devout monks wishing to reach India to acquire the original writings of the Buddha, but only very few, and none whatsoever any further.'

'Sir, are you not curious what lies at such a distance?' Nicander asked respectfully.

'We Chinese have little interest in barbarian peoples. To journey into the direction of the setting sun can only end in regions of darkness at the edge of the world. Whatever is the nature of the tribes there makes no difference to the price they seem willing to pay for our silk.'

He gave a wry smile. 'But of course, I'm forgetting the Sogdians.'

'I know little of them, sir.'

'These are peoples who make a profession of running the caravans. You will find them in every town, every stage. Your caravan master you can be sure will be a Sogdian, and they speak among themselves the intelligence to make a crossing, but never to we. The secrets of the way are theirs and they are jealous to keep them so. It is possible they do know what is beyond the mountains but we will never learn of it.'

'Then, sir, it is clear: we join another caravan at Aksu for our onward journey.'

Kuo's face set. 'Before you go further, I find it my duty to express something of the horrors – yes, I use that term – of the journey. As you move away from here, you will enter a region of madness. You will reach the edge of a desert that is an empty wilderness that stretches for eternity. You will then leave the world of mankind entirely and enter upon a place where you have nothing save what is carried on you, no friend but who is on the camel ahead, no stranger will you meet but the fiends and demons of the desert.

'The heat of the day is all but unendurable, at night the cold can petrify a man. Sandstorms arise that mount to the heavens in blackness and grief to fall upon the hapless traveller and force him to his knees to scour him mercilessly before burying him.

'And all the time there is no living thing save the caravan, which moves at the pace of a walk, yet it has to exist on its own resources until it finds the next oasis. If it does not, or misses this place, the next caravan will find its bones.

'If you think this a small risk, know that not three years ago a Turfan caravan of over a thousand camels was overdue at the Yi Wu oasis. It had vanished into the emptiness and no one knows why, it was never found nor a soul survived to tell of it. And I have to tell you this is not uncommon. I beg you, reflect on what you are contemplating. This I beseech you!'

'We go on,' Ying Mei said. 'It is my father's wish.'

Kuo hesitated, then spoke. 'Very well. I shall begin preparation. As your father would remind you, Confucius confides, "A journey of a thousand miles begins with the first step" and so it is in our case.'

'We are in your hands, Uncle.'

'Then, to the first consideration. To leave China is a serious matter – there are the customs, of course, and you will be searched for contraband, but above all your passes will be demanded.'

'Passes?'

'Signed by the military commander that you are no threat, are not spies, are known to the authorities as loyal subjects of the Empire and, most importantly, have good reason to leave. These will be sighted by the caravan master before he lets you join. I need to arrange these for you with General Wu. For that, I will have to find a story that satisfies.'

He pondered. 'Here we have a well-born lady summoned by her father to attend on his final sickness in, say, Aksu. She is accompanied by a lady attendant, naturally. That is the easier. She is under the protection of two holy men – that is the harder. These two are clearly foreigners and therefore suspect. However, she can vouch for them and carries a letter under the seal of a well-known abbot of a monastery here in Chang An.

'I think it best if these holy men carried some token of their truth-seeking, an earnest of their studies while here in China, something to take back with them to their native kingdom. By way of holy scriptures, as it were. I'm thinking of the *Great Learning* and Mencius, perhaps?'

He looked pointedly at Ying Mei.

She bit her lip then said in flat tones, 'The *Doctrine of the Mean*, Uncle. The *Classic of Changes* and of course the *Analects* have meaning comprehensible even to the barbarous.'

'Splendid! I think we have our story! Oh, your family name must change of course, my dear. That of my agent in Aksu is P'eng, you shall borrow it for now. And these faithful gentlemen have a Chinese name but this, of course, is unknown to the authorities and may safely remain.'

He stood. 'Time presses. If they seek you ardently, we may soon expect imperial agents in Chang An. This very afternoon I will make enquiries, but meanwhile you shall be my welcome guests.'

CHAPTER THIRTY

The next day a little procession weaved through the busy crowds. At its head a footman wearing an emblazoned tabard sounded a gong every five paces to clear the way. Several attendants followed and then Kuo and the two holy men, more footmen in the rear.

They had received the best of news: a caravan would leave shortly and with a letter from the abbot secured by a suitable donation, Kuo's friend the general would be agreeable, for a trifling fee, to expedite their passes.

And now they were heading for the market to fit the men out for their great journey, Tai Yi and Ying Mei in a separate party with Kuo's wife.

A maze of streets opened up; the wards were divided into lanes, each specialising in different goods. They passed singing crickets in cages, apothecaries, ironsmiths and fortune-tellers.

Kuo led them to a bazaar completely devoted to the camel caravan.

There was a welter of offerings: bridles for camel and horse, saddles of every level of comfort and expense and, of course, clothing. With the pungent aroma of new leather and fresh-oiled felt on the air they made their selections under the canny eye of their benefactor.

First was good stout ox-hide boots with extra thick soles. Deserts were not all sand and wind-scoured gravel would be trying on the feet.

Next came full-length padded cloaks with all-enfolding lace-up hats recommended for the fierce cold.

Then – peculiar sandshoes made of felt scales like a fish, lined with colourful cloth and reinforced with leather. They had a strong drawstring that bound them tight to the ankle, vital for long stretches in the dunes.

Other articles for the journey were added: personal water gourds, a clothing repair kit, wide bamboo hats against a merciless sun, gloves.

Kuo advised they delay buying hot-weather clothes, linen smocks and trousers, until they got to the edge of the infernal regions.

After a restorative snack of pork dumplings Kuo announced that they were expected soon at the caravanserai which was finalising the dispatch details of their caravan.

The offices of the caravan master were in a large cobbled courtyard, with stables and warehouses on the other three sides. Nicander's heart beat faster – in just two days they would be leaving on a fearsome journey that if all went well would only come to an end in Constantinople!

Seeing Kuo, a large dark-featured man bellowed, 'You're back!'

'I said I would, Su *hsien sheng*. Shall we talk?'

'Who are those?'

'Two of your passenger freight, should your price be right. I have another two coming later. Now—'

'Passes?'

'On their way. The Lady P'eng has been summoned to her father's side in Aksu, a final sickness – things have been rushed, you understand.'

'Lady? Aksu? Sounds like trouble to me, Kuo!'

'Not at all. These gentlemen, foreign holy men, have agreed to be her protectors and she does have a female companion. And she's of gentle birth, no competition for your girls on the way.'

'Humph. So I guess she's after top treatment?'

'I don't think so. In this time of sadness she desires privacy, not display. Tell me, is this an official trip or . . . ?'

'No, private. No hordes of slaves sucking your water all the time, if that's

227

your meaning. Carrying silks, that's raw bolts and made goods, porcelain, copper. There's a crowd o' Buddhists bearing brass images to Khotan – that'll be fun for everybody – the usual other stuff. Two hundred and twenty camels in all. You're not shipping on this run?'

'Only my two-legged freight and a few letters. Anyway, that sounds quiet enough, gold and ivory in a caravan always makes me nervous. Shall we get to details?'

'Fine.'

'What's the escort?'

'Fifty cavalry, Uighurs; twenty bowmen, Kuchean and Chinese, but these are good men.'

'Usual fee?'

'Joint, divided among all with a stake in the caravan? Yes, the usual.'

'Good.'

'So you'll be finalising? You've left it a bit late, Kuo.'

'Not so fast. I trust you, Su Li, best caravan master I know, but I'd like to set eyes on your camels if you please.'

As they were led out from the stables for inspection Nicander blinked at the first one and looked again. 'Wh-what do you call that?'

'What's wrong with him?' Su asked defensively.

'He's got two humps!'

'What do you expect of a camel, you idiot! He's going to cost you, Kuo! Troublemaker, knew it as soon as I sees him.'

'No, no. He's a holy man from a far kingdom, I don't suppose he's ever seen a camel before.'

Kuo and Su agreed final prices and fees in the office.

'Holy men, monks, like? There's a cut in it for them if they know healing. Not much, there's others I can call on . . .'

'What's the word on the route? Any worries?'

'Tibetans causing trouble east o' Niya, knocked over a garrison at Miran. Usual bother, otherwise quiet.'

'Seems well enough. You've been to the diviner?'

'Why would I not, soon as we knew the date for sure?' Su replied in an injured tone. 'Almanac gives us a fair passage, should we sight the rat star before we leave.'

'So we're settled. My party will see you at departure.'

They returned to Kuo's home to find the 'holy scriptures' had arrived from the bookseller.

Written on a curious material called 'paper', these were in an ingenious portable form Nicander had never seen before – the usual scroll flattened and folded on itself many times so 'pages' could be turned. Kuo found a gemstone specimen box of the right size to carry them and demonstrated its false bottom, used to conceal the more precious stones.

That evening Nicander felt restless, and sensing Marius was too, suggested they take in the gardens.

They walked in silence, then Marius said, 'Can see m'self setting to rights a dish or three of faggots when we get back. How about you, m' friend?'

Nicander gave a half smile. How could he put into words his sense of foreboding?

'It might not be as straightforward as all that, Marius,' he muttered. 'Something about the whole thing that makes me . . . well, it's going too well, it can't be this easy.'

'You just like it here too much, that's your problem.'

'No, I just feel—'

'It's all right for you, Greek, you picked up the lingo quick smart. Not like me, half the time I've no idea what you're talking about! I want to be back where a man knows where he's at with people, can give a straight reply, kind o' thing. For me, I don't care if I'm down to hucking the streets again, so long as I'm with m' kind!'

'Wanting something badly doesn't make it any more certain you'll get it, Marius.'

'What's your gripe, Nico? We get on a camel this end and get off some other one at the other – simple.' He chuckled. 'Might even meet up with the

229

camel wrangler I spoke to in Constantinople about getting to Seres. There's a thought – won't he gasp to see us!'

'I'm sure,' Nicander said drily. 'But look at it my way – count how many things can go wrong, then add to those how many things have to go right for us to make it through. Marius, the odds are piled high against us before we even start!

'Take just one thing. Only this – that no one, and I mean not a single soul – is known to have got through to the other side! They admit it! And I believe them for one simple reason. How many Chinese have you seen in the streets of Constantinople? None. A whole lot of Huns, Syrians, Moors and even weirder races, yes, but none from here. What does that tell you?'

'So we'll be the first! Does that frighten you?'

'I don't think you're getting my drift. We're heading out into this demon hell of a place and no one knows what's there at the end. Who's to say it's the right way home? It might be in quite a different direction and there we are, tramping on, headed for a boiling sea or frozen place somewhere.'

He stopped walking. Obstinately Marius continued on, then turned back. 'Look, Nico, I know nothing's sure. Is that why we shouldn't even try? Hey?'

'Then there's those bloody women around our necks,' Nicander said bitterly. 'When things get hard they'll come crawling to us to save them, no doubt about that. But we've sworn to Kuo that we'd stand by them, we'll never be rid of 'em.'

'You're in a funny mood, Nico – what's riding you? Day after tomorrow we're on our way and we takes what comes at us until we win. Right?'

The next day the sun was bright, but the mood wouldn't lift. Nicander took Marius aside, 'My friend. You know I'm not a religious type, but I've a feeling we need all the help we can get.'

'You're planning to go and ask a church to pray for us? Well now, I don't think I've seen a one for the last thousand miles.'

'Don't mock, Marius. We can't be sure there's anyone up there looking after us, right over in this side of the world. What I'm saying is that if we can't get to our gods, it might be a good idea to ask the ones here.'

Kuo was understanding and pointed out an impressive pagoda rising above the roofs. 'The Buddhist monastery of The Holy Turtles.'

He turned to his niece. 'My dear, do you not want to go with these holy men to seek guidance and protection for the journey?'

Stiffly she apologised that she must decline: as a Confucian she had no sympathy with a foreign religion.

Relieved to be let off, the two men set out together. A few coins for 'donations' had been quietly pressed on them by Kuo.

'But we don't know the words of the hymns,' Marius said.

'Or the order of service,' Nicander agreed as they turned a corner and went up a lane. 'But that's no matter. What we want is a lot of monks or whatever praying for us on our behalf. And that's what they'll do – for a small fee, that is.'

'I tell you what I want,' Marius said, seeing a wine shop set out in the sun under a trellised canopy. 'A sup o' something to put me in the mood.'

'Why not!' Nicander agreed.

Their holy garb provoked strange glances from the customers and a well-built waiter with one eye came across and looked at them suspiciously.

'What do you want here, then?' he asked.

'A cup of wine, perhaps?'

'You're monks – you don't drink!'

'Ah, we're foreign monks, as you can see. In our religion we are allowed.' Which was quite true of Byzantium churches.

'Oh, right. What'll it be, then?'

'What have you got?'

'Well, we've wine for them as likes that, but we do best with our ales.'

'Ales, Marius,' Nicander translated.

'Ask 'em what they have!' he said, smacking his lips.

Nicander relayed on the response – Courtiers Clear Ale, Melody of the Western Market, Old Woman's Ale and the famous and superior, Toad Tumulus Ale.

Several hours later Marius was in a very mellow mood. Nicander had to admit to a much improved perspective, even though he had held back.

They were greeted at the gate of the monastery by a genial monk, his head shaven and hands clasped together.

'Brother monk,' Nicander said respectfully. 'I am Ni *lao na*, and this is Ma *lao na*.' He had shamelessly awarded them both the honorific 'old and venerable monk'. We are shortly to set forth on a difficult and perilous journey and—'

'You are joining a camel caravan, and you wish us to pray to Avalokitesvara, bodhisattva of travellers, for your safe passage.'

'You are very understanding.'

'But of course, it is a very common thing in Chang An. There is however the custom that—'

'We will be generous in our thanks.'

'Then if you will come this way.'

Much of the prayer room was in shadows but a shaft of sunshine lit a small area furnished with well-worn wooden appointments and a large gong.

They were ushered to their places and a file of monks entered.

'Kneel, if you please.'

The soft boom of the gong sounded and chanting began. It rose and fell hypnotically and in a strange way was comforting. The gong boomed again and a single voice intoned prayers in an ancient language.

Then with more chanting it was over.

'It is my first time in visiting a monastery of your persuasion,' Nicander said, making conversation as he dropped some coins into the bowl. 'It's very impressive.'

'You think so? It is only one of very many in China. The Buddha is much respected and revered in this land.'

'I think, though, that this monastery is one of the most important, is it not?'

'I cannot dispute your words, Ni *lao na*. But this could be because of our success in our worldly endeavours which the Enlightened One bids us undertake to support our community.'

'Worldly endeavours?'

'In Chang An we have been most fortunate in the quality of our silk that we produce here. It is said to be foremost in the whole of China,' he said proudly. 'Are you familiar with silk?'

Nicander tried to look suitably unworldly. 'Not really. May I learn?'

They moved to inner buildings – where the reality of the secret of silk unfolded before their eyes. No silk trees, no seeds. Only an uncountable number of grey worms steadily munching on mulberry leaves, dozens of monks at labour with boiling vats, others at spindle frames and looms.

Nicander's guarded look of incredulity at Marius was returned with a shrug.

'And we are so renowned of our quality,' the monk went on, 'that we supply our brothers at monasteries as far away as Kuang Chou and Shen Yang.'

'Silk cloth?' Nicander asked. They couldn't possibly be shipping out wriggling worms.

'There is no need for that. We send only the eggs.' He pointed to a large stack of bamboo containers on end. 'In those. They'll stay in there for months, even years, then show them light and air and they'll begin to hatch out.'

'I see. So convenient.'

But then a thought took root, a ridiculous, wonderful, wicked thought!

He shot a glance at Marius and saw his eyes widen – was he thinking the same thing? His friend gave a slow wink.

It would have to be played right.

'Well, Reverend Brother, I do thank you for your time. When we return to our land we will be sure to give prayers for your continuing health and prosperity.'

He edged further around. 'Do convey our thanks to your colleagues who prayed for us so sincerely. We will now take our leave.'

The monk bowed politely – but then called out, '*Lao na*, what is wrong with your brother? Is he taken sick?'

Nicander turned around in concern. Marius was bent over, holding his stomach with both hands.

'Oh, dear. I fear a return of the river fever. I will help him home. Come, Ma *lao na*.'

The monk bowed again, his face unreadable.

Out of the monastery, Brother Ni and Brother Ma turned into the lane of the apothecaries and hurried until they were out of sight.

Marius laughed in relief. 'Be buggered! The monk thought I was pissed!'

'You did get one?'

He pulled out two bamboo containers.

'It's stealing,' Nicander mumbled in a sudden rush of guilt.

'I've only snitched a couple, they won't miss 'em in all that lot,' Marius said in triumph. 'And now we're going back to Constantinople – and with what everyone expects us to return with. The doings to make our own silk, for God's sake! We put 'em in our holy scriptures box – remember that false bottom? No one's going to look under our sacred writings, are they now!'

It was breathtaking. If they made it through they would have the means not only to make themselves insanely wealthy but earn Justinian's undying gratitude.

If – they successfully crossed the deserts and mountains, faced demons and barbarians, went in the right direction . . .

CHAPTER THIRTY-ONE

Kuo was waiting for them, his face creased with worry. 'Thank the heavens. Quickly – inside!'

'What is it, Kuo *hsien sheng*?' Nicander said with a sudden chill.

'Wen Hsuan – he's hot and angry, determined to find you. I've received word from Luoyang. There are imperial agents out, asking about you.'

Terrified of the Emperor's wrath, they were apparently sparing no efforts to cover the country and Chang An, one of the biggest cities in the Empire and the gateway to the outer world, would be high on their priorities.

'How far—'

'My man has only just reached here, but they cannot be long behind. I will hide you here of course, however I fear that the first place they will secure is the caravan terminus. We must pray you're able to leave before they reach us.'

With nervous apprehension Nicander and Marius prepared for their journey. In the privacy of their quarters the contents of the bamboo tubes were carefully extracted. A mass of undistinguished black earth studded with pale specks, it was easily padded down into the false bottom of the box and the scriptures carefully arranged above, in the main compartment.

Their clothing and necessities were gathered together and packed into a pair of pannier bags and then they were ready.

After a sleepless night they waited in a stew of anxiety. Kuo himself would visit the terminus to see if anything was amiss and leave it until the last moment to send for them.

It was well past midday when word finally came. It was on!

They left the house separately, the two holy men going on foot the relatively short distance to the Western Market, Ying Mei and Tai Yi in a sedan chair took a different route, their baggage yet another.

Nicander was keyed up and the noise and confusion of the bazaars and choked lanes tried his patience. When they reached the caravanserai the substantial quadrangular courtyard was packed with jostling humanity and strings of camels. On the air was a heady compound: the stench of droppings, occasional wafts of perfume, the pungency of old leather and a sense of imminent travel.

There seemed no order to the scene. Kuo found them and took them to where the ladies waited. 'It's always like this. Don't worry, it will sort itself out. The freight camels have already been loaded, there's only you passengers who are left.'

Eventually a harried clerk with a well-thumbed list came up with two stable boys. 'Kuo *sheng*! You're last, do you know that? Or nearly last. I have you down for four – two females for mule and carriage, two males for class three horses, one pack camel through to Khotan, changes at Dunhuang. Right?'

'Correct, and here they are.'

'Well, good. The boys will take you to your mounts. Please stand by them, do not leave for any reason, we will not be held liable in the event the caravan goes without you. Understood?'

The clerk made the necessary entries and they were hurried into the throng.

'Make way! Make way!' the boys yelled and suddenly they were at the long camel train.

Brother Paul and Brother Matthew's place was next in line to a snug enclosed carriage for the ladies.

Nicander looked at their two horses with dismay. They were small – halfway in size between a horse and a donkey, a different breed to any he knew.

'This is your camel,' one of the boys said.

It was a large two-humped beast with a mournful look and huge eyelashes. It swung its big head to regard him then looked away.

'What's his name?'

'Name?'

'Yes. What do I call him?'

The lad, surprised, gave a soft smile. 'This one's Meng Hsiang, on account he's always dreaming.' He fondled the beast's muzzle. It responded with a subterranean rumble and a grey tongue shot out to touch his hand.

He expertly brought it down to a kneeling position. 'We'll load him up now.'

It was skilled work; balancing the load, leading the plaited cords to counter movement and yet not interfere with the camel's gait, and having the underlying harness cinched just so.

'I'm going to be a cameleer when I'm big,' the boy said shyly as he finished up. 'My father promised.'

He tapped at its rear with a stick. Obediently the giant back legs levered the animal up on the kneeling forelegs then it straightened, not seeming to notice the load at all. He went to its muzzle and inserted a wooden nose-peg and led the line from it to the rear of the saddle of one of the horses.

'On the road the cameleers will take care of him for you – but don't let 'em treat him rough, he'll never forget. And if ever it comes on to a sandstorm—'

The booming of a large gong sounded making conversation impossible. The boy shouted, 'You're leaving!' and scurried away in a general movement to one side of all who did not belong to the caravan.

The noise became deafening with boisterous farewells, restless snarls of nervous camels and orders being shouted up and down the long snaking line.

And there was the Ice Queen, exchanging last words with her uncle. Nicander watched cynically as she finished, putting her hands together in a courtly bow. She straightened, turned quickly and went to her carriage without once looking back. She got in, followed by Tai Yi, and in one swift movement drew the curtains on the outside world.

Heartless bitch!

* * *

237

The little carriage was small and stuffy, worse when the veils were drawn.

Tears squeezed out until Ying Mei's face, expressionless and rigid, dissolved into a rictus of grief and heartbreak. She surrendered to her emotion, weeping helplessly.

Tai Yi reached for her, held her close, whispering the same endearments she had so long ago when she had comforted a small child on the loss of her friend to banishment.

But then Ying Mei fought back – she was her father's daughter and would never, ever, shame him. How could she? Such a wise, wonderful, perfect man . . . who she would not see ever again. It brought on terrible sobs welling up from her deepest being, a flood of pain and desolation that threatened her sanity.

The never-ending din outside beat in on her – but at the same time it gave her a focus. They might well have to face the world before they left and to be caught like this . . .

She brutally clamped a hold on herself, forced her body into a dignified position and managed a wan smile at Tai Yi.

Her father desired it, therefore there was no recourse to argument or self-pity. She was going to the far lands and that was an end to it.

After all, as she'd told her uncle, there were Chinese princesses who had gone this way before on their way to permanent exile, to be married for political reasons to some barbarian king. They must have gone through this agony but had nevertheless nobly complied for the sake of their country. At least she was not being dispatched to marry a horse-stinking nomad or mountain dwarf.

It made her feel better – but then again they knew where they were going, what their fate was – she didn't. Would this far country be a terrifying place of witches and goblins, barbarous civilisations who despised the delicacy of Chinese thought and manners? Would the men . . .

She crushed the thoughts.

Whatever lay in the future she would face it as the daughter of a Kuo. And, she clutched close to her heart, she was a lady, high-born and with an impeccable education and would never let her standards slip whatever the situation. If she was confronted by barbarians then they would see her quality and respect her nobility . . .

Certainly she would maintain her distance from the holy men, uncouth and rough-tongued as they were, more or less barbarians themselves. Her father had shrewdly set limits on their familiarity: 'wise direction' she would only accept as a last resort and that properly, through her Gold Lily Lady-in-Waiting. They held the chest and means to pay their way through as well as the authority to draw upon her uncle's account, quite sufficient to keep the holy men humble and supplicants for the length of the journey.

The passage would be long; she and Tai Yi would be in their company all that time and it would be essential to maintain a countenance.

From outside came a sudden massed tinkling of small cymbals and the acrid drift of incense sticks. The drone of chanting began from the Buddhists claiming protection for their journey. This was followed by the hearty thumping of drums and loud gongs calculated to keep the Taoist demons at bay.

They would be leaving very soon.

Deep within her, Ying Mei's heart began to cry out in its desolation.

The order came down the line. 'Mount up!'

Nicander swung up on to his horse. The saddle was not a supple leather one but a felted wooden frame, with a high crudely carved lion for its horn. What was so strange were the two foot supports dangling each side. He noticed others had put their feet in the iron loops and he did the same. It felt odd but remarkably steadying.

The crowds were thickening but kept at bay. Much of Chang An had come to see one of their famed caravans set out on their legendary journeys and he was one of the intrepid travellers! His excitement grew.

Marius, trying to control his horse which was gyrating and snorting at the noise, managed a quick grin.

Ahead there was definite movement, heads turning, gesturing. From over to the right people fell back quickly – and the head of a column of soldiers swung into view.

Nicander's first instinct was terror – then it was replaced by anger that they had been so easily trapped.

Run? Hide? By now the caravanserai would be well and truly surrounded.

Dully he watched the soldiers tramp around to head off the line of camels, an officer on a horse accompanying them.

They reached the front of the line, then the tall gates of the western wall of the city opened up and the soldiers marched through.

'It's our bloody escort!' Marius gasped in relief.

With a surge of shouting and cries and a tinkle and jingling of harness the front of the caravan set off through the gates.

The ripple of movement reached back to them, and in a haze of unbelief he felt the horse jolt into motion to follow the next ahead. A slight twitch at his saddle showed that their camel was beginning its plod behind them. The whole caravan was under way.

The wall neared, then the open gates – and they were through, in the outside world and on the road heading out.

CHAPTER THIRTY-TWO

In a line that stretched for over a mile the caravan wound down the dusty road, past the mean dwellings outside the gates of the town. Excited cries came from the local people.

Another drone of chanting accompanied by horns and cymbals arose from the Buddhist monks. Not to be outdone the soldiers marching in the van began a full-throated song and then the women and girls of the caravan started a spirited chorus with tambourines and drums.

The onlookers applauded, enraptured by the sight of a fabled caravan setting out for the vast unknown. Hundreds of camels mounted or led by as colourful and outlandish a mixture of races and dress as it was possible to be, all in gleeful celebration of their departing.

It stirred Nicander's soul – these people would be going about their ordinary lives again once they had watched them disappear toward the far-distant mountains, but they were destined to go where very few did, to lands and wonders, adventures and perils that would only tempt disbelief – *if* they got through.

His eyes travelled to the far-off leaders, to the escort, with the easy swing of soldiers long inured to the march. They were followed by a single file of plodding camels piled high with goods, then a string of horses, more camels and then themselves, the travellers, perhaps no more than thirty.

He swung round; close behind was their faithful camel.

A shaggy merchant on a horse followed, his effortless sway showing an easy familiarity. Catching Nicander's eyes the man launched into a raucous chorus of his own. Marius, beside him, suddenly bellowed out a legionary marching song: a relic of long ago, Rome defiantly rising up in the vastness of Sinae.

Picking up the rear trotted the squadron of cavalry, for the occasion fully mailed and with gaudy pennons a-fly. These were following behind to keep watch on the whole line such that if any point was threatened they could gallop up to be on the scene without delay.

The poorer shacks petered out and the road wound through near identical flat fields.

One by one the songsters fell silent until there was nothing but the slithery jingle of harness and soft clop of hoofs, the creaking of wheels and occasional animal snort, a hypnotic backdrop to their slow but inexorable progress.

Nicander took in the passing scene. The landscape seemed unchanging but he soon found that this was an illusion: at their deliberate walking pace the roadside passed by in an unchanging rhythm and the outer perspectives remained solid and unmoving. However, after an hour's placid motion distant features had subtly changed their shape, had revealed more of one side.

Of course, this is how it must be – great distances eaten up only by steady and continuous travel. Each new day they would press on in an achievement of endurance that eventually would see all of a thousand miles pass by.

A horse cantered down the line. It was the caravan master who reined in when he saw Nicander.

'How's your lady?' he demanded.

Irritation boiled up in Nicander at the thought of the Ice Queen in her carriage telling her lady-in-waiting to take issue with them for their conditions. 'How should I know – why don't you ask her yourself?'

The man's face tightened. 'Don't come it the fool with me, Ni *sheng*! I could make it hard for you before the trip's done.'

Nicander regretted his outburst. Su was probably under a lot of strain at the outset of a major transit and a moaning female was not what was wanted at this stage.

'She hasn't complained to me, Su *sheng.*'

The face eased. 'Good. Let me know if . . .'

Nicander nodded, resolving not to let the woman get to him again.

The sun dipped in the sky, cooling the air. Shadows lengthened, evening crickets began their chorus.

Idly Nicander wondered how they would spend their first night. The country was fully under cultivation, the intensive kind peculiar to China where fields ran close to the next with only a narrow path separating them. Where were five hundred camels going to fit?

Soon they entered a small town, pulling off the main road into a lane and through a gate into an expansive quadrangle, much the same as the one in Chang An.

Waiting for them was a line of men who moved forward as the head of the train came to a stop.

'Dismount! All riders – dismount!'

Nicander swung down painfully. So many hours in the saddle was going to take getting used to.

Under the sharp eyes of the escort the men unloaded the goods the camels carried into carts, to be put under guard until morning while the camels were taken to their stables. A lad came for their horses and they were led away into the main building. There was no alternative but to stay close to Ying Mei for this was a caravanserai and there would be costs involved.

They were efficiently dealt with: a cell for him and Marius on the lower floor with the constant stink of camels, rooms on the airy upper floor for the ladies.

And within the hour a gong announced a meal.

As this was a freight caravan the large hall was only partly occupied.

Nicander held back until he could see how things would be handled.

The monks sat by themselves at one table, the caravan crew were already at merriment at another and all the merchants and other passengers were beginning to gather together at a large communal table. There was no sign of Ying Mei or her sharp-tongued companion.

'Come on, Marius. We'll see who we've got for company. Some of 'em look interesting . . .'

Before they could move Tai Yi's voice behind them snapped, 'I've been looking everywhere for you two. Neglecting your duty, for shame! You're engaged as protectors, your place is with My Lady while she dines.'

'We're monks, not guardsmen!' Nicander said hotly. 'We'll sit wherever—'

'Even holy men can feel hungry if their allowance is cut off! What's it to be – your duty, or suffer your hunger pangs alone?'

The four were granted a table away from the others.

Nicander reluctantly conceded that two ladies on their own could be at the mercy of revellers if the night developed. For the first time they had revealed a touching dependency. It was a minor triumph and helped him put up with the stifling correctness at the table and perpetually averted gaze.

His ill-humour returned seeing Marius fawning on the woman and the shameless adulation that the caravan master showed when he came up to enquire after her situation.

However, after they had dined the ladies promptly went to their rooms and they were free for the night.

Nicander was too restless for sleep even though warned they would be on their way at first light. He wandered out into the moonlit quadrangle. It was busy with men rubbing down horses, lamplit repairs to camel tack and a long line of animals being fed.

It was a telling picture of the organisation behind an enterprise of this size and his business instinct shied at trying to calculate the overheads of half a thousand camels and horses, not to mention the costs of accommodation for the passage crew which must greatly outnumber the two-legged freight. No wonder the prices of goods passed from market to market in this way were so exorbitant by the time they'd reached their destination.

He was pleased when he spotted his camel, who'd so patiently followed them all day. He was chewing rhythmically, jaws moving sideways. The beast gave no sign of recognition and a huge eye swivelled glassily away.

A young man, probably one of the caravanserai men spelling the passage crew, emerged from the other side where he'd been inspecting one of the animal's splayed feet. He looked up in surprise.

'Do you know the name of this camel?' Nicander asked.

'Meng Hsiang,' he answered warily. 'Fifth time into the desert for this 'un. Never any bother.'

Nicander felt a jet of pride that his camel had stood out in this man's memory.

'You'll look after him, won't you?'

It came out a little awkwardly but resulted in a pleased smile. 'O' course I will. This is your first trip?'

He didn't seem at all put off by talking to a bearded foreigner and Nicander realised that for him, the exotic must be commonplace.

'First time. Tell me, why are there so many camels not loaded? There must be at least a couple of hundred not working, taking feed.'

'Oh, this is the caravan master's investment, he and his crew. Only the males take a load. There are spares but most of the others are females with their young. They'll be sold for a good price somewhere along the way, already trained.'

'Our Mr Su. A hard man.'

'Has to be. Tells the camel wranglers what he wants and can't let 'em slack off. Responsible for dealings with customs for unaccompanied cargo after every big stage. Has to know the border entry fees ahead of time, negotiate 'em down, know when to go around. If there's a run-in between two oasis kingdoms he's got to talk to both to let him through, and of course his is the last word on which direction to take after a sandstorm. Has to be hard.'

Nicander nodded.

'And did you know he's got power of life or death?'

'Oh?'

'If there's misbehaving, thievery, suchlike, he can order the culprit thrown off the caravan. If this is in the Great Desert they've no hope.'

'So, do what he says.'

'A good idea. Look, I have to go now. 'Ware of the desert demons and have a good journey!'

CHAPTER THIRTY-THREE

They were roused before dawn and after a solid meal the caravan headed out. The same steady swing and plod, the snaking line ahead a ribbon of colour in the dun-grey and soft green of the fields, the distant smudge of the mountains always there.

In a way it was soothing, the regular pace and sounds of leather against hide, the soft tinkle of bits and bridle on his mount blending with the same up and down the line. Nicander found himself surrendering to the rhythms of the journey.

As the sun grew hot, pomegranates were issued, a surprisingly effective remedy against thirst but he was glad when they left the road to stop at a well-trodden riverbank to freshen the animals. The water gourd which had seemed so big when he'd bought it in Chang An now appeared such a puny thing to set against the dusty road and he drank sparingly.

He saw Su chatting amiably with a merchant and waited his chance for a word.

'Last night I was talking to one of the cameleers. He told me something of your work and I have to admit to having no idea of what a stiff job you do. You have my respect, Su *sheng*.'

The weather-ravaged features eased slightly. 'So what is it you're wanting from me, Ni *sheng*? Something special for your fine lady?'

'Not at all. I was just wondering . . . what will we see ahead?'

'A few more weeks on this road takes us across the river and then to the edge of the desert. We can't take that on, so we turn left and stick close to the mountains – the Kunlun we calls 'em – until we get all around to Khotan. Simple, really.'

'I'm going to Aksu, Su *sheng*.'

'Well, I can't help you there. This caravan's for Khotan and that's where I stops. You'll be continuing on around the desert rim with another. Ask him.'

'I've heard the desert is a wicked place.'

'It is,' Su said seriously. 'The worst in the world. We'll be moving fast, though. Should be through to Khotan in a few months at the outside.'

'What if there's—'

'You leave all the worrying to me, holy man. We're on track and staying there. I'm a Sogdian, I take care to keep in with my friends and they'll let me know if there's trouble ahead.'

'Will it always be like this? Apart from the desert, that is.'

'Ha! You'll be seeing sights you can't imagine, feeling cold and heat like the poor bastards in hell but we'll pull through. Never lost a caravan yet – if I did I wouldn't be here, would I?'

'The next . . .'

'Crossing the Yellow River at Lan Chou. A bit of a spectacle there. Then naught much until we reaches the Great Desert and that'll open your eyes. Dunhuang, the monks'll go crazy and it's a sight if you likes that kind of thing. Then a bit empty, like, until we reach . . .'

So, months on the trail, just to reach the other side of this vast desert.

That night it was much the same. A caravanserai effortlessly catering to their numbers, another tiny cell, and away at dawn.

The ground was hilly, light forest crowning the slopes. They passed over the summit through a well-travelled cleft that exposed the fine-dust soil the Chinese called 'yellow earth' but on the other side the winds from the right increased, driving invisible particles of dust and sand to sting and irritate exposed skin. It stayed with them all day but mercifully eased towards the afternoon.

Nicander peered into the distance. Was it his imagination or were the mountains closer?

Marius had been riding alongside where he could. They talked occasionally, but mainly continued in companionable silence.

Unexpectedly, with a full hour or more of daylight left, the leaders turned off the road into a sparsely grassed field and rotated to direct the caravan into a giant circle.

'Dismount!'

Nicander gave Marius a wary glance. This night they would spend without the convenience and comfort of a caravanserai.

A fire was started, flaring and quickly growing bigger. To one side the camels were pegged out in several lines, the horses beyond. On the opposite side of the fire all unloaded freight was stacked together and guards posted.

If they wanted a tent, apparently it would be extra. Feeling the night air coming on Nicander had his views but Marius chuckled, 'We pocket the hire and kip out under the stars!'

While the daylight lasted the tents were erected and owners' packs transferred to them. Of strong goat-hide reinforced felt, they had a full eight guy lines each side as if at any time expecting a gale of wind. Peeking inside one Nicander saw that it was remarkably snug, with sewn-in hooks for belongings and a substantial ground covering.

As the chill of the evening drew in, people moved to the fire, taking bedrolls or other articles to sit on and it quickly became the centre of activity. Not far away there was a kitchen with its own fire contained in iron fittings already sizzling with activity – three vast pans, each a yard across, conjuring a hearty meal of vegetables, rice and chicken.

When the Ice Queen did not appear from her tent Nicander gleefully realised he could take his choice of companions at dinner.

The monks were together, chatting solemnly, he'd let them be. A cloaked merchant sat with his wife holding court to several around him and another group had settled around a portly man in finer dress than the others. On impulse Nicander went over to a young man sitting at the edge. Marius followed.

'May I sit here? I'm Ni K'an Ta of Ta Hsin, this is Ma Lai Ssu.'

'Wu Kuo Chin. Ta Hsin – I haven't heard . . . ?'

'A far kingdom. We're holy men on a journey to seek after truth.'

'I'm an officer of the Imperial Bannermen.'

Nicander froze. A soldier of the Emperor sent to root them out?

'Ah. How strange – may we know why it is you're in this caravan?'

'It's the usual way for officers to travel out to join their garrison at the border.'

'I see,' said Nicander in relief. 'Forgive me, this is my first visit to your land.'

'Do you know much of our past, Ni *lao na*?'

'Not as much as I'd wish to.'

'Well, understand that from the time of the Han dynasty we have held the lands to the west for the Empire, including the Great Desert at its heart. Now, since we've suffered unrest and . . . and uncertainty on the Celestial Throne, we have lost them. Only our watchtowers and garrisons at the edge of the desert stand between us and the barbarians.'

'A challenging post, Wu *hsien sheng*.'

'Indeed.'

'Not as fearful as for an official who must enter in upon these lands to regulate our lawful tribute of the lesser kingdoms!' the well-dressed fat man called across.

'Tribute?' the merchant sitting with his wife scoffed. 'This is trade's increase only! We're the one's with all the risks – and no one at our backs to come rescue if things get hard for us.'

'You've a venture on this caravan?' Nicander asked.

'I have – silk and porcelain out, carpets and glassware by return.' He was strong-faced, bearded and wearing a curious tall hat, some outlander that Nicander hadn't yet learnt to recognise.

'You'd be looking to a respectable return, then, the overheads and fees being what they are,' Nicander said without thinking.

Talk stopped and faces turned to look at him suspiciously.

'So you know these things?' the man said slowly.

'Oh, my father – he's in the incense trade. Many times have I heard him complain about them.'

'I didn't catch your name.'

'Ni K'an Ta. And yours?'

'Korkut the Rouran. Then what are you about – that is, when you're not being holy?'

'We seek truth wherever it may be in this world.'

'That's what spies do.'

'We're as well accompanying the Lady P'eng to Aksu.'

'Ah. The noble lady. It's not often we see ones of her quality on a freight run. Can you tell us for what reason she's journeying?'

'She's been summoned by her father in Aksu who is in his final sickness.'

'How sad.' He paused, 'But that's funny – I know Aksu and there's no P'eng at that level in the place.'

'She was sent to live with her rich uncle in Chang An,' Nicander said quickly. 'Her father is not of that sort.'

'Then why does she not travel in some style?'

'I think she grieves for him and does not wish display.'

'Hm. Once we've cleared Lan Chou the going's rough for anyone, let alone a high-born. You'd think she'd be advised to take camels and attendants by the dozen. Odd.'

Korkut's wife was in no doubt, however. 'Can't you see? You men are the last to catch on, as always.'

'What do you mean, Zarina, dear?'

'It's obvious. She's a princess being sent to marry a foreign king. They don't want to risk that she's captured in an official legation caravan so they send her in disguise. I've seen her face – she's stricken to leave China for ever, poor lamb.'

She turned to Nicander with a big smile. 'That's so, isn't it? Don't worry, your secret's safe with us – isn't it, friends?'

The others murmured an agreement.

Lost for words Nicander could only stare back dumbly.

Then their meal arrived. Each was given a bowl and iron spoon, and the food was ladled out. There were appreciative murmurs as they tucked in.

After finishing off with melon, they sat contentedly watching the fire.

A night under the stars was not as bad as Nicander had feared. Marius had taken their padded capes and shown him how only the hips required softer ground for comfort, the head in its warm hood needing to be raised only as much as by a rolled-up day cloak.

It was almost sensual, the feel of the chill night breeze on his face, while the rest of him was snuggled into the strong-smelling oiled felt. He heard the soughing of wind and every snick and scurry of night sounds as though part of it, yet he was tucked up in his warm cocoon.

The next day it rained: a spiteful, blustery downpour that started up soon after they were on the road, and which tested their cloaks and bad-weather gear to the limit.

Cold and dispirited, they journeyed on, the road slippery with running yellow mud, horses snorting with their stumbling efforts.

The rain petered out in the afternoon but the mud persisted. Fortunately that night they arrived at a caravanserai – a roof over their heads, piping hot cabbage soup and an early night.

Under grey skies the next morning they resumed their journey, assured that they would not be troubled by rain once they reached Lan Chou, and in fact the sun did show itself towards the afternoon.

Each day saw them a little further on, the sounds of the caravan now familiar and comforting. Occasionally there were snatches of song, a plaintive flute or a flat nasal instrument that Nicander couldn't place.

His horse walked on meekly, an occasional shake of its head and muffled whinny its only protest. Behind, their camel dutifully plodded in their wake.

One morning some weeks later, Marius spotted new mountains ahead, others to the left and then, unexpectedly, a wide river.

Swirling yellow-brown with silt, it was fast-moving – the Yellow River once more. Further along was the substantial town of Lan Chou.

The settlement had high, well-defended walls and was a frontier between the fertile plains they had been crossing and the route out into the borderlands. On the way to the caravanserai there were strange peoples with weather-darkened faces, market smells that were pungent but unknown and everywhere a restlessness, a feeling of transience.

They did not stay long. Su got them on the road as soon as he could, swearing that he would lose half his crew if they were any longer in such a town.

Not far upstream they arrived at a crossing point, under vertically fluted crags between two opposite flat areas. There were dozens of rafts manned by scores of small, muscle-hard peasants who jockeyed noisily for position, some joining several craft together to form larger rafts.

The rafts were supported by inflated sheepskins and had to be energetically paddled across against the swift-moving current.

The operation took some time; camels imperturbably standing until their turn came, precious cargoes given particular care and passengers marshalled in apprehensive groups.

Halfway across the river Nicander was fascinated to see figures in the cliff opposite – colossal carved statues ninety feet high. He hoped the Buddhas would look kindly upon their journey . . .

Their crossing complete, the mountains closed in: to the right a range of undistinguished crags with bands of red-brown, to the left a mighty rearing that had the far-off glitter of white snowcaps.

Slowly but steadily the camel train began an ascent on a stony track through the first pass. They were following a caravan route as ancient as time, out of China and into the trackless deserts and fearful wastes of the interior.

CHAPTER THIRTY-FOUR

Nicander gazed out on a flatness so vast it was limitless. A deadness – where nothing lived, the eternal grey-brown dust and sand with occasional clumps and tufts of desiccated vegetation stretching out in ever-tinier detail until it dissolved into nothingness at the horizon where the desert met the hard blue sky.

And with it a silence descended that was so profound that his ears filled the void with a soundless screaming.

For weeks – and countless miles – they had travelled in company with a solid, reassuringly visible work of man – the Great Wall of China. The wall came to an end in a tall open structure with upturned eaves above a massive portal, the Jade Gate. The act of passing through this was the formal leaving of the Middle Kingdom, China.

After this point they were entirely on their own.

Near overwhelmed with the sense of desolation and loneliness he trudged back to the safety and familiarity of the caravan in time to farewell Wu Kuo Chin, the young officer, who took his leave with a wooden face.

'A great honour for him,' Nicander murmured to Korkut.

'Ha! He's going to a living death, and he knows it.'

'What do you mean?'

'He's to command a band of criminals, slaves and broken-down misfits sent here for punishment. They have to man those watchtowers and shift for themselves, there's nobody cares what happens to them. No glory to be won here, only sudden raids by brigands and those bastard Hsien Pei Mongols.'

'The Great Wall, how long has it been here?'

'Why, this part . . . from the time of Western Han. Five, six hundred years.'

Nicander shook his head at the thought that it had been manned continuously for centuries even before Julius Caesar had seized power in old Rome.

Out of the corner of his eye he spotted Marius, and gave a hail.

His friend waved, his clothes, like Nicander's own, were now dust-stained and worn. 'Just heard. We've been called up before Su. Wants to talk about what we're going to face or something.'

It wasn't a large, formal meeting. The camel-drivers and passage crew were busy at their preparations and knew what was expected but Su was taking no chances with the travellers.

He stood at the centre of a loose circle: Korkut, his lively wife, the monks in a group, others, some thirty in all – and the Ice Queen.

She had compromised her courtly appearance and was now dressed in a plainer robe with less ornately styled hair. Her expression, however, was the same – a patrician stare above the common herd, a controlled blankness.

Su's bluff features had a serious cast. 'You're seeing me because I want you to hear me tell you what's ahead. To leave you in no doubt what you have to do if it starts getting rough.

'The first thing for you to know is that I'm in command of this caravan and therefore responsible for it. That means you do exactly what I say. Understood?'

He looked from one to the other. 'Very well. The second is just as important. Never leave the caravan. We carry only so much water, camel feed and so on and that means the caravan never stops. Not even to look for anyone who's missing, wandered off somewhere. We never go back!'

Checking to see he still had their full attention he went on, 'Up to now we've more often than not stayed at a comfortable caravanserai. That's all over.

255

We're going on our own resources by day-stages as fast as we can across the plains between oasis stops, where we rest and take on fresh victuals and water. There's no roads, no paths – if you ramble off you'll never find your way back, you'll leave your bones as a warning to others.'

He continued. 'Water. More precious than gold – you have your own gourds during the day which you'll only be able to refill from our skins at the end of the day. Never more than three sips at a go, relish it before you swallow.'

'What about attacks by raiders, barbarians?' one of the monks wanted to know.

'We're a good-sized caravan but with an escort to match. No band of raiders is likely to trouble us, but they might if they're desperate. If it happens, we'll have the camels form a circle and get down, you stay behind them while our archers and cavalry deal with 'em. Don't stray or run, stay until we give the word.'

Su continued. 'So where are we going? This is the start of the southern caravan route. The first stop is Dunhuang, then we'll be keeping close to the mountains all the way to Khotan. It won't be pleasant but believe me it's better than the northern route across the desert!'

'What will it be like for us?'

'Going's good, if that's what you mean. Plenty of water from snowmelt off the Kunluns but pretty bare else. Sooner we get through the better.'

One of his crew signalled to him.

'We're ready to move out. Remember what I've just said. The season's advanced but we're on time. Should have a good run.'

His confidence was reassuring and they mounted up quickly.

Soon the camel train was moving out, every pace setting more distance from civilisation, the world of men and order – deeper into an arid wasteland. A few heads turned back to catch a last glimpse of the Jade Gate, now a forlorn outpost in a sea of desert.

The sun reached its zenith and they plodded on. It began to descend but before the usual violet dusk of the desert stole in, Su had found his place for the night; a twist of sand and rock that had given shelter for a line of grey-green camel thorn and a flat area to settle.

A fire was quickly started and the well-practised routines of preparing for the night were begun. In respect for the cold of the desert nights Nicander and Marius had now accepted a tent.

This evening seemed in some way different. Was it the certain knowledge that they were utterly alone at the empty heart of the universe? That they would meet no others until they reached the next oasis?

The fire flared and spat but already people were moving to be near it, as all around the darkness fell silently and completely.

'Korkut *sheng*, where is your wife?' Nicander said, needing to reach out.

'As always, she paints her face as if she's to meet the king of the fairies the next hour. She'll be here – if only to hear the gossip.' The burly merchant's face was impassive as it was lit by the firelight.

'Well, Ya? Your men are posted?' Korkut asked.

The commander of the escort, a self-important and opinionated ex-soldier of obscure origins, was condescending to sit with the travellers instead of his customary holding court in his own tent.

'Of course.'

Nicander found it difficult to follow the thick accent; the man was reputedly a Uighur due to his almost Western features – and brutal treatment of his men.

Zarina stepped into the firelight in a profusion of fur and exuberantly coloured leggings. 'Good evening, everyone!' she beamed, and took up position next to her husband.

'Good to see you in spirits, *habib*,' he said, helping to arrange her cloak.

'Yes, dear. I'm always feeling better when I have so many big men about to protect me. You know the desert frightens me.'

'As I keep telling you, demons are terrified by fire – as long as those lazy beggars keep it going you've nothing to worry about.'

'Oh? You men never stop to think what it is for us ladies. What if we have to go out into the dark to . . . you know . . . what then?'

'Then, beloved, it is clear I must go with you, whatever your business.'

There was laughter but it tailed off as a figure came out of the blackness, moving gracefully towards them.

It was Ying Mei.

No one spoke as she entered the firelight and looked about uncertainly.

Until now she had kept to herself, taking her meals in her carriage and seldom seen.

She was in a plain robe and held a shawl close.

Seeing Nicander she went to him. 'May I sit with you, Ni *lao na*?' she asked in an even tone, her elegant poise not out of place at a court reception.

Thunderstruck at being addressed directly for the first time, he stood up. 'Why, of course, Lady P'eng.'

Tai Yi silently appeared with a travelling cushion.

Nicander took his place again slowly, aware that not a word had been spoken by the others. Ying Mei sat next to him, looking modestly into the fire.

What did it mean?

Zarina smiled at Ying Mei. 'You'll have had a dusty ride in the carriage, my dear. How do you keep yourself so . . . ?' The well-meant opening faltered at the realisation that she had forgotten the complex honorific due a lady – who of course in any event was not to be troubled with such trivialities.

'A woman's appearance is her chief ornamentation, without which pearls and gold lose their meaning,' was the quick reply. 'As your own appearance and dress does so well confirm. It is our duty to the world, is it not?'

'If it please you, Lady P'eng, we've been concerned you'll suffer much in this journey,' Korkut said awkwardly. 'It must be for some very important reason, I fear.'

His wife glared at him but Ying Mei answered in the same quiet, level voice. 'I'm called to my father in Aksu who lies ill. I shall obey him, I believe.'

'Oh, yes, of course,' Korkut said hastily with a quick wink at Zarina. 'We understand.'

A familiar bong started up at the kitchen and before long a steaming wheel-sized platter arrived. Nicander pulled out his bowl. The serving man hesitated then humbly went over to Ying Mei and offered the dish, kneeling with his head bowed.

'Thank you,' she said equably and reached out delicately with her chopsticks. Selecting a choice collop of mutton she offered it to Nicander.

He could hardly believe it. This was a common gesture of politeness in Chinese society – but among equals. Was this . . .

Ying Mei then did the same for Marius and Tai Yi as well, before helping herself.

Nicander struggled to make sense of what was happening. Was it because her self-imposed isolation in this vast emptiness was no longer bearable and she was craving warmth and fellowship? Had the Ice Queen melted? He didn't know whether to be relieved or scornful. But how far did it go?

'It must have felt quite a wrench to leave China?' he said.

'Yes.' Her expression was composed but she did not catch his eye.

'I suppose you're wondering when you'll hear proper Chinese again,' he continued.

She froze – and he saw that her eyes were glistening.

He tried to make light of it. 'But not before we've had a few more interesting adventures, I'd say.'

'I'd call 'em more trials,' rumbled Korkut, tucking into more mutton. 'The stretch between Cherchen and Niya is particularly bad. I remember when—'

'Are you not feeling well, dear?' Zarina said in sudden concern, looking at Ying Mei.

She got up and went to her, squeezing her shoulder gently but Ying Mei did not respond, and held herself rigid.

'The first time's always hard. Leaving behind—'

'Thank you, Korkut *tai tai*,' Tai Yi said, helping Ying Mei to her feet. 'The Lady P'eng will now retire to rest.' She shepherded her unresisting mistress away.

'Odd sort of woman,' Korkut muttered, picking at his teeth.

'No she's not!' Zarina snorted. 'The poor lamb – she's homesick, that's all.'

CHAPTER THIRTY-FIVE

The first indication they had of Dunhuang, the oasis to the west, was an increased number of mounds of dull sand clumped around scraggy sage brush.

Grey outlines of hills formed, and then out of nowhere, a single tree, gaunt, with spiky dark-green leaves.

Closer to, there were more trees. The hills were actually massive dunes – not just one or two but stretching away out of sight one after another in mighty curved waveforms.

The caravan wound past the edge of the dunes which towered above them a hundred feet in an awe-inspiring mass.

It was approaching night but Su pressed on into the gathering dusk.

Then a sight to clutch the heart: a walled town. Well-watered gardens outside, people moving, lights, distant sounds of human activity – life!

Nicander's horse snorted and tossed his head impatiently. Somewhere not far was water.

They followed the edge of the wall then picked up a track along its side and came to a river. It seemed so improbable; rearing dunes and lifeless light-grey sand, but moving through it a channel of living, sparkling water.

They had arrived in the confines of a caravanserai courtyard open to the stream. The order to dismount was given and a crew took charge of the animals and led them to water. The passengers found themselves quickly surrounded: small children running about, merchants claiming their goods, officials haranguing the caravan master, hucksters and others who simply stared in awe.

A welcoming band struck up – cymbals and lutes, a wailing pan pipe of sorts, three drummers. The crowd increased.

Nicander and Marius were told: 'You two – follow him.'

A youth with laughing eyes darted ahead to show them to their cell in the low building that reeked of the dust of ages. He held out his hand for a coin but Nicander shook his head sorrowfully. The lad ran off trailing shrill abuse.

Their kit was finally brought and they made free with a generous pitcher of water.

A little later Korkut appeared at their door, grinning. 'Look, while we're in an oasis we're off caravan victuals, look to ourselves. Now myself, I don't take to caravanserai feed, too basic if you get my meaning. Zarina thought you'd like to come with us to the Golden Peach, it being our first night. That is if you haven't an arrangement with the monks, you being holy men and so forth.'

'Kind of you to think of us, Korkut *sheng*,' Nicander replied. 'We'd be honoured to come.' He paused. 'Would it be possible to take with us the Lady P'eng? She being so cast down and . . .'

Korkut's bushy eyebrows rose. 'Well, if you think so. I have to tell you that the Peach is very much your regular oasis inn, which is to say its pleasures and entertainments might not be to the taste of a lady.'

'Zarina's going?'

'I couldn't stop her!'

'Then as she's a lady, so there'll be company for her.'

Nicander was not proud of the fact that there was also another motive behind the request: as they were a party invited together Ying Mei could hardly refuse to pay for their share – one worry disposed of.

Dunhuang throbbed with life. A caravan of colourful strangers with money to burn, fashion goods from China to buy, the latest gossip from Chang An and travellers to entertain were irresistible.

The brightly lit streets were full with peoples from every remote corner of Asia in all kinds of outlandish dress. Korkut's little band made their way through and soon arrived at the inn.

From the upper-storey balcony, girls with elaborate coiffures threw them kisses. They passed inside to a roar of noise, candlelight picking out gold-leafed carvings, scarlet furniture, intricate tapestries – and the eyes of the revellers.

Korkut took them to stairs at the rear. The upper floor turned out to be even more extravagantly furnished. They were shown to an elaborately lacquered table close by an open space.

A voluptuously dressed girl bowed with a dazzling smile. 'Good evening! I'm Mei Ling, mistress of the table, you are our honoured guests.'

They sat on low benches, Korkut and his wife in the centre with Ying Mei opposite. Tai Yi eased herself between Nicander and her mistress. Marius sat next to Korkut.

Waiters arrived with trays of delicacies. 'Wine!' ordered Korkut. 'The best!'

It came in a silver-chased jug worked with flying camels with wings, and was silky smooth, slipping down rapidly after the stern discipline of the desert.

'Not so fast!' Korkut ordered.

'We're here as guests in Dunhuang. We must follow their customs. So – will you drink my health, or will I drink yours, Ma *sheng*?' He made a fist. 'You see this?' Two fingers came out. 'Now you – any number.'

Three fingers came out of Marius's big hand.

'So the total is five. Now to make it interesting, at just the same time we throw, we shout out what we think will be the correct number. Ready?'

Marius caught on quickly to the drinking game but it was Korkut who first scored.

'Your very good health, sir!' Marius grinned and toasted him Roman fashion, moving his arm wide across his chest.

Nicander joined in and after losing twice in succession, a pleasant fuddle settled in.

The promised feast arrived. Pigeon's eggs, a fish in bamboo root, tripe in spicy noodles, the dishes kept coming.

He eased forward to catch a glimpse of Ying Mei. She was talking gravely to Zarina but appeared to be having a good time, even if her poise was as unbending as ever.

There was movement at another table where caravan master Su sat. He wore a deep-blue silk top jacket with distinctive yellow patterns woven into it and leg-hugging red trousers which were tucked into calf-length brocaded boots. And on his head was a black conical cap cheekily tilted forward.

His guests were two girls in as colourful a dress as he and both were in paroxysms of laughter.

'Bloody Sogdians!' Korkut spluttered. 'Can't keep away from 'em.'

To one side a flute began an exploratory trill. It was from a trio which included knee drums and lute.

'Ha! This is why we came, m' friends. Only thing the Sogs are good for.'

Two serving girls scurried out with a crimson and green rug which they threw over the reed-matting floor. An expectant hush fell.

The flute then joined with the pipa lute in a soft, lingering melody, hinting at mystery and allure.

Even through his alcoholic haze Nicander was caught up in the atmosphere. Mere yards away in the darkness huge silent dunes were stretching away to infinity, while here they were, cheating the wilderness demons in a celebration of their victory over the desert.

In a flash of movement a dancer appeared in a bare-shouldered silk blouse and a long, filmy gauze skirt over loose green trousers. She stepped forward daintily, her tiny jewelled slippers pointing and tapping in deliberate movements until she reached the centre of the rug where she took up a provocative pose.

Then the drums spoke with a soft but insistent beat underlying the music, steadily increasing in power until the dancer sprang to life. She threw out her arms and twirled about, setting off tiny bells on her arms and ankles, beginning a dance of sensuous whirling as the drums deepened and became more demanding in their rhythm.

At each turn she fixed her eyes on a different man who shouted encouragement until the room rang with whoops and calls.

Nicander's attention was diverted by a sudden movement. 'Come, My Lady, this is no fit place for a well-born!'

Tai Yi stood, her face tight. Ying Mei hesitated, an unreadable emotion passing across her face, then she rose and left.

The dance tightened, the turns became more abandoned, the drums deafening.

For Nicander the wine was having its effect but he was as much intoxicated with the sensual impact of the exotic scene. This was the reality now – not the desert, not the Imperial Palace, not the domes and columns of Constantinople, now but a faded dream.

The drums built to a furious climax, then without warning the dancer ran to Korkut's table. With a deft movement at her blouse she thrust her bare breasts to Marius.

There was a roar of appreciation as the legionary huskily acknowledged her. She held her pose, then turned and left.

'Don't worry, there'll be others on,' chuckled Korkut, his hand busy inside Zarina's bodice.

More wine came.

In his detached state Nicander saw Marius furtively show Korkut something.

'An Imperial silver sycee! Where did you get this?' the merchant demanded loudly.

Seeing Marius scrabble in vain for an explanation, Nicander leant over drunkenly. 'It's for doing a magical healing on the Emperor's daughter,' he burbled.

'Yes, that's right. So can you split it up, like. Coin or whatever?'

'For you? I think we can do something.'

CHAPTER THIRTY-SIX

Nicander acknowledged his friend with a smile. 'Been wondering when you'd get back.' It was well into the morning and he'd been able to sleep off the effects of the previous evening enough to take in the day.

Marius grinned, then flopped down on his bed. 'Hard work – the woman didn't know a word of any civilised lingo.'

'You've missed the excitement.'

'Have I now?'

'The caravan may be delayed.'

'What a pity.' The big man stretched lazily.

'Seems the Tibetans are coming down from the mountains and causing grief between here and Khotan.'

'How long?' The eyes were closed, the speech slurred.

'They're sending a scouting party ahead to find when we can move out. Long enough, I would have thought, for you to spend all the Emperor's silver – and half that's mine, I'll remind you.'

'I'll pass her across at the right time, don't worry.'

About to give a hot retort, Nicander saw the cheeky grin. 'Korkut says there's some famous caves close by. Feel like stretching the legs?'

'Not now, I've got some kip to catch up on. Have fun.'

Nicander demanded some coins and left him to it.

It was hot so he hired a donkey as the distance to the caves was considerable, the path winding between dunes and craggy passes for a dozen miles or more.

He went in company with five monks headed there on pilgrimage. They chattered in a barbarous dialect, completely incomprehensible to Nicander.

Left to his own thoughts he allowed it not impossible that he and Marius would make it through after all. The caravan was well organised, no doubt Su would be able to pay off the Tibetans to let them pass and then it was the lengthy journey to the mountains. There would bound to be some at that place who could tell them the direction to take next.

At least the Ice Queen was talking to him now. Never had he been completely ignored before like that. It had rankled more than it should have, the way she looked down on him.

The donkey stumbled, interrupting his musings and he saw that they had come to a winding valley with a flat floor. A shallow river meandered through and around a bend there was a little village, dominated by the pagoda of a monastery. The party drew closer; above the nestling trees there was a bluff stretching away and in its vertical face were regular square holes that must be the caves. At least a couple of dozen.

The monks disappeared into the monastery. Nicander found the path up to the cliff face. Stepped walkways projected out that led to the caves and he made his way along one.

In the first cave a scraggy, shaven-headed monk looked up and smiled. He was at work with a brush and a pot of pigment and stood back for Nicander to admire it.

It was a busy painting, full of detail. A Buddha with colourful haloes sat cross-legged, and flying above him were heavenly beings trailing swirling ribbons. Not angels as Nicander knew them, but much more full of life, so different to the static piety of Christian works.

On other walls were contrasting scenes of the Buddha's life, which meant nothing to him but which held the same vitality.

He murmured some words of praise but the monk shook his head in incomprehension then returned to his work.

The next cave along was more spacious, with several separate chambers. Sunlight flooded the outer one but the inner room was in deep gloom, relieved by just a single lamp. There was no painter at work here, only a solitary figure sitting cross-legged in the centre, motionless.

The atmosphere was stark and mystical and something reached out to Nicander. He moved closer to one of the murals. The figures came to life in the flickering illumination of the lamp. The central Buddha was posed on a lotus blossom, a look of utter serenity on his face, hands raised in a blessing. Around him were maidens in flowing gowns, mythical beasts and leaping and flying ferocious demons and warrior gods that seemed to come out from the wall at Nicander personally.

A movement behind startled him. It was the man he'd seen when he entered.

Was he a monk? His face was in shadow but he had a full beard and thick-set build.

The man growled some words at Nicander that he couldn't understand. Shaking his head he said in Chinese, 'I'm sorry to disturb you, *lao na.*'

The man came out of the shadows and replied in Chinese, 'I said, what does this hold for you?'

'Why, it's very well done.'

Nicander edged toward the doorway to the outer chamber, disturbed by the man's aura. Pretending to admire the other frescos he emerged into the light. The man followed and stood watching him. Nicander glanced at him, meeting fierce blue eyes.

'This one – I rather like the chorus of—'

'They worship the bodhisattva.' The voice was deep, commanding.

'Ah, yes.'

'You have no knowledge, no understanding of these mysteries?'

He moved closer, inspecting Nicander keenly. 'You're an outlander as I've never encountered before – and I've travelled to the edge of the world where the four winds do spring, and never have I met those who do not fear and respect these teachings.'

Nicander returned his gaze. 'And I'd say you're not a son of Han yourself.'

'You interest me, barbarian. Where did you first draw breath? What do you here, that so few set eyes on these wonders?'

'I'm – I'm a holy man from a far southern kingdom. I seek truths.'

'The south, is it!' the man whispered, then declaimed,

'O Soul, go not to the South
Where mile on mile the earth is burnt away
And poisonous serpents slither through the flames;
Where on precipitous paths or in deep woods
Tigers and leopards prowl,
And water-scorpions wait;
Where the king-python rears his giant head.
O Soul, go not to the South
Where the three-footed tortoise spits disease!'

'Well . . .'

'That is my own land, the south. I'd be curious to know what part . . . ?'

'More to the west, I'd say.'

'You seek after truths yet you show no desire to imbibe of the wisdom of this place.'

'I've not yet begun to search.'

'But truth is everywhere, as philosophers of every breed do attest.'

'Sir. I came here for my own reasons. I do not wish to spend my time in wordy dispute.'

The man bowed. 'Do pardon me, wanderer. You may know me as Dao Pa and like you, I have an unquenchable desire for truth.'

'I'm called, in China, Ni K'an Ta. I have travelled far and now return to my homeland.'

'Ni *lao na*, forgive my importuning but I sense in you a different spirit, one unaccustomed to the ways of the Middle Kingdom, unsure of the patterns of life in our existence here. The inescapable conclusion is that in the compass of your own world, you are. You will have an understanding of earthly and heavenly matters that satisfies, but which will be either in agreement with us or at variance. The answer to this is of great significance to my understanding. It would gratify me beyond saying should we walk together for a space.'

Outside he found his staff, and hitching his cloak – little more than a blanket – he and Nicander descended the cliff face to the flat sandy ground next to the river.

There was something in his manner – the intensity yet dignity, the tigerish gaze with unsettling insight, that Nicander felt stripped him bare.

They paced slowly then Dao Pa said, 'Tell me, Ni *lao na*. What is your origin?'

There could be no evasion with this man. 'I am a Greek, from a place so far I cannot tell even in what direction it lies.' He had no idea of the word for 'Greek' in Chinese, even if there was one, so used the actual word.

To his surprise Dao Pa nodded wisely. 'In India they still speak of a Hellenica, a great warrior teacher they call Aliksa Nada who many centuries ago conquered territories right up to the gates of the kingdom then received a sign from heaven and turned his back on them.'

Nicander felt the hairs at the back of his neck stand on end – he could be speaking only of Alexander the Great!

'You've been to India?'

'Certainly. There is an infinity of wisdom to be learnt in that far country, worth all the pains of the travel. Know that the caravans that ply the deserts and mountains are brought on by merchants for their own purposes but have served for time out of mind as a river of knowledge and enlightenment for those who seek truth in distant lands, such as I. These caves, the teachings of the Buddha, all these have come from India.'

'Are you – is it that you are a Buddhist teacher yourself?'

Dao Pa stopped. 'I will not tell you what I am.'

He looked once at Nicander then drew a square in the sand. 'If I do, you will have a form of words you believe perfectly describes both me and the structure of my thought.'

269

He stepped into the square. 'And by this you have made a prison for me. I cannot escape. You have confined me here and will make measure of every word I utter, every truth I reveal by the bounds of this prison for evermore.'

'Then you *are* a teacher.'

'I have my disciples, whom I needs must from time to time abandon for the pleasures of solitude. But now you are my teacher. Tell me – what is the essence of the Greek mysteries?'

Nicander felt unreality creeping in. Here he was, about to convey what he knew of Pythagoras and the rest to an oriental mystic at the edge of the wildest desert in the world.

'There are many philosophy masters in Greek thought, Dao Pa. Yet I believe you will find the greatest of these is Aristotle. At the heart of his teaching is one truth that to me lies at the centre of all things.'

'Do continue, I pray you.'

'Well, this is the prime thing we hold so precious. That nothing, no idea or belief can be accepted, without we have evidence for it. And if there is evidence in our hands, we are obliged to admit it as a truth.'

Dao Pa turned to the sea of rearing dunes. 'Come.'

Nicander followed him up the face of a nearer one, the hot sand running like water to make every step an aching trial.

Eventually they reached the top but did not stop to take in the spectacular panorama, stumping and sliding down until they were at the bottom. On all sides the dunes soared up. A trap of silence so complete Nicander thought he could hear his heart beating.

Dao Pa turned to him. 'What can you see?'

'Why, nothing but sand – the dunes.'

'Yes. You are born here and cannot leave. What evidence have you that within less than the length of a single camel train there are living, breathing humans who have their being in creating works of art of great beauty?'

'Evidence?'

'There is none. Nothing by your philosophy that reveals this alternate existence. Yet it exists!'

There could be no answer.

'And by this we have that there must be hidden worlds of man and gods that we can never know – and it would be folly indeed to reject their existence.'

Nicander felt the certainties he had lived with recede, the mental ground under him shift.

'Dao Pa – tell me now of your philosophy. What do you hold most precious?'

'This is not an easy question to answer. The Buddhists, Confucians, others, all have reached the same verity: that it is the Tao that is the first cause, the essence of existence – and our striving to understand it, that is the true study of man.'

'The Tao?'

'The way of all things. It is a great matter and cannot be told so easily. But shall we talk of it . . . ?'

CHAPTER THIRTY-SEVEN

Marius sat up, irritated. His head hurt and he resented Nicander's dig at him about the silver. He wasn't sure how much was left of their little hoard but it wouldn't be much, the woman drank like a fish.

The hard fact was that they had no money of their own. They were dependent on a noble lady for their means.

For most of his life he'd been a free soul. The legion couldn't care less about what the soldiers did out of the ranks and he had learnt many a trick of survival when they had gone unpaid, as so often they did. But this was no hard-arse army camp with only sorry-looking followers on offer, instead he had the run of a town with all the temptations a free spirit could crave – if he could find the necessary. And who knew what other oasis fleshpots there would be on the trail?

It came to him as he strolled outside to squint at the day.

The escort was quartered out of town, away from the gentle folk. He found them at the usual tasks: digging latrines, fletching arrows, mustering stores, checking harnesses.

'Hey there, soldiers!' he called. The Chinese he'd picked up was no match for Nicander's gifted delivery but these were a bunch of rough-neck Central Asians with no need for niceties.

They looked up, curious.

'Just came to check out what an army camp looks like these days,' he chuckled. 'I was a sandal-man m'self just a few years back.'

What was probably a tessararius equivalent came up, wiping a blade he'd been honing. 'Where you been a soldier?' he growled.

'Ma Lai Ssu. Out on garrison at the western frontier.'

'Aldar the Gokturk. Not Khotan way?'

'No. I said real western garrison – up on the mountains.'

'So you seen our camp. And?'

'Just interested in your weapons. We didn't go much on bows out there, more your blade. Bit more reliable, like, out in the rocks.'

'We're archers.'

'I saw. Show us your bow – it looks a bit strange.'

One was fetched. Marius recognised it instantly as a Scythian design – not one piece but made of wood and horn bonded together with fish glue in a sinuous double curve. At the ends, the nock was carved out of bone and in the centre the bow was well reinforced with animal sinew.

He took it, careful to handle it awkwardly. 'Bit small,' he said doubtfully. 'Can I have a go?'

'String it for him,' Aldar ordered.

'Show us a shot or two yourself first,' Marius said diffidently.

The edge of the dunes was the obvious target and a small melon was placed some way up. A quiver of arrows was brought which Aldar threw to one of his men.

He took position fifty feet off and drew smartly. Sighting quickly, the man let fly, but it kicked up sand inches to the left.

'Well done!' Marius exclaimed as sincerely as he could.

The man grunted in exasperation and took his time with the next shot. It skewered the melon.

'Should get it first shot,' Aldar spat. 'Bastard enemy not wait for second.'

He retrieved the weapon and handed it to Marius. 'You go!'

Stepping back in alarm, he gingerly accepted it. It was light and handy, an ideal cavalry weapon but testing the string with his finger he found the draw was formidable.

He'd noticed the arrow was shot from the right-hand side while Roman practice was always the left. He raised the bow, canting it over to emphasise the apparent awkwardness and drew slowly. It was stiff going but he could feel the power in the higher note of the sinew and horsehair string.

The dune was dotted with small clumps of sage. He sighted on one as his mark as he had no intention of hitting the target. He held his breath and loosed – the flight was fast and flat in trajectory, piercing the tuft off-centre. A nice weapon and it seemed he'd kept his eye in over the years.

'Not good. Another!' Aldar said.

'I was near, though, wasn't I!' Marius retorted. He'd need a few more to get right back to where he'd been.

He selected another tussock and heard those behind comment on his crazy left-hand shooting, which suited him nicely. This time he scored the centre of the tuft, at least four feet away from the melon.

'I think you stay with holy song, do better than this to enemy.'

'One more!'

He let it spray sand only a foot away. 'Hey! Did you see that – not bad at all!'

'You frighten him only.'

'I'm getting better at it,' Marius said stubbornly.

'No good. Have to stop. We got work to do now.'

'Wait!' He fumbled and brought out some coins. 'Look, I wager my next one gets closer. Who'll match my bet?'

He had them. He could see it in their eyes.

The next shot, to general laughter, was off two feet. Ruefully, he paid up.

'No, I want a chance to get it back. Here, I've still got more coin.'

The bet was gleefully accepted but, before he could let fly, there was a sudden stir behind.

'What's all this, then?' came the ill-tempered voice of Colonel Ya.

'Oh – this Ma *sheng*. We teach him shoot.'

'You? Couldn't hit a sick camel at ten paces! Give me that.' He seized the bow and strung an arrow.

'Watch me!' He made much of settling his stance and sighting up then down several times.

Marius could hardly believe his luck. The man was bringing the arrow down from above on to the target, a showy but useless move that ruined the sight picture until the last moment. The shot was fair however, near centre but a little above the target.

'See? That's how a professional does it.'

'Isn't this a bit close?' Marius wondered. 'I wouldn't want an enemy nearer than a hundred feet, I'd think.'

'If you insist then, Ma,' he grumbled and paced out double the distance. He loosed off, making fair practice, the arrow whistling to thunk in a foot or two to the left. 'Not bad,' Ya grunted.

'I could do better!' Marius blurted.

'A holy man handy with a bow? I've never heard of it!'

'I can! I will!' he said in a hot temper. 'Look – I'll put all this down on that I'll get closer than you!'

'You're not serious, man.'

'I am! And I'll take anything you lot can put up as well. I can get more from My Lady!'

There was a pause then a babble of excitement.

Ya cut across it. 'Very well – to teach you a lesson the expensive way.'

He pointed down range. 'Let's see what you can do, Ma.'

Marius waited until all bets had been laid, then neatly planted his arrow three inches closer to the target.

An incredulous gasp went up. 'You lucky – cannot do it again!'

'I can. But it will cost you,' he said, taking his winnings.

Ya's face suffused with red. He took up the bow. This time he scored a foot or so above.

Marius's arrow was six inches nearer.

'Steady, sir. Can't let a holy man best you.'

'Out of my way, oaf,' snarled Ya and took his time. Enough for Marius to muster bets from newcomers eager to have a piece of the action.

Ya was now shaking with anger and the hit was a good three feet to the right.

Time to collect.

These were honest soldiers but run-of-the-mill, nothing to set before the legionary who had of all in the cohort been chosen to stand with the best to bring down mighty cataphract Persian knights.

In one quick motion Marius brought up the bow for the last shot. It transfixed the remains of the melon.

He gathered up his winnings and left with a cheery wave.

CHAPTER THIRTY-EIGHT

Marius was stretched out savouring his little victory when Nicander arrived back.

He opened his eyes. 'Where've you been, Nico? You've missed the excitement.'

'What do you mean?'

'The Tibetans. It's worse than Su thought. They've cut the route and we're stranded. What a pity, when I've been to so much trouble seeing to our capital!'

He slapped down his haul, a goodly selection of every coin traded on the caravan routes of the desert.

'Where—'

'Never mind that for now.' Marius swung down his legs. 'There's a get-together tonight. All caravan members who have an interest, what we'll do next. Su isn't going to make a move without he gets backing, which means some sort o' vote.'

'To head out and take on the Tibetans with a bigger escort or wait, you mean?'

'No idea. He's going to lay out the options. My feeling is we can't wait around – if the Emperor is that set on seeing our heads on a pole he'll have agents out to the borders.'

'You've got to be right, we daren't stay here.'

* * *

The meeting was held in the Golden Peach but there was nothing light-hearted about the patrons on this occasion.

'What is it that they're such a risk to us, these Tibetans?' Korkut asked Su.

'They took Miran. We can't go around, we don't know what's on the other side and besides we can't shift enough supplies for that distance to do it.'

'So it's all off for Khotan.'

'I didn't say that.'

'Why don't we double our escort?' called one of the older merchants. 'Should be enough to sort out a lot of rogue Tibetans. Or help bluff our way through.'

'There's none available hereabouts. Southbound caravan took 'em all.'

'We wait?' suggested one of the Buddhist monks.

'Not possible,' snapped Korkut. 'I have to deliver to Khotan and can't delay indefinitely.'

'And I've got a contract to supply and can't sit on capital doing nothing.'

'But if we can't get through, everyone's going to have to think again!' growled another.

'Su *sheng*?' Nicander asked.

'I can't have a view, I'm not paying, it's not my risk.'

'Nevertheless, you have a duty to your caravan and its people,' Ying Mei's cool voice interjected. 'To assist them with their decision it's of value to have your estimate of our position. Do please let us hear it.'

Su flushed. 'My Lady, you have to understand—'

'Your opinion in this is as much to us, as the worth of your judgement is to our course through the desert. How can it be different?'

'Well said, Lady!' a merchant called.

Su frowned darkly. 'How we go on has to be your own decision! That's the way of it in a caravan.'

He sniffed importantly. 'Yet I'll give you my feelings about it. That's all!'

'Well, you've got only a few choices. The first is, you don't go on, therefore the caravan terminates here. All advance fees and monies returnable at this point. The second, you go on – but retrace and go for the northern route right around the Taklamakan desert – get to Khotan the long way.'

Mutterings arose which he stopped with a glare. 'If you do this, there's a few things to think on. It'll be high summer across the other side and there's some who'll see it a torment too far, Turfan in summer.'

He let it sink in.

'And, it'll cost you. Not only is it longer that way but there's transit fees to pay for more oasis kingdoms, although it's likely they'll be modest, they wanting to attract more caravan trade.

'Then there's those here who'll tell you, the northern route is not pleasant. In fact it's bloody hard. No horses, certainly no carriages,' he said with a glance at Ying Mei.

'No horses means no cavalry. The Hsien Pei Mongols have been quiet so far this year but we'll be passing their territory and we could get unlucky. Those of a nervous nature should think about it.'

'But I'm understanding from all this you recommend we should do it,' Korkut said.

'I'm not saying you should do anything. And as well, there's another decision you have to make.'

'What's that?'

'Don't go around the edges to get to Turfan and the other oases – strike out across the desert directly, the Loulan route.'

'Is it easier?'

'It's worse – but it's quicker.'

'How worse?'

Su rubbed his chin speculatively. 'Well, now, and I'm not the one to put you off . . . but Loulan is suffering. Their lake Lop Nor is playing tricks on 'em, retreating away and letting the dunes swallow 'em up piece by piece. I've not been that way for years, can't say for sure they're even still there, so if we go that way we could find ourselves gasping for water – at a ghost city in the dunes.'

Korkut stood up and looked about him. 'So. You've made things clear for

279

us, thank you. As I see it, there's only two alternatives. Give up right here or go the long way around the Taklamakan. No other. Am I right?'

'Can't argue with that.'

'Then I suggest we put it to the vote. Those who want to call it all off now.'

The monks voted for it to a man, as did one or two others, but when hands were counted for the longer route there was no doubt about the sentiment of the majority.

'Seems you have your answer, Su *sheng*.'

CHAPTER THIRTY-NINE

The caravan left the pleasures of Dunhuang and headed out. To cross where two deserts collided.

To the right: the hideous extremes of the Black Gobi stony desert; left: the vast sea of dunes so parched and lifeless that its name meant 'he who goes in never returns', the Taklamakan.

The sounds of squeaking leather, the muffled tread of camel feet and the desultory dinging of bells that every animal now carried seemed overly loud in the awesome stillness.

Several of the merchants rode a tarpan, the stocky steppe pony with much endurance, but they had paid Su dearly for the privilege, some were on camels but most walked at the easy pace of the caravan.

Ying Mei was in a camel howdah, a light structure between the humps with hanging veils for privacy. Tai Yi kept pace with the animal on foot, while behind, Nicander and Marius walked alongside Meng Hsiang.

It was hot, but a heat so dry that perspiration evaporated immediately. More bearable than humid heat but hard going over the sun-blasted ground. Nicander was grateful for his ox-hide calf boots that insulated and cushioned.

He felt for his water gourd. It was barely half-full still short of midday, with the hottest part of the day to come. Those unable to control their thirst would be given no extra. The next fill would not be until the evening at the water skins.

Next to him the splotched brown bulk of Meng Hsiang moved on in long deliberate paces, the splayed toes sure and firm in the sand. The beast could go for a week or more without water, and the shaggy coat that looked so hot in fact kept the burning heat of the sun at bay.

On impulse he reached out to pat his muzzle. The camel swung his head about, looking at him in mild interest.

Something resolved out of the rumpled dunes ahead. Trees! With the miracle of green on them! Some quirk in the lie of the desert had brought water to the surface – a modest spring that gouted from under a rock ledge to meander lazily on gravel for a hundred yards or more before dissipating into the sand.

The camels were released and lined the watercourse. They drank swiftly, some with deft flicks throwing water over their backs and snorting with pleasure.

At the source drinking gourds were refilled and like the others, Nicander drank thirstily, revelling in the life-giving coolness. It had a faintly sulphurous tang but at that moment it was the best water he had tasted in his life.

Suddenly aware that he was being watched he looked up and saw Dao Pa standing apart from the others.

The man was leaning on his staff, wearing a peculiar wide hat with two flaps that hung down over his ears.

'Master Dao!' Nicander exclaimed, 'I didn't know you were with us!'

'Quite so. Yet surely this is to be expected.'

'Because you . . . ?'

'That I need to reach Khotan and this is the only course open to me, yes. But more to your understanding is to perceive that of all the substantiality and conditions of this world only a very small proportion are permitted a frail mortal to know. There is an unknowable infinity of others he will never be aware of, yet most surely exist independent of his rational observation.'

'Without evidence of their existence.'

'You are progressing well on your path to the Tao, Ni K'an Ta.'

'Thank you, Master. If we—'

'Mount up!' Su's voice broke through impatiently.

Nicander reluctantly found his place in the line and waited while the caravan got under way.

He vowed to seek out Dao Pa that night; they would talk more and the frightful wasteland would retreat, if only for an hour or two.

When the sun lost its ferocity and began its slow dip towards extinction, Su called a halt by a long weathered ridge.

'As far as we go on this easy stretch. We'll leave the harder for tomorrow.'

There was speculation at his words at the evening camp.

'He means the heat. Have you noticed? As we went north from Chang An it's got hotter and hotter. Stands to reason it'll be worse the further we go.'

'And colder – at night, I mean. I don't think it's that. More like the water's going to give out.'

'Or the Hsien Pei will be waiting and we'll have to fight our way through.'

'If they're out, I don't give much for our chances – we've an escort as will see off any bandits but the Mongols are a different matter. Why, four years back – or was it five, they took a caravan and we didn't find the bodies until last year.'

The chat stopped when Su himself arrived, looking tired and distracted. 'Things on the trail are going to get worse – a whole lot worse,' he muttered to no one in particular.

With a sweep of his hand he cut short the anxious babble. 'You'll find out soon enough. Now let's have some eats.'

The mutton stew was cheering against the chill of the night and with the appearance of the *hung tsao chiu* things were definitely on the rise. Made from dried and powdered buckthorn date, the hot drink was mixed with a liquor. Su swore by its effectiveness against both cold and heat and declared that it would be on issue every night while in the desert.

Nicander was puzzled. The fierce-eyed seer was nowhere to be seen.

He asked Su, 'Could you tell me where I'd find Dao Pa at all?'

'Never heard of him.'

'Some kind of monk, I think. Comes from the south somewhere, if you saw him you'd never forget the man.'

'Look, I know who's in this caravan and there's no Dao Pa!'

'Beard, biggish fellow – and blue eyes.'

'A foreigner! I know all you buggers, and there's no one like that. Now I'm bloody tired. Why don't you leave me be, hey?'

Nicander shrugged. He'd search out Dao Pa later.

There seemed to be an unspoken acknowledgement that any entertainment in this appalling loneliness would have to come from among themselves. One of the cameleers came forward shyly, and sat cross-legged. He pulled out a flute and softly accompanied by another on a small drum performed a dreamy piece.

They played a second tune, spirited and gay.

Zarina got to her feet. 'Let cares take flight!' she laughed, and began dancing.

Shouts of encouragement came from all sides and she drew up one of the young serving girls and the two whirled and gyrated in a dance of Central Asia, ribbons swirling, dresses flaring, faces alight.

They sat to thunderous applause.

A woman who tended to the cooking was next. From one of the many tribes from the outer lands, her features were bluff, oriental and sun-darkened. She wore a padded tunic and her boots were as colourful as the long scarf that she coyly flicked as she stepped into the firelight.

Another drummer joined in. The rhythm set toes tapping as she strutted about in a high-fingered twirl, moving faster and faster until she collapsed in an exhausted heap.

Nicander was enchanted. It was so unreal: far out in the desert, untouchably remote and so dependent on each other and their animals, a bubble of humanity progressing through a hostile universe.

A gruff merchant stood up and came forward. He said some

incomprehensible introductory words and then, unaccompanied, sang in a deep voice that rang with emotion.

There was a pause; people looked about expectantly. A voice called from the other side of the fire. It was Ying Mei asking if anyone possessed a pipa, or any kind of lute. Someone brought an old but clearly cherished yu ch'in, a circular instrument with four strings.

She accepted it gracefully and experimentally plucked delicate notes.

She nodded. '"Water Lilies in the Shade of Purple Bamboo".'

The music flowed like water in a brook, tinkling and rushing, her clear, high voice complementing it. Around the fire there was rapturous attention and when the piece concluded with a last melting and affecting note held to nothing, there was stunned silence and then wild applause.

Korkut stirred in admiration. 'I'd have thought that kind of playing you'd only ever hear at the imperial court.'

Her next piece was more robust. 'Night of the Torch Festival.'

First one drummer then another picked up on the processional rhythm and the flute came in with an ingenious cross-melody.

After another two tunes she sat down, pleading fatigue.

The fire crackled and spat, its red glare illuminating the near desert with moving shadows and ghost-like shapes.

Marius leapt up. 'Damn it, I'm in!'

'Fighting song o' the Pannonians!' he roared in Latin. Marching up and down he belted out a legionary favourite, his audience bemused but appreciative.

When it was over he flopped heavily next to Nicander. 'Be buggered, but that felt good!' he muttered, taking a long pull at his *hung tsao*. 'Memories . . .'

Then he turned and shoved Nicander to his feet. 'Sing something, Greek!'

There was a patter of polite applause but Nicander's mind went blank.

It had to be something from the motherland. Perhaps from the rich traditions of Pythagoras's music of the spheres, one of the songs which he had learnt so painfully at school.

The difficulty was that there was no *kithara* to play and also the Grecian modes were so at variance with the oriental. In their classicism they could seem remote and unfeeling. He refused to compromise with Byzantine catch-songs of the street so there was nothing for it but to try to conjure something of value and moment.

He stepped forward. A vision of a scowling music dominie with a willow switch waiting for his first bad note threatened to unnerve him but he manfully launched into one of the Hymns of Apollo.

A Greek song was a series of long notes, full of feeling and intended to be accompanied by a plucked instrument which would drop notes rich with meaning into the spaces between.

There was a respectful quiet as he did his best, striving for pure and golden notes but aware that without the plangent twanging of the *kithara* the strange Greek intervals would sound baffling to his audience.

Then a soft tone sounded – and another. In the right places and while not in strict Phrygian mode, they were a very good approximation. He looked round. Ying Mei with her borrowed *juan* had come around to his side.

She stood beside him, watching intently.

They finished the song together to a wondering applause.

He bowed, touched at her gesture. 'Thank you, My Lady.'

She smiled – but without a word returned to Tai Yi.

CHAPTER FORTY

Day followed day as they passed through a moonscape of ragged sere cliffs and sand bluffs.

For all of one stage the camels trudged through a salt-encrusted surface of hard-packed clay, what remained of the inland sea Lop Nor. The spongy grit slowed them and made them spit harshly. At one point Su stopped the caravan while chunks of salt were lifted and stowed for later use.

Occasionally there were old watercourses, meandering to peter out among the sand-blown flatlands with relics of past times of plenty – low thorny bushes, stunted clumps of wiry grasses, bleached skeletons of long-ago tree life.

The heat rose and the stony plains shimmered and rippled into an uncertain distance, each plodding pace an effort of will, the only distraction the occasional whirlwind of sand moving over the ground like a dancing ghost.

How Su could make out where to go in the stony wastes was beyond Nicander. If it was by recall, he would need to remember hundreds, thousands of miles of a featureless landscape from all perspectives and all seasons – or was it by some other way, perhaps watching the angle of the sun, the stars at night?

One afternoon the camels imperceptibly quickened their pace, raising their heads and snorting. They came upon a small group of wells, each some four feet across, and with age-withered fitments including ropes and buckets.

The caravan stayed several hours, sitting under makeshift awnings while the animals took their fill. However, this water was brackish and no one felt inclined to drink it.

Then it was the dunes again – a broad tongue of the Taklamakan that had to be crossed before the Gobi beyond.

The camels wound up into the maze of vast dunes, picking their way along the crests and into the hollows between in patient, slow steps.

The yellow-grey sand was an endless succession of immense curved waves, shimmering in the heat. There was no rest, Su was anxious to be quit of the soft dunes.

At last they subsided and quite abruptly terminated in a vast wall.

The caravan wound down on to the flat desert floor and Su called a halt, then climbed to the top of the tallest dune.

'We overnight here,' he announced bleakly when he descended.

It had been some time since he had last been this way and the dunes had shifted inexorably forward. Not only that, but their shape was now quite different and they were without any kind of track or sign. After the traverse, the waterhole he had expected was not there.

They were lost.

As the camp soberly prepared for the night, Su rode out on a tarpan. He returned just before dark set in, his face long.

The travellers turned in early; who knew what lay in store for them the next day?

Even before the stars had left the sky the caravan was assembled and ready to depart. Su looked gaunt as he went over his orders yet again for the conserving of water and protection from the sun.

When it became light enough to see he would have to decide the heading: his choice would save them or doom them to a slow death.

The order was made. To the east, toward the orb of the dawning sun.

It was a different, bleaker landscape. The sand was swept clean from the desert floor; they now faced a stippled plain of stones – not the familiar water-rounded ones about a river but sharp, many-coloured gravel.

A wind arose that whipped up spiteful sand particles, stinging exposed flesh and working into clothing.

They pressed ahead. Beside Nicander, Meng Hsiang paced on, his uncomplaining calmness a reassurance, a fellow living creature who was not intimidated by their peril. There were lessons to be had even from a beast of burden, and he vowed to bring it up with Dao Pa – when he could find him.

He reached out and patted the big flank.

Out of the distance huge vertical forms coalesced out of the haze. Thrusting up out of the flatness of the desert, fluted and pillared, these seemed like the very bones of the earth rearing up.

The caravan reached the monoliths, the travellers awed by their majesty and height, their untouchable silence. They threaded through and Su called a halt in the shade of one.

They dismounted, and as if there were safety in numbers, stayed together and sipped from their gourds.

'We can't go on like this!' one of the merchants moaned. 'While we've got the chance we should take it.'

'What's that, then?' Korkut grunted, looking up from his seat on a rocky slab.

'Accept that we're lost. Turn round, go back and over the dunes. Then at least we'll know where we are.'

'Su knows what he's doing,' Zarina said. 'I trust him to get us through!' The desert had not been kind to her: dust-blown, her clothes worn, she was not the sparkling dancer of some nights before.

'If he does, then why are we lost?' the merchant came back instantly. 'To go back we lose a few days, but to go forward without knowing—'

'He's striking out until he finds the track he knows,' Korkut snapped. 'Let him get on with it!'

'Why should we all . . .'

Nicander wandered away from the bickering, remembering his foreboding as they left Chang An. He stared up at the forbidding monoliths and wondered at their meaning. Were they emerging from some subterranean hell into the world of man, a fearsome token of the diabolic realm of devils and demons – or were they the cast-down remains of giant columns that once reached into heaven?

A memory of his mother squeezed at his heart. It was so unfair; that he had shortly to lay down his life in this—

There – in the shadow under a rock slab . . .

'Dao Pa! You . . .'

The man was sitting cross-legged, his hands in his lap cupped and facing upwards.

'Where've you been? I've been asking—'

He turned slowly. 'Solitude is the highest blessing to the soul. Grant that I may so take of it.'

'Master, we're in such danger and you need to be alone?'

'You think deliverance is to be found in the company of others in like affliction? You may share their bitterness, they may feel yours – but a true release is only to be found within yourself. To understand your place in the Tao, to have your being at last one with the universe.'

'When we face . . . what we do, you still find time for such?'

'What better? Tell me; in your philosophy, Ni *lao na*, what course do you take when all else is in vain and hopeless?'

'We . . .'

'Then preparing the soul for what must come seems to me the more rational course.'

'Yes, Master,' Nicander said humbly.

'There are powers within, that you are unaware you possess. Together we will realise them.'

'We have no time.'

'Rest your fears. Su is right – soon he will find an oasis of running water and the knowledge of his position. We will have time.'

'What! How can you know this?'

'You have much to learn, Ni *lao na*, but you will achieve it. And now, for myself I crave the benison of meditation.'

He raised his head and closed his eyes.

The caravan got under way at first light, still eastwards. They would proceed on until the last possible minute of daylight before stopping on the flatness between two monoliths.

After an uneasy night they resumed their onward toil. The monoliths were left behind and the landscape became overlain with undulating ripples of hard-packed sand and further on, the fantastic sight of a fleet of sculpted rock formations, streamlined and sleek.

Too troubled to wonder at them the lonely caravan moved on into ragged, red-streaked sandhills, even the camels making heavy going of it. They had reached a gully between two lesser ranges when Meng Hsiang gave a low growl, a long purring grumble. He tossed his head, snatching at the head-rope, showing the whites of his eyes.

'Steady, there,' Nicander said, uneasy about what unseen threat out in the savage wilderness had alarmed him. He went to pat the big muzzle but it was jerked away. He heard other snorts and gnarls behind and realised the whole camel train was disturbed. A stab of fear went through him.

A little further on they came across it. A field of bones. Bleached a glaring white, obscenely protruding from rags and the mummified remains of bodies half-covered in sand, camel skeletons each arched back the same way at the agonising moment of death, their burdens still tied on them.

There was no pattern to it – the bodies lay at random in all directions. Had they kept together to the last and then . . . crept away for their final minutes under the pitiless sky?

Gulping, he went to the nearest human remains and stared down at the untidy body. The skull still had hair plastered on a leathery skin, the desiccated face leering at the world that had taken its life.

'Poor devil,' he whispered. 'How long have you been here?'

'You never can tell.' It was Marius, standing behind him. 'The desert dries 'em out, then leaves it alone. Could be one year, a hundred. Who knows.'

'We could be joining them, my friend.'

'Yes, possibly. Doesn't mean we give it away before we have to? Come on, Nico. Think what we've got in our little chest there. Some day . . .'

He couldn't find words and turned away.

There was a knot of people around Su, shouting at him in despair and anger. The voices carried clearly – Su was arguing that this only proved they were on the right track, that this was where other caravans passed, just that this particular one was ill-prepared.

He set the camel train in motion again, the imperative of survival taking priority over the impulse to provide a decent burial.

They had left the bone-field far behind but Meng Hsiang was still not happy. His eyes were rolling and he was jibbing. After what he had just seen Nicander was full of dread and the fear of the unknown returned.

The camel wrenched at his rope, snarling in temper and frustration. Nicander tried to calm the beast.

There was shouting at the head of the line and the caravan stopped. Unbelievably he saw that the cameleers were throwing off the nose-peg ropes to let the animals free. As each camel was released it made off at an ungainly lope into the sandhills on the right and disappeared.

From the crest of a nearby coarse, sandy hummock Nicander marvelled at the sight. A sizeable streamlet glittering and lazily meandering before him. And along the bank was green –breathtaking, beautiful, unbelievable green!

He and the others, delirious with the joy of life restored, were soon gulping greedily at the runnels of water.

The camels were in a solid line, splashing and slurping, giving rumbles of contentment and flicking water over themselves. They had been saved – and it had been the camels who had been the means.

They had been travelling so many miles in the gully, not knowing that running parallel, only a short distance away, was water and life. What cruel circumstance had meant that for the other caravan, the wind on that day had chosen to blow in the wrong direction, that their camels had not picked up on the scent of water, while this day theirs had?

Now Su knew where they were. Impatiently he drove the caravan across the braided stream. Then they followed the river for another five miles before they were presented with an even bigger miracle. The oasis village of Yu Li.

Willows, poplars – trees! Growing along the banks and pathways – and an orchard!

Men came out, advancing on the caravan – women too, laughing faces. Stalls of bright melons were wheeled into place under the shade of the poplars, with much chattering, greeting, calling.

The oasis had been planted centuries before, in the time of the Han when caravans traded across immense distances to bring wealth to China and needed fresh supplies and water. That it was situated on the edge of the hideous Gobi was no supernatural feat – all it had needed was the miracle of water. The natural fertility lying waiting in the soil did the rest.

There was even a caravanserai! This far from civilisation it would be too much to expect all the comforts of home but to those emerged from the valley of death it was heaven.

And they would be resting here for a whole three days!

That night as Nicander lay staring up at the smoke-grimed roof, he forgave them everything, even the red-eyed cockroaches as long as his finger, and jumping spiders with bodies as big as pigeon's eggs. He just wished he couldn't hear the crunching of their jaws as they took their prey.

CHAPTER FORTY-ONE

'It's the toughest of all, no doubt about it,' Korkut told Nicander and Marius. 'When we pass through the Shuan Ch'eng range we'll be in the Black Gobi, and that's flat all the way, completely open to the worst from the north.'

'It's late in the season, too, dear,' Zarina said. 'But once we're through to Turfan it's much easier.'

Korkut grimaced. 'Hm. Su heard a rumour that the Mongols are out. That I don't like!'

'He said that we're going to move as fast as we can,' his wife added.

'Meaning it's up early and flogging all day until the last of the light. I'm already feeling it. Perhaps I'm getting too old for this kind of thing.'

The road petered out and once again they were moving over the trackless plain, towards a distant blue-grey rumpled line. In the clear desert air distance was deceptive and it was not for another stage that they had reached the foothills of the range. The peaks were abrupt and craggy with long scree slopes. Su led the camel train through a gloomy defile, its walls sheer and forbidding.

On the other side were uplands populated with jagged boulders, and then another stone-strewn range with a gorge appeared.

As they passed through the ravine, they were met with a wind that set everyone's clothing a-flutter. Down on the level ground it eased off. The landscape was now utterly featureless. Not a hill, a dune or even a distant range, simply an iron-flat stony plain reaching out into the limitless distance.

They tramped on.

The wind picked up with force. It had a coolness in it that was strangely disturbing in the still fierce heat of the sun out of the cloudless sky. With nothing to deflect it, it came in flat and hard, making the camels lurch and stumble. It stung exposed skin with sand and rock particles, whipping mercilessly. Nicander wound cloth around his face and kept his hands inside his robe. He tried to lean into the wind but within a short time it was impossible to move.

The camels knelt down and Nicander and Marius took shelter in the lee of the big bodies, so close they could smell their rank but comforting goat-like smell. Ying Mei and Tai Yi could not be seen through the dust.

The sandstorm passed as quickly as it had arisen. Spluttering and protesting, the camels got to their feet with their riders and the caravan got under way again.

Nicander was taken aback at the sight that met his reddened eyes. On the next camel in front the familiar structure of the howdah was missing, ripped away by the force of the wind. Between the humps was a hunched figure, ragged strips of clothing streaming out in the last of the wind. Another bedraggled figure trudged gamely along beside.

He'd never given much thought to the howdah before; but he now realised it must have been a never-ending nightmare in that lurching, swaying, broiling prison. Yet Ying Mei had always come to the evening fire looking fresh and cool. What torments this noble lady must be enduring!

They set up for the night, the usual desert evening chill an icy breath that came out of nowhere, sending everyone scrabbling for their sheepskins and impatient for a hot supper.

The crew came around with iron pegs for the tents. All eight guys were rigged on each side and fully tensioned.

Soon after midnight the wind got up again, waking Nicander. The sides of the tent began flapping and banging in a terrifying bluster. The wind then turned to a devilish shrieking and the agitated flailing became a vicious thrashing.

With it was a cold that despite his layered clothing pierced his innermost being, leaving only a tiny point of warmth remaining. For hours he lay awake, frightened and shuddering with the cold.

Before first light, the order was given to form up ready as soon as a quick meal was taken. While the tents were struck by the crew, just moving shapes in the gloom, no one spoke for the misery of it all, the need for endurance. Surely this howling wilderness could not last for ever . . .

The first needle-sharp rays of sunlight appeared and they were off once more. The sun rose higher and the icy cold turned to baking heat. A general halt was called to change clothing and then it was onward, always onward, through the unvarying dreary flatness.

The sun dipped in the west and another dramatic desert sunset began building. Marius peered into the distance and growled, 'Something over there!'

With a lurch of unease Nicander spotted a series of black objects on the skyline.

Shouts of alarm came from up and down the camel train as the numbers grew.

An urgent order to halt went out.

Soon half the horizon was filled. There was now no doubt – these were a murderous horde of Hsien Pei Mongols on the move.

'Why have we stopped?' Nicander blurted. 'We've got to get away!'

'Su's right. While we're stationary there's no dust being kicked up. Maybe we've got a chance of not being noticed,' Marius said, steadily watching.

'Our escort . . . ?'

'Haven't a chance. That's cavalry, over firm ground, no cover. We'll be cut to pieces without mercy.'

'So we're . . . doomed?'

'Depends. If we offer to surrender – and if they take it, well, we may get away with slavery o' some kind, but if they're in a murdering mood, I suppose . . .'

Nicander watched the slowly moving host in a chill of horror. They were angling away as if to cut them off – but why weren't they thundering in at speed?

Up and down the line people watched transfixed like statues: there was nothing they could do to save themselves against the brutal flood.

The glorious sunset was shining full on the horde. It picked up an occasional flash of steel, the different horse colours, one or two banners – all pitilessly illuminated in grim detail. But still they made no move to ride in for the kill.

The tension was unbearable. Through Nicander's mind stampeded images of the Ostrogoths' cruel and barbarous attacks. Surely he had not been spared their callous butchery to face his end here in this hell on earth?

Marius stiffened, then turned to him with a twisted smile. 'So o' course, we just wait it out. They'll be off soon and we can get back on the trail,' he added off-handedly.

'What are you saying?' Nicander said incredulously.

'Well, any fool can tell we're right in the eye of the sunset. So they can't see us, can they?' He gestured out behind them to where the final minutes of the sun's glory blazed out.

Su waited a full hour after the Mongols had passed out of sight ahead before giving the order to set up for the night. But there would be no hot food or drink, for no fire dared be lit that might draw attention. As the icy chill stole in everyone crept into their tents in dread of the fearful horde somewhere out there in the night.

The next morning some wondered whether it was wise to continue in the same direction as the Mongol horde, but Su pointed out that the slow-moving caravan would never catch up with their steppe ponies.

The wind started up again, a hard blast that blustered and stung. Nicander felt a grudging admiration for the little figure on the camel ahead, hunched and enduring as the wind plucked and battered. This was suffering indeed and should never be expected of a woman, let alone a gentle-born one. There was nothing now he and Marius were taking that she was not sharing, and she had never once complained.

After two more days there was a subtle change in the desolate landscape: a golden-yellow sand was appearing.

It pleased Korkut. 'Praise the gods! This is Taklamakan sand, but from the Tien Shan mountains. We're nearly through to Yi Wu and from then on it's much easier.'

Nicander remembered being told that where the Kunlun mountains flanked the southern side, the Tien Shan stayed with the north – it meant that they were well on their way to having crossed from one side of the Great Desert to the other, and there it would be the famed oasis kingdoms to welcome them.

The sprawling golden-yellow dunes increased and then they were back on the softness of sand.

It was not long, however, before Nicander sensed there was something affecting Meng Hsiang. Not in the same way as when he had smelt water but there was an uneasiness, a restlessness. His big head swung this way and that, and he gave out occasional drawn-out rumbles.

'I think old Meng Hsiang is having a fit,' he called across to Marius.

'Can't be the Mongols, he didn't worry about 'em last time. Or the water – didn't they give him a swill before we started out?'

Their stout-hearted beast had never let them down. 'He's on to something, and I don't know what it is. I don't like this, Marius!'

Whatever it was, the whole camel train was getting infected. Up and down the line there were tossing heads, ill-tempered snarling, and then the caravan came lurching to a stop.

Nicander shook his head. 'What's got into them?' There was nothing ahead that looked like a threat.

Then the camels jostled together, knelt down and lowered their heads, thrusting their noses into the sand and sending up snuffling fountains.

Alarmed shouts rang out. Korkut began hastily winding a cloth around his wife's face and others were doing likewise in a frenzy.

Seemingly out of nowhere, a long wall of ochre dust and cloud towering up to the sky, dark and whirling, was advancing over the ground towards them, swallowing up everything in its path.

'Sandstorm. Get something over your eyes and mouth – quickly, Nico!' Marius cried. There was no time to look to the others.

They threw themselves down against the camel. A fitful wind started, then rapidly grew stronger, spitefully whipping up sand. Then in a sudden buffet the storm struck. In an instant they were plunged into a chaos of darkness and a hot whirling fury that howled and battered at them.

Nicander choked and gasped as dust and sand was driven into his hair and clothing and every crease and orifice. He felt a drag on his legs and realised he was being slowly buried in sand. He kicked out and tried to rise but his senses were disoriented by the whirling chaos and he fell to his hands and knees, crowded and bullied by the howling storm.

It was difficult to think: the overriding imperative was to find the camel again – if he was driven away it would be into the fearful desert where he would be lost for ever. He crawled one way. Nothing. Then he tried another direction and to his intense relief found he was clutching Meng Hsiang's front leg. He hauled himself along and buried his face in the thick fur of the neck, revelling in the pungent smell.

He clung there while the whistle and roar of the tempest went on and on but then quite as suddenly as it had come, it weakened and died. Nicander snatched a glance around him. The air was still full of dust-smoke but as it cleared the still forms of the camels could be seen, half-buried in sand piled up on one side. Here and there things began to move, ghostly shapes throwing off powdered sand.

Marius heaved himself up, spitting and swearing while Meng Hsiang spluttered and lifted his head, shaking it vigorously and snorting loudly.

Nicander stood up too and heard a harsh, barking cry. It was Tai Yi, in a frenzy by their camel. In a stab of foreboding he stumbled over.

'She's there, in there!' Tai Yi sobbed, scrabbling frantically. Ying Mei had gone the wrong side of the camel and been buried somewhere under the slope of sand.

Nicander pushed Tai Yi aside. He bent down and with his legs astride, paddled the sand clear in a continuous stream until he found a limb and knew where her head must lie. He shifted along and did it again. There was movement: he scooped quickly each side. Ying Mei's arching body then heaved clear, her head hanging while she choked and retched.

She twisted around. Her wild, dust-smeared face stared up at Nicander then crumpled in emotion. Tears slashed streaks through the dust. Impulsively Nicander held her – she clung to him, whimpering while he smoothed her gritted hair and tried to find something to say.

Then he felt a determined grip on his shoulders, pulling him away. Ying Mei held on desperately, clutching at him as though to life itself, while the sobs racked her slight body.

'My Lady! My Lady – please!' Tai Yi admonished. 'Do remember who you are!'

Ying Mei fell free and dropped to the ground.

Tai Yi then said firmly, 'That'll do, Ni *sheng*. We'll call you if you're needed.'

'No,' Ying Mei said in a weak voice.

'My Lady?'

She heaved herself to a sitting position, her face smeared, her clothing torn and ragged, a pitiable innocent taken by the sandstorm now unrecognisable as the Lady Kuo of Yeh Ch'eng.

Taking a shuddering breath she cried, 'I can't go on like this any more, Ah Lai, I just can't.'

'My Lady – it won't be like this for ever. Su *sheng* said that—'

'No, it's not that at all. Dear Ah Lai! Can't you see? I can't face being a lady any more. I can't!'

'My child, you shouldn't take on so. It'll be better . . .'

Ying Mei tried to smooth her tangled hair then replied, 'Ah Lai, I know. But you see, if we had a full court, attendants and the rest I could do my duty by my father, but out here in this frightful desert . . .'

'Nonsense! You are born and bred a Kuo of illustrious ancestry. This can never be—'

'No, I'm decided.'

'My Lady?'

'That I want to be among friends! Those who are as frayed and tattered as I am, that I don't need to put on my airs.'

'Child, this is—'

'To talk with them, bear these hardships together, enjoy things – surely you must understand, Ah Lai?'

'I don't.'

'I wish to be just Ying Mei to everyone from now on.'

Tai Yi froze in horror.

She gave a shy smile at Nicander. 'And I shall call you, let me see, Ah Yung – the brave one. Who I do now thank for my deliverance.'

Then she turned to Marius. 'And this is Ah Wu, the fierce one.'

'My Lady, this is—'

'Ah Lai!' she warned, then relented. 'Only for now, I promise. When we're in . . . different circumstances I vow, I'll behave like a high-born again.'

CHAPTER FORTY-TWO

The Yi Wu oasis appeared from nothing, a miraculous conjuring of life out of the stifling aridity of the desert. There was a clear rivulet, the sweet smell of fruits and blossoms on the air, and a little caravanserai that was eager for custom.

Their mud and straw cells were clean, the melons cool, and delicious spicy skewers of vegetable and lamb were promised for later.

'Wonder if My Lady has found her airs again, now she's back with people,' Marius said, as Nicander went to work with borrowed scissors on his thick growth of hair.

Tai Yi had contrived to keep her mistress apart from them, pleading the effects of the sandstorm on her health.

'The way she is, who knows what she'll do next,' he replied a little too off-handedly.

He splashed more water on the black locks, hoping this would make the blunt scissors cut better.

Marius gave him a curious look.

'As long as she keeps away and doesn't cause me trouble, I'll be polite enough.'

A cracked bell was the summons to eat and they wasted no time in getting to the small dining chamber and finding a place next to Korkut and his wife. Ying Mei was nowhere to be seen.

'Are you feeling better, Korkut *tai tai*?' Nicander asked Zarina. She was looking quite different to the figure that had emerged from the desert storm, red-eyed and spitting sand.

'Why yes, Ni *lao na*. And the Lady P'eng? I heard she was near to being buried.'

'Her companion tells me she is recovering.'

'Went down the wrong side of the camel,' Korkut sniffed. 'I would have thought it your job to tell her about these things, Ni *sheng*.'

'We're not her keepers!' he replied defensively.

'Never mind,' Zarina said hastily. 'Here she is!'

Ying Mei was transformed. Her complexion had a fresh, natural glow and she had acquired from somewhere a flowing pale-green embroidered dress and a short jacket in blue.

'Good evening, my friends!' she called gaily. Next to her Tai Yi wore her traditional robes and a disapproving glare.

Without waiting for an invitation Ying Mei sat down with the little group. 'I've heard it will be hotter still before we get to Turfan.'

'My Lady, if you—'

'Korkut *sheng*, I'm not to be known by my friends in that way. We've faced things together – it would please me should you call me just Ying Mei. And I will call you Zarina.'

The merchant looked at his wife blankly.

'Well, Ying Mei,' Zarina said, daring all, 'we've heard the same. It will be quite a trial for we ladies.'

Ying Mei smiled warmly. 'It will, but we'll get through, I'm sure. The Emperor decrees – that is, I've heard that the Emperor himself sends for his mare's nipple grapes from Turfan, and they come in camel containers packed in snow. They even manage to reach the capital without melting!'

'Holy Qormusta! This is what he does with our taxes? No wonder there's unrest!'

'Please don't swear, dear,' Zarina murmured, then added, 'And how about your General Wang Chih? When he goes on campaign he has a camel with a tank, just to keep his fish swimming and fresh.'

'Have you ever been to Turfan?' Nicander asked Korkut.

'No, never.'

Neither had any of the others, it seemed.

'Let's ask Su Li to come over and tell us something of it,' Ying Mei suggested.

The caravan master, expansive with wine, happily complied.

Yes, Turfan was indeed hot – but most houses had underground retreats where it would be cool enough to sleep. Yet it was close to the Tien Shan mountains where the snow would be falling feet thick while they were baking below. But snowmelt was the very reason for the existence of Turfan. It came down in torrents, streaming far out into the desert. With it, irrigation was possible and there was more than enough to sustain a whole kingdom.

The dynasty that ruled Kaochang might owe fealty to any external power that was in sway at the time but thrived by reason of one thing: competence at regulating the caravan trade. A river of precious and exotic foreign goods flowed in both directions, real wealth, with the Sogdians at its very heart making it happen.

As Turfan was allowed its independence the Chinese had no power there and therefore they should expect all the bureaucratic nonsense of a foreign country waiting for them. Fortunately, Su had Sogdian friends who would be able to help matters along – for a small fee.

With a glint in his eye Su declaimed that Turfan was to be experienced! All the races and breeds of man that ever were – long-haired Gokturks, uncouth Uighurs, the odd Tibetan, he'd even seen with is own eyes some Tocharians with red hair and blue eyes! And of course those from other oasis kingdoms – the Kuchean dancing girls were famed for their liveliness, and—

'Thank you, Su *hsien sheng*,' Tai Yi said with asperity. 'For giving us an understanding of the nature of Turfan.'

CHAPTER FORTY-THREE

After the hard experiences of the Gobi it was easier going. Days of soft, wind-blown sand and then on the horizon, a grand white-tipped mountain range rising – the Tien Shan. They had crossed from one side of the Great Desert to the other.

With a quickening of the pulse Nicander noted that now their direction was firmly to the west. At the same time the country changed abruptly from the parched glare of desert sands to the sudden green of fertility where a snowmelt river chuckled through.

The caravan closed with the mountains and then, gloriously, a great town lay in the plains beneath them. Turfan.

Within an hour a detachment of Kaochang cavalry had ridden up to escort them in, and they arrived in style.

It was on a scale they hadn't seen since Lan Chou; big, sprawling and with the vigour and noisiness of a great trading centre.

The first order of business was for Su to render his documents relating to his travellers. The pass he held for the caravan as a whole detailed their status and occupations, their intent of travel and liability for imposts.

Each traveller then had to produce their own to be levied a transit fee and issued with a permit. Ying Mei was required to sign for Nicander and Marius; underneath they made their marks – touching the inkstone as instructed, they made three horizontal lines under her beautifully formed characters.

It was a brisk, practised process.

Once dealt with, the travellers were free to go but the camel train remained until Su and the merchants had paid their toll.

The two-storey caravanserai was vast and spacious. Water trickled down one wall, cooling the rooms while the inside courtyard was criss-crossed with a grape trellis which gave welcome shade.

Nicander and Marius cheerfully freshened up. After so long on the trail they were going to have some fun!

'Now, our funds?' Nicander asked.

Their small hoard was laid out, but they were in a foreign country; what did their motley collection of silver, bronze and copper amount to here?

'We need someone who knows the place.'

'Who? Su isn't going anywhere until he's done his haggling, no one else has been here before.'

'So we'll stick together. Where's Korkut?'

'Where do you think? All the merchants have gone off to try their luck.'

'Then . . . ?'

'We step out, just we two – the boys from Rome!' cackled Marius.

Nicander agreed with a wide grin. It would be an unwise Turfanian in the backstreets who thought to pick on Marius.

'But in these?' He fingered his monk's habit, threadbare but comfortable, which he'd worn since Chang An.

'Get new stuff at some market, a bit snappier, like.'

As they left they saw Ying Mei standing with Tai Yi in the courtyard.

'Ah! There you are,' she said brightly.

'We were just going out.'

'How convenient. We need to do a little shopping and would appreciate the company in this strange town.'

'That is, we were on our way to the monastery to give thanks for our safe arrival,' Nicander said. 'But as women are not allowed . . .'

'Oh. And I was so looking forward to seeing the sights. With a friend, that is. Come, Tai Yi, we'll have to go back to our room. These gentlemen haven't time for us.'

'It might not be—' Nicander began awkwardly.

Marius interrupted gruffly. 'He's saying as women don't like to go where men do, M' Lady. And we're—'

'We'd be no trouble, Ah Wu, none at all! It's just that . . . well, you and Ah Yung being my friends I really thought you'd . . .'

Nicander felt himself weakening. 'If you came with us—'

'Oh, thank you!' she said happily. 'We'll have such a time together.'

The bazaar was vast, an arched-over covered expanse with many cross street-ways. To the eyes of the travellers accustomed to the limitless vista of empty desert it was almost more than the senses could stand. Wafting stinks and fragrances fought each other, the lure of baubles and silks competed with beaten silver and jade, animal skins with stout linen – and people of all the tribes of Central Asia pushed past in an intoxicating mix.

It was all new and exciting: an alcove with nothing but dried reptiles, another with cunningly worked children's toys, yet more with spices and medicinals and others offering sweetmeats and strange confections.

Ying Mei insisted they stop at a purveyor of holy raiment. Nicander selected a long wrap-around garment in a modest ochre. It came with an inner robe and waistcloth and was delightfully cool. Marius found a similar one in a more dashing deep red – with his beard, a striking sight.

Nicander felt in his purse but found a hand lightly on his.

'Please let me, Ah Yung. You've been so good to us.'

He was aware that her touch had lingered.

In another part of the bazaar there were goods on display that could only have come from the mountains and beyond: furs, leather capes, felt blankets. The stallkeeper was black-browed and tall and delighted in producing more – from deerskin carpets to almond pastries, *rakhbin* cheese to horse hides. Marius was delighted with his lynx-fur cap purchase and said he would put it away for the cold nights but when he picked up a bright-painted pipe with a belled end the man convulsed in mirth.

Tai Yi told him, 'That's a child's piddling tube you have, Ma *sheng*. For winter when they're under many layers of furs. He wonders that you must be so . . . poorly endowed.'

Ying Mei stifled a giggle.

They continued on, to where the vividly coloured costumes of the mountain people were on display.

'How does this look on me?' Ying Mei asked Nicander anxiously, holding up a gaily embroidered black dress.

He hesitated then beamed approval. The last vestiges of the Ice Queen had gone – in its place was a laughing, high-spirited soul who was going out into the world to see what it had to offer. Against the barbaric boldness of these dresses he saw that she was a different woman, no trace of the porcelain doll now in the natural flush of her cheeks.

They took refreshments at a stall, watermelon cider with a startling potency and grapes cold from ice pits.

It was proving a very agreeable day.

Leaving the market, they came to the entrance of a sunken garden. It turned out to be a grape forest – the fruit growing on trellises vertically and flat above them, a gratifying ambrosial shade. For a small coin they ate all they wished, straight from the vine.

Hearing a distant din of drums, gongs and cymbals they hurried out on to the streets. It was a procession. Over the heads of the onlookers they caught glimpses of part of a dazzling gold canopy, a float of some sort. The noise swelled and then into view came an extravagantly ornamented temple-car bearing a single image of the Buddha garlanded in flowers. It was accompanied by a dozen shaven-headed priests, clashing tiny cymbals and chanting.

Preceding them was a single barefoot figure daubed with red and white whorls and draped in a plain-coloured robe. In his hand he bore incense and flowers and attendants held aloft a richly decorated parasol.

The man was given great respect. People bowed their heads, others fell prostrate.

'That's our king! His Greatness Yong Ping who is on his way to the monastery to intercede for us with the Enlightened One. And then in three nights it will be the Feast of the Lanterns. You are welcome to join us.'

The ladies decided to lose no time in returning to the market to find something suitable to wear but after it was pointed out that too much admiring of female attire was perhaps not what holy men should be seen doing, the men were released.

'So what's to do?' Marius said with a wicked leer. 'All on our own in an oasis – I've seen worse. Take Syria. Damn, but they were evil. Did I ever tell you—'

Nicander frowned. 'We can't.'

'What are you talking about?'

'Not in this gear. We'd be asking for trouble. Remember we were going to buy some clothes . . .'

Marius grinned. 'Never mind that. Leave it to me – I know what to do!'

Later that evening two men in the garb of a recently arrived caravan escort slipped out into the night. After a particularly tough desert march it was quite understandable that they would be wanting to sluice away the memories with the far-fabled wines of Turfan . . .

CHAPTER FORTY-FOUR

The morning heat was beginning to take hold and Nicander threw aside the light linen bed cover. On the previous evening, unlike Marius, he'd held off on the wine, finding it sweet and cloying. He'd not appreciated the coarse gaiety of the Kuchean dancing girls, nor the lewd frolics of the performing boys. His mind was restless in a way it had never been before.

He freshened up, staring at the face that looked back at him in the bronze mirror. If they ever made it through he would be a very different man from the one who had set out. All the old certainties, his place in the world, what was possible to achieve, what was not, the value of things – were now in a state of fluidity.

Dao Pa had planted seeds of doubt. The towering genius of Greek thought and philosophy that he'd taken as the final answer to questions of being was no longer enough.

His father's expensive education had given him a thorough respect for the structures of logic and reason that lay behind decisions he made.

But now there was an alternative. Which was right? Were they both – or neither?

'Marius! Are you awake?'

'No, go away,' his friend growled.

'I'm off to take a look at that big temple we saw on the rise. Do you want to come along?'

He grunted. 'No. I need rest.'

Nicander swirled on his new robe and fastened his hair in a topknot as he'd seen on Dao Pa.

On foot it was hot-going, and the road steep. His outer robe was capacious and he drew it over his head against the fierce heat.

In the distance he heard the booming of a great drum and the flutter of cymbals, then the drone of chanting.

Was this a more effective way to claim the attention of gods and angels than the solemn ceremonies in the Hagia Sophia? Were they calling on the same god or were they having their existence in different worlds? So much to know, to learn!

He paused at the tall ornamental gate. The pagoda reared up in all its mystery.

'Why have you come, Ni *lao na*?' From nowhere Dao Pa had appeared, his features nearly hidden by the robe over his head.

'I . . . I need answers, Master.'

'What do you seek?'

'The Tao,' he said simply.

'Then this is as good a place as any to begin your path to understanding. Come, I am known to the abbot.'

They were given a room. It was austere and bare with high windows. Dao Pa sat cross-legged in the centre, motioning Nicander to sit opposite.

'Your road will not be easy. Your mind is rigid with the teachings of your race which declares rationality the only path to understanding and will allow no rival.'

'It has served me well. Why should I abandon it?'

'No one requires you discard your birth-learning. Rather to widen your perceptions and place it within a larger frame of reference where it will have its function still.'

'I'm willing to learn, Master.'

'There are many works of depth and value devoted to the striving for enlightenment, but these are closed to you.'

'But why?'

'In the eyes of this world you are unhappily an illiterate.'

'Then how . . . ?'

'There are other methods handed down to us that are quite as effective. These require that the self does rise above its containing body and in discipline gains control over the gateway to understanding.'

'Teach me.'

'The first is the truest, most potent – and is called meditation. You will attend closely: for the uninitiated, the acquiring of such a state of being is as a butterfly ascending to the clouds – not unattainable but demanding the devotion of every particle of body and soul to that end. Are you prepared?'

'Yes, Master.'

On the third day Nicander reached a point where the first tendrils of illumination had entered his consciousness, an understanding of the transcendent that could never be reached in ways that were confined to the prison of words.

It was a wondering revelation; to feel the mind float free of the grossness of the body and enter a world of purity of thought and perception. But it was as though he were newly born, unable to make sense or reason of what he was experiencing. By some means he had to seek his own way, find the truths that must lie in the writings of the ancients that had trod the same path before him.

Dao Pa came and sat beside him and said softly, 'The chief mysteries are those whose essence is sealed by time.'

'I don't understand.'

'Let me show you.'

They left the room for the glare of the sunlight, crossing to a small building apart from the others. It was dark inside, but an obliging monk fetched a lamp.

'This is the hall of relics. Look around you – there are sutras carried from

India at great cost, there is the cast of a footprint of the Enlightened One himself. And over here . . .'

Some writings were laid out which were in the form of characters descending below a continuous horizontal line. Nicander peered closely but could make nothing of it.

'This is in the native tongue of the holy men of India, the very source of the philosophy and understanding of the people of Buddha. We know it well for it has been translated into Chinese for all the world to take knowledge from.'

Dao Pa went to another, quite different, the writing vertical, with irregular jagged protrusions from the line the only indication that it held intelligence. 'It is the hand of the ancient nomads, those who had their living in the plains beyond the Tien Shan that are without limit in this world. Uncountable numbers of their people are now extinct – and we know nothing of what they say.

'It means that their world is unknowable by us. What they spoke among themselves through this writing may hold wisdom unmatched by ours but we'll never share in it.'

Despite the warmth Nicander shivered. This was touching on mysteries perhaps they had no right to pierce.

They passed to an inner room. At first he could see nothing, then the flickering lamp picked out a body laid on a carpet and covered with a richly ornamented cloth.

Dao Pa tenderly drew it back revealing a mummy, perfectly desiccated.

'This mortal – he may be one hundred, one thousand years old, it doesn't signify, for he is lost to time.'

Nicander recoiled. It was beginning to affect him, not just the mystic aura of the pagoda but the unearthly, spectral sense of having reached the borders of human reason.

'See there; he has red hair and a thin nose – like yours.'

Nicander felt a chill go down his spine. This was not an oriental at all. If anything it resembled one of the barbarous Celts from lost Britannia.

'Why do they venerate him so?'

'He was found in a city half-swallowed by the sand, buried with all the grave goods of a prince and ruler. No one can speak his name, his kingdom or his fate – he exists, yet he does not. He has substance but never a word or thought of his will we ever know.'

How had this man found his way across the world here to this unknown remoteness? Or was it that here, in fact, was the first homeland of the Celts and they had left it for a better land at the edge of the world? This was not impossible – the Huns and Goths were at the moment doing just that, sweeping out of the dark unknown of steppe and forest to take what they wanted from the Romans.

Either way this was more uprooting of his certainties, another realignment of perspectives – he had to break free and contemplate it all.

'Master – I must take my leave now. There's much to think on.'

'I will be there for you when you need me.'

CHAPTER FORTY-FIVE

Reflected moonlight splintered into myriad shards on the river as groups of people prepared their floats on the bank. Sitting on a rock ledge, watching as the Feast of Lanterns reached its climax, Ying Mei sighed deeply.

From here and there bright points of light started then a couple would go to the water's edge and launch their tiny craft. At the base of the little incense-stick mast a message was tied, known only to them.

It would gradually be consumed but not before the couple's wish had been read by the kindly gods.

Soon the whole river was a dazzling display of bobbing floats intermingling as they were carried away on their romantic mission. She watched as they sailed further and further along until the pinpricks of light began to disappear one by one.

Ying Mei was happier now than she had been for an achingly long time. On this adventure she was tasting a freedom she had never before experienced in her life. No more stifling correctness of court, rigid rules and excruciating rituals of etiquette. No longer was there the necessity to guard every word and move for fear it could be used against an innocent, and gone too was the train of those set about her, watching her day and night. Now there was only the ever-faithful Lai Tai Yi, at the moment down at the water playing with the children.

Dear Ah Lai! She had made the sacrifice of her own future to accompany her into exile and share whatever lay ahead. And she was watching over her just as she had when she'd been a child and now had gamely taken on this very different world.

She hoped that she had not disappointed too much in her behaviour but it really was impossible to sustain the front of a noble lady any more. Later, when the journey was over she would mend her ways.

She looked to where Marius, also down at the river, was rescuing a float for a crying child.

Her father had been very astute in choosing her two protectors, for apart from being from the Western Lands themselves they were holy men and therefore to be trusted.

She smiled as she remembered their arrival and transformation from holy men on a quest, into the beastmaster's star comic turn. It must have been hard for them, especially for the big Ma Lai Ssu who stood every inch the proud barbarian.

She wondered why he had chosen to be a holy man on a sacred mission for there was little that was outwardly sensitive or contemplative about him. Bold-eyed and confident he strode fearlessly through life and stepped aside for no man. This was not the bearing or attitude of the clerics she knew.

And he looked as if he'd seen a lot of the world, one not to be too easily taken by surprise, who could be relied on in frightening situations. In fact, he had the build of a warrior with that deep chest, muscular arms and those massive thews she had seen at the river as they were escaping.

She caught herself: was she physically excited by Ma Lai Ssu? He was a barbarian, uncouth and with crude Chinese but as a man he stood head and shoulders above the rest she had known. Others in the court she was familiar with were primped and pampered, knew poetry and the classics but they had little . . .

It was odd, though. The two holy men were so different to each other.

Ni K'an Ta was more of a mystery – the more perceptive of the two, he had been cooler to her. Was this because he didn't like her? Or was he holding himself distant because of his piety and vows? He had spent a lot of time at the monastery in retreat, even missing this feast. Yes, it was probably that – he was holding true to his calling, and she must respect this.

But then again, could it be that he was disappointed in her behaviour? That he expected more of the noblewoman? She vowed to be more ladylike the next time she met him.

Even so, it was strange that she had never seen or heard either of them at their devotions. This could be that they worshipped a god of the night who could not be approached during daylight. But it was not proper for her to pry.

Marius came up from the water, laughing. 'Stupid child got the frights, thought I was a hungry ghost!' he chuckled, stroking his dark beard.

'Do sit!' she commanded, shifting along to make room for him.

Surprised, the big man obeyed. She became aware immediately of the musky scent of masculinity and its secret thrill caught her off guard.

'Ah Wu,' she said self-consciously. 'The fierce one. A good name for you, I think, don't you?'

'Yes, M' Lady,' he said.

'It's Ying Mei.'

'Y-Ying Mei.'

She was touched – he was shy with her, like a little boy!

'That's better. Tell me, Ah Wu, what tribe do you come from?'

'I'm a Roman!' he growled.

'*Wo Mun.* "The culture of the commonality". Wonderful! A deep meaning indeed.'

He didn't reply and lowered his head awkwardly.

'Tell me. When you decided to become a holy man, did your family approve?'

'I didn't ask 'em.'

'Not even the . . . lady you were attached to?'

'No.'

317

'So you gave her up for a holy life. Do you miss her?'

'Why are you asking me questions?'

'Well, it always puzzles me that the first thing a holy man does is to put away his feelings for the opposite sex. Can you not feel it in you to respond to the love of a woman – that is, if it is true and honourable?'

He looked at her with a twisted smile. 'I reckon that whichever way you say it, a holy man can only be man first, holy second. Is that what you're asking?'

Ying Mei felt herself blushing. 'I didn't wish to intrude, please forgive me.'

CHAPTER FORTY-SIX

'Where the hell have you been, Nico?' Marius asked indignantly. 'I get this stupid message about you stopping at the monastery, which of course you didn't, did you? On the town with one o' those Kuchean tarts, I reckon!'

'Actually I *was* there. Learning to look inside myself, see past things into the real world . . .' He tailed off.

'So you're going to join that Buddha crew, spend your day on all that fool mumbling!'

'No, I won't. The sage who I've been talking to isn't one of those, he takes all philosophy and learning as one and—'

'Well don't start boring me with it all. Don't you know you missed the Feast o' Lanterns? Had to take the women myself, all that *ooh* and *aah* at these pretty lights on the water and stuff. Bloody fine eating after, though, believe me. Anyway, Su Li is in a fit, wants to be away off while things are right for us.'

The caravan master was everywhere, chivvying, driving, directing. Another camel train had come through from the opposite direction and had reported that there were no troubles in the oasis realms that lay ahead of them and that the going was good. Su let it be known he would be displeased at anyone who got in his way, or made it difficult for the caravan to leave for Karashahr within the next day or two.

* * *

'No, that won't be possible.' Tai Yi was in no mood to change her mind about spending good money. 'My Lady Kuo has a mount, you do not.'

So it was 'Lady Kuo' still, as far as she was concerned. 'Not even a camel?'

'Certainly not! You will walk, as will I, and there's an end to it.'

It would be sand the whole way by all accounts so they took Korkut's advice and found special shoes in the market. These laced up tight above the ankles and being made of camel skin had a flexibility the heavier ox-hide did not.

'Bugger that old woman,' Marius grated. 'What right has she—'

'She's the one with the silver,' Nicander replied matter-of-factly. 'So we walk.'

'I've a mind to do something about it. Come on.'

They went to the caravanserai where the camels were being prepared. Nicander was pleased when Meng Hsiang gave a snort of recognition.

'He's remembering me!' he chuckled to Arif, the young cameleer who was combing him down.

'If you are kind to him, of course!'

Marius didn't waste time. 'How are the females?'

'Two sick, lost five calves on the way – why do you want to know? You going to buy one?'

'How many young 'uns?'

'Thirty-two – no, six.'

'You'll get a good price for 'em all when they're ready.'

'Yes?' Arif said warily.

'I'll tell you what we'll do for you. Any young beasts as are newly broken in, why, we'll take one and by riding him all day get him used to the saddle, like. You can sell him for more that way.'

Arif grinned. 'I understand. We do this if you man enough!'

'Go and get one, let's try it.'

The cameleer went to a string of young camels at a rail and patted one affectionately before untying it and bringing it over. 'Meng Hsiao – baby Meng. One of your Meng Hsiang's own sons.'

The father gave a glassy stare of indifference but the young one pawed the ground restlessly, his eyes rolling.

'Say hello, he know who you are.'

Marius came forward cautiously but before he could say anything the head reared up and a frightful set of bared teeth clashed ominously.

'Hey, hey, Meng Hsiao, he a friend,' Arif said reprovingly, then to Marius, 'Touch his muzzle, talk.'

The long-lashed eyes were beautiful and Marius reached out to stroke the downy brown fur. The head recoiled and before he could react the camel spat at him, stinking ejecta catching him on his cheek and shoulder.

'The fucking bastard!' Marius roared in Latin, wiping his face, 'He's scored one on me!'

The camel jibbed fretfully.

'Try – hold your hand in front of his nose so he smell you, then do.'

Eventually they came to speaking terms and Arif was satisfied. 'Now we ride him.'

Meng Hsiao was made to kneel, which he did unwillingly.

'Get on.'

Marius gingerly slid between the two humps, holding on by a scruff of hair on the mane. 'Where's the reins?' he demanded.

'This not a horse, *lao na*,' Arif said. 'You ready?'

The camel snarled menacingly, its head twisting to see what was on its back.

'Yes. Get it going.'

Arif thwacked its hindquarters. Meng Hsiao gave an ill-tempered low grumble.

He gave another slap. Without warning the back legs levered up on the knuckled forefeet and Marius was jerked forward wildly. His grip on the mane was the only thing that saved him from a hard landing but then the front legs came into play and he shot backwards, hanging on grimly.

Marius found himself sitting precariously atop a nervously gyrating camel. The animal eventually settled and stood still, the hide on its back giving nervous twitches as though trying to rid itself of a foreign object.

'Well done!' Arif said with a wide smile.

Marius clung on tightly to the mane. 'How do you steer the beggar?'

'Don't worry. Meng Hsiao follow his father, who is bigger.'

'Well, then. Now make him let me off.'

There were newcomers joining the caravan: a troupe of entertainers who plied the northern route and a party of monks on their way to the oases of the west. Two of the merchants had decided that they'd had enough and after disposing of their wares planned to return as soon as possible but the others were keen to take advantage of a caravan heading in that direction.

In the morning, bright and early, they set out again.

But of Dao Pa, there was no sign at all.

CHAPTER FORTY-SEVEN

The first day promised well of their journey as they threaded along roads passing sweet-smelling melon beds, orchards with fruit in season and clumps of giant sunflowers three feet across whose seeds Korkut declared were excellent eating.

Soon however they were away from the intensive irrigation works and the familiar desert landscape returned.

Ying Mei rode a steppe pony, now with an easy grace and in colourful riding dress while the ever-faithful Tai Yi walked beside her. Then came Meng Hsiang and tagging along beside was Meng Hsiao, getting used to being away from the females and other young.

Marius had quickly adopted the lazy sway of a cameleer, finding there was no need to hang on at all.

At midday it was Nicander's turn to ride and he tried to copy Marius's easy posture as the rhythm of stately sway and rocking took hold. But when the camel train came to a halt that evening he was grateful to be able to stretch his aching muscles.

The stopping place was well chosen, between two spurs of the Tien Shan and with firm ground. The crew energetically got to work in anticipation of the entertainment. The space around the fire was widened and traveller and cameleer quickly found places.

Ying Mei felt an expectant thrill. These, of course, would not be as accomplished as performers at the imperial court but their stage was the grand spectacle of the desert at night, under the stars by the dancing flames of the firelight.

A troupe of musicians came on with their instruments and squatted to one side, opening with a lively piece.

The show started with the acrobats: young girls in crimson blouses and green tasselled trousers skilfully leaping and throwing each other aloft in time to the music.

When the applause finished they scampered off to allow a pair of dancers to steal in opposite one another. The slim-waisted woman had dark curled locks and long legs half-concealed within mysterious gauze finery. The man, in a dashing costume with sparkling gems on his bared chest, prowled like a panther around her to the sensuous throbbing of the drum.

Ying Mei stole a glance at the two holy men: Marius was rapt, watching with undisguised excitement the intertwined playing of hands and the woman's wanton pout.

Nicander was taking it in, but had a distracted frown – was this because he was disapproving or was he regretting his status as a holy man?

As the dance livened Ying Mei found herself caught up in its charged atmosphere. Beside her Tai Yi shifted uncomfortably so she quickly assumed an immobile expression in the best traditions of an imperial court.

The acrobats came on again with somersaults and juggling and were followed by three female contortionists who drew gasps from the crowd.

Ying Mei noticed Nicander and Marius lean back in conversation. Was this not to their foreign taste?

In fact, she wondered, what was?

She knew nothing about them, really – they were barbarians, from somewhere in the outer world beyond the bounds of civilisation. But did they have any culture or civilisation of their own – she doubted it, for all the peoples she had heard of shaded by degrees from the Middle Kingdom's delicacy and elegance into the unspeakable brutality of its far borderlands.

Her protectors were holy men seeking after truths, so it was understandable that they would come to China in this quest. Who could foresee that they would be caught by pirates and sold into slavery? The strange part was that now neither seemed particularly interested in the gentility and aesthetics of the greatest civilisation of them all.

Yet they were taking back to their kingdom a wonderful treasure of precious works of literature and philosophy – which neither of them was able to read! What did this say about their mission to seek the great truths of mankind?

There could be only one explanation: their searing experiences at Yeh Ch'eng had soured them on Chinese culture.

And, she reminded herself, the works they carried and looked after so well in their little chest were there only as 'holy scriptures' as a cover for their leaving China and would probably be discarded at the first opportunity.

A new set of performers pranced on, the famous Sogdian whirling dancers, entrancing the crowd with trailing ribbons and dazzling smiles.

Ying Mei glanced again at Nicander and Marius; both seemed to be enjoying this part of the show – or was it the Turfan wine?

One thing was certain: the freedoms and spice of danger was making this the adventure of a lifetime for her. It wouldn't last, though. Sooner or later they would cross the mountains and she would be duly delivered to the Western Lands and left to find a new life.

She had to face it with courage and resolve – which for her father's sake she would – but it was a frightening thought. Was there nothing that could prepare her for exile?

Then a daring thought came. She would get the holy men to teach her the language of their tribe, and as well perhaps discover what it was like to live there, the customs and etiquette of the natives. She had her gold secreted away with more to be withdrawn from her uncle's agent in Kucha but would this be enough to sustain the life of a gentle lady in their society?

How amusing to think of Marius teaching her elements of societal delicacy! It would be fun – but on reflection she realised that Nicander was more suited. He had been quicker to pick up spoken Chinese and was intelligent enough to go about selecting what were the more important aspects for her to learn on his side. But with his religious outlook would he agree to teach a woman?

There was one thing she could offer. In return for teaching her his barbarian ways she could make him literate – teach him written Chinese so that when he arrived back, the 'scriptures' would have some value.

The more she thought about it the better she liked the idea. She would make it her mission to reveal to him the enthralling beauty of the poetics and subtle strength of the prose of the ancients, to bring him to a realisation and respect of the glory that was Chinese culture.

The last act, a trio of madcap dwarfs, ended the entertainment in a riot of laughs.

'Well done!' Ying Mei called and was generous when the gratuities bowl went round.

'Ah Yung, did you enjoy it?' she called sweetly.

Tai Yi threw a reproving look at Ying Mei.

She ignored her and went over to Nicander. 'There's something I want to ask you, a favour which I would very much appreciate.'

'Why, if it's possible, of course.'

'I was just thinking. I'm to go to the Western Lands and then you'll leave me there and I'll be on my own. I'd be grateful if before then you could teach me your language, tell me what to expect and prepare for. In return I agree to teach you Chinese characters so then you'll be able to read your scriptures when you get back.'

Tai Yi bristled. 'My Lady! This is impossible! These two are barbarians and it's well known that such are quite incapable of a true understanding of the sages. A waste of time!'

'Really?' said Nicander. 'Then, Lai *hsiao chieh*, I'd be interested in your views of why Lao Tzu denies transcendence in the Tao. How can this be?'

Ying Mei laughed in delighted surprise. 'You know of the Tao? How wonderful! But . . . how did you . . . when you can't read the works of the masters?'

'I had a wise teacher.' He eased into a smile. 'It's an attractive offer. Yes, I agree – a fair exchange.'

*   *   *

326

As usual they moved out at daybreak, taking nearly half an hour to unwind into the long camel train. It was hot, the fierce heat radiating up from the sandy ground, but they were used to it now, wearing wide hats and loose robes and keeping with the relaxed gait of the camels.

Ying Mei eased her pony to the side and dismounted. She pressed it on Tai Yi then waited for the men to come up with her.

'Ah Yung – you made me a promise last night.'

'To teach you our tongue?'

'Yes, and I mean to keep you to it!'

'Very well – tonight will be lesson one, and—'

'Why not now? It's so boring doing nothing. Let's start right away!'

'But I haven't thought of the lesson yet.'

'Nonsense. Come on, we'll go and keep Tai Yi company and begin.'

She looked up at Marius riding Meng Hsiao. 'You'll be able to look after the camels, won't you, Ah Wu?'

Tai Yi twisted around in her saddle to see what was going on.

'We're going to learn about the Western Lands, and Ah Yung is going to teach us.'

Nicander frowned. It really was unfair. The woman was expecting, on the spot, a grammar lesson in Greek, the most precise and logical linguistic structure in the known world. Where was the wax tablet and stylus, the board and chalk – even the word lists of meanings? Ying Mei herself wasn't helping the situation. Since emerging from her Ice Queen personality he had discovered that she was bright and had a sense of humour that rose above the fearsome conditions. Not only that but he was uncomfortably aware that she was no ordinary attractive woman – she had elements of beauty that were classic in their lines and symmetry of the kind that he'd only seen before on ancient statuary.

She paced expectantly next to him, flashing an encouraging smile.

'We're ready, Ah Yung!'

'Well, the first thing you must know is that the structure of Greek – the tongue of Hellenica that is,' remembering Dao Pa's term, 'will be that it is—'

'No, no, the most important things first. When I arrive, will I be dressed correctly? I mean, what do the ladies wear?'

'Can we not leave this for later? There is so much to learn.'

'If you insist. But first you must tell us about your tribe and village. How big is it? Does your family own many water buffalo? In your house are there many slaves?'

Tai Yi leant down from the horse. 'She means she wants to know about the kingdoms and their history. When we get there, what will we see?'

'Yes, yes. But it's not so easy. Let me see . . . Well, we can start with the first civilisation, which began nearly one and a half thousand years ago in the land we call Greece . . .'

He was no professional teacher but he thought he'd made quite a good fist of explaining origins, the rise of the Greeks and their superior culture, and then the Romans overwhelming them yet taking their philosophy and thought as their own.

There were no Chinese names, of course, for the people and cities and he made them up. When she knew more Greek he'd correct her understanding.

'If the Roman dynasty rules Greece, why do we not learn their tongue – this Latin instead of Greek?'

He would have to be careful with Ying Mei, she was very quick.

'Ah. Well, in the top ruling dynasty in Constantinople there is little Latin left, everyone speaks Greek as being the superior form. But don't mention this to Marius, he's a Roman himself.'

'Is he?'

Nicander felt a stab of irritation at her look of wide-eyed wonder. 'Yes, but many say they are much debased now.'

'Then why is he your friend?'

'Because . . . because we set out on our mission together, that's all.'

'How wonderful! Tell me, why . . .'

Nicander didn't want the conversation to go this way and have to lie to her.

He assumed a stiff expression. 'You must know that there is one central sea. It is called the Mediterranean and is bordered by the burning regions to the south and the frozen regions to the north, and . . .'

The time passed quickly but he had to beg fatigue when the searing heat made it difficult to think.

That evening at the meal Ying Mei shyly came over to sit by him. 'I did enjoy our lesson, Ah Yung. I can see now how much there is to learn.'

'It was my pleasure.' To his surprise he found he meant it.

'And I haven't forgotten our bargain. I've talked with Tai Yi and we've found an arrangement that will serve as your classroom.'

'You're really going to teach me to write?' He was keen to have the means to read the words of the masters but he'd assumed the offer was a token one to save face. How could it be possible in these conditions?

'Yes. After we've eaten we start your first lesson.'

'My dear!' Zarina called across. 'You look so well tonight! While we're all so weary, it's not fair you know.'

'It must be the mountain air coming down, I find it so refreshing.'

'Forgive me for bringing it up, but I can't help thinking that it won't be so long before we reach Aksu and . . . well, your father might be . . . and you so . . . happy?'

Without a moment's hesitation Ying Mei smiled sadly. 'That is true – but just between you and me I've never really known him, being away all the time like he is, and when he comes home he's a beastly tyrant. I go to him only out of filial duty, you see.'

'I understand, my dear. You are a good and obedient daughter.'

Nicander's classroom turned out to be the ladies' tent. It was just large enough for them to sit cross-legged on a cushion opposite each other while Tai Yi occupied herself to one side. The master stroke was using her folding horse-mounting stool as a desk, complete with a little oil lamp.

'This is really very thoughtful of you, Ying Mei,' he said sincerely. 'I'll try to be a good disciple.'

'I'm sure you will.'

'But what will we use for the writing?'

'Ah. My teacher today told me there is much to learn first. I think these are very wise words.'

He grinned. 'He must be a fine teacher. So what must we do?'

She assumed a grave expression. 'The first is to acquire a proper respect for the power of the characters, the play between words and meaning. Please listen carefully to this quatrain.'

Closing her eyes she recited:

'Than colours of the peony
my raiment is more fair.
The breeze across the palace lake
takes fragrance from my hair'.

'You see? So sublime – and only four characters in each line. And this one . . .'

For Nicander, who only knew the tongue from workaday utility and Dao Pa's stern metaphysics, the beauty leapt out at him. She recited three more and then got out her portable writing set, an inkstone and a selection of brushes on their stand.

Taking just one character from each line she showed how a delicate shading of understanding was built up by a coalescing of the individual meanings of its elements. Then she used the same character several times in company with others. In each case the totality of what was derived had a subtle difference.

Where each Greek word was fixed and immutable in meaning, in Chinese it was a much more supple process. If in Greek there was no exact word for an intended meaning then it was too bad, the conceit could not be put across. In this language, however, something could be built up in order to match the precise requirement of what was intended; there was the possibility of an infinite variation.

It was a revelation.

CHAPTER FORTY-EIGHT

In the predawn chill the two holy men waited by Meng Hsiang, already harnessed and loaded.

'So how's it going for you?' Marius said.

'What do you mean?'

'You can't fool this old soldier!' he sniggered. 'Although how you're going to get the old biddy out of the way . . .'

'You bastard, Marius. That's not how it is at all!'

'Oh? So you're hanging about just in case she needs a fan or something.'

'No!'

'I've seen how she looks at you! She's out to make a monkey of you, Nico, take it from me – I know women, and this one's bad news.'

'You're jealous! That's what it is, you're jealous!'

'Look at her – she's a fucking high-born and there's no way she's for you. She's just playing around with who's available!'

Nicander went rigid. 'She's an honourable, intelligent lady. She knows literature and the arts and—'

'Hah! All right – tell me what you're talking about all this time.'

'Why, the history and geography of Greece and Rome, the—'

'I'll bet you everything I have . . . that she tries every time to get personal – embarrassing, like. That's what women do when they want to throw you off guard, get things started down the track they want. Am I right?'

Breathing hard, Nicander kept himself in check. 'I don't think I want to continue this conversation. She's asked me for help and I'm giving it to her, and that's an end to it.'

Marius threw off a harsh laugh and busied himself with Meng Hsiao.

Su came slowly down the line with his crew on his inspection, grunting a few words to them in the pale light of the morning before passing on.

'Good morning, sirs!' Ying Mei said gaily as she approached. 'You look a little out of sorts, Ah Wu. You are well, I hope?'

'My teacher!' she said to Nicander and gave a decorous courtly bow.

He blushed but hid it by returning the courtesy.

She touched his hand. 'I am going to have my next lesson today, aren't I?' she asked softly.

'Yes, of course,' Nicander said uncomfortably, feeling Marius's gaze on him. 'Lesson two.'

'Then I'd better be ready. What will we—'

Before she could finish someone asked brusquely, 'Are you the holy man Ni?'

He hadn't noticed the group of monks coming up, the ones who had joined at Turfan and who had until now kept to themselves.

'I am.'

The man speaking was in traditional Buddhist garb but around his neck were many strings of beads and ornate hangings. His features were hard and ruthless.

He made an elaborate gesture of greeting. 'I am Taw Vandak, lama of the oasis kingdoms. These are the venerable monks who accompany me on my journeys.'

Nicander gave a cautious bow. 'This is Ma Lai Ssu, my brother in faith.'

Marius gave an ill-tempered grunt but was nevertheless awarded a careful greeting.

The lama paused to regard them, his eyes cold and appraising. 'My brothers and I are confused. Caravan master Su tells us you are holy men from a far land. Pray do tell us something of your origins and . . . beliefs.'

Nicander realised this was no idle meeting but what was its purpose?

'Thank you for your interest, Taw *lao na*. We are from a distant kingdom sent on a quest after truth. Our beliefs are very complex to explain.'

'I see. We are confused because we expected you to join with us in our prayers to Avalokitesvara for the safety of this argosy and all within it.'

'Ah. This is because we don't include him in our pantheon.'

'This is very strange as *she* is the paramount bodhisattva to the traveller. Which kingdom did you say you came from?'

'Byzantium.' He couldn't think of Chinese words to express it and fell back on the Latin.

'Bai Zan – I cannot think to have heard of this. Another thing that puzzles us is that it has been two days and we have yet to see you at any form of devotion. In your beliefs, then, is there no room for prayer to the higher?'

Where was this leading? Nicander thought quickly. 'Oh, I can see what confuses you. Well, in our sacrament we think it sacrilegious to approach the higher except within the bounds of a consecrated place, a church. And as we have seen, there are no churches of our faith to be found here.'

Taw came back in a harder tone, 'And still another thing. You were seen at profane entertainments of a wicked nature, not to be contemplated by any who does truly profess holiness and purity.'

Nicander could feel the hostility radiating from the man's followers.

'There is nothing in our way that—'

'No? Then answer me this – you were seen entering the tent of this woman under cover of night. What does this mean, Ni?'

'We were discussing the beauty of literature and she's going to teach me writing.'

Taw spat on the ground and with a final venomous glare turned and stormed off.

'I'm so sorry,' Ying Mei said. 'You have to understand that in China monks are exempt of taxes and therefore many claim to be holy men to take advantage of this. This makes it a harder burden for the taxpayers, who then end up hating all monks. And as holy men only exist by begging alms there is so much less for everyone.'

There was a jingling of camel bells ahead: the caravan was getting under way.

'There's trouble brewing with those monks,' Nicander said in a low voice to Marius, 'I feel it in my bones.'

The early morning light showed the continuing Tien Shan range on their right at its best, vaunting snow-tipped mountains cleft with dark shadows of night not yet banished; purple, blue and where touched by dawn, a delicate rose. By contrast on their left was the deadly Taklamakan, a grey-brown sea of dunes and desolation that could swallow whole armies with ease.

Nicander caught up with Ying Mei for the promised lesson.

'This is so kind of you,' she said with a warmth that left him glowing. 'I do so look forward to our lessons. I'm hoping that today you'll give me some real Greek characters to learn!'

'Characters? Well, it's not quite like that . . .'

She was alert and intelligent but there was so much that was different in concept between the languages. The appearance of words in Greek were never the same from one sentence to another as Chinese characters always were – they altered with whether things had happened in the past or present, were single or many, even the sex of the thing talked about. Instead of a holistic meaning from the character cluster as a whole, Greek had to be analysed word by word and presented in a logical structure as a sentence.

It was a long and difficult exercise but as the days rolled on she proved herself equal to it.

For his part, Nicander began instruction in writing. He learnt that any character could be made with just eight strokes of the brush and that all these could be exercised in one: the character for 'eternity'. Then there was the comforting discovery that every character could be found in the dictionary by recognising its *pu shou* or central essence, and these were limited to just a few hundred to learn.

But after that came the realisation that writing was more than a mechanical means for rendering meaning as it was in Greek. Instead the Chinese revered it as a form of art – calligraphy, and a gentleman could be judged by his mastery and skill of it. Strength, personality, individuality – all could be deduced from the execution of a single stroke.

The writing brush had to be held just so, perfectly vertical and all the concentration and power of thought directed down into one bold action, one culmination of intent to produce a thing of beauty – or childish squiggle.

Nicander was entranced: this was much more than elementary literacy – it was a way of life that seamlessly intersected with what Dao Pa had been saying about the Tao and he felt his mind yearning for more.

The days passed while the caravan slowly made its way westward. Through the Iron Gate Pass to Korla, then along the flank of the mountains to Kucha, the sand-girt walled oasis standing like a rampart against the encroaching sea of sand.

Guarded by a pair of stone Buddhas more than a hundred feet high it was a prime stopping place for the caravans, as well as a trading post for the pack animals coming through the passes from the Turkic peoples beyond.

The bazaars were a place of magic and allure. Nicander and Ying Mei explored them together and she found him the latest *Yu p'ien* dictionary. Later, they visited the gardens of the old city and tasted peaches and almonds.

The caravan did not stop for long; soon it was stretching out over the desert and the rhythms of the trail took over once more.

Under the watchful eye of Tai Yi they continued their lessons as they walked on, Nicander spelling a Greek word in the sand with his staff and Ying Mei having to speak it in a sentence before it disappeared behind them. In turn she would form a character and he would have to do the same. It lent itself to all kinds of frivolity and they laughed together in delight.

At night she guided him while he painfully found his way about the vocabulary and applauded loudly when he managed his first lines of Hsün Tzu.

It was a breakthrough: soon he would know the masters at first hand.

CHAPTER FORTY-NINE

After the camel train had been secured for the evening Su Li came up to Nicander. Behind him, Taw Vandak and the other monks clearly meant business.

'I'm sorry to disturb, but these gentlemen have made an accusation against you as I'm bound to investigate.'

'Which is?' Nicander asked stiffly.

'They say that you're not holy men and not entitled to consideration as such.'

'A scandalous accusation!'

'If this is right, at the very least the authorities in oasis kingdoms will demand I pay full coin for you, as well as stand surety.'

'This is a nonsense! We come from a country far from here they've never visited – how can they know what our holy men look like?'

Taw drew himself up. 'You insult us with all these lies!' he snarled. 'You're no holy man. I don't know who you are but I'm going to find out!'

'How dare you!' Nicander came back. 'Our beliefs are our own concern. We've been sent by our king—'

'To seek out truths? What truths have you found so far, Ni? Any at all?' he sneered.

'These!' roared Marius, bringing out the chest. He thumped it on the ground in front of the lama, opening it so he could see the scrolls and stitched sheets.

The man raised an eyebrow and took one out. 'Lao Tzu? Confucius?' he said mockingly. 'Your common Chinese word grinders? Where is your dharma, your *Sutta Pitaka*?'

He took up another and thrust it at Marius. 'Read what it says there,' he said, stabbing an accusing finger at an embellished line of characters.

The legionary's face set.

'You!' he demanded of Nicander. It was not one he'd been working on.

A cynical smile spread. 'You can't read – you're both illiterates! You're expecting us to believe you're taking these to your king and you can't read a word of them.'

Taw glanced back at his acolytes in triumph then snapped, 'You're a pair of criminals on the run from China disguised as holy men and—'

'Falsehoods and lies!' Nicander replied hotly.

'Then you're spies from a foreign kingdom with secret orders to steal from a land superior to your own. You'll find we have a short way with such vermin in these parts, those who bring dishonour on the calling of the Buddha!'

With a venomous look he swept away.

Su hesitated. 'Doesn't do to get on the wrong side of 'em. Can't you do some miracle or something? A bit of magic, some healing, a bit of chanting? You've been no trouble to me on this trip and I'd like to help you, but . . .'

'Be buggered to it – those yellow rats can't prove anything!' Marius exploded.

'And we can't prove we're not as they say.'

The caravan moved out and Nicander hurried to be with Ying Mei. 'Those monks – they're determined on trouble. It looks like Taw can't make us out and wants to be rid of us.'

She didn't reply.

'Are you not well, Ying Mei?' he asked with a sudden stab of alarm.

She moved to one side until she was out of hearing from Tai Yi.

Biting her lip she said in a low voice, 'Last night I had a dream. I won't vex you with details but I know what it means. In a few days we arrive in Aksu. Su says it's the last oasis of size before the end of the desert and the mountains begin and it's there we must leave this caravan if we are true to our purpose.'

'Yes, this is right. This caravan moves on around the desert to the other kingdoms.'

'Ni K'an Ta, I'm frightened.'

'Why so?' he said. It was the first time she had used his name and it brought a guilty thrill.

'When we started out, we planned on going to this Aksu, the furthest kingdom on the caravan route. Now, all of a sudden it comes out that we'll soon reach it – and we've no idea what to do once we're there. No plan or anything.'

'We'll think of something, never fear.'

She glanced at him with a wistful sadness. 'Ah Yung, I've spoken to everyone I can find and there's no one can say how to get over the mountains. Or even if that is the right direction to go. They all say it's a terrible place and have never heard of any who have done it.'

'Surely not.'

'So in a very short while we have to say goodbye to our friends – and the safety of this great caravan, and it . . . I have a dread . . .'

There was not much he could say: he'd assumed they would just look around and decide on the spot what to do. It had seemed so far in the future when they had made their plans in Chang An, but now it was all too much a reality. What would it be to go on without the comfort and security of a full-scale caravan? And if it turned out camel trains could not go up into the mountains, was there any way of crossing such a fearsome barrier?

They continued on in silence and in the afternoon he walked with Marius, but in the evening there was no invitation to calligraphy.

Ill at ease Nicander wandered in the darkness, the noise of the evening entertainment carrying far on the still night air. He found himself near the camels and the long mound of unloaded cargo under guard.

A single thought came: in those dark masses were tons' weight of silk –

he'd seen with his own eyes the watery yellow skeins of the raw thread and the breathtaking brilliance of the finished bolts of fabric. These were going somewhere to the west. And in Justinian's empire there were merchants getting them from somewhere in the east. He had something he could reach out and touch that was on its way to some noble household in Constantinople. How that happened was their answer!

The Sogdians would never give up their secret of the silk route but he was a canny merchant and he would not rest until he had found a way. His fears eased.

He was about to return when something made him pause. Away from camp lights the moonless dark was held at bay by a tremulous sheen from the star field that blazed overhead. He gazed at it in awe as stealing into his mind came acknowledgement that the Lady Ying Mei was meaning more to him than ever she should.

They had worked closely together on things of beauty and humanity, had revealed to each other things touching deeply on each other – was it any wonder that he had grown close to her, found happiness and fulfilment when with her?

Or was it something deeper? He shied away from the implications and stared out into the desert.

A single pinprick of light showed – too tiny to see from within the encampment. Nicander didn't need to be told what it was and hurried towards it over the broken ground.

'How goes your journey?' Dao Pa said, looking up from his cross-legged position by a neat little fire.

'I strive for enlightenment, Master. Each day brings a fresh revealing but also a new mystery.'

'That is well. That is very well,' the sage said with a slow smile. 'I expected nothing less from you. Have you your letters yet?'

'I learn, but I'm far from construing the works of the ancient ones.'

'There is one helping you.'

'Yes.'

'Tell me, what is your conceiving of Meng Tzu, when he declares that all men everywhere are born good at heart?'

'Master, I'm torn. He brings forward an unanswerable *koan* – that on seeing a child about to fall in a well there is no man who will shrink from saving it. Yet Hsün Tzu shows that we enter this life evil and that it is only our conscious will that can rule desires, to enable us to rise above our base passions.'

'Excellent! You are manifestly on your path to the Tao.'

'Master . . .'

'You have doubts.'

'I . . . I have a problem of life that troubles me.'

'Tell me.'

'It's a woman. Who has touched my heart that I cannot . . . who has entered my thoughts and . . .'

'And you fear the purity of your quest is at hazard?'

'She . . .'

'Heaven sends lives on courses which are destined to converge. The wise do not confuse this with the chance meeting. One leads to the unity of souls, the other to lust and pollution. Do not ask me to say which it is in your case – you must look in your heart and decide.'

'You are not . . . disappointed?'

'How can this be? I am your teacher and you are a worthy disciple. You will know how to act in this, for you are well advanced in the Tao. If she is destined for you then your life is hers. If not, then it may be you will raise your enlightenment to the level where your life belongs to your disciples. That is the Way.'

'Master—'

'Your life lies ahead of you. I have set you on your path and I know you will fulfil your destiny with understanding and wisdom. I am content.'

'But . . .'

'I now take my leave of you on this earthly plane. Hold fast to what you have learnt, and you can clutch to your bosom even to the grave that you are pure of heart and intent. Farewell, Ni K'an Ta – *lao na*.'

* * *

340

Marius was in no doubt about it when he returned to their tent. 'The woman's getting to you,' he snapped. 'I told you!'

'Leave me be,' Nicander muttered. There was far too much to think on.

'You've got to do something about it, Nico. We've only to get her across the mountains to the west and then we're rid o' the woman. If you let her foul up your wits now we stand to lose everything.'

'It's not like that . . .'

'Don't you forget that half o' what we've got in the box is mine and—'

'I haven't forgotten! Now just piss off!'

He had to face that his heart was taken by Ying Mei. He should have seen it coming, the way that she had crowded into his thoughts, the rising tenderness of his feeling toward her – and the melting helplessness that her gaze on him brought.

And Marius was right: he had to do something about it. Every piece of him cried out – to let it free, throw himself down before her and declare his passion.

But this could be the worst move: it supposed that she felt the way he did, but if she didn't, he would lose everything.

Was there a halfway point – in some way or other enabling him, without revealing his true feelings, to let it be known to her that he was interested and see if she responded.

She would no doubt be scandalised at his behaviour as a holy man. He could let her know privately that he was not one, in fact, but then all the trust and confidence that was allowing her to get close to him would vanish.

He was in the worst of all worlds and when they reached Aksu he would need all his wits about him. Damn it! Why was life so complicated!

CHAPTER FIFTY

After they made their last stopping place, Taw came striding across with his acolytes.

'Greetings, Ni *lao na*.' His manners were faultless but there was an air of menace. 'Shall we talk?'

He motioned his group to one side. 'On the morrow we reach Aksu.'

'As I've heard.'

'The sutras teach us that it is more worthy to show mercy to a weevil than fawn upon a dragon.'

'Yes,' Nicander replied carefully.

'Then this is why I'm here. Should you readily confess who you are, that you are not holy men, and if you then place yourselves in my hands in the matter of punishment, then I am mindful to be merciful, and will intercede for you tomorrow.'

'What do you mean, Taw?'

'The kingdom of Aksu is staunch for the teachings of the Enlightened One, having monasteries and temples beyond counting, and is well known to me. There, the penalties for false representing are severe. Should any lay a complaint of you when we arrive it will be regarded very seriously. As lama of this region I shall be consulted and, with the evidence I have seen with my own eyes on this journey, there will be little doubt of the verdict.

'The customary penalty for those falsely representing, together with those aiding and abetting the offence, is to be sold into slavery for not less than seven years' servitude.'

With a slow smile he added, 'You have until we sight the walls of Aksu, Ni.'

'The bastard means Ying Mei as well,' Nicander blurted.

Marius stood dark and brooding. 'I should slit the bugger's throat!'

'And be a murderer? No – looks like he's got us where he wants us. He's in thick with the kingdom authorities and they'll have a short way with us. Our only chance is to do as he says and give up and confess our sins.'

'That's stupid – they'll throw us into slavery. We've got to get out of this ourselves.'

'How?'

An hour later they were no nearer a solution.

'We're going to have to tell Ying Mei,' Nicander said finally.

The two arriving at her tent was enough to alert her that something was wrong. They quickly let her know what had happened.

'This is very serious – the Buddhists are jealous of their position with the people and persecute those they think are undermining this. There's only one way to avoid being taken – we must leave the caravan. Now.'

Marius laughed dismissively. 'Mountains to the right, a deadly desert to the left. We can't go forward with 'em, so we have to go back. And that delivers us straight into the arms of the Uighur gangs following us, waiting for stragglers. Without the protection of the caravan we're—'

After everything they'd gone through. 'No! We just can't let ourselves be hauled away in chains again!' Nicander burst out.

'So think of something, Nico!'

'Put it all in the hands of Caravan Master Su.' Unexpectedly it was Tai Yi making the suggestion. 'He's going to know about it, anyway.'

'No. There's a difficulty,' Ying Mei came in. 'My father is supposed to be on his deathbed. How can I say we now don't want to go to Aksu?'

343

She smiled suddenly. 'I think I have a way . . .'

Su was not best pleased to be interrupted in his work preparing the caravan accounts and formalities for the next day and listened reluctantly.

'So you see, Su *hsien sheng*, I have got myself in a lot of trouble. All this about my father dying in Aksu was just a story – to cover up that I'm really on my way to Khotan to join my lover. Now Taw and his nasty monks are spoiling it all.'

Su frowned grimly. 'Make no mistake, this is bloody serious. I don't give a damn about your lover but if you're convicted in Aksu I stand to be charged with smuggling undesirables, and that's me finished.'

He glared at them. 'Why I listened to Kuo and his story I've no idea. Now you've come at the last minute to ask me how to get you out of this.'

He stood up. 'You get to Aksu, it's all up for you. So – there's nothing else but you don't get there – you leave the caravan.'

'To go where?' Nicander said wearily.

'Well, you can't go forward, you can't go back—'

'We know all that!'

'Or into the mountains. So there's only one way left – into the desert.'

'What?'

'You want to go to Khotan, there is a way. Across the desert instead of all around.'

'How far?'

'Oh, just a few hundred miles or so.'

'That's murder, going into the Taklamakan! We'd never do it!'

'Yes you could – the old-time travellers did it. See, there's a river, the Ho T'ien, and it crosses over to this side from Khotan. All you do is follow it. Simple!'

'If it's so easy, why aren't you taking the caravan that way?'

'Ah, well, there are a few disadvantages, shall we say. First is that this river is fed by snowmelt off the Kunluns. We're a mite late in the season and by now they'll be running dry into the sand at awkward places, not reliable, like.'

'And?'

'Away from these mountains here, the weather gets . . . strange. Bloody cold and burning hot, you need to watch it.'

'Anything *else*?'

'The rivers are very shallow, very wide. When they're dry you can't see where they are too easy, where to go. Could get yourselves lost.'

'I know what that means!' Nicander said bitterly.

'Hold on, I didn't say you couldn't find 'em again. We know what direction Khotan is, just keep going that way, you'll find the river again.'

'How?'

'You know the stars, don't you?'

'No.'

'Well, that could be a bit more difficult.'

'This doesn't sound much of a solution, Su *sheng*.' In fact it looked a lot like a move to get rid of them with no complications.

'It's got lots of advantages.'

'Oh?'

'You set off quickly, by morning there'll be no tracks to follow, the wind fills 'em in.'

'And?'

'You'll be in Khotan way before we will.'

'And?'

'You'll have no problems with Uighurs and bandits, there's none out there.'

'They've got more sense than to go where no one else does!'

'Look, you asked me for a way out! I've told you one – do you want to take it or be done up in Aksu?'

There was no choice. 'We have to do it.'

'Good. Lets get the details straight first. It'll be you four? Then you'll want at least two camels – no horses, they drink too much. I can probably find you extra kit, seeing as how you'll be on your own. Agreed?'

'I suppose so.'

'Right. Then let's tot that lot up . . . I'll be generous and only charge you rental for the camels, so long as you check 'em in at Khotan – a little deposit on each against that, of course.'

All in all it was no trivial sum being asked.

'You forgot to deduct our passage from Aksu to Khotan the long way around,' Tai Yi said implacably.

'Well, yes. You always do that afterwards, don't you?'

Su leant back. 'As this is a bit irregular, like, I have to ask you for coin in advance – so I can square m' books with 'em in Aksu, that is.'

The implications began to sink in. It was madness but they had only hours left.

Wasting no time, Su summoned their cameleer, Arif. 'Change of schedule. These lot will be leaving the caravan. Tonight. Off to Khotan along the Ho T'ien. Get their camels up and harnessed, then load 'em against this list. Oh – and keep it to yourself, got it?'

The man looked incredulous. 'They going the old desert way? That near dry up, no one go that way now! You can't—'

'Get on with it. Smartly, now!'

'They travellers only, they not know the desert. How you—'

'I told you to get those camels in harness. Do it.'

'Su *sheng*.' Arif said quietly.

'Yes?' Su snapped.

'I'm . . . I'm go with them.'

'What? You bloody fool, don't you know – forget it, that's just crazy talk.'

'I go. They need one who know camels, especially little Meng Hsiao. I'll be the one.'

'I'm warning you, Arif, if you go—'

The cameleer stood his ground.

'Right. You're off wages as of this moment. Get your kit and throw it in with theirs. You can claim your back wages in Khotan. You're out of this caravan.'

CHAPTER FIFTY-ONE

Touched by the moonlight the spectral shapes of ridges and dead vegetation held a feral menace. The crunch of their footsteps over the gravel desert seemed overloud to imaginations keyed up by their abrupt fleeing. No one spoke.

They had left in the dead of night, out into the heart of the deadly Taklamakan. The tiny flicker of the dying campfire had disappeared quickly behind them and there had been no wakening alarm. They had only to put in sufficient distance by morning to be out of sight.

There were three camels. Arif had claimed his own venture investment, a sprightly youngster he called Ordut. All of the animals were heavily laden – besides food and water for themselves and the camels, they carried extra water skins to be filled at the river, warm gear for the bitter night cold, flatbread and dried fruit for when there was nothing to make a fire and two tents.

If there was something they'd overlooked it could spell a death sentence for them all. There was no going back now . . .

A night breeze started up, brushing their cheeks with a numbing chill, driving the relentless, shuddering cold into their vitals. With it came myriad sounds – a soughing murmur, taps and clicks out in the gloom.

They pressed on. The hours passed and then the sky lost its velvety blackness, an almost imperceptible lightening that softened the harsh shadows and eased the menace of the hulking shapes.

Then the monochrome gave way to colours and with just a few fading stars the last of the night fled. The edge of the sun lifted above the far horizon in a searing blast of light.

In minutes it had risen clear. The landscape was laid bare in all its appalling beauty – a grey plain of stone fragments and sand ripples, occasional red outcrops of weathered rocks and behind them, the far away snow-capped peaks of the Tien Shan range.

Nicander knew that somewhere in that direction the caravan would be stirring, Su would be making a show of discovering them missing but adamantly refusing to start a search. It happened: a merchant would take the risk of leaving the caravan in the hope of arriving before the others and cornering the market. Sometimes it worked, but often they would be taken and murdered by brigands or claimed by the desert. No doubt Korkut and the others would be shaking their heads in disbelief that their friends had left without a farewell. However this played out, they would never see the little band again.

They trudged on, enduring. Arif broke the silence and timidly suggested they take a rest at a sandy ridge.

Meng Hsiang was made to kneel then hobbled with a rope around his folded front legs; the two younger animals would not stray far from him.

A makeshift awning was fashioned from one of the tents and the little group collapsed to the ground under it. They had gone all night and put in a full day previously and soon sleep brought surcease for aching bodies.

Marius shook his friend with a rough smile. 'Wake up! Wake up, you slack bastard!'

Nicander came to, trying to orient where he was. By degrees it penetrated: the wasteland around them, the Tien Shan still in view, and nearer, a crackling fire tended by Arif.

'We thought you were going to sleep all day!' Ying Mei teased. She was sitting with her hands clasped around her knees.

'Oh, as we had nothing else to do . . .'

'You'll never make a legionary, Nico. Every hour we spend on our arse is one less on the march!'

'So. Are we thinking of eating anything?'

'Arif has a right fine-smelling mutton hotpot ready for us – be a shame if you were asleep while we finished it off.'

'Just like to know we're on course,' Marius said, as he wiped his plate clean. 'Hey, Arif – tell me we're off in the right direction?'

'Why, make no difference, Ma *sheng*, we be up with the Tarim river which go across our path, like this.' He gestured from west to east. They were going south.

'So everything square, then.'

'There is something.' Tai Yi's tone was earnest.

'For myself and the Lady Kuo, we need to know there's someone in charge. A caravan master, even if we're just a little one. Who will this be, who'll make the decisions?'

When there was no reply she said firmly, 'I think it should be Arif. He—'

'No, no! I can't!' The cameleer scrambled to his feet in consternation. 'It cannot be me!'

'Why not?' Tai Yi snapped. 'You're the only one who knows what he's doing in this . . . this journey.'

'I . . . I too y-young.'

Ying Mei came in, 'Perhaps this does need an older man, one who can carry us through with wisdom and strength when things get bad.'

She looked across encouragingly at Nicander, whose pulse began to race. To be the hero who pulls them through against all the odds! Who would be admired and respected ever afterwards! In fact, who Ying Mei would owe her life to . . . But this was a matter of sheer survival – requiring swift and merciless decisions and hard leadership.

He pointed to Marius. 'You've marched with the legions in the Syrian desert, been up against the Persians, you know what it's like. You should be our leader in this.'

Marius stared out over the dead, parched landscape for a long moment.

When he looked back his face was grim and uncompromising. 'If I do this it'll be under one condition only.'

'What's that, Marius?'

'I'm in charge. And I mean that – I give orders and you do as I say, even if you think 'em wrong. And I make the decisions! Could be there's going to be some bloody hard ones and I don't need arguments. You want me, this is my price.'

Nicander was well aware that in an army you sent men in to die; what if there was a situation here of only enough water to keep four of them alive? Who would *he* condemn to save the others? He recognised it was a choice he could never make but he knew Marius would stand by his decisions whatever it took, seeing them through even with physical violence.

'If that's what you want, Marius. How about the rest of us?'

Tai Yi tried to object but Ying Mei quietened her and it was agreed.

'So. What is your first order, Caravan Master Marius?' Nicander asked.

'Everyone on their feet!' he rapped.

'What . . . ?'

'We're moving out!'

They reached the Tarim river late the next morning – and the miracle of unlimited sparkling water in a lethal desert. Broad and shallow, the stream lazily progressed to the east. They took their fill before resting in the shade of a group of wild poplar as the camels drank deeply and grazed on the greenery that fringed the river.

Nicander glanced at Ying Mei, who was looking out over the formidable landscape with a distracted expression.

What was going through her mind? She was a noble lady who had left a home at the highest levels of the imperial court and was now cast down to this existence, a life-threatening plight. He thought of what he'd learnt from Dao Pa. Could it be that she was more advanced on the path to Tao?

This was a woman of talents and beauty both. That it could never end in . . . a uniting, there was no reason he should not take pleasure in her close company while he could. He let his gaze linger.

350

All too soon, however, it was time to plan the next move. Marius turned to Arif. 'So – if we're looking for your river to Khotan from the south, all we need to do is follow this one until we reach it?'

'I not done it, Ma *sheng*, never this way, but this what I heard.'

'Then that's what we'll do.'

It was pleasant going along the flat, hard sand next to the agreeable sight of so much water and they were almost sorry when they spotted the much smaller Ho T'ien, sliding in to lose itself in the larger river.

Now was the point of commitment.

If they turned to the right they could rejoin the world of man. If they chose the other way, each day would take them further still into the wilderness, deep into the wastes of the Taklamakan that would see them beyond any kind of help.

'Last water for the camels – and I want to see the water skins and personal gourds filled right up. Then no one takes a drop unless I say!' Marius ordered.

He surveyed them grimly. 'Arif, you take Meng Hsiang. Nico, I want you to be rearguard, and with a fucking serious duty. If you see anyone – anyone at all – who falls out of the line o' march, you shout! Loud! They get lost, there's nothing on this earth that's going to save 'em, and I'm not going to try.'

They moved off. In the lead was Marius, stepping out with stubborn purpose. Then it was Meng Hsiang plodding forward with Arif at his halter and the two younger camels strung out behind, Tai Yi and Ying Mei walking next to them.

On his own at the end Nicander tried to dismiss the worry of what would happen if he himself took dizzy and fell. No one would notice until . . .

At day's end the comforting sight of the Tien Shan had disappeared. There was nothing to show their direction in the unknown landscape apart from the sprawling glitter of the Ho T'ien, meandering from the south in great curves into the distance.

Marius declared a halt and briskly detailed duties. While Arif saw to the camels Tai Yi and Ying Mei were to collect the scraggy dried bushes dotted about for firewood and prepare the food. He called Nicander to help him with the tents and then made a muster of their stock of stores and water.

The days passed and the landscape changed around them. Before, they had travelled over a hard gravel desert – now the dunes and sand ripples were growing, wind-blown crescents that had fine grains whipping from their crests. The only flat area was the bed of the Ho-T'ien as it made its way in vast sweeps through the depressions between the dunes.

Arif was vague about exactly how far off Khotan was, possibly some hundreds of miles. There was a precious connection with it, however, that they could reach out and touch – the Ho T'ien. It had begun its life as snow in the Kunlun above the town, and had made it right through the desert to the other side, their assurance that they would eventually arrive.

The dunes grew larger; swelling hundreds of feet from valley to crest they marched away into the desert in silent array yet through it still threaded their lifeline. At places water was visible at the surface of the now drying river bed. At others, the water thinned and braided, forming many small rivulets that joined and split.

Where the water was plentiful there was lush green, where it was not the bleak grey drabness of the wasteland went unrelieved.

Ying Mei was the first to notice Meng Hsiao stumble. He gave out a low, almost inaudible moan before raising his head again. She frowned, it was level going and should not have caused him problems.

Ordut responded with an irritated snarl at the break in pace. Meng Hsiang just phlegmatically paced on.

It happened again. 'I think Meng Hsiao has hurt himself,' she called in concern.

The caravan stopped and Arif went to see for himself. The animal seemed fractious and resisted his probing hands.

'His stomach. He eaten something bad. He get over it.'

They got under way again but it was clear that the camel was in some discomfort and in the evening it refused feed. During the night it was heard groaning and in the morning it jibbed at its burden being loaded on again. No allowance could be made, however, for the other two had their own full loads.

Ying Mei walked beside it, patting the young animal's muzzle and talking to it but it was clearly still in distress.

Arif had a worried frown when they made camp. 'I not like it. He not better.'

The morning came, a cold grey dawning.

Ying Mei looked haggard – she had spent the night with the suffering creature.

'Let's go!' Marius showed no sign of sympathy.

'Can we not wait for Meng Hsiao to recover? I'm sure he'll be better in a day or so.'

'No. Get him to his feet, Arif.'

'Ah Wu. Have mercy on the beast, please! He's tried his best for us and now he needs us to be kind to him.'

'Get him up, Arif.'

Ying Mei turned away as the switch was used mercilessly. The camel screeched and writhed but did not get up.

Meng Hsiang loped up and nuzzled him in perplexity and had to be dragged back.

'He weak, Ma *sheng*. The load, it hold him down.'

'Take it off him.' Marius glanced at the other camels. 'We can't wait, there's only rations for another ten days. Unload 'em all, sort out which is the most important and they'll go with these two, the rest is left behind.'

'And Meng Hsiao?'

'If he can stay with us . . .'

Marius stood with folded arms as the pile of rejected stores steadily grew until it was one-third of the whole.

The other two camels were reloaded and Arif finally managed to drive the sick camel to its feet where it stood, trembling.

'Move,' Marius ordered.

They started out again, Meng Hsiao in the rear with Ying Mei.

But after a mile or so the camel was staggering; its humps drooping, the area between its legs and ribs concave and gaunt.

'Keep up!' roared Marius.

'He can't!' called Ying Mei brokenly. 'He needs a rest!'

The caravan halted.

Meng Hsiao fell to his knees, then to his side. His mouth was foam-streaked and his eyes dull.

Marius strode back. 'Arif?'

'He not go any more,' he said with deep sadness.

'Then we leave him. Cut him free.'

When nobody moved Marius grated, 'He can't keep up, so he takes his chances on his own. Just like any of us – right?'

Arif slowly untied the rope.

'Move on!' Marius urged.

'I'm staying with him!' Ying Mei cried.

'No, we must go on.'

White-faced, Tai Yi went to her mistress and gently led her away.

The tiny caravan moved off, Ying Mei's tear-streaked face looking back at the receding shape.

Heartrending bleats came faintly over the still air.

After a short while Marius halted them again. 'Arif, you know what to do. Do it.'

The cameleer looked away, reaching for control, then took out his knife and paced back to the sick beast, which quietened when it saw him.

Ying Mei fell to her knees but held herself to a soundless grief.

Arif was with the camel for some time, hunched over the still form, working at something.

Then he returned. In his hands was a bloody haunch of meat.

Ying Mei retched helplessly.

Nicander tried to quell his pity; this was the cold logic of desert survival.

CHAPTER FIFTY-TWO

The next day the river died. Flat and broad it had been their security with the glittering water path always with them. Now there was just the wadi, wind-blown dust and a spreading desolation. The only water was in their precious gourds and water skins. And if the dry bed disappeared entirely, where was their path?

They kept on. The dunes were now at a stupendous height – towering to over a thousand feet between valley and crest.

That night, as soon as the camels were seen to, Marius lined Nicander, Arif and the women up and, one by one, granted a single gulp of water, a ceremony he had performed at strict intervals during the day. 'No boiling, no cooking in water, nothing.'

The wind got up. It droned and whistled, finding every hole and slit and filling the tents with a fine dust that settled a gritty coating over everything.

Nicander lay with his covering over his head, unable to sleep. Had they made the right decision to come to this hellish land, where humans had no right to trespass? The alternative was seven years' imprisonment. That bastard Taw would make sure of it. But they at least would be safe, not in this demented wilderness.

The wind increased, shaking and flapping the tent – but then there was something else. Tremors through the ground, a deeper pitch to the wind and at the back of it all . . . the sound – of a great army on the move.

'Did you hear that, Marius?' he said breathlessly.

The noise wavered and strengthened, the concussion of thousands of feet, the rumble of wagons from out of the darkness.

'They're coming for us!'

'I hear it,' came Marius's voice, sounding not as steady as usual.

Intertwining it was a distant calling, a sad keening, the words not quite understandable.

Nicander's mind whirled – for he could make it out now. They were calling to him, pleading with him to go outside and come to them.

'It's the demons of the Flowing Sands!' gasped Arif. 'They after us!'

Nicander stared into the near impenetrable dimness where only the indistinct shapes of Marius and Arif could be made out.

Outside the wind blustered and moaned and the calls grew more desperate.

Then he sensed a presence – close outside. A scrabbling and movement.

He lay rigid with fear.

A dim shape passed across the laced-up entrance working at the loop.

Then into their tent burst first one then another giant demon. Nicander opened his mouth to shriek but one sobbed, 'We couldn't sleep, we were frightened.' A cringing Ying Mei and Tai Yi crouched before them in the crowded tent.

The next day they set off in a still blustering wind with stinging particles that had them winding cloths around their heads and hands. It relented as the day's heat began but the river bed was getting indistinct. They followed it around in a long sweeping curve and there ahead was a speck of green. This meant water – they were still on track!

The camels got the scent and increased their pace.

'Thank God!' croaked Nicander, as he made out a pool thirty feet across, with a few reeds and tamarisks growing at the edge.

Marius held up a warning hand. 'I'll try it first.'

He touched the water to his lips but quickly spat it out. He gave a grim smile. 'We can't have it but the camels will.'

Meng Hsiang and Ordut were soon showing their appreciation, throwing sprays of water over their bodies and giving hoarse roars of satisfaction as they drank.

Nicander and Arif sluiced water over themselves while Marius went to the other side of the pool and cast about. But there was no river bed to follow at all now, just dreary plain, ending against the slope of a massive dune.

He returned to the little group. 'I won't hide it from you. We're in trouble. We can't be sure this is the main river or if we've been following a branch off it to its end. Now we can turn round and go back, looking for signs in the river bed where the main went off in another direction – if ever it did.

'Or we could go back on our tracks to reach the last place with good water. Either way we'll run out of rations because we'll be three times covering the same ground. The other side o' the coin is to go on, see if the water comes back to the surface further on, hoping it's the main stream. Which direction do we go to find it – the last way it was headed? Or do we give up looking and strike south and hope we pick it up again?'

'It's your decision, Marius,' Nicander said almost in a whisper. 'Which will it be?'

'We stop here and set up for the night.'

'Marius, it's only the morning!'

'Now why didn't I notice that?' the legionary said with a wintry grin. 'No, you bastards are going to wait here in comfort while me and Meng Hsiang go up that dune and spy out the land.'

The crest was a thousand feet above them. The trip would take hours.

They stood watching as the lone camel angled up the dune, a tiny dot on the immensity of sand slowly ascending until it disappeared around the flank.

In the late afternoon Marius was spotted again and by evening he had returned.

'No news,' he said tersely. 'Can't see a thing that's for sure a river. Only these fucking dunes like waves on a sea. They go on and on and you can't see

357

down between 'em to check if there's a river there. I'm . . . I'm sorry.'

They were lost.

'Thank you, Ah Wu. You did try – for all of us,' Ying Mei said softly.

Nicander wondered how she could be so calm. Did she not know . . . But then he realised it was the strength of her character, the same self-discipline that had made her the Ice Queen as she had struggled to keep her appearance before the world in hideous times when others would have given up long before.

And now she was maintaining a normality that was calming their anxieties and preserving their humanity for the final trial.

His heart cried for them all.

CHAPTER FIFTY-THREE

Marius gave his decision. 'We head south.'

They moved off quietly and soon came to the first dune. They began climbing at a shallow angle, their feet sinking into the soft sand at every step.

Marius positioned the women to the left and right of Meng Hsiang, Nicander and Arif either side of Ordut. The camels hardly noticed the soft going and were able to help pull them along bodily. He remained in front, stolidly pacing ahead.

They eventually reached the top – an infinity of dunes stretched in every direction. No mountain ranges, telltale oases, winding rivers or flat plains.

The hot wind was brisk on the crest, driving sand in curling spindrifts to the lee of each. But at least they would be spared the agony of constantly toiling uphill – the giant crescents were oriented in their favour, to the north and south.

'Ma *sheng*,' Arif said diffidently.

'Yes?'

'The sand harder where the wind blow.'

Nicander was grateful: a little below the crest on the side from where the wind blew it was firmer going with the more compacted grains.

Unspoken was the realisation that their desolation was complete. Not a single living thing other than themselves and the camels, nothing but dunes and the cruel unblinking sun.

With every step he could feel the sloshing about in his precious gourd of water. How curious to realise that there was a simple equation that ruled everything: water in the gourd equalled life, none equalled death.

The odds were now very much against them pulling through.

He found himself thinking: what would Dao Pa have said? There was no way of knowing but he vowed to meditate that night and prepare his soul.

The resolution cheered him a little.

In a way the dull repetition of their slogging progress insulated him from despair. Each dune was different, all the dunes were the same. Sometimes it blew harder than other times, one time Ying Mei would be to the left of Ordut, then it would be the right.

She was muffled in flapping clothing but he knew and cherished the image of her valiant trudge.

At the end of the day the tents could not be put up as there was nothing firm to take the pegs so as darkness closed in they were reduced to curling up in the lee of the camels below the crest with every piece of clothing they could find against the bitter cold.

Nicander's dreams were always the same: sparkling, refreshing water. But as he raised it to his lips he would jerk awake, parched.

Each morning they would take a gulp of water and refill the gourds at the water skins, trying to ignore the sight of their increasingly flaccid appearance.

Marius would then yet again go to the highest point and meticulously scan every quadrant. He would give a quick shake of the head and growl, 'Move!' and they would lurch into motion.

Finding the general direction of south was easy enough: at night the dazzling display of stars revealed it while in the day the centre of the arc of the sun was always south. But when would their agony end?

Thirst became a torment. The single-gulp discipline took inhuman control but under the eyes of all it was impossible to cheat. For a brief few minutes the mouth would be moist, the tongue free – then in the pitiless heat it would thicken and loll, the taste of dust always there.

Another day and night passed.

And in front, always, Marius striding on.

He would grimly administer the water ceremony at the stops, his voice hoarse but still hard, his skin wrinkled, his eyes sunken and feverish.

They were all suffering but none complained or criticised. Ying Mei was a slight, stooped figure with flushed face and hands that trembled as she took her water. A sun-ravaged Tai Yi kept close by all the time. Arif had taken to dropping his head in silent misery as he went about his duties.

Now the last water skin was empty – what they had in their gourds was all that remained.

Still there was no sign of deliverance. The nature of the dunes was becoming complex, the edge of the crests splitting and joining and making a straight course impossible even if they seemed to be becoming less massive.

They plodded on through another day, the hot wind got up again and scoured their exposed skin but they dared not stop.

That night Nicander suffered from painful cramps and headache, finally slipping into a fitful sleep in the biting cold.

In the morning and with their gourds barely half-full they got under way.

When the sun rose high, Nicander's cramps returned. In pain, he reeled about. On the other side of Ordut, Arif, head bowed in endurance, didn't see him and the little caravan carried on without him.

He dropped to his knees, his hands tight on his stomach as the spasms racked him. He closed his eyes in pain.

There were faint shouts and he opened his eyes to see Marius trudging back towards him.

Nicander struggled to his feet but without a pause Marius knocked him down.

'I said no one falls out of the line o' march!' he rasped. 'Get back in the ranks!'

Nicander caught up, ashamed that he had let Marius down.

'I can't trust you lot out o' my sight!' the legionary croaked. 'I'm following behind, and God help any as drops out!'

They pressed on, ever to the south, this time without the comforting sight of Marius in front.

With a tongue swollen to twice its size and cruel aches in every joint it took Nicander heroic resolve to keep moving. He knew it was the same for the others.

Every step was an effort. His head hung and he saw one foot go out then the other in hypnotic succession.

A strange whimper made him look up. Ying Mei was gesturing behind them.

A dark huddle lay still on the sand thirty yards away. Marius.

It couldn't be! Of all of them . . .

Nicander somehow summoned strength to hurry to his friend who lay face down in the baking dunes. The others followed.

'Marius!' he whispered hoarsely, turning over his body. He was breathing but unconscious.

'Get his gourd and give him water!' Ying Mei pleaded.

Nicander lifted it up and found it empty of even a drop. It didn't make sense . . . then it hit him like a blow. Marius had made great play at the water skin but had not filled his own gourd, letting others have his share.

His eyes stung – Marius had not had anything to drink the night before.

Logic demanded that they leave him and go on, playing out the drama until its end.

'Ah Yung. You are the leader now,' Ying Mei said unsteadily. 'What do we do?'

'We stop here for the night,' he croaked. It would buy time to think.

'Try to get him to take some water,' he muttered, handing over his own gourd.

As he had seen Marius do so many times, he went to the highest point and looked out over the endless dunes, now shadowing as the sun fell. Ahead – south – the curving crest they had been following was splitting into two going in alternate directions. It meant that there were three valleys now – one ahead and one on either side.

Marius did not regain consciousness, lying still, barely breathing. Ying Mei fanned him but there was nothing to be done.

Nicander sat upright against Meng Hsiang's hairy bulk staring into the night. This was the end, there would be no more hopeless striving. One by one they would drop in their tracks. Then their bones would be left until they too would be covered by the restless sand.

He felt a great sadness that it all had to end like this.

His head drooped as weariness claimed him but something made him look up – and as if in a dream he saw a figure, a robe covering its face.

Shaking his head to try to clear it he saw the vision remained. The robe was thrown back and Dao Pa stood before him!

Nicander hadn't the strength to do more than wonder what he wanted but the image grew stronger and more real.

'Why are you here?' he managed to say.

Dao Pa made a solemn sign of blessing.

'We're in our last travails, Master. What can we do?'

The sage mouthed something.

'I can't hear you.' Nicander said, his voice barely above a whisper, but it hurt to speak louder.

Dao Pa shook his head sorrowfully and spread his hands.

In a sudden spasm of hope Nicander pleaded, 'Where must we go – ahead, to the left or right . . . ? As a last chance!'

The figure extended a hand – and pointed firmly to the right. Then he made the gesture of drinking.

The river!

'Thank you, thank you, Master! For the others, I thank you!'

With a last farewell, Dao Pa turned and vanished into the blackness.

CHAPTER FIFTY-FOUR

Marius still lived but would not last the morning without shade and rest. Nicander knew the cruelty of flogging on the two women was beyond him. Therefore there was only one course. 'I want everyone to stay here today,' he croaked. 'I'm taking Meng Hsiang to look for water. If I'm not back by tomorrow then Arif's in charge.'

He felt lightheaded and strangely calm as the camel stepped off. Was the vision of Dao Pa real or was it a dream? One way or another their problems would all be over before the end of the day.

He followed the crest for about a mile to where it divided. Confidently he kneed the camel to the right. Soon he could look down into the valley and there he would see the flat of the river bed and the unbearable glitter of moving water.

Meng Hsiang plodded forward patiently and they drew nearer – and then the whole valley opened up before him.

He searched eagerly – there was no sparkling water. No flat river bed. Only another drab bottomland.

Disappointment slammed in, followed by a dull and bitter resignation. Even Dao Pa had let him down. Did he turn back now or try another direction? He couldn't bring himself to think about it.

Then something caught his eye: deep down and near the bottom. A series of dots.

They moved.

With a desperate intensity he stared down and made out a string of camels in a line, travelling slowly along.

He tried to yell with all his strength but it came out only as a harsh croak.

'Go!' he urged Meng Hsiang in an agony of hope. The animal reluctantly began to step and slide down the steep slope towards the camel train. They saw him and stopped.

'Faster!' he gasped but his camel had its own speed. They drew nearer and he could make out several men dressed in outlandish coloured tunics and turban-like headdresses, gaping at his approach.

Nearer still and his vision blurred with emotion. Then he was up with them nearly crying with relief. 'Who are you? We need help, desperately, please!'

They looked at each other and shrugged, babbling something that had no meaning to him. 'Please! Water – water! Please understand – we're looking for Khotan and—'

'Ai, ai! Khotan!' they said, vigorously pointing back to where they'd come from.

Near delirious, Nicander tried to get off but slipped and tumbled. One of the men slid to the ground and hurried over. Nicander pointed to his mouth. 'Water! Please – water!'

The man untied a small skin pouch and placed it to his lips.

Nicander drank then he fell back, wanting to weep with the emotion of it all but unable to.

The man looked down at him and with the utmost tenderness tried to ask him something.

'There! Up there!' Nicander managed, indicating over the crest. 'More of us!' He held up four fingers and gestured again.

'Ha!' The man snapped a rapid-fire command. A water skin was flung over one camel, another mounted. Twitched into motion, the animals angled up the dune.

Nicander slumped back – and the world dissolved to nothing.

CHAPTER FIFTY-FIVE

'Be buggered to you!' Marius protested. 'I'm not staying in this bed rotting for ever – we have to get going.' He threw aside the threadbare cover.

'Not until they say you're ready,' Nicander said wearily, pulling it back again.

'Have you checked the silk eggs, Nico? I've got to know they're safe.'

Reassured, he closed his eyes again.

The two men had been left at the lamasery as a deserving charity, poor travellers on a caravan that had been set upon by brigands and who'd made a desperate escape into the desert, arriving with little more than the clothes they wore.

Not daring to reveal the contents of Tai Yi's chest in a strange place they had humbly accepted the hospitality of the lamasery. It was not a richly endowed one, however, and there had been pointed remarks about their future plans.

One vital piece of information they had gleaned was that Khotan was a major trading centre on the rim of the Great Desert. From here argosies set out for many destinations, especially Kashgar. Situated where the Kunlun range in the south curved up to meet the Tien Shan from the north, Kashgar was the transfer point for goods coming from the desert to the mountain crossings.

No one seemed to know exactly what lay beyond the mountains – India was somewhere past them, in another direction was the land of horses that sweated blood. Yet another route, it was said, led to the home of the barbarous nomads.

As it happened, Kashgar fell in well with their story: that the journey to Ying Mei's sick father's bedside had been interrupted by their fleeing across the desert to escape marauders and now she wanted to resume it by going to Aksu the other way around – to do so, they'd have to pass through Kashgar. They still had their original documents to back up their tale.

Nicander did not want to vex Marius until he had regained his strength but he had much on his mind. He recalled Su's worry that it was late in the season – did this apply to mountain travel too? And there was the fact that as Marius lay recovering, Su and the caravan was on their way here around the same desert edge. If they didn't get to Kashgar before them, they'd meet somewhere along the route. And were Tai Yi and Ying Mei safe? They had been separated when the ladies were led away to a nunnery to recover. So many concerns . . . but at least they had been able to reward Arif for his loyalty with the gift of Meng Hsiang's deposit.

There was every reason to be gone at the first opportunity. Nicander had heard that in these parts caravans were more frequent and the abbot had been quick to point out that one was on its way north in only a few days. But Marius—

A firm knock at the door broke into his thoughts. With a disapproving frown a monk informed him that they had visitors, but being female they could not enter the lamasery. Nicander gave a start: it could only be Ying Mei and Tai Yi.

He was escorted to the gate. Ying Mei stood outside wearing borrowed novice's robes. Apart from the high colour of a sun-touched face she seemed none the worse for her ordeal. Tai Yi had not been so lucky and her swollen features obviously gave her pain.

Ying Mei gave a hesitant smile. 'Tell me, how is Ah Wu?'

'He's on the mend. Complains all the time of lying still. We've been told he's too weak to leave yet, so I worry we're going to miss the next caravan.'

'That's why I came to talk to you. I've an idea to get us on the caravan. Why don't we hire a camel or a horse just for him? When he's better we can take turns on it.'

'He won't like it, but it'll get us going.'

She hesitated. 'Ah Yung – would you walk with me? There's something I want to say to you.'

Tai Yi gave her mistress a sharp look.

'This is private between Ah Yung and me, Tai Yi, please understand.'

Nicander's heart skipped a beat. Could it be that she had similar feelings for him? Damn his monk's disguise. Was she going to . . . ?

They began walking; Tai Yi fell behind at a distance.

'It's . . . well, we've come through a horrible time and it was all of us together, wasn't it?' Her tone was stiff, unsure.

'Yes, it was,' he answered carefully.

'And if it wasn't for Marius we wouldn't have . . .'

'We owe him much.'

They walked further in an awkward silence.

'Ah Yung.'

'Yes?'

'We've been good friends, haven't we? I've learnt such a lot of Greek, about your country and . . . things. And you've come along a long way with your Chinese characters. You've a natural gift, do you know that?'

'And it's been a pleasure, always,' he said softly.

She hesitated, then said so quietly he had to strain to hear, 'I want you to know, Ah Yung, that I will never forget you as long as I live.'

'And . . . and I also, Ying Mei. I will remember these times until the day I die.'

This caravan was far bigger than their last – a cavalcade of nearly a thousand camels and horses, stretching for miles. It was a rich one with not only the usual precious jade of Khotan but tons' weight of finished silk goods, ivory and spices from India, carpets and tortoiseshell, ornaments and toys – and, it was rumoured, quantities of musk which was known to be four times the value of gold, weight for weight.

So close to the great Kunluns there was no shortage of water run-off and horses were plentiful and easy to sustain; not just Marius but all four were able to go by horseback.

This was an official caravan. High-ranking bureaucrats from Khotan and Tibet were going north on diplomatic business and the escort was impressive, a column of Turghiz cavalry. There was also a promised oasis caravanserai every night – no tents for this caravan. And with the need to keep the dignitaries at their accustomed level, the rations and entertainment were of the highest order.

With such comforts, time passed congenially.

On their left the Kunlun range kept pace, snow-capped and majestic. After some days they began to change: to loftier, more complex jagged peaks – some said that for those with the courage, fabled India lay far beyond.

They continued following around the mountain's flanks on the left and across the vast plain to their right, another white-tipped mountain range rose above the horizon.

The two gradually converged – and there ahead was Kashgar.

'Not as if it's a place I'd like to spend my days in,' Marius muttered when they arrived. It was big, sprawling and had an air of hard trading and squalor.

As their caravan made its stately way through mean streets to the vast caravanserai, a chill squall flapped their clothing. From an unrelieved humid and grey sky, rain began falling and the streets soon ran with mud. Quite unprepared for a heavy downpour, they were quickly soaked and arrived at the caravanserai dripping.

'How wonderful,' laughed Ying Mei. 'I feel like a child again!'

Although small, their cells were adequate in which to refresh after their journey but Marius wanted no time wasted. 'We get together, ten minutes!' he ordered.

It was more like half an hour as the ladies begged time to make themselves presentable.

369

When they were all assembled Marius got down to business. 'This caravan moves out in two days – and we're not going to be on it. Instead we're going over the mountains!'

'We know all this, Marius,' Nicander said gruffly. 'What we don't know is where? I mean, it's all very well saying we're going across the mountains, but in what direction? We choose the wrong one and we'll end up in India or some place the world hasn't heard of.'

'Simple! Like you said, we follow the silk. It's eventually going to end up in Constantinople.'

'Not so easy,' Nicander came back heavily. 'From here they've got camel trains going everywhere under the sun.'

'We ask, bugger it!'

'Ask what? "Are you going to Constantinople, sir?" Nobody here's even heard of it!'

'For fuck's sake! We ask to go somewhere on the way, o' course!'

'Do you know any town on the way? You can't, because the Sogdian's keep very quiet about it. They don't want any outsider connecting east and west and turning into a business rival, so they keep it all a great secret. No one else knows because they pass the silk between themselves. We're stuck, Marius, admit it!'

'Please try, gentlemen,' Ying Mei pleaded. 'I've heard camels can't walk in snow. What do they have to carry the loads? If we can find a caravan without camels perhaps we can see if—'

'No idea. You, Marius?'

He scratched his head. 'Never really thought about it. Hannibal did well with his elephants but I've not seen many around here . . .'

Ying Mei looked blank at the foreign words.

'I'll explain later,' Nicander said hastily. 'Right now time's short. Su's caravan could be along at any time, and this one will be on its way soon.'

Marius lifted his chin and growled, 'I've made a decision.'

'And what's that?' Nicander said archly.

'While the ladies and I go to the caravan master and tell him we're stepping off and need to settle up, you, Nico, will go around the caravanserai and, any way you like, find out about mountain caravans and stuff. Right?'

Nicander smiled wryly – all the blame would be his if he couldn't find a way out.

He returned late with mixed news. 'I made out I had a cargo needing to be shifted west and they all said the same thing – that it would be going through the Terek Davan Pass. Wouldn't say where to, but at least we've got a direction.'

'That's wonderful, Ah Yung. But you also said bad news?'

'We're too late. The last freight has gone through and now the pass is closed by snow. Nothing now until the following travelling season, next year.'

'Next year?'

'About seven months to wait.' He paused. 'But I did hear from one of the cameleers that if they've got need to get hold of more carrying capacity, they hire a small crew on a temporary basis to follow on independently. This lot are Kyrgyz and while unreliable, know the mountains well. Could be they're running for a little while longer . . . ?'

Marius beamed. 'We find 'em! Ask what they'll take to get us through!'

'Ah. Now there's a problem.'

'Bugger you, Nico. Always coming up with something as will queer things! What is it now?'

'Our friends the Sogdians. Nobody's saying, but it's clear that if they're keeping their whole system end to end a secret they'll slit the throats of any who let through spies. And we look just that – a couple of western barbarians and their Chinese concubines.'

'Ni *lao na*! I resent that!' Tai Yi spluttered. 'In front of the Lady Kuo, as well!'

'Yes, yes. But look at this from our caravan master's point of view. Is he going to risk taking on spies and having the Sogdians down on his neck? I don't think so. We have to come up with a good story.'

Ying Mei gave a little smile. 'What if I'm a Chinese princess who's been taken with a lover. I flee from the palace but my father is so angry he vows to slay me. I fly, but his vengeance follows me everywhere I go. In the end, accompanied only by my faithful attendant and two foreign slaves I find I have to seek exile in the only place he cannot reach – beyond the mountains.'

'A disgraceful tale!' remonstrated Tai Yi.

Nicander beamed. 'That's just the story we want! How can such as we be business spies? And it shows we have to move fast and secretly – well done, Ying Mei!'

Early the following morning Marius and Nicander hired two horses and headed towards the foot of the mountains.

They had a name and a place and quickly found the outlying compound. A modest collection of snug timber buildings, it had a bare pasture at the back with many horses and a few donkeys. Was this an operation that could cross those titanic snowy peaks and take them to the Western Lands?

They were met outside the largest building by a young man in red and black with ornate boots and tassels. He was not of any of the races of people Nicander had come across and his fierce, dark-tanned features had no trace of the oriental. He carried a whip which he passed from hand to hand as he snapped a question at them in a strange tongue.

Ignoring it, Nicander asked in Chinese, 'We come to offer business. Who shall we speak with?'

'In here!' came a reply.

They entered a smoky room and sitting at a table was the most ancient old man he had ever seen. He barked something at them.

Taken aback by his vigour Nicander repeated what he had said.

'Who are you to come here asking stupid questions?' The man replied in near-faultless Chinese.

'Are you still crossing the Terek Davan Pass?'

'If I am?'

His heart skipped a beat. Dare he hope?

'You were recommended by Kashgar to take a late freight. I've got one that has to get over before the end of the season. Can you do it?'

'Why aren't you using an agent?'

'Because this is a special, I want to organise this myself.'

'No.'

'Why not? You're crossing still, aren't you?'

'You're new around here, stands out like a tree in a desert. The Sogdians have a hold on everything here, that's why. Don't want trouble with 'em, they spying me taking a freight away from them. See?'

'I can understand that. But this isn't cargo, it's people. Let me explain . . .'

Before the man had chance to interrupt he launched into their story, telling of harrowing times fleeing unjust retribution, the constant fear, the trust they were putting in himself at that very moment.

'. . . so all she asks is to be taken beyond the mountains until his wrath is spent. Surely you have enough pity in your heart? Your Sogdians wouldn't care if you took just four across – they're only being taken there into exile, it's not as if you're robbing them of freight.'

The man stroked his straggling beard then shook his head. 'I've never taken travellers. It's too hard on them who aren't used to it. And a princess! No, this is not for me.'

Nicander, however, saw an opening for a commercial negotiation. Names were exchanged and within the hour a deal was done.

He, Yulduz, would take them for a fee and on conditions they dress as Kyrgyz and supply their own gear, which he specified. It would be a freight run, the usual when not hired by the Sogdians, which comprised goods needed by the mountain folk on the way up and taking theirs to sell down the other side. Therefore there'd be no fancy treatment as they'd enjoyed in a proper camel train.

'Osh! Did you hear that, Ah Lai? We're going to Osh!'

'Now, don't get too excited, Ying Mei,' Nicander cautioned. 'Yulduz told me it's going to be the worst journey we'll ever take and he can't do much about it. And there's not long to get the gear he said we'll need.'

'Why can't I be excited? We're saved!'

'How do you know? Where's this Osh anyway? – I've never heard of it,' Marius rumbled.

But there was no suppressing the general optimism.

They quickly arranged to purchase new kit – mainly warm clothing; leather boots, a double-thickness padded coat and a peculiar felt pyramid that wrapped around the body. With a pair of fur-lined leather gloves and their existing sheepskins, they were ready.

Yulduz met them with a gap-toothed grin. 'Which one's the princess?'

Ying Mei froze him with a glance.

The smile disappeared and he gave a clumsy bow. 'Is Your Highness ready to depart, M' Lady?'

Their mounts were led out to barely stifled gasps of dismay. They looked like runts; donkey-coloured, they had bushy manes and long tails. Nicander heaved himself up on one, which didn't appear to be troubled by the burden.

Their baggage went on a pack mule and with the other ponies, five drivers and Yulduz they got under way.

CHAPTER FIFTY-SIX

As they skirted the base of the mountains, they were overawed by their dark bulk thrusting vertically to arrogant heights. The limitless immensity of the desert floor stretched out to the other side.

After an hour or so a river valley opened up and they entered the world of the mountain.

Bare, forbidding grey cliffs dropped precipitously down to the narrow valley floor and a small jade-coloured river.

On each side the cliffs began closing in and before long they were threading their way along an uneven rocky track by the side of the river. Ahead through the winding defile Nicander caught breathtaking glimpses of snowy peaks.

A constant cool wind funnelling down from the uplands through the ravines obliged them to find warmer clothes. As they wound ever deeper into the mountain fastness it turned to a sun-bright cold that was piercing.

Sure-footed, their ponies made their way forward on the rough terrain, delicately, like cats. It was now obvious why these were used in preference to the big-boned horses of the plains.

By the end of the day their track was appreciably steeper. They stopped at a flat area, a saddle between two valleys. It had spectacular views of the interior, the soaring peaks now tinged with a delicate rose as the lower areas shadowed before nightfall.

On this caravan there were no crew to take care of the domestics and while Nicander and Marius set about rigging a heavy black tent Tai Yi and Ying Mei took their pot to where a tiny cooking fire crackled.

Quite swiftly the mountains turned purple and then all disappeared into the shadows of night.

With no campfire, no entertainments and no fellow travellers there was nothing for it but to retire. To reduce the load, a single communal tent had been brought – and sleeping arrangements agreed. The ladies would enter first and when decency allowed, call out, on their honour to face away as the men did likewise.

The tent was roomy but stuffy with a strong odour of animal. Nicander threw the door flaps wide but the night air was frigid, feeling far colder than the desert and with a humid edge to it, much more cutting. He quickly laced them up again.

They lay back in the dark and after a round of stilted 'good nights' each was left alone with their thoughts.

Across the saddle they descended to another valley floor trending in a different direction. It widened and after a while they took a steep path that led out on to a sparse meadow. The ponies were given their head to crop the grass.

Without any warning a squall came up and fat drops of rain began falling, icy cold. It passed as quickly, leaving the grass wet and glittering and the sun beaming in warmth.

Suddenly Ying Mei pointed to the sky. A pair of great eagles circled high up. 'Wild creatures!'

They were the first such they had seen after months in the dead heart of the desert.

'And there.' Marius's keen eyes spotted a montane sheep perilously picking its way along the side of the far mountain.

They spied more and the time passed agreeably until they found themselves entering some kind of upland kingdom between the crags and peaks. Pleasant grassy sward, trickling crystal brooks and here and there the tiny dash of colour of a wildflower.

Then a settlement came into view with blue smoke spiralling up from squat stone huts, flocks of sheep and a cluster of gaily decorated round tents off to one side.

Their arrival brought out children in ribboned pigtails and little black trousers screaming in delight and women eager to see what goods had been brought.

But they did not stay long. Yulduz chivvied on the proceedings, glancing repeatedly at the sky.

Soon they had left the grassland. Their track took on a marked upward gradient and the animals strained at their loads.

They passed through a towering canyon, a dismal place of cold dankness and shadow, and out into a broader valley where they continued their ascent.

The ponies were now making heavy weather of it, panting. Yulduz got off his mount and led it, ordering Nicander and the others to do so too. Puffing and wheezing with the high altitude they tramped over the stony path, now littered with boulders and treacherously wet.

Often the sun was obscured by clouds streaming over the peaks, instantly sending the temperature down to a numbing cold.

Further on they came to their first snow, scattered slush that made it hard to see what they were stepping into and in their bulky sheepskins difficult and slippery going.

They passed over the rise and a wide upland area opened out before them. On it many long-haired beasts were grazing peacefully on the slopes before a small village. Yulduz gestured towards it with a smile. As they headed there the first flakes of a light snow came whirling down.

They stopped at the largest house, a wooden two-storey structure with lean-to stables and animal pens.

'My son's house!' Yulduz said proudly.

Inside, aglow with the ruddy glare of a fire, it stank richly of animals.

After he was greeted by a succession of sun-browned relatives, Yulduz introduced a shy woman in filigreed headgear and voluminous dress as his son's wife.

Then came a number of wide-eyed children to greet them and a deeply wrinkled old woman. 'Her mother.'

The travellers were greatly relieved to be in the warm, and with no shared language, but with Yulduz translating, chatted happily to the family.

A frothy concoction of tea, salt and butter was served. This was followed by a delicious feast of many dishes – horse-meat sausages, sheep's liver, a spicy rice dish of chicken and fried shredded carrots in a huge cauldron.

After everyone could eat no more, Yulduz commanded, 'We sleep!' A rickety ladder led up to the open second floor with beds and tables in one communal area.

In the morning they all helped in the main task: transferring the goods and baggage to the yaks. Yulduz explained that at the higher regions where they were headed the ponies could not stand the altitude.

The yaks were of impressive bulk: even Marius could barely see over their humped shoulders, and with a dense and hairy undercoat they looked well fitted for the cold. Their horns were a yard across but the huge beasts were imperturbably docile, taking their saddle-frame without pausing as they cropped the snow-littered grass.

The yak train was sizeable – thirty-five of the shaggy monoliths in all, laden down with salt from the plains, worked silver goods, carpets, baubles from Kashgar's bazaars.

Nicander and the others were helped into the saddle by giggling boys. The massive beasts stood unmoving, firm as a rock. Nicander flashed a nervous grin at Marius and the ladies.

There were no ropes stringing the yaks together as with a camel train. When shrill shouts announced the start of the trail, each animal obediently followed the one in front. The lead yak, which did not carry any load, walked forward and placidly turned to left and right on command as they wound across the upland plain.

They were easy to ride, reassuringly steady with none of the airy sway – or the goaty smell – of a camel. Yaks were almost scented, even with their slightly oily hair, which hung down below their bellies.

Ahead, Ying Mei twisted round to wave an assurance to Nicander.

The plain contracted and then they began following a narrow, stony track around the steep bare flank of a precipice. Nicander saw to the right the mountainside falling away in an awesome drop to a river below. All it needed was a misplaced hoof and . . .

The yaks were seemingly unconcerned, plodding forward, one behind the other.

Before they made the next pass the snow began again, whipping about spitefully in the hard wind. They were all now shuddering with cold. Still the big beasts walked on, their only concession to the bluster being to lower their heads.

At one point they forded a river in a perilous stumble. On the other side, they picked up another narrow track that led to open upland again, not agreeable meadows but a rocky wilderness.

Yulduz pointed to the end where a solid white mass half a mile across filled the valley from side to side. 'Ice river.'

They traversed the stone-strewn slope, the rounded hoofs of the yaks clicking and knocking as they went. The snow returned, swirling ever thicker it made it impossible to look up and they had to trust to the yaks to follow on after the bell of the one in front.

Nicander was becoming more and more breathless. The gasping strain gave him a pounding head.

The chill began a remorseless clamping in. A trial of endurance.

Still the yak train wound on, past a craggy outcrop that suddenly loomed out of the snow squalls and up to another level.

Nicander could just see Ying Mei, a dark hump ahead in the swirling snow. She was no doubt suffering as much as him. Was it worth it? Was this really the way to Constantinople and home? In the misery of the unrelenting cold he sank back into his enduring, head hung.

The yaks came to a stop. Looking up Nicander saw that they were halted in the lee of a bluff which cut off the wind like a knife.

Frozen and torpid he fell off his yak into a few inches of snow, vaguely sensing someone leading away his mount.

'This snow, I not like!' Yulduz grunted, squinting up at the heavy grey sky. 'We have to make Terek very soon or we in trouble!'

Nevertheless it was decreed that the night be spent there. Miraculously there was a fire: one of the drivers had been tasked to carry a pottery bowl under his cloak with precious embers of charcoal which were blown into life. Dried yak dung was added to make a small blaze.

They huddled over the life-giving warmth, the flames lurid and golden against the bleak grey of the stony landscape in the falling night. Yak-butter tea was doled out and for a brief time spirits rose.

There was no question of erecting a tent on the loose scree. The crew wrapped their felt pyramids close about them, pulling the 'hood' over their heads then hunching down, clutching their knees to their chests.

Marius made sure he and the others had their own felt protections on and made use of the tent against the bitter winds that flapped and blustered through the long night. It was opened up and laid over them, held down from the inside. The shelter was suffocating and odorous, but the alternative was worse.

There was a blizzard in the morning but Yulduz was insistent they start. 'I worry the Terek!' he muttered.

CHAPTER FIFTY-SEVEN

The snow eased but there was a new hazard. The yaks could not see the track under the fresh snowfall and slipped and staggered as they missed their foothold.

'Not far now, Terek Davan!' Yulduz said.

Unexpectedly the snow ceased abruptly and the sun glared unbearably bright in a deep-blue sky.

As the little train continued on around the side of the mountain they squinted against the dazzling white. Before them was the broad snow-covered saddle between the buttresses of two cloud-torn ranges – the long-sought Terek Davan Pass.

But only two miles below it the snow began again, squally flurries and then solid, driving flakes that blinded and choked and lay a chill deadness thickly on ground and beast.

It was impossible to go on – blundering over a precipice was a real possibility.

The train stopped and the yaks quickly came together in a huddle. Forcing their way inside, the humans took refuge from the icy wind in the steamy mass as snow steadily built on the hairy backs. Nicander caught a glimpse of Ying Mei's pinched but expressionless face; holding on, enduring.

The snow continued remorselessly.

It was so unfair – only another couple of miles and . . .

Nicander tried to ask Yulduz their chances but in reply only got an ill-tempered gabbling and the man turned away.

With the pass so close would he wait for the weather to clear and make a desperate attempt to transit, or return to the village and wait for spring?

The fearful cold made it difficult to think. The yaks could probably wade through a couple of feet of snow but who could tell if conditions the other side of the pass were better or worse? They couldn't stay where they were indefinitely. The longer they delayed returning, the deeper the snow behind them, and he remembered more than one patch that . . .

Had they left it too late either way?

Nicander felt a swelling dread.

Time passed and he slipped into a reverie of images and impressions.

He was abruptly brought back to the present by hurried movement out of the huddle – the snow had stopped!

Yulduz stared at the grey sky. Then he bent and picked up some snow and let it fall to the ground, watching it closely. His gaze returned to the line of the summit.

'We go!' he snapped.

There was a fevered scurry of activity. This time there would be no riding; each would walk beside his yak.

They set out for the distant top of the pass, stomping the soft snow with every pace and knowing the stakes if they failed.

The sun came and went. Everyone periodically glanced warily at the sky, dreading what they would see.

Yulduz was ahead, testing the way and calling out shrill commands to the lead yak.

The crest drew nearer and, praise be, they were atop it – a slope led gently away on the other side into the same grand panorama of great mountains and far valleys. Yulduz took a wide, sweeping zigzag down, going as fast as he could get the yaks to follow.

Nicander, like the others, was numbed and exhausted and it wasn't until they stopped at a sheltered crag that he realised they were safe.

Yulduz, now in fine spirits, handed out a ration of *chhurpi*, a bar of dry yak cheese that took hours to chew.

'Not so bad, now. I don't think they come after you here, M' Lady!' he added with a cackle.

Nicander found himself smiling. They were through the mountain barrier and were on the road to the west!

Yulduz gave the order to remount, their way now was a continual downward winding track along the wide flank of a mountain to where green peeped through the snow on the uplands.

In two days they left the snowline and reached the lower foothills whose terrain made for fast going. Later, wide river plains led through increasingly fertile regions with nomad tents and flocks dotted on the slopes.

They stopped at tiny settlements for fresh provisions and news and to exchange their trinkets for furs and handworked trifles and then passed on to a majestic river valley.

'To Osh,' Yulduz said proudly. 'He goes to my town!'

They followed him up a steep track littered with sharp stones. It wound around then through a cleft – and they caught their breath. Below was an immense plain ending in a blue-grey haze at the horizon. They could see every detail, the glittering meander of a river, the dots of trees, the smudge of forests and the far-distant sprawl of a city.

The travellers beamed at each other. The landscape was alive and green, even roads could be picked out. They had left Chang An for a desert of sand, then from Kashgar endured a desert of snow and rock. Now they had won through to what could only be – the Western Lands.

CHAPTER FIFTY-EIGHT

Directly before them was Osh.

Ying Mei did not speak but her eyes darted everywhere: this was the crowning moment of her journey.

Nicander glanced at her. Against all the odds they had made it through, over the endless miles. And now she was in the Western Lands he had fulfilled his bargain.

The ground levelled in the last mile or two and the caravan joined a tree-lined road. As the travellers drew closer however, they could see that the houses were mean and seedy; the streets and lanes unplanned and dirty, full of ragged children and herds of pigs. Noisy, uncaring and stinking.

By the time they had come to a halt in the big caravanserai it was clear that this was a trading outpost, a town perched on the frontier.

Seeing Ying Mei's set face Yulduz said defensively, 'Osh is a fine place, M' Lady, but I'm thinking, not so good for a princess.'

She gave a confused look to Nicander.

He had only a hazy idea of the geography. 'Where is Constantinople from here?' he asked Yulduz.

The man just shrugged.

'The Mediterranean – the great sea?'

'I am a man of the mountains, I know not much of what is across the plains. But there is a great city many times the size of Osh. This is the home of the Sogdian people. It is called Samarkand and is only a week or two away. There you will find every kind of comfort and civilisation that would suit you, M' Lady.'

'How will I . . . ?'

'My brother, he runs caravan there. I will see him directly, you wait.'

After he had gone Ying Mei forced a smile. 'Ah Yung, we are in the Western Lands, you have completed your mission.'

She paused. 'But can I ask . . . will you go with us to Samarkand?'

What else could he do? In all conscience he could not leave Ying Mei and Tai Yi in this town alone. In Samarkand she could settle down in some comfort, yet still keep her ear to the ground for news that it was safe to return to China.

At the same time hanging over him was his own quandary – how to get to Constantinople from here. What more likely place than the capital of the Sogdians to find out?

That night Nicander found sleep impossible.

He now knew it was more probable than not that he and Marius would eventually succeed in getting through to Constantinople. It was no longer a fearful adventure with no end.

But it was only a very short time before the moment when he would never see Ying Mei ever again.

He had accepted that their friendship, warm as it was, could go no further. She was a noble lady and would see out her exile in Samarkand. He and Marius would continue on to Constantinople.

Yet she had entered his heart and mind in a way that no other woman had. A disgraceful thing to admit for a holy man, he reflected ironically. The holy man conceit, of course, was as much a defence against what could not be, as to allow her the trust to be close and he had to see it through. In any case, it would be a shameful thing if he had to admit that he'd deceived her all this time.

No, it had to be faced, there would be a parting soon and it would be final.

It were better for both, therefore, that from now on he keep away, withdraw from her company. Be polite – but distant. The only way to get through it.

Yulduz came back with good news. 'He can take you. Like I said! If you quick.'

The caravan was already on its way and they had to chase it on horseback, rendezvousing in the early afternoon with a colourful line of laden camels, packhorses, all the familiar jingle and panoply.

The caravan master, looking nearly identical to his brother, accepted their fee and it was arranged that their baggage would catch up with them at their first staging.

Ying Mei's face was flushed with anticipation. 'Will they speak Greek in Samarkand, Ah Yung?'

'If it's as civilised as they say.' He rode on without taking his eyes from the road.

'I'm so relieved! A new land with all these things to see, to learn about – aren't you excited, Ah Yung?'

'Yes – I suppose so.' He couldn't bring himself to look at her.

'Oh, you worry too much! The bad part is all over now.'

When he didn't reply there was a tiny frown. 'Are you feeling unwell, Ah Yung?'

'No.'

'I wouldn't want to miss our Greek lessons, now we're so close to Samarkand.'

'I . . . I don't think I'll have time tonight. I have to . . . to meditate.'

'Oh. Well, when you're free you'll find a ready pupil.' She quietly fell back to Tai Yi.

As the days passed, Nicander found it harder and harder.

In her place, alone in a country that was as different from her own as it was possible to be, he would be clinging to anything that was familiar, secure. Yet she never allowed her fears and anxieties to drag her down, standing before the world as the high-born lady she was.

He nearly weakened several times over resuming their Greek lessons but he knew he couldn't, the closeness would be too difficult to bear.

He told himself that in any case he'd been teaching under false pretences: he'd assumed that here, as everywhere in the civilised world, Greek would be spoken by all but the barbarians but this, it seemed, was not the case. She'd trusted him and . . .

If he and Marius safely made Constantinople, in their box of holy scriptures – now mustered daily by Marius – was the means to make both of them insanely rich, never to be troubled by anything again. He should be rejoicing, looking forward to the climax of their adventure.

Instead, he was being torn in two at the thought of parting from a woman who he now knew he loved but who saw him only as a friend, albeit one she had said she would never forget.

They were soon approaching Samarkand. The verdant plain was populated by farms – irrigated peach orchards and greenery stretching on and on. In the hazy distance a single massif thrust out of the flatness.

The caravan headed towards it and as the roads thickened to streets and the traffic choked the way it came into plain view. It seemed peoples from every conceivable corner of the world were streaming there.

A walled city with impressive towers and monuments was atop the rocky eminence. After they had passed through the caravan gate they wound along a wide flat area to the prodigious-sized caravanserai.

There were two other caravans in the bays and their arrival caused little interest.

Nicander dismounted. This had been the last time he would be with Ying Mei in a fabled caravan on the silk route. From now on—

Suddenly she gave a squeal. He wheeled round in alarm to find her pointing to a shabby sign above an alcove that read, 'Andros and Sons, Merchant Factors' in Greek.

She ran across into the office, Nicander quickly following.

'Good morning!' she said breathlessly in Greek to the clerk.

'What do you want, lady. We're busy, can't you see?' he replied in the same language.

'How wonderful!' she breathed.

She turned to Nicander, 'You see? I can speak – I can talk! Isn't it marvellous!'

A lump came to his throat at hearing his native tongue. He thrust outside hoping she did not see the tears welling.

Ying Mei followed in concern and put her hand on his arm. 'Something's the matter, isn't it, Ah Yung?'

The touch was all fire and flowers and he strove for control. 'Oh – only that – someone speaking Greek after all this time.'

The others came hurrying up.

'Anything wrong?' Marius wanted to know.

'No, nothing,' Nicander managed. 'Well, we're here, aren't we?'

'Yes, o' course we are, Nico! Now, there's to be no caravanserai for the ladies any more. This is going to be their home, so we've got to find 'em a place to start off.'

'I was just about to ask here if there's a Greek-speaking lodging house nearby. Somewhere to stay while they find out what they want to do.'

There was one such, and in a better-quality quarter up the steep slope above the caravanserai.

The door was answered by a maid who quickly sent for her mistress, a Mrs Malech.

She was a pleasant-faced woman who took to Ying Mei immediately. A guest of quality who knew Greek: it would be an honour to have her.

It was a modest but comfortable house, faintly reminiscent of the antique Euboean style with its mock porticoes and inner courtyard. Quiet, away from the lower streets, it seemed to fit the bill perfectly.

'What do you think, Ying Mei?' Nicander asked, puzzled that she had suddenly gone pale and withdrawn.

'Yes. It will do,' she said woodenly, then enquired, 'What are you asking for the rooms?'

Mrs Malech named a value in Sogdian soms which Nicander's quick merchant's brain quickly converted to a usable reference, but before he could speak Tai Yi snapped in Greek, 'That's too expensive!'

Nicander wheeled around in astonishment.

'Who do you think I was practising with?' Ying Mei said with a small smile.

He shook his head in admiration as an arrangement was satisfactorily concluded.

'Then you'll need your gear to settle in. We'll have it sent to you from the caravanserai. Is there anything else . . . ?' The lump in his throat had returned.

Ying Mei turned and looked at him for a long moment. 'You promise you'll come back and say a proper goodbye before you leave?' she whispered.

Nicander nodded slowly, unable to speak.

Marius chuckled. 'O' course we will! There's the little matter of settling up for the rest of our trip, we haven't forgotten. Come on, Nico, we've a lot to do.'

'Well, how did you get on?' Nicander asked Marius.

'There's a caravan, sure enough, but the master needs clearance from his agent before he'll put us on the books. How about you?'

'Good and bad.'

'Tell me.'

'I know more about where we are now.'

'Oh?'

'Marcanda of Transoxiana.'

'What?'

'This is what Alexander the Great called this place when he conquered it. And it's why they still have Greek here. You wouldn't believe it but he put in another week's march from here towards Osh but when his generals saw the mountains we came down they mutinied and wouldn't go on any further.'

In a way Nicander felt a kinship with these ancestors of his and a comforting realisation that at last they were on known territory. On this very ground

Greeks and Macedonians had set their boots and in a line that stretched back to Greece itself, a saga of conquest that was unmatched in history.

'You also said bad,' Marius prompted.

'Yes. The way home is due west in a straight line. Just a small obstacle we have to face.'

'What?'

'We're the wrong side of Persia, it's in the way and we have to get through it – Justinian's greatest enemy and we don't quite look like harmless Sogdians.'

Marius was not going to be put off. 'Well, let's see what happens with the caravan. We may have to go in disguise or something. We'll work it out – after coming all this bloody way there's nothing going to stop me now!'

Nicander tried to be enthusiastic for his friend's sake.

It was tedious, having to remain at the caravanserai for word, not being able to get out to see sights that might take his mind off things, or visit a wine house to drown his sorrows. Hanging over everything was the crushing thought of having to see Ying Mei one last time.

Nicander pulled himself together. It had to be done. Then he would try to get on with what was left of life.

'Marius. I think I'll say my farewells to the ladies now. No sense in waiting to the last minute. Will you come?'

'I don't think so. I'm not much for goodbyes, and some bastard has to stay around here. You go, tell 'em I wish 'em well, that sort o' thing, you know. Oh, and don't forget the settling up!'

CHAPTER FIFTY-NINE

Ahead was her lodgings: in a way so sweet-sad in its Hellenism of another age, and from now on where she would have her being. How could he just go in and end it all?

Nicander shied away as if he'd come to the wrong address. But this was just delaying things. He turned back, determined to see it through; he would make it short and final, be strong and resolute – it was the only way.

His hand hovered at the door then he knocked firmly.

Ying Mei opened it uncertainly, pallid and tense. Her face lit up on seeing him. 'Ah Yung! You came!'

'Why, yes,' Nicander answered, taking in the image of her standing there; he would remember her beauty for as long as he lived.

'I promised . . . to say goodbye before we left.'

'Please come in!' she said happily.

The room had been transformed: there was now an elegant throw over the long couch, a deep-pile rug in green and gold on the wooden floor. And after her desert travails: flowers everywhere.

'Would you like some wine? Here it is all made from grapes, I find.'

'That is kind of you.'

He sat diffidently at one end of the couch.

'Tai Yi is not here at the moment,' she called from a side room. 'She went out with Mrs Malech who's showing her all the local shops and bazaars. I . . . I couldn't really face it myself but they said they'll be back for supper.'

He stood up. 'There's nobody else here? I should really leave.'

There was a sudden clatter. She hurried in. 'Please – please don't go!' she blurted, her face strained and the glint of a tear visible. Nicander steeled himself – she was taking the reality of her exile harder than she was admitting to the world and it was all he could do to prevent himself going to comfort her.

'I – of course.'

'I'm such a silly, it's just that . . .'

'Ying Mei, you don't need to explain. I understand.'

His heart began to weep for her – and what could not be.

'Yes, I know you do. We always did get along well, didn't we?'

He struggled to answer. 'You were a good pupil.'

She came and sat on the opposite end of the couch. 'And you! Do you remember how quickly you understood how Hsün Tzu and Confucius could be enemies, yet friends at the same time? I was amazed at you!'

'It must be that my teacher was a very wise and patient . . . being,' he said, unable to keep the feeling from his voice.

She looked at him, her expression unreadable, her hands working together.

In the silence the emotion in his breast swelled.

'Ying Mei – I can't help it. I have to tell you this or die!' he cried out suddenly. 'I . . . I love you so much! I can't bear for you to be taken from me, God help me!'

She froze at the words but he didn't care. In a few minutes it would all be over anyway and if it was the last thing he did on earth he wanted her to know how deeply, passionately and hopelessly he felt about her.

'I . . . I'm sorry, but this is how I am. I've tried but I just can't stop it! My love – it keeps getting stronger and I c-can't help it!'

Tears came and he gazed at her in dumb misery.

She still sat rigid; then, very deliberately, moved over and knelt down in front of him.

'Ni K'an Ta. I . . . I didn't know!' she said with an infinite tenderness. 'You should have told me.'

She took his hands, raised them to her lips and kissed them gently, looking into his eyes with a compassion that was unbearable. 'For I would tell you . . . that I care for you too,' she whispered. 'I have for a long while but I mustn't show it. You see, I have to say it: I . . . I love you too.'

A storm of feeling broke and he tore himself free and stood, his chest heaving. If he didn't run – flee from the room instantly – he would be overcome.

But before he could move, she was clinging to him, her face buried in his shoulder, weeping brokenly.

His arms went around her in an instinctive comforting but he felt her body pressing into his.

With a roaring in his ears he held her closer.

The warm, soft form yielded to him and they slowly slipped to the floor in each other's arms.

Images intermingled: robes in disarray, a flash of nakedness, a shoulder, a young breast.

Ying Mei looked up at him, her face impossibly beautiful, dear and precious.

He kissed her again and she responded passionately. Her body under him came alive, awakening and arousing his own in a sweet agony.

Finally, in an uncontrollable ecstasy, they came together in a hard, thrusting convulsion, leaving them both spent.

They clutched each other for a long time as if desperate to hold on to the moment; wild-eyed, ecstatic – fearful of the storm that had passed.

Nicander gathered his robe about him and rose to the couch, fighting back tears at the sight of her naked form, still shuddering with passing spasms.

She collected her scattered garments and joined him, both lost in a haze of unbelief and joy.

Her hand crept into his. 'I-I'm sorry,' she said in a small voice. 'I'm truly sorry. It . . . it just happened, I couldn't stop myself.' Her head fell.

'Ying Mei, don't say that!' he stammered. 'I love you! So much, so very much – this happened because we love each other, we need each other!'

'I have disgraced you. You will hate me for seducing you like a common whore.'

Hardly believing his ears he seized her hands and forced her to look up. 'What are you saying? I don't understand.'

She looked up at him tearfully. 'You will never forgive me, for I've done something that is wicked, yet I ask you to—'

He stared at her in amazement. 'You're saying things that don't make sense. Please tell me!'

'Your calling is now affronted. As a holy man you have your standards and—'

'A holy man!' he gasped. 'Is this . . .'

'Since that time in the desert you pulled me out of the sand, I've looked up to you, admired you – and then loved you as I knew I must not. Now I've dishonoured you, shamed you and I bitterly regret it.' Her eyes filled, imploring his understanding.

At first he couldn't answer, struck dumb with what he was hearing. Then he tenderly lifted her chin and looking deeply into her eyes said simply, 'My love, I never was a holy man.'

'You . . . you're saying this to comfort me.'

'No, it's true. I couldn't admit I was not a holy man or you wouldn't trust me. And then it went on for so long, if I admitted it you'd despise me for an impostor.'

'Then you're really not . . .'

'No.'

She flung her arms around him and wept in release.

'My very, very dearest, it should be me who should beg forgiveness. You are a noble lady and . . . and have a future . . . and I . . .'

Touching his lips she murmured, 'When we're married . . .'

'Married?' he stuttered, overcome.

'When two people love each other, it's the usual thing, I believe.'

In a whirl of emotion he blurted, 'My darling! I . . . I . . .'

'Dear Ni K'an Ta, we've always been meant to be together! And now we shall!'

'I . . . I . . .'

'And you're not Ah Yung any more. I'm going to call you the same as Ah Wu does – Ni K'ou. It's a fine ancient name, and one for the man of my heart.'

He swallowed, hardly able to speak. 'And you, my very dearest, I shall call you . . . Callista, the most beautiful.'

She looked long and deeply into his eyes. 'We will live and love together, you and I, for always and always, to the end of time.'

In a delirium of feeling he pulled her to him, crushing her with tenderness.

'But what now?' she whispered.

'Well . . .'

'We'll live here in Samarkand, but . . . but I really don't know that much about you, Ni K'ou. If you're not a holy man then . . .?'

'It was only a means to protect us while we went on our mission.'

'For the king! How wonderful – do tell me about it!'

'Later, Callista. Shouldn't we . . . ?'

'Oh, yes. They might be back early.'

She gave him a kiss then left the room, calling back, 'I won't be long. Don't go away, Ni K'ou!'

When she returned, sparkling and radiant, he had restored his outward composure but inside he was nearly overwhelmed in an unstoppable tide of happiness.

She came and sat by his side. 'When will we tell everybody, Ni K'ou?' she said dreamily. 'It will surprise them both, don't you think?'

'Ah. This could be a problem. Could you hold off telling Tai Yi until after I've spoken to Marius? He's going to need careful handling.'

CHAPTER SIXTY

Nicander walked down the road to the caravanserai in a blissful haze. To have been granted by the gods the highest felicity in this life . . .

But his mind suddenly slammed in to the present. If he was to live in Samarkand, what was he to do? They couldn't live off her capital indefinitely. Would it be enough to start some kind of business?

And there was the matter of the grand mission he and Marius had embarked on all those many months ago. Was it right to let his friend go on alone when he'd sworn to stand by him? He would have no regrets about letting Marius keep the secret of silk for himself, but he had to make it to Justinian first. And while the proud legionary had his strengths, this arguably needed both their talents.

Did this mean he must see it through first then return to her? Would she wait for him? Was it fair to expect her to?

But to leave her now was more than he could bear to think about.

The thoughts raced through his head and as he came up to the caravanserai cell he made a decision. He owed it to his friend to tell him about Ying Mei right away; he'd work the other things out with him afterwards.

He opened the door but before he could enter he was slammed to the floor.

'What the . . . ?' he spluttered, staring up at Marius.

'I thought it was . . . bugger that. Where've you been? You took your time saying goodbye!'

'Well, I've—'

'Save it. We've got big trouble.' Marius went to the door, checked outside, then closed it quickly.

'That clearance the caravan master had to get? The fucking Persians now know there's someone here who's come from China and heading through. There's rumours of foreign devils talking to Sogdians, holy men who aren't what they seem . . . Nico, they're out looking for us. We've got to get away!'

'You mean leave Samarkand?'

'Of course I do! What's wrong with you? This is bloody serious – we've got just hours before they find us.'

'But if we can't go by caravan then—'

'For Christ's sake! I'm saying now! Get out by any means as long as we're gone from here!'

'What about Ying Mei?'

'Those two takes their chances, o' course! Nico, there's no time to argue, we've got to move.'

'They have to come with us.'

'Are you crazy? Whatever plan we come up with things'll be rough, women'll get in the way and we'll be caught. No, they stay behind.'

'Marius, we agreed to deliver them safely to the west. This is the west, but they're not safe. I'm not leaving them here while they're in danger.'

'*You're* not?' Marius rapped.

'No.'

'So I go alone?' he said with a steely edge of menace.

'And break your word to Kuo?'

Marius flinched then gave a twisted smile. 'You bastard. All right, they come. But let's get out of here fast. We'll hide with them while we come up with something – anything!'

Ying Mei opened the door. 'Ah Wu! How nice to see you!'

After a quick look up and down the road, Marius pushed past her. Bewildered, she flashed a glance at Nicander who put a finger to his lips.

Wheeling about in the centre of the room, Marius demanded, 'Where's Tai Yi?'

'I'm here!' she said frostily, suddenly appearing.

Nicander caught Ying Mei's eye and she gently shook her head. She'd kept her secret.

'Tell 'em,' Marius grunted, going out to check the back of the house.

It took little time to explain the situation and as soon as Marius returned it was agreed that they had to move fast. Their options were pitifully few. Any caravan would be watched, including the ones returning to Osh, so even falling back to where they had come from was not possible.

'Creep out into the country and hide?' hazarded Ying Mei.

'We've got to look at the bigger picture, not just the short term,' Nicander replied.

'He's saying we've got to get out o' where the Persians are, to somewhere they're not!' Marius said flatly.

'Like . . . ?'

'Let's face it, Nico. We're going back to Constantinople, whatever it takes. We've got to get around the Persians and I don't know how. And that's saying if the women are coming with us, they're going there too.'

Nicander glanced at Ying Mei. Samarkand was to have been where the two of them were to have lived, and where she could listen for news of China. There were no such lines of communication out of Constantinople and she would therefore never know . . .

'We go,' Tai Yi said, surprising the others with the force in her voice. 'These Persians know we were with the foreigners when they came. So, My Lady, we have to decide if we trust these two to get us somewhere where we will be safe. I do.'

Ying Mei bit her lip and avoided Nicander's eye.

Knowing nothing of the country, the larger world, even the city outside, where would they begin to plan? It seemed hopeless.

Then she brightened. 'Why don't we ask Yulduz, you know, the caravan master we had? He's sure to know if there are other ways.'

'Damn it – she's right!' Marius agreed. 'I'll wait until dark to go and find him. Nothing we can do until then.'

Marius came back with disastrous news. 'This is bad – no, it's fucking terrible! I gets to him and asks him, nice and friendly like, to help us. Then he turns white, says he doesn't know us and in any case there's no way he's going to help any who are wanted by the kingdom. I don't give a single obol for our chances now!'

Tai Yi stood up. 'We must go. Right now – into the country, find a farm or something and stay there while we think what to do.'

'What if—'

'Shut up! Quiet – all of you!'

Marius listened intently. 'There!' he whispered, pointing up to the ceiling.

The others heard nothing: but then there was a nearly inaudible scrape. And another. Marius beckoned Nicander and the two crept toward where the steps led down from the roof garden.

'They're here!' Marius grated. 'I'll take the first, you—'

A dark figure dropped into view to a muffled scream from the women.

'Wait!' Marius hissed, holding up his hand, but there were no more following.

The figure threw back its hood. It was a bearded man, his eyes wary and suspicious. 'You the four?' he barked in broken Chinese.

'Who are you?'

'Mansur, son of Anjak. He say you want . . . get out of Samarkand.'

Quick as a cat, Marius crossed to the steps and looked about carefully, then returned. 'How do you know this?'

'My uncle, he say.'

The caravan master must have told him of their plight – and the opportunity for gold.

'We have to leave right now. Can you . . . ?'

It took some explaining but when Mansur had finished there was a deathly hush.

What was being proposed was audacious, dangerous and terrifying, but it might just work. Centuries before the Persians had clamped their hold on the caravan routes, there had been trade between Rome and China on the seasonal trails. One of these went north about the Hyrcanian Sea, what the Persians called the Caspian, and from there across to the Pontus Euxinus, the Black Sea. And then it was only a direct voyage by trading ship to the city of Byzantium itself.

There was a catch. The route had been long abandoned for fear of the Huns and Goths who had come out of the howling wilderness of the steppe lands on a path of pillage and destruction among the rich pickings of Europa. What was being suggested was that they journey into the homeland of these brutal nomads.

Mansur, however, specialised in trading with these peoples and knew them well. He was able to move freely about the more settled tribes for they liked the bright baubles of civilisation he exchanged for their furs and worked goods, and in fact he was off on a trading run now and could offer them safe passage for a price.

In terms of distance it would add little to the miles they would have had to travel by the usual route and the going across the steppe lands would be easier than the deserts and rugged lands of the south, but in terms of risk . . .

To stay was out of the question. It would be only a matter of time before they would be found.

Ying Mei had drawn heavily on her uncle's note at the last possible place, Khotan, and Mansur's price would seriously deplete her resources. However, there was nothing for it. To leave under eye through guarded gates was not to be considered, even in a disguise of some sort. As part of a caravan perhaps two had some chance of breaking out but as a conspicuous party of four . . .

'How will we escape the city?' Nicander asked.

'Leave to me. First, you give me your mark.'

This was to be something that would recognisable to them later. 'Marius! Your Mithras.'

Unwillingly the legionary took off his iron ring and passed it over.

'Tonight, someone will come with this. You will do as he say! Your baggage – you leave in this room, so. Go with nothing.' With that, Mansur slipped away.

It proved to be a long wait but, just as the first light was beginning to lift the darkness, a boy appeared at the steps.

He handed over the ring. Nicander gave a nod.

Nervously the lad beckoned. They followed on to the roof and down the rear in the predawn stillness. The boy darted ahead, peered around the corner, then motioned for them to make haste.

Nearby a cock crowed making Nicander's pulse race but there was no holding back now.

The small group hurried down the street and turned into a narrow lane. It led to a communal well.

Pausing, the boy looked about – then feverishly cranked up the bucket and gestured to Marius.

'In there?' he muttered with incredulity.

The boy stabbed a finger at the bucket.

'Stand on it, hurry,' Nicander said with urgency.

Marius did so, holding on to the rope and the lad let him down quickly. He leant over to see, then cranked up the bucket and pointed to Tai Yi. She went down too, followed by Ying Mei.

As the bucket was being pulled up, Nicander heard footsteps behind. He whirled round – but it was only a woman with a large pitcher looking at them curiously.

The boy gabbled something and she came forward with a smile and took her time getting a fill of water, then left.

Nicander clambered on and the bucket was lowered quickly into the darkness, past slimed stonework that stank of mineralised water.

At the bottom was a light – a tallow dip set on a ledge giving a ghostly illumination to the three standing together in water to their knees.

'I didn't reckon on this,' Marius quavered. 'What're we doing here?'

Nicander recognised the ancient method he'd seen in Petra for bringing life-giving water from distant snow-covered mountains to arid lands. 'This is a *qanat*. You see that tunnel?' He pointed to the low subterranean passage hewn out of rock. 'It feeds a line of wells that goes far into the desert. I've a notion we'll be going for a long wet walk.'

The boy shinned down the rope and splashed next to them. He picked up the light and led the way into the tunnel.

Bent double, they inched forward, following the wavering light and stumbling on the uneven floor.

In the gloom the sound of their splashing progress was loud and echoing.

Was the crushing weight of rock above them waiting to collapse and bury them?

Nicander had contrived to be behind Ying Mei whose mechanical movements betrayed her fear and in the darkness he ached to hold her, to comfort her. He realised that Marius, too, was affected by the confinement of the narrow, dark passage. He tried to keep up a steady conversation, complaining at the numbing cold of the water, the constant splashing forward and demanding that the sun had better be shining good and hot when they eventually came up.

Then far ahead there was a change in the Stygian blackness. As they made towards it, it resolved into a delicate splash of light from above. They drew nearer until they reached it – they were at another well and far up was a perfect disc of pure brightness.

Marius stared up, the light pitiless on his contorted features. He gave a hoarse cry and pounded on the side of the well.

The boy hurried back and urgently signalled that this was not the right one, they must continue on.

But Marius was near the end of his tether. Nicander pushed over to the legionary and swung him around. He scooped icy water and dashed it into his face. 'We're all still here, Marius! Let's finish it together!'

The man's chest heaved and Nicander could sense the struggle taking place as his friend strove to conquer his terror.

'It's time to march, *caligatus*,' he said gruffly. 'Now!'

With fixed, staring eyes Marius shuffled off down the tunnel.

They splashed on and on. It wasn't the next well but the one after that when they were motioned to stop.

The boy whistled twice. There was no response.

He whistled again, agitated. No answer drifted down to their echoing dungeon.

Nicander felt panic rising. If there was a misunderstanding and no one was there . . .

A sudden dark shape broke the blinding circle of light above and a shout echoed.

In a giddy wash of relief the young boy shouted back and soon a bucket on a rope was clattering down.

'Marius, you go.' Nicander guided him forward.

'No!' he replied in a hoarse, off-key voice. 'Ladies must.'

Ying Mei was first and the bucket was winched up. Then it was Tai Yi, but Marius would not be budged, it had to be Nicander next.

The squeaking windlass swayed him up into the ever-increasing light until in a blinding flash he reached the surface. Willing hands helped him over the lip of the well and in the warmth of the morning sun he found himself looking out over a parched landscape back to the walls of the city.

He turned to the well but it was the young boy who stepped out.

Marius was the last to emerge. He fell to his knees and kissed the warm earth. 'I'll rot in hell before ever I get down there again!'

Mansur was waiting for them with mounts ready saddled up, along with his packhorses and mules and a goods wagon piled high. 'We stage at Aktash. Your baggage will catch us there.'

CHAPTER SIXTY-ONE

Nicander's heart was bursting; there were so many things that he wanted to say to Ying Mei, but she was riding ahead with Tai Yi.

He found his chance at the midday break when they stretched their legs together under the spreading willow trees along the river.

'My dearest, dearest Callista,' he murmured, 'we haven't had a chance to talk.'

'Dear Ni K'ou – it's hard for both of us, but you see—'

They were startled by one of Mansur's drivers as he brushed past on his way to wash a water skin.

Nicander collected himself. 'I'm sorry you had to leave Samarkand where you would have been able to listen for news of China.'

She gave a small smile. 'Don't worry about that, Ni K'ou. I've thought of a way. You told me that the caravans end in Constantinople. Travellers can't get through Persia, but messages can. I'll send a letter to Yulduz and ask him to deliver it to my uncle's agent in Khotan. That way my uncle can get it to my father in Shaolin. You see? So when I'm in Constantinople I can tell him I'm safe and happy – and perhaps that I'm Ni K'ou *tai tai*,' she added shyly.

His eyes misted and his hand went out to hers.

'Please don't, Ni K'ou.' She drew away and her face clouded. 'We can't be . . . close . . . It would shock Tai Yi and I would hate to hurt her. And it wouldn't really be fair to Marius . . .'

'My darling love – how can I—'

She looked at him tenderly. 'Ni K'ou, I love you and I want nothing to spoil it. Why don't we keep things as they were until we get to Constantinople? Then, when we're safe, we'll tell the world and be married.'

'B-but it'll be so long and . . .'

'I'll be strong and you must be too,' she said, easing away from him as they walked.

'For you, I'd . . .' he gulped.

But a thought came: was she in fact testing him? To discover whether it was love – or lust – that his feeling for her would be the same in far distant Constantinople before she gave her heart?

They continued on in silence for a short distance.

'We should join the others, Ah Yung.'

'Yes, Ying Mei,' he said sadly.

After more than a week of heading ever deeper into the dusty, empty plains they reached the great Oxus river then followed a pathway north for another week.

There, they came across two shy but curious shepherd children tending a flock of sheep. Mansur called to them familiarly and they sang out a reply.

'Hah. The Turghiz, they ahead, wait for me.'

He jolted his horse forward. 'That a good sign. If trouble, they not there.'

After an hour the gentle rise fell away – and below was the extraordinary sight of the sea.

It was so unexpected that Nicander felt disoriented. He went up to Mansur, 'I thought we were . . .'

'What the Turghiz they call the Aral Sea because many islands.'

Along the low-lying coastland there was a village with a few modest timber houses and numbers of yurts, substantial round tent houses, from which wisps of smoke were rising.

405

A wave of people came out to greet them and soon they were surrounded by laughing, chattering strangers in outlandish and colourful garb. Far from the pitiless savages they'd feared, mused Nicander.

'We feast!' Mansur announced.

The next morning Mansur's wagon was made the centre of an enticing display of his trade goods and he stood back to let the villagers see his wares. But as the afternoon drew to a close, Nicander saw he seemed in no hurry to conclude his stay.

'When do we start out again?' he asked politely.

'Again?'

'Why, yes. We want to get going as soon as we can.'

'Nothing stop you. Over there –' he indicated vaguely away from the Aral '– you reach the Caspian. Around, and you meet your Black Sea.'

'No, I meant all of us together. When do we go?'

Marius heard the talk and came up. 'That's right. We're not paying you to lay about and peddle your stuff all day!'

Mansur stiffened. 'I don't know what you talk, foreigner! You pay me, leave Samarkand, through nomads – I do it! Tell you where to go on old silk route, I do it! Not hold your hand all way to Constantinople.'

'Tell me you're not saying this is as far as you go?' Marius said dangerously.

'I say. This is Dost. I stay one month, return to Samarkand. You don't like, you come back with me.'

'Why, you fucking cheat! I'll—'

But Nicander had seen several Turghiz men moving closer, fingering weapons. 'Marius! Not now,' he muttered.

Mansur snapped some words at the Turghiz who remained nearby, watching warily.

Nicander held Mansur's eyes. 'Let's get this clear – you say this is as far as you go with us?'

'Is right.'

'So if we want to go on, we go alone.'

'Yes.'

'Through the steppe barbarians – just us.'

'They leave you alone. Mongol or Turk, they get no honour for killing weak, helpless. Only if you have treasure – but you not have.'

'We don't know the way!'

Mansur shook his head as if to an imbecile. He pointed in exaggerated fashion to the west. 'You go there, you meet Caspian. Big! Cannot miss! You go around. Finish!'

'How far?'

'I give you good horses. Two week, you go slow. Other side, I don' know, never go.' He folded his arms.

'We don't know the barbarian tongue. If we need to . . . ?'

The man simply shrugged.

They had no choice but to set off alone. Six horses, two mules and four travellers, moving over the dry, featureless plain in the general direction of a vast inland sea that none of them had seen.

Ahead were the lands of the restless Turks and Mongols that were so terrifying that the Huns and Goths who had wrought so much carnage in Europa had fled before them.

The little band stopped for the night by a slow-moving watercourse.

Nobody spoke more than the odd word – was it the towering silence of the stark, empty landscape or their utter helplessness in the face of both nature and man?

And their painstaking politeness to each other – was this to keep the fear of the barbarous primitives at bay?

The stars came out, a scintillating splendour overhead, but with it a chilling cold. They shuddered and drew closer to their fire until it began to die.

There was only one tent and without weapons it made no sense to take turns to be on guard outside so each lay down to their sleep.

* * *

407

They travelled deeper and deeper to the west.

The going was good and there was fine grass for the horses. But always the thought that somewhere out there was a Mongol horde on the move – not the tame Turghiz settled pastorally around the Aral, but the cruel and all-conquering warrior Turks from the unknown interior vastness of Asia.

On the fifth day the morning began like any other; the vast blue bowl of the heavens cloudless, nothing moving. Then the hazy line of the horizon became imperceptibly stippled, restless, followed by a subliminal rumble – the beating of thousands of hooves, louder and louder. Out of the dust a broad wall of riders appeared, spreading out to the right and left, an unstoppable torrent.

Hearts thudding, Nicander and the others dismounted and waited for what must come.

The flood parted each side of them in an appalling thunder. Brutish, swarthy-faced riders with lank hair, wearing long coats and upcurved boots surged around them.

Ringed by the horses, edgy and fidgeting after their gallop, one man vaulted out of the saddle. He swaggered up, stopping a few yards in front of them and barked something.

Nicander shook his head with incomprehension.

The man threw an order over his shoulder and in one fluid movement a hundred bows were readied and aimed.

He snarled at them again.

In the last moments of life granted to him Nicander turned to gaze on Ying Mei's precious face – but was dumbfounded to see her begin striding forward, proudly carrying her staff. Looped on it was the ornamented yak-tail her father had given her.

She stopped in front of the Mongol, raised the staff high and proclaimed the words of an imperial court admonishment that they be allowed free passage.

The man's eyes opened wide in astonishment, first at the yak-tail, then at her slight figure. The moment hung then he motioned the bows down.

He made a curious gesture across his chest with a slight bow of his head and indicated the four should remount.

However, as his warriors took station on each side it was clear they were meant to follow.

It was a ride of some hours. Late in the afternoon a sight few had ever seen unfolded before them: on the gentle grassy slopes ahead was a vast nomad city of densely packed yurts, lines of wagons, tethered oxen, and on the outer fringes, flocks of sheep and goats.

The dominating rise in the centre was covered by an inward-facing rectangle of large yurts decorated with flags and pennants.

They were led forward to the most ornamented one of all where a number of richly robed Mongols stood on each side of the entrance.

By this time there were hundreds of onlookers, agog to see what would happen to these brazen intruders.

A majestic figure in green satin emerged from the grand yurt. All around bowed low until a lordly wave released them.

Their captor scurried forward and prostrated himself, reporting in a staccato series of grunts.

The grand figure came forward. It seemed prudent to bow low as well, and when Nicander looked up again a statuesque woman, in turquoise silk and with a headdress of gold and pearls had appeared by the figure's side.

He spoke, gesturing to Ying Mei's yak-tail.

'He asks your origin, your business.' It was the woman, speaking in perfect Chinese.

Ying Mei, in faultless courtly phrases, answered that they were innocent and harmless travellers and were perplexed by their treatment.

The woman smiled coldly. 'I knew you were Chinese, my dear. You speak to the Wei princess Chang Le as was, and this is my Lord Bumin, Khagan of the Gokturks, who you'd do well to fear.'

Nicander froze. A Chinese princess, sacrificed in years past to seal some barbarian alliance.

She was either for them . . . or against. Only Ying Mei could . . .

409

'You know why you were brought here and not slaughtered outright?'

'No, Your Highness.'

'You flaunt the sign of an ambassador.'

'It was given to me by my father who trusted that the mighty Khagan would respect it and allow me free passage.'

'The penalty for falsely going under the sign is to be torn asunder by four horses!'

'Is the great Khagan so fearful of we few that he must forbid us his realm? That he needs to—'

'Enough!' She drew away to one side and beckoned Ying Mei. 'Come here, child!'

The two spoke together for some time and the noble lady returned to her husband, whispering something in his ear.

He held up his hand and in ringing tones made a pronouncement.

Nicander tensed at the answering roar but saw that the princess had the glimmer of a smile on her face.

Relief rushed in – but why had they escaped?

Ying Mei hurriedly explained that Princess Chang Le had extracted a promise from her to get a reassuring message back to her family in China. In return, she had reported that they were indeed ambassadors, from a mysterious kingdom over the mountains to the east to one in the west, where she, like her, was to be wed. They had been set upon by brigands and rather than turn back begged the great Khagan for his protection.

A small polished bronze plate was produced with jagged lettering incised upon it. 'This is a diplomatic pass of sacred power,' Princess Chang Le told them solemnly. 'Whenever a Gokturk sees this, in the name of the Khagan Bumin he is enjoined to render all assistance to you. You're free to go on your way!'

CHAPTER SIXTY-TWO

Nicander's eyes misted as he took in the rumpled green plain far below and in the extreme distance the lazy sparkle of a great sea. It had happened – this was the actuality of what he had thought could never be. He was gazing at Europa once again!

He looked down to where, on the other side, ancient Greek settlements had been since time began – the shores of the Black Sea.

'This . . . this is it,' he breathed. 'Colchis, the land of the Golden Fleece! The hero Jason and his Argonauts – but we've travelled infinitely further and have . . .'

'Forget your history! It's what it's now, that's the wonder of it all!' Marius triumphantly punched the air.

'What do you mean?'

'Ha! This is Lazica, the furthest out of all Justinian's outposts. Nico, this means . . . we've done it! This is Byzantine territory!'

'Well, nearly,' Nicander said, orienting himself. 'It's still on a bit to the trading port of Trebizond. That's the place we take ship to Constantinople!'

Ying Mei gave a squeal of joy. 'After all our journeying – to be here . . . it's . . .'

Their winding progress passed quickly and they found themselves threading through well-wooded meadows and fields of corn.

In the little town nestling in the foothills it seemed not worthy of remark, colourful strangers in barbarous dress coming down from the mountains, and they wasted no time finding a place to stay for the night. In the morning they went to the market and procured clothing more in keeping before setting out on their last journey.

Trebizond was a small, pleasant town, which as a Greek colony had been trading for many centuries, and there had been no difficulty in finding a place aboard a fat trader bound for Constantinople.

There had been curious questions but Nicander was ready with an answer. This was an exotic lady from far parts, accompanied by her attendant and two monks for the sake of propriety, destined for the household of a well-placed Byzantine noble whose name need not concern the enquirer.

It had the merit that it was not at all an unusual import for the pretentious wealthy, and there were no more questions.

Marius was beside himself with impatience. Less than a week's voyage and they would sight the marble dome of Hagia Sophia, the towers, the palace – all of which now had a very different meaning to two returning with the prospect of riches beyond anyone's dreaming!

The ship was not due to sail until the next afternoon. The ladies made free with the baths in their rooming house, and with Marius a caged bear, Nicander found himself wandering down to the harbour.

He sat on a bollard and looked across at their ship, still loading.

It was a fairly ordinary Black Sea *corbita* of medium tonnage, trading mainly in grain and wine. Their quarters were as might be expected: for the ladies a poky cabin aft and for himself and Marius the usual temporary cloth deckhouse. But – in less than a week those dull black timbered sides would be touching port in Constantinople!

Emotion began to wash over him as for the first time he had the leisure to contemplate things, to get to grips with all that it meant to have left the known world and gone to unimaginable realms of the perilous and exotic – and returned.

Now, the great adventure was over. No more torrid heat, bone-chilling cold or lying under the stars on a stony desert floor; no more fear and terror, fatigue and pain, thirst and hunger. And no more fireside companionship, the sharing of trials and triumphs – that had brought them all so close.

And his beloved. She had been right to insist they keep their distance while the final journey was completed.

But she had seen him in the most demeaning and wretched circumstances during their long odyssey: had she since cooled in her feeling for him?

And if she still cared for him, that would mean setting up their lives together in Constantinople. It was of course Ying Mei who would have to do all the adjusting – would she turn her back on the rowdy circus that was the city and set up as an exile until she could return to her own kind?

How would she take to the rude, thrusting nature of Byzantium, so unlike the studied, contemplative subtleties of the Chinese? He remembered the dignified elegance of Grand Chamberlain Kuo with a stab of poignancy, and what he had learnt at Dao Pa's feet showed that the ancient Greeks had no monopoly on pure thought.

But then he knew that Ying Mei was made of stronger stuff. If she gave him her heart, she would give soul and body too, and would become a Byzantine herself. Had not women since the beginning of time cleaved to their menfolk? Her exotic appearance would cause no comment, for this was the biggest metropolis in the Roman world, where so many races were to be seen.

And Tai Yi? When she heard about their plans would she be shocked – or heartbroken – at what her charge had become? No more in temporary exile, she might decide to set out alone and return to her homeland.

And, of course, Marius. Bluff, great-hearted Marius, to whom they all owed their lives. How would he fare, with his greatest friend taken by a woman? What would be his role in any economic and political convulsions caused by their introduction of silk production? His direct thinking and forthright ways could damn him . . .

And who knew what position he would find himself in. As outsiders in the maelstrom of intrigue and treachery that was Imperial Byzantium he and

413

Marius could both be easy targets in the struggle for power in the new world of silk. In fact there was every chance . . .

He threw off the dark thoughts. He should be rejoicing at their homecoming, not letting imagined conspiracies spoil it.

When he got back Ying Mei chided him for being a dreamer and told him that he was to get himself ready – everyone was going for a splendid celebration dinner the night before they sailed.

They were given a room to themselves and the ladies were introduced to their first taste of Greek cuisine, slow-baked lamb with garlic and lemon.

The country wine was robust and dark and went far in adding to the jollity.

The dishes were cleared away but no one seemed to wish to leave. Another jug of wine was summoned.

'Our first good meal since . . . when was it . . . ?' Ying Mei asked happily. She was looking more beautiful than he had ever seen her, thought Nicander.

'That would be in Samarkand, I'd think,' Nicander recalled. 'But it wasn't as you'd say a good meal, we being so distracted. I think it would have to be that funny little place in Osh.'

'The goat was revolting!' Tai Yi replied quickly. 'Not fit for a lady. No – it was over the mountains in Kashgar, at the caravanserai when we arrived.'

'That rice muck?' Marius spluttered. 'Queer idea of filling a man's belly, that crew!'

'Well, it has to be Khotan,' Nicander said with feeling. 'Out of the desert and fit to die – and a meal of melon slices and thin-cut mutton. That's to remember all my life!'

It was carried unanimously and they drank to Khotan.

'I'm really going to miss us being together like this,' Ying Mei said quietly. 'We've seen so much and . . .'

A hush spread, each deep in their own thoughts.

Tai Yi was the first to speak. 'Well, we'll be going our different ways when we reach Constantinople. You two will be returning to your monastery, Ying Mei and I will have to find somewhere and—'

'Hey, now! We'll be seeing each other at times, won't we?' Marius growled.

'I really don't think it possible,' Tai Yi said with a slight edge to her voice. 'Lady Kuo will be setting up her residence and as you are both holy men it would be unseemly to be seen too often in our company, I believe – however much we'd wish it, that is.'

Nicander couldn't catch Ying Mei's eye. 'It's been a great adventure – don't you think so?' he said to the table in general.

'No one will forget it,' Ying Mei said wistfully. 'It's all over now.'

Trying to rescue the mood, Nicander turned to Tai Yi. 'What do you remember most about it?'

She frowned. 'Why, I suppose when we left the imperial court in a hurry and my heart sank so, that we were to be going with a pair of barbarian clowns for company.'

'You still have them!'

'Ah, this is true. Perhaps I'll change my mind. Is it too late to say I'm sorry for calling you *kuei lao* then, even if you really are foreign devils?'

Nicander laughed. 'Forgiven! And you, Ying Mei? What do you remember?'

'I think it must be that time we were hit by the sandstorm and you had to pull me out.'

There was a general murmuring of sympathy for she had been all but buried alive.

'No, it wasn't my nearly dying, it was that when I came out in such a state I knew I couldn't be a proper lady any more!'

Nicander led the laughter that followed.

'Marius, tell us your memory of our great adventure.'

'Well, I think the worst of all has to be . . . let me see . . . it was when we left the hippodrome after . . .'

'No, not that,' Nicander said hastily. 'The ladies are not interested in chariot racing. What else was a hard time for you?'

'That's easy. It was playing the fool like that and all the time thinking of my marching comrades in the Pannonian legion, that if they saw me then I'd die o' shame!'

It needed translating so the others could appreciate it and join the merriment.

'And what about you, Ah Yung,' Ying Mei said sweetly. 'What do you remember?'

'Well, it must be the one who taught me that there are many paths to understanding, that the mysteries of the earth and the heavens are never to be mastered by mortal man, but the aspiring to such is the highest purpose of the human soul.'

'Who was it that brought you to the Tao? You never told me,' Ying Mei said softly, her eyes wide.

'It was . . . one called Dao Pa. I don't know where he came from, or where he went, but I'll never forget him or his words.'

Marius stirred impatiently. 'Damn it all, this is all getting a mite too solemn for me. I want we should drink – to us! To us as came through so much together!'

CHAPTER SIXTY-THREE

Nicander stared out over the water in a deep depression. He'd not had a chance to see Ying Mei alone and the talk at the dinner before they sailed had brought something into focus that was a dire threat to their future together.

He was living a lie. This mission was not the noble one of seeking truths for the Emperor of Byzantium, it was the grubby and shameful stealing of the secret of silk from the land of her birth. And when they arrived and it was revealed that they were the perpetrators . . .

The very thing that had set them on their way in this venture, that had served to bring them together, would in the end be the means of destroying their love.

It was now the third day since they had left Trebizond and she had kept to her cabin. Had Tai Yi's talk of setting up a residence swayed her? Why had she not even explained her feelings to him? Perhaps she had decided to end their relationship but was reluctant to tell him.

He had taken to seeking the very nose of the ship, the rearing curve at the stem and the solitude to be found there.

Astern, to the east, was the dawn and the blossoming day; ahead to the west, was the dying day, sunset and darkness. Was this a sign, a metaphor for his fated destiny?

Wrapped in his anxieties he didn't hear her come up. 'Ni K'ou – not you too! It's really so unfair.'

He swung around.

'You've been queasy with the sea? I've been so unwell these last three days I couldn't face anybody. Tai Yi is still lying down, poor thing.'

'So you weren't . . . ?'

'And now I'm better – and feeling quite hungry, I have to say. How long is it to Constantinople do you think?'

She was looking so beautiful with her rosy cheeks and the light wind playing with wisps of her hair. It brought a catch to his throat.

And she was standing uncomfortably close.

'Oh, the captain says after two more sunsets,' Nicander tried to say matter-of-factly.

'That's wonderful!' she exclaimed, then turned grave. 'It doesn't leave us much time to plan, does it?'

'Plan?' he gulped.

'Don't be a silly, Ni K'ou!' she teased. 'We're to be wed – or had you forgotten?'

The clouds of gloom and anxiety fled. She still wanted him! Nothing else mattered!

His grip on the rail tightened as he fought an overwhelming urge to hug and kiss her – but then, like an accusing ghost of the past, came the one thing that could and did matter, the secret he had kept from her, which he could do nothing to prevent coming out in just a few days' time.

The only choice left to him was whether she found out from others – or he told her himself.

'Ying Mei, Callista. I think we should talk.'

She picked up that this was not to be light chit-chat and tensed. 'If you say so, Ni K'ou.'

'I have to tell you something. About myself. It's only fair I reveal it now, before we're . . . married.'

She said nothing, her serious expression deepening.

'I . . . I'm not who you think I am. I've done something that I'm very ashamed of and now . . .'

It all came out. Their mission had not been a sacred one. They had been sent by the Emperor, true, but for a quite different purpose – the stealing from China of its most valuable secret; the idea had been his in the first place and the expedition funded on his plans.

'They're in our box,' he said in a low voice. 'Protected and sealed in a secret compartment under the holy scriptures. This is why Marius is so excited, we're probably going to be very rich indeed. You see, before we were very poor and low people and now . . .'

He stopped at the confusion and bewilderment on her face. He couldn't blame her if now . . .

'Ni K'ou – I don't understand.'

'I'm so very sorry to have deceived you, Ying Mei.'

'No, no, not that. What is it you are trying to tell me? I-I . . .' she trailed off uncertainly, searching his face.

'Don't you see?' he said. 'We've stolen the secret of silk. Nobody in Byzantium knows how to make silk and now they will. It will take all the profit from China and—'

'This is what you are telling me? That you're a bad man because you brought silk eggs out of China?' She looked incredulous. 'Only this? Tell me Ni K'ou, please!'

'Why, yes. Isn't this an evil enough thing to do to China?'

She shook her head in disbelief then broke into a delighted smile. 'My dear Ni K'ou, no! Never! I cannot thank you enough. You've given me such a precious gift – you've given me revenge on the beast who did all that to my father!'

Tears sprang while Nicander tried to make sense of it all.

'You see, at one stroke you've cut off the riches he makes from sending silk on the caravans. It's a terrible blow to him, for it's the major part of his tax revenue. Now he won't be able to pay his army to attack and plunder and they'll turn on him!'

'What about the people – the common people who make the silk?'

'Oh, Ni K'ou. If they knew they'd thank you, as I. They labour for nothing to make the silk, it's a burden put on them by the Emperor, even at the end of a day toiling in the fields. If they don't produce enough they're punished.'

'Then you're not—'

'My darling Ni K'ou – I'm proud of you! For centuries many have tried to do this but have failed. The penalty is execution but you've seen it through without telling me so I wouldn't be worried.' She dabbed her eyes. 'You're very brave, my dearest Ni K'ou, and so clever to have thought of this in the first place. I'm very lucky to have won such a man!'

'Callista . . . can't we just—'

'No, my darling. I want it to be very special. It's only a few days, then when we're there we'll set up all the arrangements – and then tell them!'

His heart overflowing with happiness, he would do anything for her, and he watched with the utmost tenderness as his future bride went below to see to Tai Yi.

They had the rest of their lives together, after all.

CHAPTER SIXTY-FOUR

'But it's my custom, I insist!' Their genial captain would not be denied. 'We raise Constantinople in the morning – this is our last night and you are my guests.'

It was an odd gathering in the cramped and dimly lit cabin. Besides their host there was Nicander and Marius, then in came a priest. He was in severe clerical garb and looked about disapprovingly before sitting. There would be no women allowed in this company, of course.

'Well, now,' the captain said breezily as he poured some wine. 'And I'm honoured indeed, aren't I.'

'How so, sir?' the priest said stiffly.

'Why, it's the first time ever that we've shipped an all-holy set o' passengers, Reverend sir.'

'All holy? What do you mean?' snapped the priest.

'These gentlemen are holy men, too, aren't you?'

'Yes. That is to say—'

'Holy men? Are you monks or priests?'

'Brother Paul, Brother Matthew.'

'What church?' the priest rapped.

'We're from the kingdom of Artaxium Felix, beyond Hawazin. The Church of St Agnes.'

'I've never heard of it.'

'As was isolated after the reign of the blessed Septimius Severus when our river changed its course.'

'Isolated – is that the reason why you're garbed in so disgraceful a dress? You've lost sight of the precious values of the One True Church, you've—'

Marius growled, 'What we do in our own church is our business, not yours!'

'Hah! You're then a heretic.' The voice had risen several notches. 'You've strayed from the course of righteousness – you're apostates. You know what is visited upon those who stand not in the true faith . . .'

Nicander felt a flush rising. 'Are you so narrow-witted you can't see there are other ways to wisdom? I'll wager you've never set foot outside Justinian's realm, seen for yourself how they order things.'

'Of course I haven't. Heathen, unlettered barbarians with as much understanding of higher matters as an animal!'

'They're not all barbarians!' Nicander ground. 'I've travelled . . . widely, and I can tell you there are savants and philosophers beyond the mountains that could put our own Pythagoras to some serious thinking.'

'Rubbish! If there were any of these I would have heard of them.'

Nicander saw red. 'I can prove it to you. As it happens, I can— wait.'

He returned with the first 'holy scripture' he had come to in their box. He waved it in the priest's face, who recoiled with distaste.

'Listen to this.' It was the fourth scroll of Lao Tzu and Nicander painfully rendered in Greek the ringing paean to the denial of selfishness in exchange for a mystical union with the ultimate.

'Give me that!' The priest snatched it from Nicander.

'I've with me more of those, all of which can stand with the very finest of our scholars.'

'I can't read it!'

'That's because it's in Ch—, I mean it's in a foreign tongue.'

'Hmmph! It's too dim in here, I'll take it outside.'

'You're welcome,' Nicander replied cynically.

He waited until he had gone then said, 'There's no medicine I know that can cure blindness of the mind.'

'We'll have trouble with him later,' Marius muttered. 'Better not get him going, Nico.'

'With what we're bringing back,' he said with a satisfied smile, 'we'll have friends that'll see him posted out to some far desert in an instant if we so desire.'

The captain blinked with incomprehension but said stoutly, 'More wine, good holy men?'

They proffered their glasses, relaxed in the warmth of the knowledge of what the near future held for them.

'Taking his time,' Marius said. 'Seems not to be getting anywhere, the fat prick.'

Nicander was about to reply when there was a disturbance at the door and it was flung open. A terrified crew member shouted, 'Sir, sir – fire! Fire on deck!'

The captain thrust past in horror, closely followed by Nicander and Marius.

They were confronted by an appalling sight. Lit like a demon from underneath by red flames the priest danced about a small fire: somehow he'd found their box with the remaining holy scriptures.

'You're too late! I've consigned your sacrilegious scribblings to the tongues of hell where they belong,' he crowed.

'Over the side!' screeched the captain. 'Ditch it! Quickly.'

A crew member hurriedly levered the still burning box into the sea where it sizzled for a moment then slowly sank.

It had happened in seconds. The horror of fire in a ship at sea gave way to a rising frenzy at the realisation of what had happened.

That which they had cherished and protected over all those so many miles of mountain and desert for a year of their lives was now gone. For ever.

With an inhuman screech Marius leapt forward and fell on the demented priest.

Horrified crew tried to pull him off – it took five of them before he could be subdued.

CHAPTER SIXTY-FIVE

In the early morning light the marble domes of Constantinople came into view.

Nicander stood watching, a far-away expression on his face.

'Ni K'ou!' Ying Mei begged. 'Speak to me – please. Why are you like this? Is it something I've done? Do please tell me! I don't care if the silk is lost, I love you and still want to marry you, even if we'll be poor and . . .'

She was fighting tears, not understanding.

They were now close enough to see the wharves, which were not far from the palace. In a very short time their travails would be over.

'Ni K'ou! Talk to me. I've a feeling something terrible is happening. Tell me!'

'Ying Mei. Things have changed. I'm . . . I'm not a man to be seen with. You'll have to manage without me.'

Her face paled. 'Not . . . not that, Ni K'ou, please don't say it!' she blurted.

'It's true. Over there is Emperor Justinian, the most powerful man in the world. Since we've been away he will have discovered that he's been tricked, we're not really from a far land and we're not really holy men – and our mission was . . . not altogether as we said. He's a vengeful man and will show us no mercy.'

'We'll run away together! We must flee to—'

'Callista,' he said sadly. 'We're marked men. Justinian has agents and spies everywhere and it would only be a short time before we're recognised and brought before him. If we had the eggs we would have fulfilled the mission in full and made him very content – without the eggs we have nothing but a fairy story.

'Our only chance is to go to him and throw ourselves on his mercy and . . . and I don't believe it will be shown in our case.'

Her tears were open now. 'P-please, Ni K'ou! Don't send me away, I beg.'

'My dearest heart! It's for your own good. I'm finished, but you have a life to live and—'

But she had fled below, sobbing.

The vessel bumped and juddered as it came alongside. Ropes were thrown and secured.

They had arrived – a journey of impossible distance was over. Marius came and stood beside him. 'We'll be hunted down whatever we do. We have to face the bastard.'

The lump in his throat made it difficult to speak but Nicander replied dully, 'Let's get it over with.'

The gangplank went out and they started towards it but were stopped by a call.

Turning, Nicander saw that it was Tai Yi. She was on her own.

'I won't be long,' he told Marius.

'What is it, Tai Yi?' he asked.

She was obviously finding difficulty with words. 'Ni *lao na*,' she said eventually, looking into his face. 'Ying Mei has told me . . . everything.'

'Oh. I . . .'

'I have a question for you that I beg you'll tell me truthfully, for on your answer hangs much.'

Her eyes never left his.

'Very well.'

'Do you . . . truly . . . love . . . my Lady Kuo Ying Mei?'

He stood back in astonishment but quickly answered, 'As my life, Tai Yi! It's why I asked her to leave me, for I would not have her in danger on my account.'

'Did you truly intend to marry her?'

'Tai yi! Of course! But it's impossible for us now, did she not say?'

'She said to me that after what we've all been through together, she can see you would be the only man who could ever make her happy.'

It caught him unawares and he choked back tears.

'Enough of that,' she said briskly. 'I have decided – her happiness is the only thing that matters to me at my age. Now listen to me very carefully. Go to your emperor and . . .'

As she explained, Nicander could hardly believe what he was hearing and when he turned back to Marius he was suffused with the most pure joy.

'Come on – I'll tell you on the way.'

The grey bulk of the imperial palace was ahead, quite unchanged. They stepped it out. 'Leave all the talking to me, Marius. Agreed?'

Suddenly there was a shout. 'Stop! Stop those men in the name of the Emperor!'

It was a voice from the past, one that still brought a cold wash of fear. Marcellus.

His men clamped a hold on them and he swaggered up. 'Well, well, well. Look who we have here,' he said with a lazy smile.

'We've come to see the Emperor,' Nicander said unsteadily.

'How convenient, as I know since he discovered your little . . . naughtiness, he would very much like to see you! Come along, don't dawdle! I've a feeling there's going to be much entertainment to be had, once His Resplendency claps eyes on you two!'

They were marched directly to Daphne Palace where they had last seen the Emperor and where they had laid out their crafty scheme before him.

'Wait here!' Marcellus barked and entered Justinian's private room.

'This had better bloody work, or we're cooked – and over a slow fire!' Marius said nervously.

426

Marcellus came out with a tigerish smile. 'Go in, both of you.'

Guards escorted them into the Presence.

Justinian looked up from his table. The same austere, brooding look, the hard lines, the terrifying reality of the Emperor of Byzantium.

His eyes widened. 'We stand amazed, Marcellus, but you're right. This is the pair! Good work – good work indeed. Don't go away – we may have something for you after we've done with them.'

He leant back, taking them in.

'You've played us false, and you won't be suffered to get away with it, you know that? What we can't puzzle out is why you came back? You knew you'd be found out. For the sake of our curiosity, pray tell us why you've returned to Constantinople?'

Nicander gave a dignified bow. 'Your Clemency, there is but one answer to that.'

'Oh?'

'Sire, it is that, ashamed as we were of our villainy, we stopped and prayed together. An angel then told us that there was only one course we could take that would repay Your Majesty's kind favours.'

'Tell us, this should be interesting.'

'We were directed to go forth and complete what we had said we would do – perform the mission in full, all the way to the land of the Seres. Sire – this we did, and are now returned.'

There were disbelieving murmurs and muffled laughter but Justinian cut across them. 'Then this means you've come back with seeds of the silk tree.'

'No, sire, we have not.'

The laughter was now general and Justinian frowned dangerously.

'We have not returned with seeds of the silk tree, sire, because it does not exist. But we have returned with the secret of silk and you shall have it this day to begin making it whenever you desire.'

There were puzzled gasps and Justinian leant forward. 'If by this you are seeking to prolong your miserable lives—'

'We have it here, sire.'

'Show us!'

Nicander strode to the empty area in front of the table. He looked about him significantly, daring any to challenge him.

Then he raised his knee – and snapped his staff across it.

In a glittering black cascade, packed earth spread over the floor before the Emperor. And in it could be seen scores – hundreds – of tiny worms, pale and squirming.

'This is the true secret of silk, sire. Not from trees but from these lowly creatures which, when grown, will spin a nest which is made of the finest, most delicate . . . silk thread.'

He stood back as courtiers and attendants crowded about to see the miracle.

'Thank God,' he whispered to Marius, 'the Chinese monks were right about transporting the eggs. When I broke the staff I nearly wet myself thinking they'd all be dead.'

'I don't get it,' Marius hissed back. 'How did—'

'It was Ying Mei's father. He wanted to give her security in the Western Lands, and what better than this? Remember he gave us each a staff – but he told only Tai Yi what they contained.'

'Why her?'

'Because he needed to be sure that it would be revealed only when the situation was right.'

'And Tai Yi thought that this was the situation?'

'Well, Ying Mei and I want to marry, and . . .'

'You cunning dog! I'll be—'

'Brother Matthew, Brother Paul,' Justinian began. 'Or whatever you'd like to be called. We find you've honoured your obligation beyond all reason. This empire is for ever in your debt.'

They waited politely.

'We're vexed to think what reward is in our power to bestow. Could you . . . ?'

'Sire, the friend of my bosom is a true soldier, a legionary of old Rome. If there's—'

428

'Quite. Well, let me see. Ah! I do believe the Procurator of Syria is due for retirement, don't you think, General?'

'A very suitable appointment, Resplendency.'

'Then as of this moment, legionary, you are herewith installed as Procurator with the immediate rank of Patrician. Do you think you can whip my army into shape there?'

'S-Sir. Clemency, y-yes!' spluttered Marius.

He turned to Nicander. 'And you?'

'It would be of the very greatest felicity, sire, should you grant me the honour of being wed in the hallowed Hagia Sophia.'

'Well, it's very irregular, however if that's what you desire. But perhaps also something a little more . . . material?'

'Then, sire, an estate of quality, not too close to the city, perhaps – and suitable for the bringing up of a family.'

'That seems very possible. Very well – we thus decree it be so.'

Justinian looked thoughtful, then leant over to address his learned court historian.

'Good Procopius. We do not wish any odium attached to these fine men's otherwise misguided actions or motives.

'Let history simply record that the secret of silk was brought here by two selfless monks who then did vanish.'

ACKNOWLEDGEMENTS

I owe a debt of gratitude to the many people who have contributed in one way or another to the writing of this book. Space precludes naming them all but they have my deep thanks. I am particularly appreciative of the assistance given by my new Turkish friend, Ziya Yerlikaya, and for the helpful information offered from Tacdin Aker in Ankara.

This is my first book with Allison & Busby and it's been a delight working with Publishing Director Susie Dunlop and her team. And last, but certainly not least – heartfelt thanks to my agent Carole Blake and my wife and literary partner, Kathy.

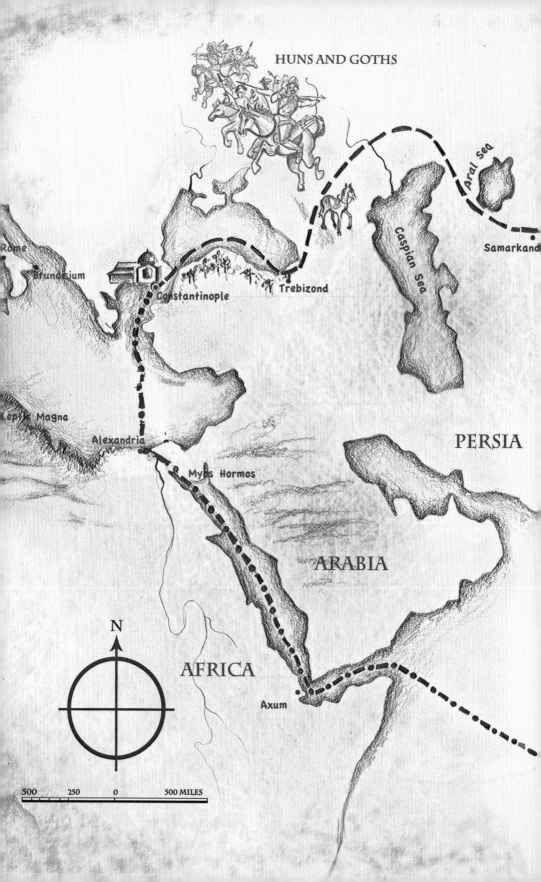

HUNS AND GOTHS

Aral Sea

Samarkand

Caspian Sea

Rome

Brundisium

Constantinople

Trebizond

PERSIA

Leptis Magna

Alexandria

Myos Hormos

ARABIA

N

AFRICA

Axum

500   250   0   500 MILES